THE

TELL

ALSO BY HESTER KAPLAN

Kinship Theory: A Novel

The Edge of Marriage: Stories

THE
TELL

A Novel

•

Hester Kaplan

HARPER ◑ PERENNIAL

NEW YORK • LONDON • TORONTO • SYDNEY • NEW DELHI • AUCKLAND

HARPER ● PERENNIAL

HarperCollins books may be purchased for educational, business,
or sales promotional use. For information please write: Special
Markets Department, HarperCollins Publishers, 10 East 53rd
Street, New York, NY 10022.

FIRST EDITION

Designed by Fritz Metsch

Library of Congress Cataloging-in-Publication Data is available
upon request.

ISBN 978-0-06-218402-3

13 14 15 16 17 OV/RRD 10 9 8 7 6 5 4 3 2 1

For my parents and my sisters

Grateful acknowledgment is made to the National Endowment for the Arts and the Rhode Island State Council on the Arts.

ART WORKS.
arts.gov

THE
TELL

I

====

For weeks he'd waited for the wild lilacs arching over the carriage house to bloom. Then, back from teaching and a plodding swim at the Y that afternoon, Owen had spotted the first fat plume with its buds rising like a thousand fists. The driveway's pea gravel had protested underfoot as he broke off a sprig. He'd put the lilacs, delicate and strong-perfumed, in a pitcher on the sill over the sink for his wife, Mira, and saw now, as he looked up from his hands circling under running water, how their hue matched the lowering sky, the drooping sun. In the tinted early evening, Providence was washed with improbable color, lulled by a phony urban calm, the arterial whoosh of the highway and the digestive rumbling of the train moving out of the station down the hill toward Boston. Behind him at the table, Mira read in the paper about the city's boasts and failings, its crimes and peculiarities. His wife's head would be at that absorbed angle as though every story was interesting and in some way personal, but he understood that this sense of knowing her completely was wrong.

"Listen to this," she said, and read to him a story about a man who'd beaten his neighbor's dog to death with a shovel because the animal had bitten a five-year-old girl on the face. "All it took was three whacks." Mira banged the table in an echo of finality.

"A *Rott*weiler," she added.

Owen was so struck by her presence at that moment—the way she bent over the paper; how she spoke, emphatic and raspy; her engagement that kept her in the middle of things, sometimes incautiously—and by this prized evening routine of theirs that a palpitation rose from his chest in a cough. Some essential air flew out of him and left him breathless.

"You okay, O?" Mira peered at him over the top of her green almond-shaped glasses.

O: his name in her mouth. He slapped his ribs and nodded. But his pulse had been strangely rampant too during his laps in the sweet pool water earlier, and it had fluttered with a familiar beat of expectation. It was fortune reminding him of its moody balance, of chance's visit, and of how this house very recently had been atilt with apprehension. Five weeks earlier, they'd been broken into for the first time. They were asleep upstairs and then awake to hear the snap of the ancient lock on the kitchen door, the rummaging and banging around, the uninvited whispers that were gone in a minute as though a bat had flown through. Owen had rushed, terrified, to the window, saw nothing, but heard the sounds of escape down Whittier Street. Mira's bag and laptop had been taken, and shoeprints were left on the rug to discover in the light.

Owen leaned into the sink and gulped water, leady and lethal, from the tap. Then some movement of white, gone before he could fully detect or confirm it, drew his eye past the unfurling pleasure of the lilacs to the empty house next door. Its windows were violet mirrors. In the year since the place had been on the market, Owen had sometimes used the house to animate wisps of his imagination the way people used empty battlefields. Where they saw the fuming charge across the hard-packed earth, the clash, the fallen in the grass, the victorious mob shaded by incoming clouds, he pictured his future children on the oak stairs, bodies passing in front of doorways, and the motion of family life he hoped to have here in this house, someday, with Mira.

He'd been inside only once, after the ancient owner had croaked in her bed and the place had been efficiently emptied by her officious out-of-state children. The apocalyptic vacancy of the rooms, the fissured ceilings, the washcloth on the floor of the tub, the isopropyl chill in the air, had awed him. There was something about all those aristocratic details of leaded glass, inlaid floors, and lights hanging like distended organs that made him think of an old man, useless now in a threadbare suit and expensive shoes whom no one wanted to talk to anymore. He couldn't imagine who would want to take on the colossus—smaller and less elaborate than the one he and Mira lived in, but still daunting and ridiculous enough—who would want to coddle it and tend to its bounty of needs, its pickiness. Mira always reported to him when people came to look at the property. She imagined the narrow inhales of prospective buyers who would be unnerved to find their own reflections caught too often in beveled glass or their voices skittering into corners. They might have thought they were the right kind of people for a house like this—bold, quirky, dreamy, rich—but when it came down to it, they couldn't imagine themselves or their children, chairs, and collections living there. They had to admit that they liked clean lines and straight vistas better. Mira had lived in her house for her entire thirty-four years, even during her time at the art school that was just down the hill, which meant she sometimes overlooked the architecture's Victorian haughtiness and how it could make people wonder about their own ambition. Wonder about themselves. Last week she'd told him that there'd been a guy in a tan Windbreaker taking pictures of the house as he walked the perimeter with a clipboard and a tape measure, occasionally blinking up at the high peaks of the roof lost in the vaporous sun of a Rhode Island spring.

Owen saw now that what had been a flash a moment before was really a man moving by the low iron fence that separated the properties. He lost him for a second in the vines and rhododendrons, and then the white shirt winked through the lilac's heart-shaped leaves of rich green. It was hard these days to know who was harmless, who was an intruder, a buyer or a thief.

"Someone's next door," Owen said.

Mira pushed back from the table and slipped between him and the window. Her shoulders drew up. The crime in their house had changed the way she kept watch; this was no longer the neighborhood of her past, the one she knew perfectly and benignly. It was a shock and disappointment for her to find that her goodwill in the world and longevity in the house had not made her invulnerable or earned her protection against the brutal side of city life. The crime had disturbed her and stolen her conviction, left her nights spiky, her days antsy. She took the break-in personally. Owen, eager to obliterate his own particular fear—the proximity of violence—had installed a heavy new lock on the door, security in the form of a glinty dead bolt. This man, though, with his lack of furtiveness, his leisurely step and crisp white shirt, didn't look as if he were anything to worry about.

"What's with the pacing?" Mira asked.

"Maybe he's measuring something. A lap pool, a dog run."

"A batting cage," she suggested. "A bomb shelter. Maybe he wants to park an RV there. He wants to buy the place. Tell him to go away, O. I like it empty."

"You tell him. Tell him the neighbors are assholes."

"Tell him how unfriendly they are." She leaned back against

him. "Tell him they won't take in his mail or water his plants or feed his cats. Tell him they'll never even bother to learn his name."

"Tell him how the old lady died in her bedroom and wasn't found for five days," Owen said.

At six-foot-six, he was more than a foot taller than Mira and had to bend to get his hands around her swooping waist, his pinkies grazing her inviting hipbones. She had spent the day at Brindle, the striving art school she owned and ran on the other side of the Point Street Bridge, and her dark, chaotic curls held the smell of clay and poster paints. This was her perfume—industrious, ambitious, alluring, the scent of best intentions. He adored her in a way that made his legs go watery.

"Tell him it was a horror show," he whispered, and took another deep inhale of her scent mixed with the sweet lilacs. "The corpse with open eyes, the rotting body, the damp bed."

As though this detail of death that Owen had spoken out loud, this notion of the old lady alone and undiscovered, was the one that finally caught his attention, the man in the yard turned to look at them. His face was a coin coppered in the last angle of the sun.

Mira pulled in her breath. "Oh," she said. "O."

"You know him?" Owen asked. He could be one of a number of former boyfriends, an old classmate, a friend of her dead parents. Rhode Island was a speck of land, and sometimes it seemed that Mira knew everyone on it—while he knew no one.

"For a second, I thought I did." She rubbed her eyes behind her glasses and rose on her bare feet for a better look. "But now I'm not sure. I can't really see."

"He definitely sees us," Owen said, and raised his hand.

The gesture was ambiguous and Owen wasn't sure what had compelled him to make it in the first place, but it was all the man needed to lift his own hand in return and move to the scrolled gate as though he'd been summoned. Instead of opening it, he swooped one long, thin denim-clad leg over and then the other. He was wearing soft leather shoes without socks—not at all the style of the sloppy, sneakered natives. In a moment, he was at the back door they'd left open for the scent of spring, sighing in relief as though he'd just crossed a roaring highway.

He dragged his forearm across his high forehead. "Thank God. There are actual people here. I was beginning to wonder where everyone was."

"Actual enough, anyway," Owen said, moving toward him. The setup was amusing and the man definitely out of place and harmless, but he still tasted the sourness of suspicion. "Can we help you in some way?"

Between narrow, almost maroon lips, the visitor's teeth flashed like a ticker tape of good news. Owen had a feeling that he knew the guy in some distant way, that he'd sat next to him on an airplane or they'd waited in the same doctor's office or on a bench at the DMV. His face was half memorable in the way handsome, strong-jawed men sometimes were—they looked not so much like themselves but like others.

"I hope you can help me. I've just bought the house next door. Here's the question: Do either of you know how to get the hot water going?" His eyes roamed the kitchen's shabby elegance and distant, shadowed ceiling. What was there but a round milk-glass fixture and years of unreachable cobwebs? "I'm not the most competent when it comes to domestic matters. Switches and buttons, that kind of thing. But we all have our failings, and mine's not the worst, I'm guessing." A contrite, suggestive smile snaked across his face. "Dials I can probably handle, though who knows?" His laugh was an expensive bauble.

Too many words, Owen decided. Too much padding around it all, too theatrical, too chattering. What was the guy really trying to say? And who talked like that? Mira was about to say something but pulled back. The dip just below her throat pulsed with questions. She was likely trying to figure out how she'd managed to miss the entire real estate transaction happening right next door when, in the past, nothing had ever escaped her.

"But look at this. My timing's perfect, as usual." The man nodded to the steaming pot on the stove, the sparkling lettuce in the colander, the doomed garlic on the cutting board. When he shook his head, his hair followed stylishly like a little poodle. "You were about to have dinner. I'm sorry for just appearing like this. Should I come back later—or would you prefer never to see me again?"

The question was pure flirtation. You could stop the future cold and unadventurously, it suggested, or take a chance on what might happen next. Which kind of person were you? The man, in his midsixties, Owen decided, spoke with a kind of put-on accent of breeding and affluence, half high-up East Coast, half something fake British, and as though he meant everything and nothing at the same time. A vaguely ridiculous person, Owen thought, a man too much about himself. The standard blue eyes were watery, the blade of nose off-balance, not the result of a fistfight—he was too wispy for something like that—but from aging imperfectly and maybe dissolutely, and there was the first slackness of skin on his neck. His wiry body had an almost dissipated look to it, the former muscles gone stringy as if his personal trainer had recently defected. He looked like he'd once been strong. But it was the pose, the boneless posture and thin wrists, that were most familiar to Owen, though he still couldn't say how or why, and the way the man's shirt hung open to reveal a smooth expanse of tan clavicle and a few gray chest hairs.

"No, it's absolutely fine. Really, this is okay." Mira had been holding her breath so long that the words came out in an enthusiastic and uncharacteristic rush.

"That's good, then. Because I can do without a lot," the man said, and leaned forward as if this were a coy game they had played before. "But not a hot shower. A man's necessity, don't you think?"

"A woman's, too," she said.

He didn't take his eyes off her. "You're absolutely right."

Heat flamed the tops of Mira's ears and she bounced on her feet. "Look, I just can't believe this. I have to say something, okay? Why should I pretend to be cool about it?" She threw Owen a look that suggested he should join in with her, that this holding-back act of theirs was over, but he had no idea what she was talking about. "How amazing is this? I watch you every night." She ran her hands down the front of her corduroy pants. Her toes curled to hide under the flared bottoms. "On television, I mean."

Their visitor gave a shrug of humility. "You're probably the only one."

"I doubt that." Mira's laugh was airy and eager.

Owen was still lost, and he didn't understand what Mira's jittery excitement was all about until the man ran a deliberate finger around his jaw and chin. That was the gesture that gave him away. Owen stepped back for a wider view, one that might also take in the years and compress them into a single second.

"Jesus Christ, you're from that show, years ago, that sitcom," he said. He sounded too fervent, but he couldn't help himself. He didn't *feel* like himself. "*Ancient Times*—am I right?"

"Right, and yes, years ago." A lift in the man's smile suggested he was pleased to be remembered. "That damned television."

"You're Bruno Macon," Owen said, the name landing on his tongue. How strange it was to know him then—in a way.

"Isn't that a terrible name? I never liked it. Sounds like some kind of burned-pork product. Actually, I'm Wilton Deere—Bruno was the character I played."

The correction prickled Owen; he liked to think he was no member of television's addled class, though he had been an avid member at one time. But Wilton Deere—was that any more of an authentic name? He marveled at how the presence of celebrity, even a one-time, one-show kind, could fluster him like this when usually he was checked and hard to read behind his reserve. He kept his enthusiasms close, his restraint closer. But here was that thrill of seeing someone who'd been on television in real, fleshy life. It was the enthrallment of proximity, the assumed glow, and it was intimacy, even if false, a put-on, like the man himself.

"But it's an interesting idea," Wilton said. "Which of us is actually the real person? But that doesn't happen so much anymore." He gave Owen an unhurried gaze that seemed to take in his thready chinos, faded blue T-shirt—a gift from the Spruance Middle School PTA—his averted dark eyes, his thick-veined arms, his loose hands, a flop of hair just starting to gray at forty. The sweat of scrutiny appeared above Owen's lip. "Most of the people who are old enough to remember my show are the same people who are old enough to forget. That's the irony of history. Those who've lived it have forgotten how it went." Wilton wagged his head, levered himself off the doorway and opened his hands, as if to say you couldn't do anything about the way some people were.

The notion wasn't untrue, but it had a rehearsed feeling to it, Owen decided. The man was actorish in a way he found embarrassing, with the too-expressive face, the stagey intonation. And all that feeling, that hammy honesty. The blowsy clothes, the feminine ankles. He wondered if the man was gay.

"History doesn't matter—not when there're always reruns," Mira said. Sleepless in the middle of the night since the break-in and watching the TV newly installed in the bedroom, she spoke like a recent convert. Her face flashed with authority. "One, two, three o'clock in the morning. Seven days a week, if you want."

"Insomnia?" Wilton asked. "Insomniacs and the Japanese. My fan base these days."

"I couldn't figure it out at first," Mira said, taking a step back and weaving her fingers through her curls. "You were completely familiar, so familiar that I couldn't really see you, I couldn't make sense of your face. Were you someone I knew? I wasn't exactly expecting you to show up at the back door." She recounted their meeting as if it were already their delightful history. "And then."

"And then," Wilton said. "Here I am."

Owen caught Wilton glance at himself in the mirror by the basement door and disapproving lines etched around the man's mouth. He was a less robust version of the star he once was years before, but he puffed up his chest and Mira rounded her shoulders to catch his attention. And who wouldn't look at her the way Wilton did just then, returned from his own troubling reflection, at how her pants sat so swingy on her hips that you couldn't help but calculate the rousing rise of her bones, the braless statement of her full breasts, the way she moved like she was on a boat commanding the waves and whales? No, the man wasn't gay; he looked carnivorous, a drop of moisture at the corner of his mouth. Mira's eyes were a remarkable, colorlessly pure element and expertly focused. She never wasted her attention and she could be fierce with her loyalties, fierce with her stubbornness. Wilton blinked and blinked as if she were a very bright signal.

"So, you bought the house next door," Owen said, taking a step closer to Wilton, to get him away from his wife.

With exaggerated concern, Wilton back-stepped out of the doorway to look at his hulking purchase. They followed him out onto the cool bricks of the patio. "You say that so ominously. Why? Is there something wrong with the place?"

"Nothing wrong with it at all," Mira assured him. "It's an amazing house, one of the few old beauties still left and not chopped up into condos. You're very lucky."

"An old beauty," Wilton repeated.

"Did they tell you that the previous owner died in it? Let's just say no one checked in on her for a few days." Owen offered the details as a challenge, a way to bend the air and see which way Wilton might sway, or if he would sway at all. "It wasn't pretty. Five days in the heat."

"Wow, O. He needs to know that?" Mira laughed, but she seemed to understand the test and turned to Wilton expectantly.

The man examined the ink-stained clouds as the city minutes ticked off. "I suppose she had to die somewhere, and isn't it best to die in your own bed? After all, it wasn't her problem that they didn't find her for a while. That's how I want to go, in my own bed. But I just hope they got the body out and let some fresh air in. Maybe a few squirts of air freshener." He wiggled his fingers under his nose. "Anyway, it gives the place a certain pedigree, its own drama. Every house should have a story. This is my first time here," he continued, "which should explain why I can't get anything to work. That's what happens when you buy a house over the phone after visiting a few rooms online. They call that a virtual tour, but it's virtually useless. Anyway, a wad of cash, a leap of faith, and here I am. I'd never even been to Rhode Island before today, and now I own a piece of it. All very efficient and perfectly American."

There was no *we* in the details, Owen noted, and Wilton had

tempered his voice to make the story sound empty of attach-
ments, roots, responsibility, lovers, and in the process, arouse a
kind of sympathetic curiosity. Who was so untethered and free to
buy instant residence anywhere he wanted? No one just landed in
Rhode Island, after all, not the first settlers looking for refuge in
a forgiving patch of earth and shoreline, and not Owen. It was a
place to go when you needed to escape something. And not this
guy either—who'd already told them how he'd like to die. What
else did they need to know?

"By the way," Wilton said, cradling his elbows and smirking,
"you haven't told me your names yet. That doesn't seem quite
fair."

Mira put her hands on her head in happy surrender. Her glasses
slid to the end of her nose. "You're right. That's just terrible. I'm
Mira Thrasher and he's Owen Brewer."

Wilton turned and his gaze climbed up the shingles of their
house to the many eaves and the slate roof's highest, homicidal
point, where the copper sail of the wind gauge was frozen in its
north-south axis. He took in the carriage house and the weighty,
surrounding houses. He took in the evening's uncertain hour and
both of them, Owen's arm around Mira a little too tight.

"Thrasher and Brewer," he said. "Like exhibits in the Museum
of Industry."

Mira laughed, unhooked Owen's hand from her waist, and offered to take a stab at Wilton's hot-water heater. "I'm sure it's nothing, just a switch. Or maybe a dial," she teased, elbowing Wilton
without actually touching him. Owen marveled at her ease—and
was uneasy with it. Mira was not usually won over so soon.

"Good, because I'm completely hopeless," Wilton said and followed Mira across the lawn, content to be led by her. Mira called

to Owen that she'd be right back, then she kicked open the gate
with an athletic flourish and they disappeared into the vast house.

Back inside the kitchen. Owen kept an eye on Wilton's house while
he dried the lettuce, boiled the spaghetti, and waited for Mira to
return. He chopped parsley but the distracted blade nicked his
thumb. Blood dotted his paper towel bandage. How long did it
take to turn on the fucking water heater? He watched lights next
door go on and off in one room and then another. Finally, there
was a diffuse glow on the third floor within the recesses of the
eaves. What was Wilton showing her? Or was Mira pointing out
city sights to him? Restless, Owen took his students' papers from
his bag to the room Mira called his study, as though he were a
studier, a scholar, when he was nothing close. But this was the
same room, the same chair even, that Mira's father, grandfather,
and great-grandfather had used. Two tall windows faced Whittier Street, their dusty velvet curtains pulled apart like revealing
skirts. Every Thrasher male must have watched his own timely
parade pass by and felt like its master and leader. Mira's family was like that—proprietary and boastful. Owen, though, felt
more like a parade follower, still an intruder in this house, in this
city and state—and on rare and troubling days, even in Mira's
life. It appeared that no woman, in generations of high-minded
Thrashers, had ever claimed a single room as her own study. Even
Mira used the bed or the kitchen table when she was working
even though there was plenty of other space. Was it because every
woman already thought of the house as entirely hers?

　　He turned in the desk chair, still not sure after five years of
marriage how he was to think of this house and its contents.
Whose cracked rubber bands were these, whose blackened and

ancient pennies in an ashtray from the Hope Club, whose keys without locks? Whose marble busts, Chinese porcelain bowls, inlaid boxes, and masterly paintings? Were they his, too? Most of the books on the shelves were not his, and neither were the many pieces of art that interrupted the room's green-banded wallpaper, not the oak desk with its cavernous drawers, not the swiveling leather chair grown shiny from years of commanding, virile body heat. He didn't know much about the endless booty in the rest of the house either. He slept in a bed that had belonged to people long dead. He was surrounded by their bureaus and pillows, wrapped in their linen sheets. He bathed and shaved and shit where they had. He made love to their very last daughter. Mira's father's family—a long line of aggressive lawyers and businessmen with too much city influence—had been single-mindedly acquisitive. They'd hoarded and stuffed every room in the house, even the far back ones never used, as if collecting were a family disease passed down. His own father, Edward, covered the splintered sills of his aging pond-side cottage with an ever-changing collection of the natural: sticks, shells, bleached fish skulls, shriveling apples. When he was bored with it, he just opened the door and tossed the junk out. Nothing was ever tossed out here; it only grew in value and inapproachability. Owen didn't know anything about the one object he coveted in a dark, felonious way: he'd named it the squid pen. Tentacles were etched onto the silver sheath, and two red enamel dots on the tapering cap were collusive eyes. The fountain pen's long black bladder was cracked and limp, vaguely sexual and bereft. He was fairly certain Mira didn't know the pen existed, resting in a velvet-lined coffin at the very back of the desk drawer where it had probably been forever, and where she had no reason to venture.

Tonight, though, his students' papers, soft pencil on smudgy lined sheets or florid pink or purple ink, were definitely his and needed to be read for tomorrow. He looked at the one on top: *My mother washe peoples haredos in a store. Her shirts is always covered with hares.* He asked his students to tell the stories of their lives, but sometimes reading them made him feel hopeless. It was the one crucial lesson he could give his sixth-graders—how to explain who they were and where they came from, what encouraged them—but he was stolen away now from their accounts by the long absence of his wife. He knew that his growing disquiet was apelike and primal, his woman with another man. Wilton was strange but not exactly a stranger, and he had the indemnity of fame. It would be easy enough to go next door and yell for Mira, but to do that would be indelible and he would be the macho, barking husband forever. The jealous one. Neighbors had only first impressions and gestures to go on; everything after that was silence and spying. He read on. *She sweeps the floor and thros the hares in the garbij. Her hands smell like roses and kokonut when she come home to me.*

When he'd first moved into the house, an enthralling, improbable world, he'd brought only a few things from his two-room apartment in Fox Point. He could offer some books, a few brown towels, the fibers stiff, and his beat-up television. Amazingly, there had never before been a television in the Thrasher house. The antenna had long ago been snapped off, leaving a sharp, silver scab. Until a few months ago, the thing had sat cold in the study, unwatched except during the world's disasters, war blunders, and good games, its blank screen attracting dust, ugly in a room with a much higher class of objects. But Mira couldn't sleep after the break-in, her insomnia twisting around her like an old nightgown, and when she refused pills, the dreamy Starstella or the practical Dreamatin, Owen had carried the television upstairs, the smell of dusty electronics spiraling through his nostrils. He put it at the foot of their bed on a small table he'd found in one of the many unoccupied back rooms with their legions of empty beds. When you wake up in the middle of the night, he told her, turn it on and give it a try. She was skeptical and didn't like to be guided, but she didn't mind his concern.

She admitted that her sleeplessness ate away at her mood, dulled her, and left her to worry not just about more break-ins (that had only set off other things, she claimed) but about Brindle—never enough money, the fickleness of its century-old building, the at-risk kids getting riskier, the trembling old people falling, the addicts shooting up behind the Dumpster. She might end up letting them all down and losing the place that was everything to her. At other times, on particularly alert nights when her feet jiggled under the sheets, her worries were more fantastical— flames shooting with three-alarm exuberance from Brindle's front door, an epic flood that would breach the Fox Point hurricane barrier and float her school out to Narragansett Bay. It was this amorphous prediction of disaster that seemed closer to the truth of her middle-of-the-night restiveness, because what was fear of ruin really but a glimpse of abject loneliness and the very end of things, of death? Owen knew the fear. He'd lived with it until he'd met Mira, and he wanted to save her from its dark, invading force. Sometimes he'd wake for an instant and see that she'd put on her glasses as if they'd help her make sense of the errant illumination crossing the ceiling. What she'd landed on in those sleepless hours to soothe and amuse her was the newly installed television and *Ancient Times*. And now Wilton Deere was here in

the pallid, pampered flesh, and she lingered on the third floor of
his new house, doing who knows what. The clean confluence of
events left Owen a little light-headed. This was like Mira in a way,
to disappear, to leave him wondering.

In the kitchen again, he looked at their sagging dinner and
then outside at the yard begging for the season's first cut. He went
downstairs for the mower. The basement was a chilled museum
of old tools and freakish, mushroomy growths and fuzzy cocoons.
The metallic bite of the air barreled through his sinuses as he
dragged the machine up the bulkhead stairs. It was a clattering
old thing, one of an array of worn tools with wooden handles
rubbed smooth from use, not by anyone in Mira's family, but by
those they hired. The family's aristocratic aspirations ended when
Mira's parents died with the definitive shock of a car accident
when she was nineteen. To them, a son-in-law teaching at a public
school would have looked like no aspiration at all. They wouldn't
have approved of Owen, a tall, silent cipher. But his ambition was
to unburden himself, to ignore tragedy's daily reminders, to descend and settle within this house and this marriage and their
future children, and into this precise hour and every other to follow. It seemed vastly ambitious to him.

The yard was full of weeds and volunteer shoots and alive with
the night tripping in to fill up the spaces where day had been. The
lone dogwood tree, ripe to bursting, had a shim of slate from the
roof lodged in its trunk, and the plot where he grew tomatoes, Big
Boys and Beefsteaks and Early Girls, was ready to be turned over.
Mira loved tomatoes and anything sweet. The mower choked on
the rocks that appeared after every winter as though they were
what those last, stubborn piles of snow turned into. At this hour,
the neighborhood had settled into something dense and drawn in

on itself. Unlike Mira, he hardly knew who lived in the houses surrounding him. He was still—and might always be—a newcomer here.

"Cutting grass in the dark," Mira said, coming up behind him. "That's a new idea." She pressed her cheek against his backbone. "I asked Wilton for dinner. He has nothing to eat in that house. And no car to go anywhere. He doesn't even drive," she added with strange intensity, as if this detail suggested something much bigger.

She said nothing about why she'd been gone so long. Her breath against him was warm with anticipation, but it chilled his skin with the same premonition of disaster he'd had earlier by the sink. No, he wanted to tell her, this will not turn out well. Tell the man to go away.

"It's okay that I asked him, O, isn't it?" she said. "He's all by himself over there. The place echoes like crazy, there's no furniture, nothing but a blow-up mattress. And it will be something different, a change." Her eyes were lit from behind. Was change what she was after?

"What were you doing for so long over there?" he asked.

"We talked, that's all, and looked around. He hadn't even been on the third floor yet."

Wilton appeared at that moment, a white-shirted, perfectly timed apparition with a bottle of wine in each hand. His house wasn't entirely empty, apparently. He pointed at the mower and moved the bottles under his arms like cocked rifles. It seemed to Owen that he'd overheard their conversation. "Please tell me I'm not going to have to do that. I'm not the mowing type."

It was hard to imagine Wilton with all his domestic bafflements and his prissy shoes ever pushing a lawn mower or cleaning a toilet or boiling an egg. "Not if you pay someone to do it for you,"

Owen said, and looked at the man's profile, which had become pensive for a moment. Was he wondering how he'd managed to find himself here of all places?

After his show had gone off the air, Wilton Deere had disappeared. If Owen ever heard his name again, he'd forgotten the face to go with it. He considered what it meant to fade away so thoroughly like that, to be known and then hardly known at all. Would you know who you were anymore, would you know your own pretense if no one was there to tell you? The man had gotten an infusion of celebrity, and once unhooked from its IV line, he'd slipped, desiccated, under the bed. And now, to end up in Providence, a city that claimed to love progress but didn't know what to do with outsiders, a place that was proudly peculiar and proudly backward, in a house he could never fill by himself. But Mira had given him back some of his color and blood. He'd found his fan and his admirer, and his face softened. Wilton's sigh sounded almost content, and he turned to give them a broad, hungry smile.

2

Wilton perched in the kitchen doorway until Mira waved him in and showed him where to sit, and then he ran his hands across the scarred wooden table as if reading the hieroglyphics of a family history. He was captivated by the simplest dinner they served; by the chipped plates, last survivors of old, gold-rimmed sets; by a chrome toaster on the counter with its hairy black cord, nothing new or gleaming here; by the mismatched chairs. It was as if he'd been boxed up for years, shut out of a peopled life. *So this is a pepper grinder. This is a marriage.* Mira lit two candles and Owen savored Wilton's red wine. It was like nothing he'd tasted before and made him melt into the flickering hour. He knew he was being seduced.

"There was one episode I liked a lot," Owen said, when they'd been at the table for a long time and the candles were sputtering stubs. He was loose with the drink, the time, and the talk about *Ancient Times.* Wilton gave them no more than they asked for, claiming there was nothing more idiotic than an actor going on and on, and about television, no less. Though Owen had not seen the show in more than twenty years, the story lines and pictures came back to him with surprising clarity.

Ancient Times had been about the inept staff of a nursing home that sat high up on a bluff in a plantation-like building.

The residents often spent entire episodes sitting in rockers with blankets across their soggy laps, mumbling semidemented comments. Bruno Macon was the well-intentioned activities director who wore Italian suits that were always smeared with canned corn by the time the credits came on. With his elastic expressions of haplessness and self-deprecation, he tripped over boxes, flew down stairs, and got caught in the workings of adjustable beds. He landed face-first in butterscotch pudding. He was an acrobat of humiliation and grace, a man who could take mortification's blow as long as it came softened with love. He gazed at his decrepit, snarling charges as if they were the boundless Atlantic Ocean, things of beauty.

"Which episode was that?" Wilton asked. He was a slyly unenthusiastic eater, attending to each strand of spaghetti and maneuvering the slivers of garlic to the side.

"When you discovered a stash of vodka bottles one of the residents was hiding in his closet."

Mira looked between the two men. "I don't know that one."

"That's the beauty of reruns," Owen told her. "Wait long enough and you'll eventually see everything. It could almost make you believe in reincarnation."

Wilton turned to Owen. "I'm getting the impression you watched a lot of television in your day."

At thirteen, fourteen, and fifteen years old, watching endless television while his father shut his door and wrote his books about the mysteries of beach erosion and toad populations, Owen had felt a little better about his motherless life in a drafty cottage in Cape Cod in the thick of locust and scrub pine. The ruminating pond was in front of him and at his back was all uncertainty, a landscape of highway, dunes, and shuttered summer houses. The woods had natured on without him and the season's clouds had drifted by, while in his face was a different kind of life on the screen—loud, colorful, and riotous with ads for things his father would never buy. He hadn't cared what was on—sitcoms, dramas, baseball games, news. He'd liked the late-night talk shows with their parade of shiny guests and all that jocularity, all that fake persuasion. He drank more wine now and considered television's peculiar power over memory. It imprinted a picture because a rehearsed moment was as close to perfect as you could get. You could watch a scene over and over and it was always the same, while what was true and troubling was never fixed and wiggled out of your hands every time you tried to grasp it.

"I watched all the time," Owen said. "Anything and everything. Half of my understanding of the world I got from television."

"And the other half?" Mira asked.

"The other half was knowing that what I saw was on television wasn't true at all," he said.

"Which left you," Mira paused, and gave him a teasing smile, "where, exactly? Half-formed?"

"A mess?" Owen said.

Wilton frowned at a drop of oil on his shirt. "Don't you think that vodka episode was in bad taste, though? Poking fun at demented old people in wheelchairs, ladies who soiled themselves? Old drunks? I was just the actor. I did what I was told, so what could I say?"

"He opened the guy's closet door and the bottles just kept tumbling out," Owen explained to Mira. "A hundred bottles. He was log-rolling on them."

"Yes, senility used to be a real scream. People take it much too seriously now, Alzheimer's is a real conversation killer." Wilton refilled their glasses. "Alcoholism used to be a laugh riot, too. And I should know—my father was a barrel of monkeys."

A small crack opened, allowing them to peek into the man's history—and they were meant to look. Mira chased a fleck of green across her plate with her fork. Wilton rolled up one sleeve with exaggerated care. On the inside of his almost hairless arm, scars crisscrossed the skin in fine embroidery. Candlelight made the damage look like scribbles.

"What you didn't see," he said, laying his arm out like a pale offering, "was what happened when I came down on the bottles. They were supposed to be plastic—but they weren't."

Mira ran her finger down the raised lines. Her lips moved as she read the scars. Owen was struck by the idea of how Wilton had paid for their amusement, but more so by how Mira was touching this man with intimate curiosity. A tickle danced at the base of his skull. He hated the feeling. Mira drew her hand back and put it on her lap. Wilton's eyelids drooped. He looked sated.

"Let's move into another room," Mira announced into the charged silence. She stood and grabbed the second bottle of wine. "This huge house and we only live in a small part of it. We like the idea of space, but then we don't know what to do with it when we have it. We might as well live in a cell."

Moving down the weighty oak hallway to the front of the house, Wilton stopped to consider the art, the details of the architecture, the newel post and panels, the table lamp that cast a glow over life's mess: a spattering of papers, keys, change, a collection of Mira's fluorescent orange parking tickets. He tapped the lamp's glass shade and looked at the colors it threw onto the high ceiling. A Merchanti, he said, and sucked air in through his teeth. He appeared to know his stuff—or was pretending to. Who or what the hell was Merchanti? Owen wondered. There were two expansive rooms at the front of the house. One contained a seldom-played piano and a stiff arrangement of furniture. In the other, where they gathered, Mira turned on a single, low lamp. When she and Wilton sat on the velvet couch, the cushions exhaled the endless dander and dust of Mira's dead relatives. You couldn't escape it in this house, a DNA windfall. Owen sensed the room's permanence in the solid, patrician arms of his seat, a chair that had been in its spot much longer than he had and would still be there long after he was gone. The many objects in the room regarded the three of them with superior disinterest. During the day, sun poured into this room, but to Owen, the house would always be a little cold and dark.

Mira worked the corkscrew. Her green shirt, dotted with paint, swooped low at the neck and the rise of her chest shimmered with the faintest mist of sweat. She was beautiful in a way that didn't always strike people immediately. What they first noticed was that her eyes were exaggerations, stretched wide, and that she had an overstated, ardent mouth. Owen knew she was embarrassed by her mouth's fullness at times, by how people assumed its ripe offering was her, and she pressed two fingers to her lower lip to hide herself. She gave herself away like this, her private moment of retreat. But when you watched her in action, relaxed like this—as Wilton watched her now—you saw a face that was somehow more than any other. Mira was more than any woman Owen had ever known, more intent, determined, more completely herself and still at times not known to him. Which is how he knew it should be with a woman you loved. To know her completely would be the end of trying.

"Tell me more about Brindle," Wilton said, still watching her.

"Oh, I don't know," she laughed evasively. "You really want to hear about that?"

Wilton nodded, and Mira's flattered mouth was glossy with wine, the lower lip exposed. The cork made a satisfying pop to match an enthusiasm about Brindle that came on like a summer storm and filled the room. Owen hadn't seen her this expansive and loose in a while, certainly not since the break-in. She talked about the school's fundraiser coming up next month, the life-drawing class for the residents of an assisted-living facility bused in from Lincoln, and the ceramics class for the boys from Noah House who arrived in the battered van two afternoons a week, sometimes so agitated that she could only guess at what had happened at school or at home. They were always hungry, so she fed them and gave them clothes when they didn't have enough. Some had terrible stories.

"You have no idea," she said.

Wilton shook his head. "I'm sure I don't."

"You can't imagine," Owen said.

He knew that Mira thought of those who had passed through Brindle and her curative, instructive hands in the same way a salesman marked his successes on a map with colored pins, conquests that dotted the city. You looked for density, entire shaded areas, progress. He admired how certain she was of her work and her impact, when on many days, he doubted his own effectiveness in the classroom. He was probably not meant to teach children; he still didn't know what he was meant to do.

Wilton sighed theatrically. "Good work must make all the difference in a life. Personally, I have no ambition myself." He smirked, but his expression suggested a resigned truth about himself. "I'm just a man who was once on television. And what's that ever done for anyone? Television's for shit. That's not the real kind of good work."

"Good work?" Mira said. "I don't know that I do good work. Necessary work, maybe, though very small in the scheme of things. Way too small." She sipped her wine. "The trouble is, there's never enough money to do even this miniscule part. And it's getting tougher and tougher out there every day. And the way things are now? All those multicolored kids with the funny accents and all those shaky recovering drug addicts—they just don't bring in the bucks like they used to. My donors are suffering from compassion fatigue. And the older they get, the less they care. Old people love their pennies all over again. They hide them under their pillows at night." She sat back and rested her feet against the edge of the low table. On the wall behind her were drawn portraits of the Thrashers with their arrowed noses and platinum eyes. They were gazelles, regal, elegant, a haughty species on the plains of Providence. Mira was one of them, the last of the herd for now, an orphan without siblings, a woman without children. Car lights washed over Mira and Wilton, turning them ghostly for an instant.

"Amazing to have grown up with all this," Wilton said, and opened his hands to the room. "This was my fantasy as a kid. To grow up in a place full of beautiful things."

"But look at it," Mira said, without looking at any of it. "A million things to know about and I am no expert. It's enough to remember to clean the stuff occasionally and lock the door."

Sometimes Mira, struck by an urgent, wordless mood, whipped around the place in her bathrobe, with her hair wild, wielding an ancient feather duster. Nothing in the house had been chosen by her, but it was all profoundly hers at the instant of her parents' deadly car accident, and she was mostly cold to it. She didn't think in terms of liking something for its associations or memories; she wasn't sentimental or nostalgic in that way. She was captive and curator, weary but responsible. Her tenure in the house was for now; someone else's would follow. Her children, when she was ready to have them, she said.

"But to be surrounded by it," Wilton insisted. "It would change the way you see the world. It might look like a more forgiving place."

"Or less forgiving," Owen said.

Mira gave Wilton a long and serious gaze. "We're not rich, if that's what you're thinking." Her eyes shifted for an instant to Owen, who saw that she was well on her way to being drunk. "Really, we don't have any money, almost none. Owen teaches in a public school, and I don't exactly make a profit at Brindle. We eat lots of spaghetti, and we keep the heat really low. What? It's true, O. Don't look at me like that."

She wasn't wrong: they were always short and too much was left untended. Their cars were lousy, rusted, close to death, and the house ate cash and time. Their clothes were old. Brindle was always hungry, too. What Owen earned—including the many evenings he spent out each week tutoring kids—disappeared. He was tired of being so strapped, so conscious of every dollar. But it was ridiculous, insulting even, to cry poor sitting in this house and in this room that reeked of deeply rooted affluence. And to worry about Brindle the way she did when a single item, maybe that Merchanti lamp, might float the place—or an entire family—for a good while.

"You know you could always sell something," he suggested.

"Let's not get into this again, O, okay?" she said. "It's boring. A stupid conversation."

"But you could, Mira. You could sell something. Who would stop you?" Though he pushed at her now, a little reckless from too much wine himself and her stubbornness on this point, he knew it was a subject he couldn't really touch. What was here, after all, did not belong to him. "Sell the fucking lamp out there, for instance. No more spaghetti."

"Stop, please," she said. "Enough. I'm sorry I brought it up."

Wilton looked from one to the other, then leaned against Mira and lowered his voice to a seductive hush. "I have lots and lots of money. I have way too much. It's obscene. Residuals are recession-proof." He threw up his hands over and over as if he were tossing a million bills into the air. "Oodles and oodles of it. Cascades. Avalanches." He paused. "Duck! Here it comes!"

Owen had the feeling that Wilton had seen the gap open up between Mira and him, measured it, and then maneuvered himself into the space between. He wanted to kick the guy out now and get rid of him. He didn't like what was happening to his wife, who was acting out this goofy play with a man she didn't even know. But Mira was delighted by Wilton's miming, put her head back, and let the imaginary money wash over her. Owen pushed himself out of the armchair. He'd had enough. The late hour and the wine were going to hit him at some point tomorrow in the classroom, and his gaze would float over the heads of his students, looking for somewhere soft to land. Even the kids who never paid attention, the ones who slumped on their desks in the morning as their breakfast of Doritos and Sprite worked its soporific magic, would notice his missed beats. He remembered the papers he'd meant to finish and raised his arms over his head in a stretch, showing his length. His shirt lifted to expose inches of his skin above his belt. He meant this display to be nothing subtle to Mira—or to Wilton.

"Time to wrap it up," he said. He tried to meet Mira's eye but she looked away, though it was clear she understood exactly what his gesture was about: I want you to leave this man and come to bed with me.

"I have to be up in a few hours," Owen said to Wilton. "You have to go home now."

"That's rude," Mira said, and laughed.

"No. Of course it isn't. It's late. I understand." Wilton sprung from the couch. "Sometimes I forget people actually get up in the morning, get going, have jobs and do things, be productive." Nothing was slumped or wrinkled about him, nothing tired. "That was a wonderful dinner. You don't know how long it's been since I had a meal at anyone's table, in anyone's house. I'd forgotten how significant it is. And I'm just a man who barged in, out of nowhere. My excellent luck, it seems."

"What will you do tomorrow?" Mira asked. Her voice had an almost plaintive edge to it.

Wilton slipped his hands into loose pockets. "You're wondering about my plans, why I'm here."

"Yes, but it's none of my business," Mira said. "Forget it."

"No, it is your business. I'm you neighbor, you should know these things." He pressed a hand to his chest. "I have a daughter, Anya. She's moving here in a few weeks, starting medical school."

"She'll be living with you?" Mira asked.

"Well, not at first. I hope at some point soon, but for now, no. To start, I'm just hoping to see her from time to time." There was more to say, but not tonight, his indulgent expression suggested, another dose of seduction soon to come.

Owen inched Wilton to the front door and walked with him to the sidewalk. Whittier Street was overhung by oak and linden branches. The musk of aroused boxwoods and now the drifting perfume of the lilacs in the yard, was the season's return and softened Owen toward Wilton. There was something about the man that made Owen think he might understand how the murk of sadness could blur the stars. When he was a kid on a night like this, he told Wilton, he would smell the slime of tadpoles and hear the ferns unfurling around the pond where he grew up and believe that everything was possible in his life. Later, a night like this had shown him how that possibility could be over when a friend had died. He looked away from Wilton, disarmed by how easily he'd offered this piece of private history to a man he wasn't even sure he liked or trusted.

"You're young. Life's still all ahead for you," Wilton said, and put a companionable hand on his shoulder. "I think you and Mira are pretty remarkable people."

"You don't know us." Owen balked at the easy flattery.

The houses surrounding them were dark and fortified in sleep, except for Alice Jessup's. Alice was over a hundred, Owen said as they walked past Wilton's, a friend of Mira's grandmother who was now attended by round-the-clock nurses who placed alien green nightlights in the hallways as if to give their charge a glimpse of her spectral future. At the end of Whittier, on the corner of Hope, chain link confined the high school. The clock was frozen in its peeling tower. Owen pointed across Hope and deep into the expensive, leafy neighborhood where Spruance Middle School sat like a stripped and broken car on a grassless hill. It had been abandoned by its neighbors years ago, he told Wilton, and was now populated by poor kids who were bused in from harder parts of the city. Children who weren't white, he meant.

They turned back. Wilton had left his front door unlocked. Owen told him that the city might look innocent, but it wasn't. He should watch out for coyotes loping up from the river, sniffing around for cats left mewing on doorsteps. Criminals slid by in silent cars, headlights turned off. Houses were broken into all the time; the smash-and-grab was a Rhode Island specialty, like frozen lemonade and clam cakes. He told Wilton about the crime in his own house. He hoped to scare the man some and make him pull back into himself, to make him slightly less sure that he belonged here.

When Wilton went inside, Owen stood on the street and watched as a light went on in the bedroom where the former owner had slept—and died. When he looked at his own black bedroom window, he knew that behind it was the warmth of his wife waiting for him. In the kitchen, the plates were still on the table, the pots tumbled in the sink with their handles reaching out to be rescued. The room was filled with the mortal scent of extinguished candles.

Upstairs, Owen stood in the dark bedroom and undid his belt. The brass buckle clinked.

"That sound," Mira said, sleepily. "It's really the most erotic one on earth. Come and fuck me."

"Christ, Mira. What's up with you tonight?" He got in next to her. A salty smell escaped from the sheets, another gust when she rolled against him, another when she exerted the greatest power in the smallest pressure to move him on top of her. Her skin was an urgent temperature. She liked to be weighed down by him. She made him breathless in how she touched him, her fingers at the base of his spine. His face was at her neck, his erection insistent now. He listened for what she was thinking.

"So you didn't really answer me before," he said, parting her legs and sliding into her. "About what took you so long over at Wilton's."

"Was it a long time?" She spoke distractedly, her body suddenly distant. "Wilton didn't really need any help with the water heater, you know. I think he just wanted some company for a while, someone to walk with him through all those empty rooms. He was a little spooked by the place. Who wouldn't be?"

Owen stopped moving and pulled back to see her face. "What did you talk about that whole time?"

"God, who knows? And that shirt, open too far like an ancient swinger," she said. "No one will know what to do with him here, what to make of him." She rolled Owen off, her desire ebbed. He was left at sea, treading water, while she'd rowed to shore.

"When does anything like this happen?" she asked. "When does someone like him just appear at your back door? I don't know how to explain it, O, that he's here now when he was just there." She pointed at the television at the foot of the bed. "I don't watch television for my entire life, and then, in the middle of the night, I see a show that's been off for decades, I laugh at this guy, and all of a sudden he's moved next door, of all the places."

"You don't have to explain it," Owen said, irritated. "He has to live somewhere."

"Yes," she said, "that's exactly what I mean. And somewhere is here."

"Because his daughter is here," Owen said, but he knew she wasn't really listening. She was busy with her own logic. "I thought we were making love, Mira."

"I'm suddenly really tired. I'm sorry. I feel like an idiot." She touched his face. "You know, it's like I conjured him up. I made him out of my imagination, a real person."

Was Wilton who she needed in some way? The wine drummed in Owen's stomach. He was far from sleeping, but in a few moments, he heard Mira take her dive into dreams.

He imagined he heard Wilton shifting and sighing on an air mattress next door, imagined the sound of his heartbeat echoing in the empty house. If Mira believed she had plucked Wilton out of the television screen—conjured him up, but for what?—he believed he had plucked Mira from the distant rooftops six years before. Because he'd needed to, needed her. Through the wire-etched window of his first classroom at Spruance, before they'd ever met, he'd spotted the contour of her house a mile away. With his back to his students, he'd looked every day at the determined roofline and stately chimneys above the trees and telephone wires, and it had been like reading his own EKG. Its rhythm was vibrant, alive with highs and lows and history, but it was also out of sync in places, with an extra beat or a missed one, quiet and then sometimes howling with grief. But he couldn't look away, and every time he saw the same thing.

The year before he'd fled overnight and wordless to Providence, leaving his job, his students, and his friends, he'd come so close to being killed one night in May that he'd tasted the briny end wash over him. The cold had bathed his eyelids. With Mira breathing lightly beside him, he couldn't help replaying the moment the bullet announced its intention, not for him after all, but for Caroline, the woman he'd been having dinner with. His life was held in the gun's slightest shift to the left. He could have moved, he could have shifted to meet it, but he hadn't. He'd saved himself.

Caroline was not his girlfriend, though they had been sleeping together for almost a year. It was a strange, chilly arrangement. She was prickly and quick to defend herself, while he was evasive and sarcastic, and together they made a sticky mixture they couldn't extract themselves from. They went to movies and museums, a Knicks game she hadn't liked because her sweater kept getting caught in the flip-up seat. They ate at El Sombrero, where scorched cacti and a faded piñata crowded the front window. That night, Caroline chillingly bit off the point of a chip with her front teeth. This might be the night to end whatever it was they were doing together; he'd been chewing on the notion for a while. Dissatisfaction had finally begun to mobilize him.

But she spoke first. "We should discuss us," she said, as though she'd gotten advance warning about the dinner's topic. She was measured, exact. She didn't intend to hurt his feelings; this was nothing personal, she said. "But people who sleep together should at least like each other."

Owen's tamale was impossible to swallow. He knew he should be relieved, but there was still the gut punch of surprise. He gulped his Corona and saw her very reasonable expression. He said something sarcastic and vaguely hurtful. A voice rose and a chair scraped at the front of the restaurant. She asked if he wanted to try her chicken and held out her full fork to him, but she didn't want him to take the fork itself. She would feed him instead, always holding on to what was hers. Somewhere, a plate fell and shattered on the red tile. Fork still aloft, Caroline swiveled to get a view of the action. Her face grew grim and old. Hair swept behind her ear fell forward. A man wearing a cheap black ski mask, the eyes and mouth holes outlined in red yarn, approached. A gun was attached to his right hand, which rose toward an imaginary horizon, Owen's head pinned like a kite against it. This was a cartoon stickup, a joke as synthetic as the threads rising from the mask in static electricity. Owen had the urge to laugh. Caroline's jaw thrust forward urging him to do something. But what? His heart was under his tongue, his bowels retreating fast. He struggled to get his fingers around his wallet and extract it from his back pocket. He put it in the man's hand. Caroline took her purse off the back of her chair and held it on her lap. Water rushed innocently in the open kitchen behind them. The skin around the gunman's eyes glistened and his lips pushed forward. He gestured with a tick of the gun for Caroline to give her bag up. She said no, and then: *fuck you.*

This finally was the reason they shouldn't be together; she said no when she should have said yes. Later on, Owen realized that moments of terror can have their own solipsistic lucidity. Back then, though, he began to piss down his leg. Caroline gave a look that seemed to say that the entire world was a disappointment, Owen at the top of her list—he, a big man and still a coward— and then she fell off her chair like a furious little girl, her hands obstinate on the tile, her skirt up to her waist revealing black un- derwear, her legs straight out, one shoe off. She had a startled expression. The sound of a jet roared through Owen's head—but long after the shot had been fired. The timing was off and these were the moments that still stuttered until they slipped away from him out of frustration. It was disastrous, almost seven years later, to still detect the basaltic odor of Caroline's death and he could only press his arm across his face to block it out. He couldn't see her face anymore.

He'd met Mira a year later, and then not on Whittier Street or in her house, but on Ives Street, outside his apartment in Fox Point, on a summer's nighttime glittering sidewalk where she nearly hit him with her bike. They had an unhurried conversa- tion, she still straddling the bike's cracked leather seat, while they watched traffic drift down Wickenden. She'd come to find the boy who'd stolen ten dollars from Brindle. There was something defiant and assured about her, with her old-fashioned, clattery bike, her torn sneakers, her deep red lipstick, her funny, bright, and strange clothes. When they turned in the direction of the bay, Owen snuck a few sideways glances at her. He liked how she kept pushing her glasses up her nose with her index finger. It was bookish and sexy. He liked her long neck and high clavicle, her smokeless smoker's voice. She was on a mission to save the kid by having him own up to what he did, but it was really Owen she'd end up saving. She'd drawn him out of his gloom and made him happier than he imagined he'd ever be. He believed he'd conjured her up to take him to this house, this bed, this body, that his heart already knew from a distance, because he'd have slipped away without her. He wouldn't have survived otherwise. She'd suffered tragedy's long legacy after the death of her parents, and she treated what had happened to him as something cherished and fragile, the bubble that held within it the belief that they were safe when they were loved and loved back.

3

On the third floor of Mira's house—servant quarters when there had once been servants—a series of small rooms ran off the hallway. There was a bed in each with a tamped-down mattress and air that was dusty with old grudges. In one room, Owen looked out at the State House and the dome's Independent Man, a proud, gaudy marker. The hour glazed the edges of industry and blurred the city. It was a view he sometimes took alone, a way to see where he was.

When Mira had shown him this same view on his first-ever tour of the house, he had wondered why it was that people in a new place always gazed outward first, inward second. For his part, he was half afraid to stare at Mira too much, as though he might wear out the slightly scary exhilaration he felt looking at her. She'd pointed out landmarks and ruins and said that when the city was smoothed out like this, she could imagine she was living in any century. She could put herself in the place of someone standing at this window a hundred years before, a great-grandmother, maybe. Owen hadn't asked what she really meant by that, not because he was incurious but because he already sensed he was going to have a hard time sharing her with her history. It was everywhere in the house, and in the accommodating, careful way she moved through and around it. He could not separate her from it.

He'd been the one to suggest she give him a tour that first evening. She'd had on a red sweater that zipped up the front but not
to her throat, and her hair was collected with a piece of kitchen
string, an attractive, careless touch. She was always barefoot. That
she'd lived contentedly alone in the house for more than a decade after her parents had been killed made him question if there
was room for someone else in all of it. If silence and echoes and
still air didn't make Mira hungry for company, then what would?
Why would she ever need him? When they came to the third-floor
stairs, she'd tucked her thumbs into the belt loops of her pants and
announced there was nothing to see up there. Empty rooms, she
said. Peeling wallpaper, an old bathroom with a claw-foot tub. Her
tone had intrigued him for what she wasn't saying. He'd backed
her up a few steps, and she resisted only a little when he guided
her the rest of the way with his hands on her hips. He'd wanted
to stand very close to her and still feel the distance above and below and around them, while she was suddenly interested in pushing out the smallest space left between their bodies. Come closer,
she'd said. Hold me tighter, take your clothes off. Press your chest
to mine. He had put his shirt on the floor to protect her from splinters and she teased him about his manners and his armor of goose
bumps. He was shivering for a few reasons, and he asked why they
weren't making love on one of the beds, or couches, or even rugs
instead, somewhere warm, at least. She laughed and tightened her
legs around him; she liked the chill contrast to his hot skin. He
dwarfed her in a way they both were awed by. His hands were huge
on her. They were cold in the ecstatic drafts blowing up between
the floorboards. There was nothing casual about what they were
doing; he didn't want to mess this up, to be half-hearted, half-
asleep, or afraid. She knew who he was and what he'd suffered,
and how he suffered still. She wasn't scared of his past—just the

opposite. She wanted to understand it, but she admitted she'd always be, at best, looking in from the outside.

She told him that night how she'd seen him on Wickenden Street one evening when she was coming back from Brindle, his shoulders hunched as though he'd been trying to disappear. It sounded like too many evenings to him when disaster tailed him like something stuck to the bottom of his shoe. She said that she'd like to make him less forlorn, if she could, and pull happiness out of his gloom. That he would be the best work she might ever do.

Later that night, she'd looked ghostly, moving pale and naked to the far end of the hall, where she stopped in front of a closed door. This seemed to be a sort of ritual of hers that suggested something terrifying behind the door. A month after he'd moved in, she'd shown him the angled space where the ceiling zoomed low to meet the pitch of the roof and went on forever, but she wouldn't go in. He smelled the closet's morbid breath while she'd giggled uneasily, dismissive of herself and her babyish fears, and explained that the dread was just something left over from her childhood. But she did not want that erased or revealed; she was content to leave it alive and intact, and she'd pulled him back when he'd tried to take a step in.

Tonight Mira was staying late at Brindle again, getting the place ready for the fundraiser. Owen sniffed at the loamy stink of the four artichokes he was steaming on the stove and imagined the smell zigzagging across town to reach her, stirring up her appetite, which always waned in these anxious pre-party days. Down in the kitchen, he shut off the flame and noticed how the last sunlight hit the many bottles of wine Wilton brought each time he came for dinner, washing the wall in a thirsty red. Wilton gave them other gifts as well that he ordered online and had delivered to his porch by UPS—buttery steaks packed in huge

Styrofoam boxes of dry ice, cheeses, glowing golden kiwis, cakes from Chicago, black bread from Poland. And most recently, along with the artichokes, a quartet of honeydew melons, one already soft in the box.

Owen packed dinner up and walked to Brindle, taking his usual out-of-the-way detour through Fox Point, where he'd lived before he'd met Mira. The view from his third-floor apartment there had given him a slivered glimpse of the bay. There were times in that bleakest first year in Rhode Island when he'd felt he was drowning on land, and he counted on that spot of Narragansett Bay, black and streaked with red warnings from the Allens Avenue gas tanks, to keep him afloat. Every morning around five o'clock, the scent of baking Portuguese bread had woken him, making him intensely hungry. At the bottom of Wickenden Street, crowded with students and people out for a cheap dinner, a dim underpass led below the highway. Fifty yards of sidewalk were tacky with shit from the pigeons that perched and cooed on the steel beams. A truck roared above, shaking Owen. The Point Street Bridge in front of him was a structure beautiful in its dereliction. It was one of Mira's favorite places—the epitome of Providence, she claimed. The city had been fixing the bridge forever, and the fact that she didn't think they'd ever finish it delighted her. The bridge was the city's private joke, and like the city itself, corrupt, possibly dangerous, and endearingly rusted. The hurricane barrier, Mira said, was the city's single admission of vulnerability—and only then to the forces of nature. Orange-and-white traffic barrels and a regiment of cement barriers made the bridge appear amputated in midspan. The water caught every reflection so you felt as if you were floating above the city rather than standing at its base. On the other side of the bridge, past the fluorescently bright Hess station with its fortified cashier's booth, past Planned Parenthood devoid of its daily protesters at this supper hour, and one block in, was Brindle with its front door wide open to the warm, deserted street, and across from it, an empty lot surrounded by chain-link fencing.

Large windows on each of the two floors spread across Brindle's brick façade. The building had once housed supplies for the costume jewelry industry. Later, it had stayed vacant for decades, except for the occasional squatter or rat. Mira's father, in the family tradition of mindless acquisition, had bought it for reasons unknown to Mira, though she'd said it definitely wasn't because he saw an art school in it or her future. Occasionally Mira would still find a sparkle or chip of ruby or sapphire glass between the wide wood planks. She collected them in a jar she kept on her desk.

The foyer held a counter Owen had built out of plywood and given three coats of glossy white paint. Mira called it the snow bank. When she wasn't running around, Joy, her assistant, sometimes sat there. Unclaimed items were always piled at one end: a greasy Red Sox cap, a mitten, shirts, socks, a gutted cell phone. Mira's compact office was secreted behind a turn in the wall, and to the right was the gallery that ran the length of the building. The high ceiling was mapped with pipes and beams that had been painted a hundred times. The room was chaotic now with ladders, bulbs, tools, pieces of pottery, pictures, water bottles, the curling remains of a pizza Mira had ordered for the kids who'd stuck around to help her earlier. Diffuse circles of light fell on bare walls and on Mira, who was nailing something in a far corner. She lifted her face to him and put down her hammer. She sat back on her heels, smiling.

"The door was open," Owen told her. "Is that really such a good idea? Anyone could just walk in."

"And so you did just walk in. Anyway, Brindle *is* open to

anyone, O." She stood. "You're always afraid something bad is going to happen."

He wanted to say, remember our own break-in? Remember
how besieged that made you feel? He sensed violence's proximity
everywhere. "You're not offering sanctuary here," he said. "And it
seems like you're asking for trouble, inviting it in. What's the point
of that?"

Mira fiddled with one of her hoop earrings, a tic of patience
and a reminder to him that she did fine on her own. But the skin
under her eyes was puffy, and her expression was straining to be
light. "Maybe I am offering sanctuary here. Anyway, I thought art
was supposed to be a refuge. Like a church."

"Not true," he said, and smiled.

He didn't like that she would jeopardize her safety to make
her point or excuse her nonchalance with a joke, but this was her
realm and he knew he shouldn't say any more. She gave him a
light kiss. Her breasts urged against her thin white cotton shirt
as she put her hands at her waist and surveyed the room. Owen
was struck by how peculiarly possessive he felt at that moment,
as though he needed to pull her back from somewhere else. He
wanted to take her into the office and claim her as his and only
his, and cage her with his body.

"It's a disaster in here," she said, "but in a few days this place is
going to be sparkling and packed with rich people and big spend-
ers who want nothing more than to give Brindle their money."
She spread her arms in front of a bare wall. "Right? Paintings
here, pastels there, ceramics around the edges. People will be surrounded by things they can't resist bidding large sums for."

"Bigger than large," Owen said, slipping off his backpack and
unloading dinner. "Massive and colossal."

"Humongous," Mira added. "And if they don't bid? Then what?"

Owen presented her the giant artichokes in their tin foil coats. They looked like steaming jungle oddities. Her delight was gratifying.

"Wilton brought them over," Owen explained. "He said you'd told him you loved them. That you two were talking about your favorite foods."

"True. Sweet."

Did she mean the food or the man? Behind her, past the window and the awkwardly shaped parking lot and the Dumpster, he saw the bend of the river, the newest tent city erected by the service road, and beyond, the swell of College Hill. Somewhere in the darkening trees was their grand house, but he couldn't make it out.

"You seem a little tense," Mira said, and ran a hand down his back.

He said he'd had a frustrating day at school; he'd had to send a couple of kids to detention for fighting, which always depressed him with its uselessness, and he was tired. The truth was, he didn't know why he was impatient with her, or what he was feeling, except unsettled.

"I'm sure I kept you up with the television," she said. "I'm sorry."

Last night, Owen had been awake with Mira watching reruns of *Ancient Times* again. Pollen had filtered through the window screens and hung in the colored light. The past of his childhood and the present with his wife next to him, there on the pond and here on this bed, Wilton an image then and a fact now next door, was a transfixing midnight confusion. Mira was absorbed, laughing, giving encouragement to Wilton. Owen's hand and the action's shadows played across her slim bare legs. His fingers had trolled her inner thighs, but finding no invitation in, had finally stilled.

"I was watching with you. That was me, remember? That was my hand on your leg?"

"Come on, O. Don't be snippy. You know I'm always like this before the fundraiser. I get a little crazy and scattered. So I leave the front door open. So what."

Joy appeared in the gallery, soft-footed in her sneakers, red like Mira's. Her shy pink face was babyishly round at twenty-two, and she reached for her long ponytail like it was her consoling stuffed animal.

"I hope you like artichokes," Owen said.

"I've never had one," she said, growing pinker. Owen liked that she blushed at everything, as though she were just waking up to the sensual world all around her.

"Then I'll have to show you how to eat one," Mira said, putting her arm across the girl's shoulders. "It's an art."

She dimmed the lights, and they sat cross-legged on the platform at the front of the room. "Like this," she said to Joy. She scraped off the soft meat with her bottom teeth. She took another leaf, and this time rolled the flesh around on her tongue, presenting it as a soft, green ball. Joy pulled off a leaf and slipped it into her mouth, miming Mira. It was like watching some fascinating, vaguely erotic ritual. Owen had always detected something charged about Brindle, even in his first visit. Maybe it was all that wordless intention poured into the lopsided clay pots and shaky pastel drawings. Maybe it was Mira's passion and purpose, the refuge she offered.

She stood and began to pace the room, her fingers dug into her pockets. She went back to the corner where she'd been nailing earlier and considered her hammer. "I don't know what I'll do if I have to close this place, but I think about it all the time now," she said. "Don't you think it would be easier if I did shut it down?

I could get a regular job. Or maybe not. But I could have time. I could have a clear head. I could let someone else do the worrying. I'd be free of it."

Mira pressed her back against the wall. "I just wonder what it would be like not to feel as if everything were teetering on the edge all the time. As if *I* were teetering on the edge and about to fall off and pull everyone and everything over with me. Other people are a lot of responsibility, it turns out. There are so many problems, things I can't do anything about, no money. It's a struggle and it's getting overwhelming." She pressed her hand to her chest. "I feel it right here. Maybe it's just heartburn, though." She laughed. "Those artichokes."

"But isn't this exactly what you like?" Owen asked, going over to her. "The teetering? Because it makes you feel alive? You like the edge." He put his hands on the wall behind her, framing her face, and hiding her from Joy. "We'll find the money," he insisted quietly, "and I'll do whatever it takes. I'll do more tutoring at night. You're not going to lose this place. I won't let it happen." Why was the specter of defeat so close this year when the pressure had always been there? What did she now imagine was barreling toward her?

"You're lovely and even heroic, but you don't have to fix it for me, O," she said, touching his cheek. "Maybe it's just time to do something else. Nothing so wrong with that, is there?"

"No, but listen to me. Brindle makes you happy, and you'd be miserable without it. I know that about you. I want you to be happy, Mira."

She rankled at sentimentality and its thin solace, and her look said she suspected him of it now. She pressed her face to his forearm, not to console but to quiet him, then ducked under his arm and went to the open front door. "I feel rain," she announced, returning to the gallery. "Rain on the night of the party. Lots of it. The whole stormy package."

"That's not going to happen," Joy said, working hard to sound upbeat. "We'll have perfect weather. We always do. It's going to be great, just like every other time."

Owen went to Mira to pull her away from her foreboding, but stopped where a huge, lumpy, brown clay pot sat like an unloved mutt. Mottled and covered with blemishes of glaze, there was something especially furious and shitlike about it. Its ugliness was impossible to miss, and hard not to admire.

"Doesn't it look like it's going to come to life and attack?" Mira said, her enthusiasm rising now that she was talking about something solid and real. "I think it's amazing. The kid who made it—Cory—is this skinny little guy and he can't even lift it by himself. He loves the thing, but he told me he's ready to part with it if it brings money to Brindle. He was so serious about it, his first act of charity. I want to put it right there, in front. I want people to see it first thing." Tears slid down her face. "I want everyone to see it and see what it's worth."

"Mira," Owen started, "what's going on with you?"

She waved him away. "It's nothing. Just pre-party stuff." She wiped her face with the neck of her shirt and smiled. "How about no more work for today, okay?" Mira said. "Suddenly, I'm completely exhausted."

During the last weeks of the school year, a profusion of flowering trees circled Spruance Middle School like hopeful cheerleaders. Smeared blossoms of pink littered the front steps. Owen struggled with a window in his classroom and imagined that if he could ever get it open, he'd be able to cool the stifling place but he might also let in the stink lurking outside that was closer to the truth

of things; the rumored death of the school was like something
rotting in the trees. There was the fretful buzz again that morning from teachers huddled by the shushing copying machine. The
chatter suggested the city would finally close Spruance at the end
of the next school year for its continued inability to improve, for
its dwindling enrollment and attendance, for its failures year after
year, its poor performance, discipline problems, teacher dissatisfaction, its impossible detention rate, its plummeting test scores,
for what-fucking-difference-did-it-make-in-the-end. The building
would be razed, plowed under like a bad idea, the kids scattered
across the city, abandoned again. Teaching here now was going to
be like caring for a terminal patient.

The kids read silently from *Winter Wheat, Summer Corn*, the
banal but mandated novel about a city boy sent to live on a farm
in Iowa. It meant zero to his students. The boy might as well
have been sent to Cairo or the moon. More than a few of his
twenty-eight kids stuffed into the classroom had already drifted
off somewhere else, and who could blame them? Some couldn't
read at a first-grade level, or speak English, but there were all the
signs of transport in the lowered lids, the open mouths, their profound stillness. And where had they gone in their heads? Owen
would have liked to know, because he would try to talk to them
there. The afternoon sun smacked the lima bean–colored walls
and the photos of wheat and cornfields he'd tacked up, though
nature mostly annoyed these kids. They squirmed at bugs and
shrieked at thunder and lightning, trusted only concrete, glass,
and cinderblock, and raspberry flavor that was turquoise blue.
Owen admired their city attitudes but lamented the fading optimism that came with age.

Since the start of the period, he'd had the uneasy feeling that
someone was on the other side of the door, but saw no one when

he looked out. His defensive colleagues papered over the glass portholes so they couldn't be watched, while others wanted a clear view to keep an eye open for trouble. It was most likely a parent out in the locker-lined hall, furious or confused. Teaching was never just about the kids. Behind them, over them, far away from them, there were always one or two parents, grandparents, an overburdened aunt, an ambivalent guardian. Some gave him their concerned hands, some turned their backs, others kept a tight grip on their children. Some wanted soothing, some came to argue. Sometimes he'd look into the eyes of a kid and detect generations of brutal history staring defiantly back at him: I dare you to change the course of my life.

A chair scraped against the floor, and Jacqui, in the center cluster of desks, pink tank top and black bra straps, ponytail of hair pulled back into a glossy helmet, shot up. In the amazing variation of skin color in his classroom, she was somewhere in the middle, between pale sun and wet earth, now with a greenish tint. All heads shot up with her. Hand over mouth, she wove between the desks to the door which she yanked open in time to vomit in a trash can placed with odd prescience just outside. Owen left his own desk as the kids began their derisive hooting and twisted in their seats to get a view of Jacqui doing her fearsome business. Owen put his hand on Jacqui's rounded back to absorb the jolt of the heaves. Sweat polished her neck and hid in the padding of baby fat. The smell of strawberry perfume mixed with puke. Where his finger met an inch of bare forearm, she was hot.

"It's okay, sweetheart. Just relax. You'll be okay," he soothed. Efficient footsteps approached the turn in the hall, and Owen pulled his hand back. Touch was a loaded word, a lethal action here. The girl shuddered and shivered. "Breathe, Jacqui. Take your time."

Mrs. Tevas, the librarian, hadn't been rushing to the scene, but had happened on it. Waylaid, she stopped, an ancient encyclopedia volume pressed to her chest. Her thin eyebrows dipped as she noted the posture, the trash can, the open classroom door, the stink of puke. Just last week Owen had been in the library and picked up a book about space exploration for one of his students. The first line read, "Someday man will walk on the moon." He'd showed it to Mrs. Tevas, but she hadn't found it nearly as funny as he had.

She passed off the encyclopedia to him so she could hold the girl's shoulders. He sensed that Mrs. Tevas didn't think all that much of male teachers. Still, there was something assertive about her that he admired. She tended the library like it was a garden, a place you might someday enter and be surprised by. Like most of the teachers in the building, she was a native of the city and had a pragmatic surface, a Formica demeanor. Her accent sounded like a piece of bright melted plastic. She always eyed him circumspectly, as did his fellow teachers, as though he'd come to Spruance with an unfair advantage, as though his height and size alone could scare kids into compliance. Almost instantly they'd decided that his ability to control a classroom hadn't been earned—though it had been, in harder, tougher schools than this one. That he might actually be able to teach was a secondary consideration. He was from out of state, always an outsider, and so suspect of other things, too: aloofness, his own ideas about how to teach, maybe even the sin of mystery. Moments of affinity with his colleagues were rare. He didn't regret this very often.

"What happened?" Mrs. Tevas asked. Her mustard yellow blouse and blue skirt had the toxic sheen of dry cleaning.

Wasn't it clear, the smell rising in yeasty waves? "Jacqui was reading, and . . ."

"I got mad sick." The girl spoke from the echoic depths of the trash can. A cell phone in her back pocket pulsed with light.

"Maybe something from lunch," Mrs. Tevas said, and looked at Owen. "You taste those fajitas?" She rolled her eyes.

Over Jacqui's back, they silently rifled through what they knew about the girl: mouthy, fifteen, bright, twice repeated grades. She'd given Owen cookies at Christmas; she laughed wickedly, often cruelly, at other kids. She never did her homework, and shrugged as if to say, *Mister, you know how it is.* He was fond of her, but what he knew about any student, even the ones he knew best, was treacherously full of holes, and too often meaningless when a kid was eclipsed by problems. They called him *cocksucker* and *motherfucker* and mostly *Mister.* Some were sweet and bright, others were sullen and dull-eyed, impossible to reach. They all came and went too fast anyway, a new crop filling the seats in September and emptying them in June, each taking another's place in startling repetition. Here was America's true limitless natural resource—squandered. Owen wondered if Mrs. Tevas was thinking, as he was, that the girl might be pregnant. He hated his quick assumption that if Jacqui wasn't doing her homework, if her bra straps showed, if her lip gloss was too pink, if she was poor and throwing up, then she must be fucking, and fucking carelessly, too. But he'd also been teaching a long time. He'd seen it before.

Mrs. Tevas took Jacqui down to the office, though this wasn't the one day a week the nurse was in the building. What remained was the soupy trash can in a ray of sun and the encyclopedia in his hand. The stink had made its way into the classroom. The kids waved their books in front of their faces and yelled they were dying. Reading was impossible now, surrendered to the more relevant drama of Jacqui and the fact that bodies in distress were the most fascinating of all. He tugged again at the window. He wasn't sure why he kept at it after all this time, all these years. Justin yelled that he should just break the thing, that it was an emergency.

"I think I have it," he said.

"Fuck you do," a boy shouted. "You're a pussy."

His fingers strained. His shirt stuck to his chest, his arms trembled. Once, Spruance had been the home of soldierly virtues with its medieval arches and heraldic designs stamped in brass above the doors. Everything was dull-colored and indestructible these days, soldierly now in an entirely different kind of way. How many kids had also heard the distressing rumor that the end was near? He gazed out over Lincoln Street, its well-kept houses and wide stone driveways that led around to back doors and gardens. The NASCAR whirr of lawn crews at work came from every direction. He closed his eyes to imagine Mira at Brindle just then, waiting with a mixture of determination and care—that was pretty much what you needed—for the afterschool kids to arrive, and then someone said that there was a guy outside the door. Owen turned to see a face pressed up against the glass, goggle-eyed, lips smashed, a deranged mouth, pink tip of tongue.

"You said if I was interested, I should come by and see what you do," Wilton whispered, when Owen opened the door a few inches. "So here I am."

Owen hadn't actually expected the man to take him up on the offer—because he hadn't meant him to. It was just something he'd tossed out at the end of another one of their long dinners together. The man had become a regular at their table, a regular in their house, a regular in Mira's days and conversation. And then sometimes Wilton would go away for a couple of days, and his house would remain as mysteriously dark as his destinations and desires. Mira would be left blinking at his porch light left on.

"Look, the period's almost over," he told Wilton. The kids were itchy and noisy behind him, straining to see what was going on. "This isn't a good time."

Wilton's face sagged as if a tension line had been snipped. "I wanted to see you in action."

"There's no action. They're reading."

The room was anything but quiet, the restless tenor rising with Wilton's grin. "That's some loud reading. I'll sit in the back. I won't say a word. Besides, you can't leave me out here with this." He gestured at the trash can.

Spruance's front office staff was impossible to break through, but Wilton had done it because here he was, wandering the halls alone. Owen imagined that he'd charmed the women as he leaned over their high counter, thumbed their attendance book and asked their names, imitating their Spanish *r*'s, and today he looked like a rich, generous uncle in a lapis blue linen shirt and pressed blue jeans. Owen pushed back his reluctance and ushered Wilton into the classroom. He introduced him as an actor. Other guests had withered under the kids' scrutiny. Last month a reporter from the *Journal* had come to talk about bullying. She had cleared her throat incessantly as wet spots spread under her arms. Wilton was a combination of coyness and composure, self-confidence and humility. He leaned against Owen's desk with his legs crossed at the ankles. He allowed himself to be stared at, every piece of him scrutinized and judged. He was priced, assessed, evaluated, and enjoying it. The attention fed him. He plumped and glowed.

"You on TV?" Kevin asked. "Because I never seen you."

"Yes, on television, but way past your bedtime."

The kids laughed at that infantile idea. "What channel? I'm going to watch," China said, and waved her lime green pencil at him. "You got rich, I bet."

"How do you know I got rich?" Wilton asked.

"Because you have some fancy-ass shoes," she said.

"These things?" Wilton looked down at his feet. "Fancy-ass? Is that a brand? Is that like Nike?"

"And your shirt, too. Fancy-ass."

Wilton flipped up his collar, playing to the kids, and hooked a thumb at Owen. "What do you think of this guy? Is he a good teacher?"

"He's good. He's okay. He's big, but he's not so strong." The kids continued to shout their opinions, some standing, waving their arms and leaning over their desks, slapping the chipped plastic veneer with open hands to make sure they were heard. They threw in what they didn't like about him—too strict, too tall, too much writing. Too white, someone said.

"Too white? He can't do anything about that. But he's the best teacher you'll ever have," Wilton said. "He's one of the top in the country. It's a proven fact. I'm not making it up. The experts say so. Believe me."

The kids were baffled by this. Maybe their teacher wasn't exactly who they thought he was. Or maybe this man was just playing them. Owen was irritated. Why do this? What was the point? Authority was mostly an illusion; it couldn't stand too much fiddling with and poking, too many shifts in light. The bell rang and the kids burst out of their seats. In a second, the place echoed with their escape.

Wilton crossed his arms over his chest. "You look out at these kids and it's like the UN. Amazing. All those colors, so many hues and tints. What are they, Puerto Rican, Dominican, Guatemalan, Cambodian, Haitian? Other?"

"Yes, other," Owen said. He was sorry he'd let the man in. "The kids knew you were bullshitting them. They're not babies. All that crap about best teacher and proven facts and experts. They can smell it a mile off."

"But I meant everything I said. It wasn't bullshit. You are one of the best teachers."

"That's bullshit."

"Is it? For weeks and weeks, I've heard you talk about your work, I've watched how animated you get, I've felt your dedication. You can't fake that. I saw how you handled that poor girl out in the hall." He leaned in closer and whispered. "What's wrong with her, by the way?"

"I have no idea." Owen knelt to pick up the Starburst and gum wrappers blooming under the chairs. The kids were like birds, leaving their bright droppings behind.

When Wilton squatted next to him, his joints popped. "Look, sometimes I overstep," he said. "So I apologize. I just wanted the kids to see what they have in you, that's all. People like you never get enough recognition."

"People like me?"

"Teachers, I mean." He paused and gave Owen a narrowed look. "Mira warned me that you're impossible to give a compliment to, that you'd fight me about it. She wasn't kidding."

It was startling to hear, not because it was untrue but because Wilton had quoted Mira and that meant that Mira had been talking about him with Wilton. The man's eyes, a glacial blue, were too earnest and invasive to meet, and Owen began to straighten the desks. He told Wilton he'd see him in front of the school in fifteen minutes.

When he stepped outside, one bus was still waiting to ferry kids back to less verdant parts of the city. Affluence, and the lack of it, Owen had once been told by the man who flew the traffic helicopter for Channel 10, could be measured by the densities of springtime green (and in these few weeks, pinks and purples and buttery yellows)—not in black or brown or white or any other color that existed at street level. A few kids trudged up the steep hill that crested at Hope Street, petals falling on their shoulders like confetti for heroes. To his left, just beyond the corner of the school, a lens of kids had contracted. He pushed through them—in moments like this, he was the imposing giant with giant strides and a deep voice—and pried George and Oscar apart. Skinny boys, full of shaking rage, throwing punches and kicks. Their sweatshirt zippers were bared teeth. He gripped their wrists, measured the brutality in their pulse, and felt the sap of it rise in him. He suspected that just under his own cool restraint was a capacity for violence, something he wasn't ever going to tap. Dark hair was beginning to whisk the boys' upper lips, and their bones were thickening as they waited for him to do something. They didn't know what pride was, or what to do with it, but it obscured them like their hoods. They groped at their slipping pants, checked their shirts for smudges and injuries. Oscar blinked furiously and tried not to cry.

"So, you guys had enough?" Owen asked. He waved away their attempts to blame the other.

Tears and fury was a particularly poignant middle school brew that left the spectators, many of them girls pressing cheap necklaces to lips, unsure where to look except at the hard-packed, grassless dirt. He hoped Oscar wouldn't blubber. George called him a bitch and a baby. The pugilists made a half-hearted attempt to shake Owen off because it was expected of them, just as it was expected of him to take them back into the building and write them up. But he didn't see the point on most days—and on this day particularly. He looked past the boys' heads and the identical knobby structure of their closely shorn skulls, now that he'd whipped their hoods down to make them nakedly accountable, and he saw Wilton standing under a flowering tree. Owen made the boys shake hands and told them to go home. They walked in opposite directions, backpacks entirely empty of books and homework, shoulders hunched like men and pants dragging in the dirt like children.

He and Wilton walked in the direction of the leafy boulevard. The afternoon had lost some of its electric edge. In front of the Oasis Market, Wilton read out loud the signs for a million urgent needs plastered on the glass. Milk! ATM! Fax machine! Cigarettes! Charcoal! He wanted to go in. It was a squeezed convenience store that smelled of milk gone bad and pine tree deodorizers, with a dizzying array of candy, energy drinks, muscle magazines, mini fruit pies. Wilton walked up and down the short aisles, running his fingers over the goods. The woman at the counter watched Wilton on her surveillance monitor; he was on television again and loving it. He waved at her. By the cold case, three girls who'd been in Owen's class the year before wiped the glass with their hands to view the lineup of drinks.

"You girls going to buy something?" the woman at the register yelled. It was common knowledge that she didn't like Spruance kids.

"They're with me," Wilton called back.

"We are not with you," one of the girls snapped to set him straight. She glanced at Owen. Was this fool with him? He nodded. They banged their bottles of soda on the counter. They added two scented candles, lollipops, and a lighter at the last minute, which Owen put back. They didn't look at Wilton when he paid or when he held the door open for them so they could skitter past. Only when they were outside did they yell thank you and collapse into one another, laughing as they wove down the sidewalk.

Wilton stared after them, dopey with astonishment. "Such spirit in those kids. I've seen more today that's amazing and real than I have in a long, long time," he said. "Ah, Owen, you don't get it, do you? You're just jaded." He slapped Owen on the back.

The man was completely out of step with the world and the year. Where have you been, Owen wanted to ask as they turned onto the boulevard. He didn't know what Wilton lacked exactly, but he was starting to sense it was enormous. Another person's deepest need to have his sorrow soothed could either draw you in or repel you. It was what drew Mira to Wilton—was what had drawn her to Owen as well—but to him, it was something that could pull you down and drown you. Wilton struggled up the incline of Lloyd Avenue and took a puff of an inhaler he pulled from his pocket. At Hope Street, where they would part so Owen could go to the Y for his swim, Wilton sat on a low stone wall to catch his breath.

"You're staring at me," he said. "Not that I mind, of course. But who can ever read that face of yours? Not even your wife, I bet. Who can ever know what you're thinking?"

"I was wondering about why you didn't work after your show went off, why you just disappeared. What happened?"

Wilton watched the kids from the swim team push through the glass doors. "I loved what I did, and then one day I didn't. I woke up with this suffocating feeling, like my chest was being crushed. I could hear my ribs cracking. The dread was enormous, ER-visiting, heart-clutching dread. It was terrifying. I thought I was about to die. They called it a depressive episode. 'You mean a nervous breakdown,' I said, and I told the doctors that I just hoped there weren't reruns. Good joke, right? So after a couple of weeks in the hospital, I spent the next decade and a half hanging out by my pool and trying to figure out what I was going to do with my life." He sighed dramatically and picked at the knee of his jeans.

Owen knew the details were vague on purpose, the story meant to be heard, an incitement to wonder. It might be morose and worrisome, but it was gilded with false California ease, a blue swimming pool, an expensive recuperation. Who could take fifteen years to think about something as amorphous as life?

"And did you figure things out?"

"No, but I got a nice tan." Wilton shrugged. "There are no epiphanies in real life. You know that. You get to a certain age when the why doesn't matter so much. There isn't time for that. It only matters what you do next, because you don't have so many nexts left. And I didn't want next to be more of the same, so I stopped acting."

"But you were good at it."

"Lots of people are good at things they don't want to do."

Owen paused to let the roar and exhaust of a bus pass. "Actually, most people want to do things they're not very good at. But most, if they had a talent like you do, they'd run with it." He would have liked a talent himself but accepted the aptitude for living.

"Talent doesn't mean purpose and work, which are much more important," Wilton said. "Talent is just a trait, like my thin fingers or your height, the luck of the genetic draw. You have purpose, Mira has purpose, you've both found your way to something important. And what I did was just television. Meaningless stuff. Is there anything of less value, less purpose than a sitcom? I don't regret what I did all those years, but I understand exactly what it was. I'm under no illusions anymore that I matter." He made an exploding motion with his hands and followed the fallout as if looking for what might be left. "I was at the drugstore yesterday," he continued, "and this woman, all hair and huge, scary teeth, was gawking at me." He imitated her hawkish lean, still an expert mimic to make Owen laugh. "It happens all the time. People know they've seen me, but they don't know from where. They don't know my name or if I'm someone they should remember. That's not impact—that's not even a tiny dent."

"But that's because you're out of context. It happens to everyone. Who would think you'd be hanging out in the toothpaste aisle in Providence?"

"But in real life, I'm always out of context. No television screen, no context. In which place am I the real person? In which do I really exist? I can see the entire thought process run through these people who recognize me. Is he someone from high school? Did I used to work with him? And why does he make me feel a little funny?" He forced a full body shiver. "There was a time when people knew exactly who I was. They knew I made them laugh." The line of his mouth grew straight. "But that's long over."

"Do you miss it?"

"That part I miss very much. You stand in front of your students and know exactly who you are."

Owen looked down the long stretch of Hope Street that dipped and then rose again in the distance. The stoplights were out of sync. "Has there been anyone for you, someone you've loved?" he asked. Wasn't this what the man was really talking about, the agency of love to pull you back from that kind of confusion? "Someone who's loved you?"

"Loved? Not in a long, long time."

"Tell me about your daughter." Owen hadn't intended to ask— though the daughter was something he and Mira speculated about all the time—but the moment seemed right. Wilton was all about his daughter, Owen suspected, the central piece of his story, and yet the man told a story entirely empty of her.

Wilton stood. "Another day. Time for your swim. I don't want to hold you up anymore than I already have."

The sun revealed the two tones of his hair, still brassy on top but now gray-brown at the scalp. After only a few months, Wilton had lost some of that shine he'd had when he first arrived, and his time in Providence could be measured in the strata of fading vanity.

By midafternoon of Brindle's fundraiser day, a quilt of humidity hung low over the city. The metallic river had stopped flowing. Mira, in a black silk dress that clung to her like an anxious child, was spooked that her prediction of rain was about to be borne out in exaggerated fashion. Deluge was only minutes away, she said as she and Owen stood in the doorway and the steamy air contracted around them. It would pour, and her guests, her patrons, her aging donors, friends of her parents, would throw their car keys back on the front hall table and decide not to venture out in this weather. They'd stay in and tell themselves they'd mail a check in the morning. Which they would never get around to doing.

Owen went into the gallery where each drawing, painting, and piece of pottery was tagged for silent bidding. Pens were poised on the bid sheets. Owen looked at the charcoal drawings of nudes done by the class that came in from an assisted-living facility. There were elated contortions of breasts and smudged bellies on newsprint, preposterous nipples, and split melons of ass. The model's body was charmed by bad eyesight and wishful thinking. He'd once peered into this class and seen a field of white heads. An occasional dry cough or the unwrapping of a lozenge had broken the silence. A model was posed on a platform covered with a rug Mira had brought from home. Her body was in a slouch, the sun sliding down the sizable bump in her nose and landing on her rough knuckles. She wasn't beautiful, but she was dramatic and doomed, and Owen wanted to push past the people on their stools and help her up. The same urge was also there on the faces of the old women and the few robust men in the class: desire, envy, memory, a chance to do something big. Their days of seduction, of romance and heroics, might be long gone, but not for that hour. It was, Mira insisted when he told her, one of art's most powerful subversions.

The asphalt turned black even before the rain hit it. It already smelled of spoiling fruit and the inside of cardboard boxes. As a kid, Owen would watch the pond beyond his house prepare itself for rain, and he detected the trees holding their breath, their leaves upturned like Mira's hands were now, waiting for that first drop. At the back of the gallery, Joy arranged plastic cups and poured big bags of generic pretzels into a bowl. Her eyelids were swiped with the color of eggplants. A green halter dress was engineered to hold her breasts, while a gold chain with a cross caught in her cleavage. Owen had never seen her so intrepid. They watched Mira straighten pictures that didn't need straightening.

"She's been like this all week. I keep telling her things are going to be okay." Joy cut herself off; she knew her job might depend on how this night went. "You know how she is. You can't tell her anything at all when she's like this. You don't think she's really going to give this all up, do you? All that stuff she was saying the other night?"

"No, I don't. Things are going to be fine."

As he spoke, the rain started and the gallery took on an eager glow. A wet gust blew in and with it a group of seven middle-school boys from one of the afternoon classes. Black, Hispanic, white, they wore smoothly buttoned shirts or spotless white tees over loose shorts. They looked scrubbed. They clustered around the tallest boy, who at thirteen was already a man, with thick, defensive shoulders and a hand quick to fly to his crotch. Mira jostled and joked with them. She was completely at ease as she led each boy to his piece of artwork so Owen could take pictures. They posed themselves, a hip thrust out, a tilt to the head, a gesture with the hands. "Just be normal," Mira laughed. These boys made her happy.

Their wet sneakers sang a chorus of pride across the floor. Cory, skinny, short, pale brown skin, with a lopsided smile and ears that stuck way out, bent to hug his hideous clay pot. He stuck his head in its monstrous mouth, yelling echoes into it until Mira told him to cut it out or he'd get stuck. Cory charmed her; he was one of her special ones. When others began to arrive, Mira went into her fundraiser mode, part solicitousness, part intimacy, always a hand on someone's arm. She corralled people without their noticing and then looked them straight in the eye to disarm them. Occasionally, she glanced toward the street to take the measure of the weather.

Out in front, white water churned in the gutters. The Point Street Bridge, all but its single smeary light at the top of the span, had disappeared in the cascade. Windshield wipers berated the rain. People shook themselves off in the foyer. Owen took raincoats and umbrellas and mopped the floor. Humidity clung to the skin and weighed down clothes. A few tough old birds from the assisted-living facility, dressed in pastels, came in looking bewildered. If they recognized the model they'd sketched, they didn't show it. They were more interested in the groups of roving kids who kept checking the bid sheets and moved around like schools of fish. One old man touched Cory's head as he darted by, as if to suggest there was nothing to getting old—it just happened when you weren't watching. The room was filling up with noise and body heat.

Some people in the gallery—annual donors—had been friends of Mira's parents, and they exuded a sense of belonging anywhere, but already they gave away an intention to leave early. They flinched at the noise. Owen had been introduced to them before—lawyers, watercolorists, urologists, all part of a rosy, good-postured elite. Mira was smooth and deferential with them and played the part of William and Cecelia Thrasher's daughter. Their orphan girl. She knew that many of her parents' friends, especially the women, were uneasy around her, though they'd known her forever. There was nothing mysterious about the speed of the car her parents had been in, or the tree they'd hit, or the deadly impact made to bark and body, but she struck them as evidence of tragedy's random fall. Mira was bad luck. Owen crossed the crowded room and put his hand around her waist.

"For these kids, these people. Well, enrichment is essential," a man was saying. "We can't quantify the effects, but we all have to support *that*. Or else—"

"—we know what will happen then," his wife said, with curious brightness. She squeezed her shiny black purse against her ribs. What exactly do you imagine happening, Owen wanted to ask. His face was locked in a stiff smile.

A mist of patience hung on Mira's upper lip as she waited through the meaningless talk and then led the couple to look at the drawings on the far wall. She didn't see the point in challenging people like this, or calling them on what they really meant, or backing them into saying something they'd regret. Best to nod and look receptive, she'd told Owen; it didn't cost her anything this way, and might even get her some money. Ellie Cotton, who was imperious and horsey, with arms loaded up with gold and jade bracelets, waylaid Mira and wagged a finger as she talked. This was the woman Mira had once seen her father eating out on his couch at work. She'd described for Owen her father's pants puddled at his feet, his head bobbing at Ellie's crotch, while Ellie still had her green espadrilles on, and her underpants dangled on an ankle. Mira had stayed long enough to see her father slide up the woman's body like an alligator slithering onto the sunny shore. Ellie always gave a donation to Brindle as hush money, Mira said, though there was no one left to keep the secret from.

Mike Levi, who had taught at Spruance until he went into the lucrative college prep and tutoring business that Owen worked for several nights a week, arrived with his wife, Faye. He shook off the rain like a wet dog. Walter Brazil, a man Owen was friendly with from the pool at the Y, arrived looking uncomfortable out of the water and his Speedo. A few teachers from Spruance—including Mrs. Tevas with her librarian's gravitas—showed up. The gallery was filled with friends they hadn't seen in months, and the party was celebratory in spite of the weather. Owen replenished the ice, set out more cups, and emptied another bag of pretzels.

A man in a drenched army jacket shuffled his way around the edges of the gallery. His head was pushed forward, but he wasn't adept at going unnoticed. He pulled at the snaky coils of his dirty beard. The room contracted in his presence. Talk slowed, the hum lowered, shoulders rose. You didn't have to see menace to know it had joined the party. It brought its own weather system. As Owen watched, Mira left a circle of friends and walked over to the man whose fists rested like grenades in his jacket. Owen wanted to call her back, but he didn't. His mouth was dry, and the base of his skull ached with holding himself in control. Finally, the man skittered away from Mira and, on his way out, bumped into Lusk, the boy mayor, who had just arrived and was pushing the rain through his hair.

Lusk smiled diplomatically, as always. Mira hooked her arm

through the mayor's as she led him into the room. Though he was a few years older than Mira, the two of them had played doctor and naked patient when they were kids and their parents were drinking cocktails together downstairs. Lusk likely thought of this every time he saw Mira. She did—Owen could see it in her pinking cheeks now. It was funny to him how this old game would always connect the two of them, and how decades later, it could still spark some jealousy in him. Owen knew that his understanding of Mira's past, her lovers, the shape of her life before he met her, would always be slightly off.

Mira had only a few minutes with Lusk to make her pitch for city support. He could make things happen—this was Providence after all, and nothing got done by going through the obvious or correct channels—but he gave her a look of no promise tonight. The city was broke, the state and the country worse. Mira's frustration was a resolute horizon that appeared across her forehead. Lusk scratched his neck. A young girl pressed between them and pulled Lusk over to her drawing. He gave the room a dazzling smile, arm around the kid, then made a dash for the door and his waiting aide who already held out an opened umbrella. For a moment, Mira froze, watching Lusk—and maybe Brindle's future—skitter away into the rain. Owen checked the bid sheets; he wasn't happy to see how few entries there were. If Mira knew this already, she wasn't going to show it. Owen entered his own bid for each of the kids' pieces; he didn't want any one of them to go home dejected, unwanted.

The noise in the room fell and the humidity seemed to drop as Wilton appeared at the gallery entrance in a voluminous white shirt and pants. He'd wafted in like some cloud the storm had whipped up, and people turned to look at him, their faces lifted to the meteorological wonder. It was true about actors and politicians, Wilton and Lusk: they had a shine unlike anyone else, and you couldn't fake that magnetism, that radiance. They made entrances where other people simply came in. But Owen considered how the man in the army jacket had changed the room's weather, too, for a minute. Wilton waved at Owen to help him with something outside. He had a cab idling in front, with platters of food in the backseat and trunk. There were shrimp, fussy sandwiches speared with toothpicks made to look like paint brushes, strawberries dipped in chocolate, blueberry tarts, wedges of cheese to take the place of the wilting pretzels. Joy came out to help and smiled shyly when Wilton said something to her, his mouth close to her ear.

"This is amazing," Mira said, looking at the bounty spread across the table. The room began to surge toward it. Any minute, the frenzy would begin. "You didn't have to do this, Wilton."

"Feed the people, and they shall give," he said, and found an empty spot of wall to pose himself against, slightly damp white against white. "Isn't that what they say?"

When Mira went to stand next to him, black against white, something shifted. To Owen, it was as though the light had become thinner, or his eyesight worse. The affinity between Wilton and Mira was not about sex or romance, he knew, but something much less ephemeral, something both imperceptible and obvious. Their young friendship had the oldest roots. But why and how it had happened like this he didn't know. He stood back, afraid in a way to get closer and learn what kept others out. Soon, a semicircle had formed in front of them. Many people recognized Wilton. Wet shoes were suddenly easier to stand around in because of Wilton's charm, his bounding talk about Brindle, his wheedling for donations and bids. Ellie Cotton watched with regal distance and distaste, but she watched anyway, a lowering chin a sign of her thaw. For all those who said television was a black hole that spit out shit and trivia, who claimed there was nothing worthwhile on, who spoke with condescension about those who did watch, there were always more people who recognized Wilton. Watching television had become a private sin; they'd been secret viewers— Edward had once caught Owen in front of the television slack-jawed—but they gave up their secret now. Wilton caused a spike of laughter; looking over his admirer's heads, he winked at Owen, then Joy, who blushed.

When the last people left an hour later, Owen went out to lock the front door. The rain had stopped and the city was washed and gleaming. The man in the army jacket leaned against the chain-link fence across the street, more beaten than menacing now, his face unevenly shadowed and wet. He gave Owen the finger. Without the crowd, the gallery looked exhausted, the artwork curling in the humidity. Wilton and Joy swept the hundreds of shrimp tails and strawberry stems into the garbage, while Joy used one hand to press the front of her dress to her chest. Her face was a fiery red from Wilton's predatory attention. Owen didn't know anything about the man's sex life—if he had one at all—but he knew he should not devour this soft, sweet girl like a marshmallow. One swallow and it's done. Joy looked up to catch Owen watching her, and the colors of Wilton's flattery drained from her face. Owen had snooped on her desires, spied on her romantic fantasies, and caught her admiring herself in Wilton's reflection. She crouched to pick up the balled napkins from the floor, but her dress made the movement awkward and she had to catch herself from falling forward. Owen knew he'd humiliated her in a way neither of them was ever going to forget. In a few minutes, she gathered up her things and left Brindle, but not before Wilton insisted on kissing her cheek.

Mira, who'd noticed none of this, slumped on a chair. "I'm so beat. I don't even want to deal with the bid sheets now. Tomorrow I face the truth after a cup of coffee. But not tonight."

Owen turned away; he already knew the night's failure. He was the highest bidder on everything. He felt stupid now for having put his name down. What was the point of that?

"I just want to see one thing, one bid I'm curious about," Wilton said. He studied the bid sheet for Cory's giant, hideous pot. "It looks like I'm the high bidder on this, thank you very much."

"Let me see that." Mira held out her hand and studied the paper for too long. "No, Wilton. Absolutely not. No fucking way. Forget it."

"What do you mean 'no'?" Wilton said.

"I mean no, as in no, you can't do this."

"I most certainly can," Wilton said. "I am the highest bidder, aren't I? Then it's mine. There are rules about these things, Mira, fixing the bidding, fraud, and so on. Don't make me turn you in." He laughed. "You'll take a personal check?"

Mira handed Owen the sheet. Wilton had bid $35,000 for the pot.

"You're kidding, right?" Owen asked. Wilton shook his head.

"I'm completely serious," Mira said. "I'm not going to accept your money. If you want to make a small donation, I won't say no. But this is too much. It's not right."

"Who's to say what's right?" Wilton asked. "I've done nothing except take dumb money and make it smart. I want to do something meaningful in my life, something for other people for a change. I've led a very selfish existence. Let me do this. At least so I won't feel like such a slug."

He bent to scoop up his expensive piece of pottery. At first he struggled with the thing and mumbled that maybe he'd had too much wine to stand straight so quickly. Mira begged him to be careful, and for a few steps, he was steady, the tip of his tongue on his upper lip. But then his legs folded jointlessly, he slipped and skated and whooped and righted himself. The room held its breath. Police sirens wailed down Point Street, and when Wilton looked up to see the throbbing colors pass over the glass, he took a step forward and slipped on a strawberry. The pot rose in the air. He lunged forward at an inhuman angle and his knees hit the floor with a sickening crack. His arms were outstretched as though he were catching a baby thrown out of a burning building. The pot landed in his hands with a slap. His acrobatic dive was astounding. He hadn't ever been about to let the thing smash; this was all an act. Wilton put the pot down and fussily adjusted his shirt and pants, now dirty at the knees, as though nothing had happened and no one was watching. But he had to know they were fixed on him. He was Bruno again, with that slightly melancholy, elastic face. He was comedy meeting tragedy, or just barely dodging it, and he was as surprised as anyone by what felled and befell him. It was like being in love. Humor showed no reverence for the guileless or the good-hearted. His expression suggested that everything that could be made fun of—himself included—was also true and real.

"Shit," Owen mumbled and turned away. He wanted to kick something for how he'd been played, for how he'd held his breath and counted his heartbeats.

"Not so funny, Wilton," Mira said, but she was laughing now, her hands on her knees. "Really, don't do that again."

"Do what? If you could do one thing for me," Wilton said, turning to Owen. "You can drive this back to the house because I'm going to walk. I could use the exercise; you taught me that the other day. I have to get in shape. Just make sure my pot wears a seat belt. I don't want anything to happen to my beautiful new baby."

Just before Wilton left, Owen saw him out in the foyer with his hands on his knees, working to catch his breath and ease some obvious pain when he thought no one was watching. His spine had an ancient, brittle arc to it, and it occurred to Owen that maybe the near-disaster had not been such a distant possibility at all. If he'd hurt himself, that meant he'd lost his touch, and the man was too proud to admit that. Mira stood looking at a shelf of small ceramic objects. Her head was angled with dissatisfaction as she flapped Wilton's check against her thigh.

"That little clay dog," she said to Owen. "The one that doesn't look like a dog at all? It's gone. Someone stole it. Why the hell would someone do that?"

Owen suspected the guy in the army jacket, but he didn't say anything, and instead led Mira up to the roof so they could look at the night. He always stayed back from the two-foot-high edge while Mira always stood against it to look down. His stomach flipped. He couldn't bear to watch her bend forward with her heels lifting slightly.

"I wish Wilton hadn't given me this," she said, letting the check wave in the breeze. She could easily let it go. "I'm locked in now, O. I can't be done. Not with this."

"Locked in? If you feel that way, then give it back."

"Is that what you think I should do?" She slipped off her shoes and walked through the puddles. "Tell me. Tell me what I should do, O, because I have no idea."

"What do you want to do?"

"I'm lost. I don't think I've ever been so lost. And yet here's the answer." Mira waved the check again and held her dress up above her knees, as though the water were deeper than an inch. She rarely got dressed up, and he was struck by how elegant and beautiful she could be without trying. "It's enough money for a good while, so how can I not take it?" She let her dress fall. "Really, how can I not?"

Owen was afraid of the gift's unspoken obligation to Wilton, what the man might expect in return. "You could give it back and sell the Nadelmans instead." They were a pair of white marble busts in the living room with eerie lensless eyes. Wilton had mentioned them one night.

"The Nadelmans?" She gave him the kind of skeptical look that was part curiosity and part suspicion. "I can't do that. Anyway, there's no art market these days. It's tanked like everything else." It was a while before she said anything more, and then not to Owen, but to the city before them. "Do you want to know why I can't sell them?"

"Yes, I would love to know. I've always wanted to understand."

"Because I'm still waiting for my parents to come home. They went out for awhile, but they'll be back. And if I start getting rid of their things, what does that mean? That they're not coming back."

Her confession stunned him. "They're not coming back, Mira."

He put his arms around her, close enough to the edge to make him light-headed. But it was as if she dissolved against him, so that when the wind died down, he was holding only some notion of his wife.

4

As he backed the car out of the driveway, a narrow black shape, motionless as an assassin, appeared in Owen's rearview mirror. He jammed the brakes and pebbles flung themselves against the underside of the car. His whiplashed heart banged against his ribs. Wilton was inches from the bumper.

"What the hell are you doing?" Owen demanded. Adrenaline's watery rush left him parched and furious. "You scared the shit out of me. Do you know I almost hit you?"

Wilton came around to the driver's side. He half tamped down a grin. "Never. Would I let that happen? On the day before I finally get to see my daughter? Would that make any sense?" He studied Owen. "Ah, you're angry. I've never seen this before in you. And look at how you're sweating."

"That's because it's ninety-five fucking degrees out here." Owen hated being played like this, and he had the urge to step on the gas so that Wilton would be flung backward. He took a deep breath instead. "What's up? I'm sort of busy."

"I can see that. Have you ever seen what surprise looks like? This is you." Wilton stretched his mouth wide with the hooks of his index fingers and made his eyes bulge. His hair was a static cloud the sun peeked through. "Somewhere between ecstasy and agony."

"That's really great. Thanks a lot. What are you doing out here anyway?"

"Waiting for my daughter."

"I thought she wasn't coming until tomorrow," Owen said.

"That doesn't mean I wasn't waiting."

Since the day he'd arrived, Wilton had been waiting—for his daughter, Anya, his packages (UPS had just delivered another Styrofoam box of steaks for the dinner tomorrow), for the start of his life here. Now he was like a kid before his own party, trying to fill up the anticipatory minutes by squirming into every one of them. Mira had offered their house as neutral territory and themselves as buffers for tomorrow's reunion of father and child. She offered everything to Wilton these days, post fundraiser, the donation check cashed. His money's grease was impossible to wash off her hands.

Wilton pointed at the bent arm from the first floor's leaking toilet sitting on the passenger seat. "I see you're fixing something. May I come with you? I know how nothing works. You can show me."

Wilton's eagerness could be hard to deflect, and Owen told him to get in. At Home Depot, Wilton acted like a man who'd never been out of the secured desert compound. He gawked at the aisles of bathtubs and sliding doors, followed the sedating twirl of a hundred ceiling fans, ran his hands over the rug samples, tile samples, aluminum siding, lightbulbs, giant sponges. For a few minutes, he watched Owen match parts for the bent arm, and then he disappeared. But in his peach-colored polo shirt and long white shorts he was not hard to spot at the front of the store, where patio furniture, umbrellas, grills, and tiki torches were set out awaiting imaginary guests. Awaiting Wilton, who reclined in a chair that offered a matching rest for his feet. His arms were linked behind his head as though he were poolside, waiting for his iced tea.

"Look at those birds," he said, and pointed to the rafters. "They love it here."

Owen gazed up. "What makes you think they love it?"

"Would they be singing if they didn't?" Wilton wasn't about to give up his optimism or get up from his bird watcher's seat, and he patted the chair next to him for Owen to sit down. Owen was uneasy with how people stared at them, and he scratched his chin, bristly from not shaving. His shirt had holes. The school year was over and the days had a different rhythm. He tutored a few nights a week in air-conditioned houses.

"The birds must come down and eat when no one's around," Wilton said.

It was an attractive scenario, but the truth was, Owen told him, that the birds either made it out, taking a kamikaze dive for the sliding glass doors, or they died. Owen had once found the stiff, weightless body of a finch in a box of rheostats.

"How is it that you've never been to a place like this before?" Owen asked. "I don't mean just here, but out in the world. Everything you see is something new to you. You come to Rhode Island and you act as if it's a state full of miracles."

"Maybe it is. Tomorrow night, for example. That could be a miracle. And I don't mean the kind with angels either, because I don't believe in that stuff. But Anya. She's my miracle." Wilton looked into the distance as if he were contemplating a dip in the waterless hot tub. "By the way," he said, "that lady over by the grills is giving you the eye. Has been for a while now."

A middle-aged woman in a pink tank top leaned on her cart, out of which stuck the long red handle of a mop. But she wasn't eyeing him at all. It was perfectly clear that she was looking at Wilton, who had to know that, but still needed Owen to see.

Many people, in fact, had slowed to look at Wilton. They knew he was someone they recognized.

"You ready to go?" Owen asked, and stood.

"This question of miracles," Wilton said, "is an interesting one. Mira says you also came to Providence looking for something miraculous to happen." He plucked at the webbing under him, and said he was going to buy a few chairs for his porch. "She said you were in rough shape when you two met."

"Maybe." Owen's impulse was to dodge, evade. He was unnerved by Mira's having told his most private story to Wilton. "No big deal. Let's go."

"The first night we met, you said something about a friend who had died. Mira said your friend had been murdered and that you were there. She said you don't like to talk about it."

"Jesus. Why would I?"

"You're much better at asking questions than answering them," Wilton said. "They say talking is healing, but that just sounds like something a gossip came up with. Mira told me you don't have many friends, by choice, that you're the most private person she's ever known. But I hoped that maybe, as my friend, you'd talk to me. You'd open up some. But I won't push."

Owen sat down again and listened to the birds. They sounded trapped. If he gave a little, Wilton might be satisfied. "I was in a restaurant with a woman, a friend, when a guy came in to rob the place with a gun. He shot and killed her. That's the whole story." The words left a breezy space in his skull.

"Mira said she was your girlfriend."

Was disaster more understandable, more meaningful, if love was involved? Was that how Mira made sense of it? "They never caught the shooter and they never will. It's been way too long.

There's not a whole lot more to say about it." Owen watched the woman in the pink tank top circling back.

"What about you? What happened to you, Owen?" Wilton asked. "There's much more to say about that. Do you ever talk about yourself? My god, that's all I ever do."

Owen had come to Rhode Island because he knew no one there, because no history would follow him, and no grief would need tending if no one knew about it. He would arrive cleanly. But there was something about Wilton now, a man who was awed by life's unexpected beauties—mica in the sidewalk concrete, crack vials they'd seen on their way in, the geometry of artichokes, doomed urban birds, Mira, perhaps even Owen—who might understand how an instant of hesitation was all it took for life to change. He made Owen think it was okay to speak out loud, just this once, what he could never say before, what he'd never even told Mira. Was it how the man played with danger—the car's bumper inches from his legs—so adeptly? Was it all about timing?

"I didn't do what I should have," Owen said. "I froze when I should have moved. I should have said something, done something, but I didn't do anything. Nothing at all. Useless."

He saw again Caroline's pinched face when she said *fuck you* to the man, her expression when she hit the floor, and how her disappointment was not about being shot—that was over and done and she was strangely serene—but about him. She'd looked through him as though he were nothing.

"And if you'd done differently, then you would have gotten yourself killed," Wilton said.

"I was a coward. Too terrified. Too selfish. I wanted to save my own life." He hesitated, sensing danger in his confession "I've never even told Mira this." How could she love a man she couldn't trust to save her?

"Who knows if you could have done anything anyway? Are you that powerful? You can't blame yourself."

"But I do."

He didn't know what he wanted from Wilton just then, but the man's attention was gone anyway, turned instead to the circling woman who was coming at him. Wilton issued a bright hello. The woman, caught, yanked herself out of her famous-person stupor, but as she swung her cart around, the mop handle swiped through a pyramid of plastic citronella bottles. The collapse had a nice beat to it, the bottles on top plunging over like cliff divers, the others wobbling and gulping as they hit the floor. She paled and then turned fiercely red. This was free entertainment, and people stopped to watch. Wilton went over to her, whispered something, and righted a couple of bottles for effect.

In the baking parking lot, Owen struggled to fit the chairs Wilton had bought at the last minute into the back of the car. Wilton was already sitting in the car—it wouldn't occur to him to help. He wasn't much for physical labor. Once a week, he stood on his porch and watched like a king as the yard crew attended his already perfect grass. Owen gave the chairs an irritated push and slammed the door. Hadn't he just told Wilton something he was never going to tell anyone? He felt played by Wilton for the second time that morning.

Traffic blocked the road out of the lot and heat rose from the blacktop in infernal waves. Wilton fiddled with the air conditioning that hadn't worked for years. Owen turned north instead of home; he knew Wilton wouldn't notice the city's modest skyline receding. He hoped the wind off the water in Lincoln Woods might cool him in more ways than one. He wasn't happy that Mira had told Wilton his story, as if his private anguish were just another instance of something she felt she owed him, a way to pay him back. In a few miles, Owen pulled into the park and took its winding, shaded loop around the pond. Wilton smiled and looked out the window as though being driven around without knowing where he was or where he was going was fine and usual. Deep in the piney woods, people scrambled over enormous boulders. On a patch of land farther on, canopied by trees and carved out like a campsite, a kid's birthday party was underway and balloons bobbed in the branches. A bottle of orange soda glowed fluorescently on a bench.

"You and I have something in common," Wilton said, after not having spoken since they'd gotten in the car.

"What's that?"

"This feeling of having made a terrible mistake is always with us. Would you like to know why I don't drive?" Wilton spoke to the trees.

"Tell me."

Wilton seemed not to notice Owen's tone. "Anya and I were in a car accident years ago, when she was a little girl, just five. I was driving and I nearly killed her. I never drove after that. I couldn't bear to. I was too afraid."

Owen pulled to the side of the road and they got out of the car. The breeze, scented with sunscreen, carried shrieks from the swimming beach across the water and whipped up tiny whitecaps. In front of them, old women had set up chairs at the water's edge, where they cooled their feet.

"I'd taken Anya to a party one night, a terrible, self-pitying party full of people who all wished they were better than they were in every way: younger, sexier, more famous, richer. The air was full of the poisonous spores of discontent. It got into my lungs. I could barely breathe."

Like many of Wilton's stories, this one had a rehearsed feeling to it, the words too loaded and staged. The women had stopped talking and listened.

"Anya was in the hosts' bedroom, asleep in her party dress," he went on, pulling Owen away from the eavesdroppers. "When the party was over, I put her in the front seat of the car, and about twenty minutes later, I drove into a wall."

"What? Were you drunk?"

"Who knows, but I believed I was thinking very clearly. Drunk wasn't the problem." Wilton took off his shirt and splashed his skin. With his sunken belly, long arms and face tilted up, he looked ready to receive some kind of visitation. "Anguish was, depression was. I was a mess. The truth is," he said, "I drove into the wall because I was trying to kill myself. "

Owen's lungs squeezed. "But you weren't alone."

"I wasn't. I wanted to take Anya with me. I wanted a big tragedy, a big story; I wanted the world to know. But the instant before the car hit the wall, I knew what I'd done, and I told myself that if she lived, if I lived, I couldn't ever see her again. That would be my punishment." Two joggers passed behind them. "Almost twenty years of it so far."

"But it wasn't an accident, then. It wasn't a mistake," Owen said, furiously. "You tried to kill your own daughter. Jesus Christ."

"You're shocked."

"Shouldn't I be? It's fucking shocking." He felt little for Wilton's regret, his description of despair; another man's pain was a pale, abstract thing, an impression made of words. The child, though, asleep in the front seat, was something real. "Your own daughter. What the hell is wrong with you?"

"Yes, I know, my own daughter." At the last moment, Wilton

explained, he'd lost his nerve and only swiped the wall, busting a headlight. "I don't deserve to be alive, but fortunately, I was a failure at killing myself, too."

"Stop pitying yourself." Everything was drama with the man, everything a need to be looked at and listened to. "You knew exactly what you were doing."

'I could say the same to you," Wilton said sharply, surprising Owen. "You knew what you were doing when the gun was pointed at you, so no more self-pity. Time to move on, Owen. Time to stop using your story as an excuse."

After a few silent minutes, Wilton explained that he had taken himself out of the picture after the accident. Sick with what he'd done, he had his breakdown, got himself treated and drugged up, and when Anya's mother—who was never his wife; he barely knew her and they had slept together only once—got married and left California a few months later, he didn't fight it. He had no right and no energy, no heart. Every year he'd send Anya's mother money and cashmere sweaters for his daughter's birthday, and early on he'd write to Anya and she'd write back, but he didn't see her because he didn't think he could bear it. And because it didn't seem fair to her. Anya had another father then, and soon another family, so who could blame her now for being so elusive and cold with the father who'd let her go without an explanation?

One of the women in the waterside chairs let out a grunt and splashed the water with her heel.

"And then she wrote me a postcard to tell me she was moving here," he said, "and that was my cue that it was time to be with her again. I've waited and waited. And now it's time."

Anya's single postcard had taken on the grandest proportions, a call back from exile, even redemption, when maybe she'd only wanted money to pay for medical school. Wasn't it possible she

had no interest in seeing him, and all this expectation and optimism on Wilton's part was just delusion and wishful thinking?
Owen could not imagine what it would be like to wait for a child
all those years, but he knew that instead of diminishing, the missing would only intensify. In the way you could not imagine your
own aging, it was impossible to imagine the aging of your child.
How could Wilton know who this child had become?

"Does she know what happened that night?" Owen asked.

Wilton's jaw slid forward and he shook his head. "Maybe she
remembers the accident, though probably not. That her own father tried to kill her? No. And she will never, never know that.
What she knows is that I dropped out of the picture because I'm
a selfish prick. Let her think I'm the worst kind of bastard. Better
she hate me forever than ever know what I did." He gave Owen a
warning look—do not tell.

Finally, the three women twisted to see who was talking behind them, but Wilton had already turned and was walking to the
car, ready to go. When they neared Whittier Street fifteen minutes later, Wilton asked Owen to pull over for a minute.

"Mira doesn't know the story," he said. "No one but you knows.
I don't think Mira would ever understand it, just like she wouldn't
understand yours. She's like that—impossible standards, impossible loyalty. She expects a lot from people. I'm not sure we'd live
up to her standards." Wilton laughed uneasily.

"I know my wife," Owen said.

"So then I can only ask you now, as a friend, not to say anything to her. Don't tell her the story. I trust you with this because
I think you understand."

"But you're wrong, I don't understand it at all. I don't understand how you could know what you were doing," Owen said, "and
then do it anyway."

Wilton tapped his knee. "But so did you, Owen. You knew what you were doing that night with your friend and you did it anyway. You didn't save her. We both live with that shame, and who else can we tell but each other?" He stretched his arms up. "Confession feels good, doesn't it?"

Owen felt trapped. The obligation of confidence was dangerous, and Wilton's secret was a piece of glass in his pocket. Wilton was asking him to lie to Mira, and he supposed he was asking Wilton to do the same thing—enter into these sins of omission. Didn't Mira have a right to know?

When he turned into the driveway, he saw that his grass had been mowed, the bushes trimmed tightly, the corners naked of dead leaves and plump with deep brown mulch. The pea gravel had been raked to Zen garden perfection. A man with a leaf blower on his back disappeared around the far side of Wilton's house.

"They were coming anyway," Wilton explained, as he slid out of the car, "and I asked them if they wouldn't mind doing your yard. *Por favor,* you know, and *gracias.* In preparation for tomorrow night. I want it to be perfect, and I didn't want you to have to do any work."

When Owen got back from tutoring later that evening, Mira wasn't home. He called her cell phone, but it rang on the kitchen table. Wilton's house was dark. The air still smelled of fresh-cut grass. He sat on the front steps with a beer as the private nurses changed shifts over at Alice Jessup's: a man arrived, a woman left. The two had a cigarette and talked quietly in the center of the street; alone for an instant, the old lady might take that opportunity of solitude to croak. Mira and Wilton pulled into the driveway, windows open and singing to the radio. Wilton had a high, almost operatic voice. They didn't notice Owen on the steps as they got out and danced to the music on the pea gravel. Mira was not wearing her glasses and her eyes looked lit from behind. She was giddy, kissed Wilton on the cheek, and watched him go inside.

Owen called to her and she came and sat next to him on the steps, wrapping her arms around one of his knees. "You look like you're having a good time," she said.

"It's nice out here tonight. Where have you been? You didn't take your phone."

"I forgot it. It was so hot we went to Lincoln Park. Wilton said he'd been there with you earlier and wanted to go back."

Owen laughed. "Not Lincoln Park—Lincoln Woods," he said. "The park has the dog races and the slot machines. The woods have the water and the trees. Small difference."

"Well, yes," she said, laughing with him and taking a swig of his beer. "I figured out his mistake in about a second, but by then, we were already there, the AC was wonderful and we decided to check the place out. It's one of Rhode Island's finest cultural institutions, though the dogs looked pretty mangy. I've lived here all my life and have never been there, can you believe it? It seemed almost my civic duty to check the place out."

That summer, it was as if two forces had come together: excessive heat and excessive speculation about the state getting its very own giant casino that would compete with the ones in Connecticut. Like converging weather systems, the two forces fueled endless debate and frequent, sometimes violent thunderstorms. A casino would either ruin the state or save it, and what went on inside, depending on where you stood, was either gaming or gambling, harmless or moral destruction. Letters in the paper talked about jobs and revenues and the rights of reservations, while others pointed out the proximity of proposed sites to schools, churches, and nursing homes, as if kids, parishioners, and the feeble were most vulnerable to the evil vapors.

"And so how was it?" Owen asked.

"Horrible. Really horrible." Mira laughed. "But it turns out Wilton likes casinos. They're full of his fans."

She and Wilton had bet a few dollars on the greyhounds and lost. Then Mira had played the slots. "There's one called Cleopatra," she said, extracting a few wrinkled bills from her pocket and displaying them on her palm like stolen flowers. "There's a game called Linda's Lobsterfest, but a slot machine should not be about crustaceans. Where's the romance in that? Cashola—multistate progressive video slot machines. That's what they're called. Cashola. I love that."

"Seems like you had a good time," he said. "A good, horrible time."

"I did. It was kind of exciting, actually. Something different. All that dumb luck, that dumb rush you get from it. Very easy stuff. There was something strange and wonderful about being so mindless for a few minutes. A very mini vacation. You should try it sometime."

"It doesn't appeal to me at all. I don't get why people gamble any more than why they climb mountains," he said. "Who finds the prospect of losing—or dying—exciting?"

"Maybe it's the prospect of winning or living that's exciting," Mira said. "Depends on how you look at it." She elbowed him. "Either way, you feel *something*. And feeling something is better than feeling nothing. Risk is thrilling. I get that part." She tilted her head back, exposing her throat to the stars.

"Not me," he said. "Risk is just risk."

"Ah, my safe husband. Just try it sometime."

Owen was glad to see her mood so high. She'd recovered from

the disappointment of the fundraiser. Owen was grateful to Wilton for some part of that, at the very least that his money kept Brindle afloat for now. He looked over at the man's house. A shape moved behind a window, a dark reminder to Owen of the confidences they'd traded, the ones they would both keep from Mira. But what was Mira keeping from him? Wilton could be one thing to Owen and another to Mira, the man each of them wanted and needed. But you could not ask a man to keep a secret from his wife without also coming between them as a reminder of that promise. He felt Wilton's presence caught in the trees, and now falling over them.

Only the grape tomatoes were ripe. Owen cut a handful in half and sprinkled them with sea salt. He showed Mira how red and muscular their insides were, like chambers of the heart. For hours the sky had slouched under the threat of rain; the kitchen was moody with a purple hue and the fan's incompetent breeze. Earlier, Owen had watched Wilton set up the new chairs on his porch, angling them one way, and then a few minutes later coming out again to angle them differently. He'd been over twice already, once with the four steaks in their bloody vacuum-sealed packages, once with enough wine for ten people. His lips were pale and dry. A few curls hung damp at the back of Mira's neck as she looked over at Wilton's now, alert for any sign of Anya, who was already forty-five minutes late. She ate a tomato, a baby's heart. Owen kissed her shoulders, inhaled her smell of salt and almond soap.

"Let's go make a kid," he whispered. "Let's do it right now."

"Right now?"

"Why not? We can do it fast. We can do it on my desk. Push everything onto the floor. Come on. Let's be risky. I thought you liked risk."

He reached for her, but she wriggled away and began to set the table. We can't because we're supposed to be getting ready for dinner, she said, because Wilton and Anya are coming over any minute, because we still have things to do, because you need to finish cutting the tomatoes, because, she said. Because you have terrible, unfair timing. He tried to read her true reason in the way she first placed the forks and knives around the plates, and then in the way she slapped down the napkins and filled a pitcher to overflowing. She was full of ambivalence and knocked over a glass that shattered on the floor.

"I don't understand why Wilton doesn't just call her and ask if she's coming or not," she finally said, as if to preempt Owen's pushing. She got the broom and reached it under the table. "It's simple. Yes or no. Coming or not. He's just prolonging the torture. Like he likes it." She swiped angrily at the floor. Sweat sparkled on the back of her neck.

"Give me that," he said. "You're not wearing shoes. You're going to cut yourself."

She continued sweeping. "Wilton's so hopeful, and now it looks like Anya's changed her mind about tonight. I feel terrible for him." She motioned for Owen to hold the dustpan. "The girl's put him off so many times, always ready with an excuse, and he puts up with it. He keeps trying, but the whole situation's not right. It stinks."

"Maybe he doesn't know what he wants," Owen said.

"Spoken like a true man." Her jaw was set at a furious angle. He wasn't going to tangle with her now. "You tell me then. What does he want?"

But didn't Mira have a false version of the story, one that put Wilton in the softer frame of the supplicant, the innocent, a man who missed his only child? She had no idea of the truth. From the way she looked at him, he was sure she detected his evasion. He didn't like this skirting and hedging that was new between them, this shapeless obstacle, and he went outside to check on the crumbling embers in the grill. In the near dark of his perfect yard, Wilton was a wandering ghost in his usual all-white. When Owen called to him, he stepped over the fence and held his hands over the fire even though the night was stifling.

"It just might be that she's not coming tonight," Owen suggested.

Wilton nodded. "That's pretty clear by now."

"Have you called her?"

"I don't see the point." His voice was thick with disappointment. "If she wanted to come, she would. What's there to say? I don't want to beg."

The embers shifted, incinerating the night's plans. "I should cook before the fire goes out," Owen said. "You hungry?"

"I've lost my appetite. You understand." He looked at Mira, who was standing in the doorway listening to them. "You two eat without me."

He moved in slow motion. Even his door closing made a mournful gulp behind him. Owen and Mira sat on the kitchen steps and ate with their plates balanced on their knees. What was there to say about tonight or about Wilton's distress? It leaked out from between the clapboards of his house. It robbed the food of any taste. The meat was tough and stringy and turned Owen's stomach.

And then Wilton appeared again, this time dragging the four new chairs from his porch. Four steaks, four chairs, four melons, four artichokes, wine for four, but the fourth person hadn't appeared.

"You should have somewhere better to sit than the stairs," he said, and set the chairs up on the uneven bricks. "I hope it's not too late for me. Half an hour ago I wouldn't have been very good company. But I'm fine now." His eyes were turned up high and clear. He'd been crying and didn't try to hide it. "I've waited a long time. I can wait some more."

"I'm sorry, but that was a shitty thing for Anya to do," Mira said. She'd gone inside to get Wilton a glass of wine. "I wouldn't put up with it from anyone."

"She's not just anyone," he told her. "She's my daughter. It's different. You'll understand when you have one. You two will have such pretty children." He sat down and looked into his glass. "We put up with everything from the people we love. We'll wait forever, and we always welcome them back no matter where they've been or what they've done or how long it's taken them to get here. We'd only want them to do the same for us. Maybe you don't understand, but this is the end of love for me, the very last chance."

It was a sobering idea—that there might be an end of love some day, that you'd no longer see it in your future. It was only human to believe there'd always be more, there'd always be another chance for it, even at the very end of life.

"That's not true." Mira put her hand on Wilton's knee. "Let me get you something to eat."

"No, you sit. I'll do it. God knows, I know my way around by now."

As Owen measured the hour, he thought about how Wilton stirred something in them, questions and ambitions and desires. Wilton took the torment of his daughter's silence like a loud penitent, and how could you not respond to that? Owen considered, too, how there are people who appear in your life in bursts so brilliant they're almost too much to look at. And then they burn out and you're left rubbing your eyes to fill the empty space.

5

"hat's going on with you?" Owen asked Mira, when their boat was at the pond's center. The sun dripped syrupy into the water on this Sunday of Labor Day weekend, the first half week of Spruance already come and gone. "You look unhappy."

She gave him a considered gaze. "I was just thinking how the summer went too fast, another one gone too soon. The older I get, the faster they go and the less I get done. I can barely get my hands on anything before it slips away."

He sprinkled a handful of water over her bare feet and she smiled in the cooling pleasure of it. Years ago, in the month before they were married and out in this same boat, he'd first tried to show Mira a dweller rising from the bottom of the kettle pond. The dwellers, women in dresses of weeds, came in and out of view as their feathered hems and hair moved in the currents. He'd been enchanted by them as a kid, only slightly less so now. The dwellers had always been about his mother; she was one of them, they were made of her, this is where she'd gone when she'd died when he was not even two.

"Look now," he told Mira, "a tall one in a column of sun." But he could tell that what she saw was her own reflection trying not to disappoint him. She slapped a mosquito at her neck.

"There, right below us," he urged her, his voice edged with frustration. "See it?"

She inched to the center of the seat and offered up her open hands. She squinted at him like he was a distant street sign and she wasn't exactly sure where she was supposed to be going. "Maybe it's time I just took your word for it. Or maybe I'm seeing it and I don't even realize."

The dweller had ghosted away, or the boat had moved past it. You might feel you'd come to a dead stop in the water, but that wasn't ever the case. You turned and drifted until you found yourself near the opposite shore. Spots on the perimeter of the pond—the few houses already closed for the season, some vulgar new construction, towels draped over a line, his father's many cats like sentinels in the bushes, the dog Rey swishing his tail in the sand—were hours and minutes on a clock. Maybe these imaginings, these morsels of private logic, weren't ever translatable. Once put into words and exposed to the air, they would lose their shape.

Mira wanted to appease him but not give in. The source of his real displeasure was no secret. Since the night Anya had not showed up for dinner, Mira had started to go to Eagle Run Casino in Connecticut with Wilton during many of the evenings that Owen was out tutoring. They had nibbled around the edges of a full-blown fight about it on the drive from Providence; they'd been nibbling at it for many weeks now. She'd offered him her reasons for going—to keep Wilton company, bereft without his daughter; to spend a few hours gawking at people; to stretch the summer out to its last air-conditioned end; to play a few harmless games on the slots. Not a big deal. Owen had struggled to dislodge the picture of his fiercely intelligent wife brainless in front of the machines, under the halogen stars she'd told him about, one among the pastel and denim mobs she'd described—but it was something more than that. She came home stinking of cigarettes and the bitterness of other people's losses, but also the sour sweat of her own strange excitement. She was too animated on those occasions, too full of stories and observations about a place that sounded like hell to him. Smokers dragged their oxygen tanks behind them. Old ladies came in groups of three and four, their hands trembling. Buses speeding in from Chinatown disgorged a hundred eager players. She'd described for him how Wilton sat at the bar by the waterfall flirting with women and fans while she played the machines, how his face was open and tilted up as though taking in celebrity's false sun hanging from the rafters. This waiting to be recognized—by his fans and by his still elusive daughter—was Wilton's work and fuel these days. It made him happy. Was there something wrong with that? Mira asked Owen in return why he was so uptight about the place and her going there, especially when he refused to check it out for himself, even once. She said he was being close-minded and a snob.

But now the pond encouraged harmony and kissed the underside of the boat, warming the wood under their feet. As Mira rowed, he was rocked by the rhythm of the dipping oars and the warm vegetal smells of the pond. He liked the straining tendons in her neck, and the cleaved line of taut violet bathing suit between her legs. Wouldn't Brindle start again in a few weeks, and wouldn't she be too busy then to go to the casino anymore? He leaned forward and touched her knees in conciliation.

"Are you ready to swim?" she asked.

"Pretty soon. Maybe someday you'll let me teach you how. You'll see how incredible it is. You'll believe me then."

She rowed them to the far edge of the pond and the floating dock he liked to dive from. The dock belonged to Porter, who'd been his father's friend and the only other year-round resident on the pond, until he died that past November. The dock had always been Owen's to invite others onto. In his childhood summers, he would set himself up on the bleached wood, challenging kids from the rental houses to diving and swimming contests, and later on, asking girls to meet him there at night, where they both shivered with their tops off while the moon exposed them and mosquitoes attacked fresh skin. The muddy, fishy smell and the soft warmth of water trapped in a bowl of leaves had made him crazy with longing. But he'd never had sex on the dock, though it was still what he'd like to do one day. Maybe now, even: he and Mira hadn't made love in a month, and sometimes he pretended to be asleep when she came back late from the casino.

When they were feet away, they saw two people on the dock absorbing the last vain hour of sun. The couple was naked, identically ripened to a persimmon glow. The man's erection stood up like an unreliable sundial.

"He's obviously having a good dream," Mira whispered and began to turn the boat around when it tapped dockside. "I bet you it's not about her." Her maneuver was clumsy, and the man flipped over while the woman stayed still.

"Hey, how about a little privacy here?" he barked. His face was fleshy and aggressive.

"That's the idea," Mira said. The boat knocked against the dock again. "Oops. I'm not so good with these oars." She was only pretending to be inept. "Thanks for being so friendly, by the way. Have a nice evening."

The man rose on all fours like a dog, his ass high in the air and his balls swinging. Blood surged to his face. "I don't have to be friendly."

"Relax," Owen told him. "There's no problem here. We're leaving."

"Right, there's no problem. This is my property."

"I don't fucking think so," Owen said. His voice was tight; he could have sprung at any moment.

"You're very wrong about that."

The man had forgotten he was naked, until he remembered and slapped down on his stomach. The woman still hadn't moved, but Owen caught a glimpse of her brilliant orange hair hanging off the edge. Mira gave the dock one more definitive whack before steering away. In a few minutes, they were in the middle of the pond again.

"He had a very small dick," Mira said. "Maybe I should have said something about *that* property." Owen's laugh drained his anger. Rey barked on the beach. "Now are you ready to swim?" she asked.

When he stood, Mira playfully rocked the boat to see him teeter, then he arced up into the water. Sometimes he delayed this first swim as a kind of wonderful torture. The water was soft, like fur against his skin, with just the slightest note of cool deep below the surface. It took the edge off his anger at the man. He scissored his legs, and his feet looked like pale fish in gold water. With his ears under, he picked up the electrical vibration of the pond and the purr of its shifting sandy bottom. He was tempted to circle back to the dock and swim under it. He might punch the wood just to feel the man jump, just to wake the woman, just to disturb them, but he floated on his back for a while instead and felt the sun lowering on his eyelids. When he lifted his head, he saw Mira pulling the boat onto his father's small beach. She scratched Rey's head and disappeared in the tunnel of honeysuckle without looking back. She had always waited for him before. This was new and disturbing. He swallowed a mouthful of pond water.

When he got back to the house, the familiar mulchy smell of stewing lentils hit him. He was still dripping from his swim and the parched floorboards sucked up the water. His father was hunched at the counter, his head at a hawkish level as he sliced the tomatoes Owen had brought from home. At seventy-five, Edward's bones didn't want to work as hard anymore to hold his tall body straight. Age had whittled away the softer parts of his face and left his nose and chin sharper. The tops of his ears were almost transparent. His wild white hair clung to his head. When a kitten prowled across the counter and ran its tail across Edward's face, he gave it a tug. His spirits were high; he loved their visits.

"Where's that wife of yours?" he asked.

"Sounds like she's in the shower," Owen said.

The only shower was outdoors, boxed in by shingled walls and canopied by trumpet vines in the summer. In the winter, Edward insulated the pipes and steam rose from the enclosure in giant, shivering clouds. As a kid, it had been both exotic and impossible for Owen to shower outside while the pond creaked under a thick layer of ice. As a teenager, it was less spectacular, bordering on hatefully weird, but his father had stubbornly never seen a need to move the shower inside.

"Yes, I hear her singing," Edward said. He wiped his hands down his front and left a trail of tomato seeds on his shirt. His clothes were ancient, like most things in the place, and not necessarily clean. Sometimes it was hard for Owen to tell just how derelict his father was, or if he was derelict at all, when his head was anything but. He still put out a new book every few years, articles and reviews in between. His mind was fertile if not always well-tended. Owen heard no singing from Mira, just the sound of the water hitting the shingles.

"Things okay between the two of you?" Edward asked.

Owen surveyed the narrow kitchen with its open shelves of old cans and boxes and bottles. A bunch of wildflowers was stuck in a jelly jar on the table, not a gesture he would ever have expected from his father. "Sure. Things are fine."

"Just wondering." Edward's voice was gravelly but suggestive. "You know how I pick up on these things. Something's just a little off. I can tell." He toggled his hand. His eyes were a pale flecked green and unusually bright, even if rimmed with age's red crayon. There was something different about him, something tuned and tightened. "I know even when you don't say anything. Which you never do, by the way. Still my silent, guarded son." He touched Owen's shoulder. "It wouldn't kill you to talk."

"You never know," Owen said. "It might."

Edward considered Mira a rare, heroic species of bird and believed she had saved his only child by swooping in to pluck him up when he was so far down he could hardly be reached. She was the antidote to Owen's tragedy, and he was grateful to her in a way that made him weepy. He kissed her hands. He didn't hide that he was afraid of what would happen to Owen if they ever split up. What kind of parent, Mira asked, amused, actually talks about that out loud? She loved Edward in return, in a way that she hadn't ever been able to love her own remote and bullying father. Edward's big emotions sometimes toppled him like a rogue wave, which was why it made sense for him to live on the dry land of solitude.

"She came up here while you were still swimming," Edward said, "and she always waits for you. She knows—you both know—that it's not a good idea to swim alone. People drown that way. I've seen it happen." He tapped his knife on the cutting board. "They drown when they think that being alone is exactly what they need."

"I wasn't going to drown," Owen said. "The mosquitoes were vicious down there."

"This is their hour. You have to respect that." Edward sliced another tomato.

Owen went into his father's bedroom to change out of his wet bathing suit, but he kept the door open.

"So what's the problem then? " Edward asked, still at the counter. "And no bullshit now. Just talk to me."

"I like the flowers. Nice touch."

"I get the point, I'm no idiot. I won't ask you anymore if you don't want to talk about it. Maybe I'll just ask Mira instead. When you're not here. At least she'll talk to me. She always does. You? Forget it."

Edward still detected Owen's moods like he detected bird song or the scent of a bay breeze. He could tell you if the bluefish were running. Owen felt intimately exposed. It had always been too tight here; he couldn't swallow without his father asking what he was eating. Why not say something to the man now? It was easier when they weren't looking at each other. He told his father that Mira had been going to the casino with their new neighbor, Wilton, and that he didn't like it. As he talked, he noted that the bed was made, an unusual enough thing in itself, and the room was neater than he'd ever seen it. Clothes had been put away, piles of books straightened. The curtains had been washed. A fuzzy violet blanket hung over the footboard. Gold-plated nail clippers were poised like a grasshopper on the bureau. Christ, he thought, his father has a girlfriend. And they cut their nails together. They lay under the purple blanket. She picked wildflowers and put them in a jar. They watched the curtains lift in the air. He was astounded. Did Edward think he wouldn't notice?

"So what? Sounds innocuous enough to me," Edward said, standing in the doorway. He rubbed a basil leaf between his fingers and held them out for Owen to smell. "How often does she go?"

"I don't know—once, maybe twice a week." Last week it had been three times.

"Your mother played poker. She had a weekly game, nickels, dimes, nothing much. It was a social thing. So what's the problem exactly?"

"I don't like it. I don't like the place. I don't like how it makes her act."

"But that's you. Look, sweetheart, I know Mira, and the more you get worked up about this, the more she'll bristle. Let her do her thing, no harm done. It doesn't have to be your thing. You don't know that by now? What do you want her to do? She's a good girl, leave her alone. Don't suffocate her."

Owen laughed—a good girl. His father spoke with authority on women, when he hadn't been with one for decades, or not until recently, under the purple blanket. He often came up with information about Owen's mother at the precise time it was needed to form a unified parenting front. *Your mother hated the city for its violence. Your mother never swam alone. Your mother wanted you to live here with me forever.* Who could ever know what was true and what wasn't? Owen finished dressing and poured his father a glass of the wine they'd brought from home, one of the many bottles Wilton continued to give them, sometimes using the key Mira had given him to come into the house and drop them off. Edward held his glass up to admire the color, which he said was the color of expensive.

Mira appeared then, dressed in shorts and a tight black T-shirt, toweling her hair. Owen was struck by how beautiful she was, with her skin holding the sun. Her arms were long and elegant, her single gold ring shining. He didn't want to be angry at her anymore. She told Edward about the naked couple on the dock and how she had expertly run the boat into it several times just to piss them off.

"You should have seen the guy," she said. "He was lying there with a hard-on and he started barking at us."

"I know him. He looks like a bulldog?"

"A rottweiler."

"Right, a real bastard." Edward smoothed his hair, a gesture of care for Mira. "Porter would have hated him. He would have burned the land before selling to a prick like him. Did you see the monstrosity of a house he's building? An eyesore."

"Owen told him to go fuck himself," Mira said. "Or something along those lines."

Edward kissed her forehead, his hands on either side of her face. "My son makes us so proud."

Mira sat on the sagging couch. She stroked the orange cat in the corner. Books and papers were pushed under the armchair and the low table. The wooden walls of the cottage had aged to a deep, oily brown, while the tacked-up photos of Owen as a kid had faded to x-rays. Edward had left New York at thirty and moved to this cottage, one never meant to be lived in year-round, before he met Owen's mother. They'd lived together in the months before Owen was born, twenty months after until she died. Of a drug overdose, Owen had always suspected. Edward replaced things in the house only when he absolutely needed to—the sink faucet or the screen door—but never added anything new. And that in-cluded a woman. Except now there were the flowers, the blanket, the nail clippers. Owen noticed a box of tissues on the mantel above the fireplace. His father usually used his sleeve. An array of shells and fish backbones and one delicate mouse skull covered a sill. The Museum of Natural History, Mira had dubbed it after her first visit. It was nothing to like as a kid, the skeletons of tiny animals hanging from walls so thin he could hear his father talking in his sleep, hear him farting. It was no place he'd ever wanted his friends to see. But Mira loved it.

Owen went outside to watch the sun pull away from the locust trees as he walked the dirt road toward Route 6. The sky was too bright to look at, while his feet were already in darkness, so the night appeared to rise from the ground instead of descending from the clouds. Rey followed him. Returning home often brewed up an unstable mix of melancholy and impatience, the acknowledgment of life already passed and the expectation of life ahead. He knew that the death of his mother ranked as tragedy, but he hadn't ever really felt that. He'd never known her, and she had never been more alive to him than she'd been dead; they were equal states.

As a child, his constant view had been of the water ringed by trees. He'd seen the way the surface of the pond reflected even the smallest change in the weather's temper, and he'd felt captive to a moody spirit. He'd always been restless here. And this time of year brought back the pinch of loneliness. During the summer, the houses around the pond had been full and busy. The children all looked beautiful and lucky to him, the older girls exquisite in their bikinis. The renters brought life and clamor and junk food, bags of red licorice and tubs of cheese balls, and their goal for their vacation week or two was to not think about what they called "real life"—when this was his very real life all year long. What did it mean—except his father's profound relief—when they'd all left

and the pond was silent again? It was like standing still while a
very fast train blew by you and lifted your hair. What remained
was what had been forgotten or abandoned: a towel in the bushes,
a single sneaker, a cat, a brightly colored plastic ring still drifting
on the pond.

The year he'd turned thirteen, he became desperate to leave. It
was as if something had invaded his blood overnight. Where before he'd listened patiently to his father talk and read his work in
progress out loud, and he'd offered his opinions, now he couldn't
stand another word about tide pools and perch populations. Nature irked and bored him. His temper made him itch. He had
no interest in trudging down the beach to see a whale that had
washed up and lay swelling in the sun. Where the hell were the
people? Where was the noise of life, the romance and sex and action? There must be something wrong with his father if he could
stand this, he decided. Owen had turned on the television to dis-
courage his father from talking to him, and he didn't plan on turning it off until he left. For a while, Edward had continued to yap
over the television's racket, and then he'd stopped, and he stopped
asking Owen to take walks with him, to listen. He'd stopped reading out loud what he'd written. Often their dinners were wordless
and painful.

The television was an ancient thing bought by Edward so he
could watch the Watergate hearings, and when the set finally began to die, Owen's campaign to get a new one was relentless. Edward suggested a book instead. When he said, *Your mother didn't
approve of television,* Owen said he didn't give a shit about what a
dead person thought. Edward picked the television up, walked it
down the path and through the arbored tunnel, and threw it into
the pond. Owen had laughed weepily at first, mostly out of dis-
belief. He was furious with his own helplessness, though he was

already as big as his father and much stronger. The thing stayed in the pond, one sharp corner breaking the water's surface like the bow of a shipwreck, its cord a useless line snaking onto the sand. Sometimes a bird perched on it.

It was March then, still very cold, and Owen trudged to one of the houses on the other side of the pond. He'd been inside one summer, invited by a brother and sister who'd rowed their rafts over to him one day. Their parents had fussed over Owen like he was a strange specimen and fed him Pop-Tarts and hot dogs. When he looked in the windows, he expected to see the bowls of bright food still on the table and, most importantly, the television. He kicked open the side door. His strength was new and still surprising, like his own hard-ons. He took the television and brought it home. That night, Edward baked fish that stank up the place, and Owen insisted on leaving the door open to the cold night air as his own retribution. As they were eating, he looked over Owen's shoulder at the water and extracted another fish bone from his mouth. He laid it on the table, reconstructing the skeleton. The next morning, Edward dragged the old waterlogged television out of the pond and left it in front of the house under a sheet like a corpse. When Edward finally bought a new set, Owen took the stolen one back to the house across the pond and repaired the busted door. Neither of them ever said a word about it, this test of their opposing wills.

Owen led Rey back to the house. Inside, Mira had lit two mysterious pale pink candles. They ate the lentil soup, the bread, the tomatoes, and the chocolate cake Mira had made. Owen opened another bottle of wine. Mira leaned back in her chair, pushing off from the table with her palms, and told Edward about the adult life-drawing course she was going to offer soon, maybe just after the New Year.

"It makes sense," she explained. "If Brindle is going to survive, I have to start getting a different crowd in there. You know, one that can actually pay, one that doesn't cost me money. One I don't have to also feed and clothe. The place can't survive on goodwill or liberal guilt anymore." She talked about replacing the leaking windows in the gallery, updating the two bathrooms in the building, hiring another teacher or two.

"Where's all the money going to come from?" Owen asked. It was the first he'd heard about any of these plans. "You're talking about some very serious work. The windows alone—"

"I know, Owen. Lighten up. I'll get it. Listen, I have to make some decisions about the future of the place. Expand or fold." Mira demonstrated like she was opening and shutting a book. "I can't keep waffling. It's making me crazy. Wilton and I've been talking about how it doesn't make any sense to be in the middle anymore. It's just too hard, too wearing."

"Were you going to let me in on this?" he asked.

"Life drawing," Edward said, cutting in between them. "Some artists learned by looking at cadavers. Audubon did. Do they call that death drawing?"

Mira pressed cake crumbs under her thumb. "Men and women, everyone's just crazy to look at naked boobs."

"Maybe you should try the class, Owen," Edward suggested. "Expand your horizons. Loosen up a little. Relax."

"I'm all set for naked boobs, thanks." Rey's long snout rested on his thigh.

Edward shrugged. "I'd like to meet this Wilton. He sounds interesting."

"You'd like him," Mira said. "He's been incredibly generous to us—and to Brindle. He's basically floating the place now."

There was something about the way she said it that made Owen pull up short. "Has he given you more money?" he asked her. "More than at the fundraiser?"

Mira tapped her fingers against her lower lip. "You know he has, O. I already told you that."

"No, you didn't."

"I did, but you forgot." She spoke slowly to make her point. "With school starting and all your tutoring, you've been distracted and busy. It's okay."

"No, trust me, I would have remembered." He supposed it was possible that he hadn't been listening when she'd told him—his mind focused only on the casino business—but he didn't think so. "Maybe you're the one who forgot."

"There's nothing wrong with money." Edward smoothed the air again. He'd retreat rather than fight or listen to one. Mira determinedly forked cake into her mouth and swallowed his collusion. She wouldn't look at Owen. "You're not sleeping with this man, are you, Mira?" he asked.

Her laugh was an explosion. Crumbs flew onto the table and her hand covered her mouth. "I can't even believe you asked me that."

Edward looked at Owen. "Okay. She's not sleeping with him. Then I don't see what the problem is. Everything's fine. Your neighbor sounds generous, that's all."

"It's a little more complicated than that," Owen said. "Maybe you should stay out of it."

"Owen," Mira cautioned. She ate another piece of cake.

They slipped down in their chairs, a retreat. The season's last cicadas revved up. Edward pulled the candles closer. "Any word from the police?" he asked Owen.

The question was inevitable, even seven years after the

shooting. It was always just a matter of when his father would ask. There hadn't been any word from the police or anyone else involved since the first months after Caroline's death. No one had ever been arrested and no one ever would be.

"It's always the same. No word," Owen said. "Maybe it's time you stop thinking about it." He stood to shake off the unease his father's question always provoked. "Stop asking, while you're at it."

"I can't very well control what I do or do not think about," Edward said, made petulant by the wine and the hour. He held Mira's hand in his and looked at her. "We're much closer to tragedy than we ever think."

"But sometimes we see it coming and we move away. O dodged it, didn't he?" Mira asked. "Nothing happened to him."

They'd had this conversation before. She wanted to relieve Edward of this oppressive sense of precariousness and erase for him the notion that Owen could just have easily been the one killed, that his only child wouldn't be there, just inches from him. She did more than Owen ever could to calm his father, whose eyes had begun to well up. He blinked out the tears. Mira stood behind Edward and placed her hands across his chest. She kissed the top of his head.

"It's okay," she said, looking at Owen. "He's okay, we're all fine, we're all safe."

Edward sniffled. He was fiercely attached, a man who'd been left with a child without knowing how to care for one. He'd been clueless a lot of the time, but Owen had never doubted his father loved him. Maybe it was that particular brand of love that had made Owen feel so suffocated in a place where there was plenty of everything but never enough air. It was the essential problem of two— one would always leave first. That inevitability had hung over them from the beginning. Mira went over to the radio and dialed through the stations until she found some slow music. She pulled Edward up to dance with her, and they laughed together at how clumsy he was. She told him not to look at his very ugly feet. They made a funny couple, one alert with evasion, the other brittle and tentative and moved by life's fragility, with skinny pale legs and shins scabbed by thorns and branches. After a few songs, Edward disappeared into his bedroom. Mira stood with her hands on her hips.

"Looks like he ditched you," Owen said.

"Seems like that, doesn't it."

"Wait for me. I'm coming back," Edward yelled.

He emerged, cradling something in an old towel that he put on the table. Owen unwound the towel and stared at a handgun, an obsidian black against the faded yellow, small and fearsomely precise.

"What the hell is this?" Mira asked, flipping the towel over it.

Edward disrobed it again. "Well, it's a gun, wouldn't you say?"

"We get that part," she said. "Why are you showing us a gun?"

"Why do you even have a gun in the first place?" Owen picked it up. The weight was exciting.

"Put it down, O," Mira said. "I don't even like to see you touching it."

"I'm giving it to you, to both of you," Edward told her. "In case you need it. You should be prepared." He put a handful of bullets on the table.

"Who are you, Charlton Heston?" Owen asked.

"I hope not. He's dead." Edward fished a chewed-up tennis ball out from under the couch. He opened the screen door, and threw it out. Rey tore after it. "If you get broken into again," he said, "you'll be glad you have it."

"Glad? Why, so we can shoot and kill the guy this time?" Mira asked.

"Yes," Edward added. "What's wrong with that?"

"Everything is wrong with that. We're not going to take it. This is absurd. Please, O, will you put it down?" She turned away. She didn't want to see his hand still wrapped around it.

I've had a gun stuck in my face, Owen thought. I've smelled its mineral sweat, and heard it rip open the air. I've seen what it can do to flesh, but I've never held one before. He hadn't known how much he'd wanted to until that moment and he gripped it harder.

"Don't worry," Edward said. "It's not loaded."

"That's what everyone always says," Mira told him, "and then boom, someone gets his head blown off. If there's a gun in the house, it goes off. We are not taking it home, Edward. We don't want it. We're not gun people. For god's sake, please, Owen. Put it down."

Owen covered it decorously and pushed it to the far end of the table. He asked his father where he'd gotten it.

"Sit. I want to tell you something. I met a woman in April. Katherine. At the salt marshes. Seeing anyone out there that day would have been pretty surprising—it was freezing—but there she was, taking pictures. You'll see them sometime. She was wearing these funny gloves without fingers so she could adjust the lens. I'd never seen anything like it." They'd shouted in the wind until their cheeks burned, and then they'd gone for coffee. The next week, she'd made him dinner at her place in Brewster. "She's an interesting woman. She used to teach high school math. I like her. Very much in fact."

"Wow," Mira said. "This is great news."

Owen turned to his father who still stood behind them. "It's been months. And you never said anything until now?"

"We wanted to give it some time before we told anyone—to see how things were going. You'll meet her soon."

We. Katherine: the flowers, the tissues, the pink candles, the tightly made bed. His father was in love. "And then what, you two went gun shopping?" Owen asked. Which was more shocking, the gun or the woman? "Is she your girlfriend or your arms dealer?"

Edward laughed as he went to the door and whistled for Rey. The dog crashed through the woods and skidded into the house. He dropped the slobbery tennis ball at Owen's feet. "Katherine had the gun," Edward explained. "Actually, her son gave it to her for protection after a student attacked her—landed her in the hospital. It was terrible." He winced as if her past was now also his. "But she said no one was going to bother an old lady in a condo complex on Cape Cod and she didn't want the thing around anymore. I don't think she liked the idea of her grandson finding it in her underwear drawer some day. I told her about your break-in and she wanted you to have it."

His father was ripe with his news, and later, after he had talked about Katherine with the kind of enthusiasm he usually conferred on piping plovers and riptides, after he'd exhausted himself and gone into his room, Mira and Owen made up the pullout couch and lay down. Owen watched the moon admire its reflection in the pond and slink into the house. It was an evocative night and the air was tempered with his father's belief that anything could happen at any time. Letting his anger at Mira dispel was just a matter of choice. Anger had no life on its own—you had to give it shape with your own breath. And what was his problem really that wasn't about his own fears of losing her? His father's news made him feel hopeful.

"I don't want to fight with you anymore," he said and rolled on his side to look at her. "Go with Wilton to the casino. Do what makes you happy."

She faced him. "It's just so much of nothing, Owen."

"So much of nothing," he repeated.

"Nothing's going to happen to me," she said. "You have to believe that, trust me on that one."

"I do."

"You'll get rid of the gun?" she asked. "Promise me you will."

"I promise."

"Because we can't have it in the house."

For a while they listened to the sounds of the woods and the nocturnal wanderings of the cats. They whispered about Edward and his new girlfriend, and their speculation and release from their own discord made them giddy. Owen knew you couldn't talk about someone else falling in love without feeling a pinch of envy and a need to confirm what it was you had. He kissed Mira and stroked the length of her silvered body, which felt vaguely resistant to him, like the skin over a rising bruise, tight and too warm. He wondered if she was worried about Edward hearing them, if she felt, as he did, like a kid in this house, but now a kid who wanted to possess, control, and devour, without knowing what any of that really meant. When Mira opened her legs, the sheets whispered their routine beneath her, but it sounded wary to him, or maybe more like a rehearsal. He locked his mouth on hers, and she was insistent then as she released herself from the top down so he didn't so much enter her as slip down her throat and into her. But her insistence wasn't about desire or that tingly, aching drive; it was about appeasing him in some way, for what she hadn't told him, for how she was moving away from him; and he came powerfully, loud and selfish and married, and he didn't care if his father heard him.

"Nice," Mira said, softly, distractedly, and it broke his heart.

6

I don't like the book because it makes me tired to read it." That sounded about right to Owen, who looked up from Reggie's paper, tired himself. One school year was getting to be too much like another, the repetition of aspirations and their gradual deflation. He turned in the desk chair to the window onto Whittier Street and saw a woman coming down the sidewalk. The rolling walk that presented slim hips first, long upper body next, the casual angle of elbow and forearm—this was Wilton's essence in female form. She had to be Anya. Her head, angled slightly up, might have been a kind of overconfidence until she stumbled on an uneven seam of sidewalk hidden under October's first crisped leaves. Her grace was clumsy, her clumsiness graceful, and she looked at her feet, those long Wiltonesque culprits. She stopped in front of her father's dark house but didn't move toward the door.

When she crept around to the side porch, Owen went out to the backyard where he could watch her from his garden of puckered tomatoes. If she saw him there, he wouldn't look like he was spying on her. The season over, most of the fruit was overripe, split and dribbling, while some was still an implacable green that would hold on through the first frost. There was a flash of hair, more reddish than brown, and a gray sweatshirt in the reaches of his vision. He was eager to see her face, but she cupped her hands

against a window, her back to him. Wilton's rooms were mostly
empty still, with a distracted placement of furniture and the boxes
that contained all the things he ordered online but didn't always
bother to open. In one upstairs room, there was nothing but a pair
of new leather shoes in the middle of the floor, as if the person
wearing them had evaporated. In another was the clay pot Wilton
had paid Brindle so much for. Owen guessed that what Anya saw
to make her hands fall to her sides was the unsettled, bereft life of
her father, a scattering of intentions that could leave you chilled.

"He's not home," Owen called.

Anya's hand flew to her throat as she took a step back from his
voice emerging from the foliage. He saw only the side of her face;
the balance of forehead, nose, and eye was coolly beautiful. He
came to the fence to show himself. "I'm sorry if I scared you," he
said.

"Well, you did." She jammed her hands in her sweatshirt pockets and started for the front of the porch. "You really did."

He apologized again to keep her from leaving and showed his
hands, not empty but full of unripe tomatoes—nothing to find
menacing. Her face was not icy at all, but soft in the wide expanse
of her cheekbones and chin. He realized, though, that he was
expecting the child in Wilton's stories, a little girl in pajamas, a
three-year-old swimming in the pool, a child in a party dress the
night of the accident. He knew about the birthmark on her hip,
the size of her baby hands. He knew that she used to stroke her
father's cheek. He knew nothing about the adult.

"Do you know him?" she asked. "The guy who lives here?"

"Wilton? Yes. I'm Owen, by the way. And I think you're probably Anya, right?"

She gave him a skeptical look and then nodded. Her body, at a
three-quarter turn, was ready to run but was also curious about

what else he might know. Did he know the troubled history of father and daughter? "Just him in here?" she asked, ticking her head at Wilton's house.

"Just him in all that space. Crazy, isn't it?"

He didn't know what more to say or how much to reveal, but he wanted to keep her there. She shivered in the dubious, cool air, while his heart thumped away. Would she like a glass of wine, or some tea, while she waited? he asked. Anya was clearly trained to consider all the dangers in the world to a woman, and here was a man she didn't know, but who knew who she was, asking her in for a drink.

"I don't think so, but thanks anyway," she said. "I'm going to go."

"Another time, I hope." He hesitated. "Your father will be really glad to know you stopped by."

"Actually," she started, and in her hesitation assessed his hands full of tomatoes, his rangy, nonmenacing height, his mention of Wilton, and she took him up on the offer. He pointed to the gate that was permanently angled open these days. Where its foot had drawn a ragged scar into the grass, thick clover had grown. As Anya passed through, a corner of her sweatshirt pocket caught on an iron curlicue. It yanked her back with a hiss. She held up the inch-long tear and rolled her eyes. The way she poked fun at herself and put mishap next to poise was pure Wilton. Where was her mother in all this biology?

In the kitchen, she leaned against a counter near the door and took in the room's dated details in the same way Wilton had done his first time there. She held the beer bottle below her chin. That morning, Mira had lined some tomatoes up on the table in ascending order. The last was no bigger than a green pea. The Edible Vanishing Point, she'd called it and kissed him on the mouth before going upstairs to get ready to go to Brindle. She'd been

breezy, hard to hold down. Owen picked up the two biggest tomatoes, which were almost purple in density. He was self-conscious
about the way they sat so plump and cleaved in his palms before
he cut them open. He showed Anya the best way to eat one, always at room temperature and sprinkled with sea salt. The gelati-
nous pillow of seeds surprised her as it slid over her lower lip and
fell to the floor. They talked about food, a neutral passion—the
Portuguese bread she'd found in Fox Point, where she had an
apartment, the meat market on Gano Street that reeked of fresh
blood—as they ate crackers, goat cheese Wilton had ordered from
Vermont, a jar of jalapeño almonds. Fancy, ridiculous food, all of
it from her father. Anya sucked spice powder off her fingertips.
She wore a ring—a silver band—around her thumb. Owen knew
he was staring; she was very pretty, with a streak of seriousness
that cut across her forehead and her father's determined jawline.

"These were also a present from your father," Owen said, spilling some chocolate-covered espresso beans onto her palm. She bit
into one with her front teeth, as if she were halving a pill. "And all
that wine." He pointed to the collection on the counter.

She looked over at her father's house. Her wavering confidence
was appealing—and young. "Why does he give you all this stuff?"
she asked.

Owen shrugged. "It's what he does. He orders online and gives
in person. The ASPCA and Amnesty International and Oxfam
and Planned Parenthood and the food bank send him letters and
he gives. The Fireman's Fund and the Sierra Club and PBS call
and he never hangs up on them."

"My father and I aren't exactly close," she said.

"I know."

"You do? Do you know we haven't seen each other in years?"

"He's told me some things. I know he's been waiting to see you for months."

"You're not scolding me, are you?"

"Nope."

Anya nodded and seemed to understand that she had nothing else to go on but what he told her. Owen was aware of his vaguely corrupting power, if he opted to use it. What it was like to have a father drop out of your life, and what story had Anya been given or told herself about why it happened? Whatever it was could never fully satisfy. Especially the true story. Death was one thing—his own mother was dead before he even knew her—but this wasn't death. This was so much murkier, and still alive and beating. Wilton's remove from her had to be a kind of chronic pain for both of them. Anya held her hair back with one hand, exposing two piercings and two tiny diamonds in one ear as she examined the painting of a sturdy, sour woman with a dark upper lip.

"Mira's—my wife's—grandmother," Owen said. "The esteemed Agnes Thrasher. She could use a shave, don't you think?" Anya smiled. "My wife is out somewhere with your father, as it turns out. They're very good friends."

Somewhere being the formless word Owen said to himself these days when he knew exactly where they were together. It was always the casino and about Mira's keeping company with Wilton, who was so deprived of his daughter that he needed her constant consolation. And how could she say no when he continued to be so generous to Brindle? And if she liked to play for ten or fifteen minutes on the slots when she was there, well so fucking what, right? It was an exhausting, stupid conversation. Owen had stopped counting how often she went; inexactitude was like a mild painkiller, just enough to take the edge off but not enough to forget the ache was there. It distressed him, but what could he say anymore? It wasn't about the money; she didn't win anything and she didn't lose anything, she claimed. But he knew gambling didn't work that way: everyone lost eventually, and usually lost big. Was Mira being dumb, or did she just think he was dumb enough to believe it? Gambling was the stuff of a million tragic stories, he told her, and he didn't want it to be hers. She shook her head at his crazy exaggerations, and said he was ridiculous; she said she hardly played at all. He hated that she liked the packaged towelettes they gave you to wipe the muck of money off your hands, and how she always brought some home and left them on the kitchen table as if she'd picked them up as souvenirs for him. *Thinking of you. Wish you were here.*

One night last week, Mira had called from Evil Ruin, which is what he'd renamed the hellhole, to say how much she loved him, and that she'd be home soon. He'd just that minute come back from another mind-numbing session of tutoring, that hushed, coercive profession, and he'd flinched at how her voice rose to be heard above the chiming clamor of the slot machines. Was she just making sure he was still there to return to, that he was something real when everything around her wasn't? Was he a safe home base?

If he delivered Anya to Wilton, would Wilton release Mira?

A car door slamming on the street made Anya look up. It was enough to make her announce that she had to go. She was anxious to get out of there, and her eye was already on the front door.

"Are you sure you don't want to wait?" he asked.

"I'm sure." She stepped outside. "Will you tell Wilton I was here? I'm going to call him soon. Maybe. I don't know when." She paused to acknowledge his confusion and her own. "Look, I know it sounds kind of crazy. He's my father, and all, but I can't explain it."

"You don't have to explain," he said. He thought she might understand that you couldn't cure the throbbing of loss with reunion—you might only make it beat harder and hotter. "I'll tell him you were here."

But Anya didn't call Wilton the next day, or the day after, and Owen didn't tell him that she'd been by. He didn't tell Mira either, but held on to the fact like a prize he might have to trade in later. Tonight, he was out tutoring, restless in the kid's room as he watched the dark eat up the Cranston neighborhood. Behind him, the boy, leaning back in a chair, was too stoned, once more, to notice anything disappearing, including the expensive minutes his parents were paying for. Down in the kitchen, noisy family life was taking place and a dog barked, but it felt far away from Owen's own life and this carpeted bedroom that still reeked of pot. When Owen gave up trying to rouse the kid, he went downstairs to explain to the boy's father why he was leaving thirty minutes into the session. Your son is high again, he said, one foot already out of the house. Nothing was familiar in this silent neighborhood, not the tight air, not the streets named after the developer's eight daughters, not the perfect lawns, not the fuming, pitiable father who was watching him out the window by the door. Owen got into his car, and at the end of Phenix Avenue, he realized that he had a choice that suddenly seemed novel and significant to him, though he'd been at this same intersection many times before: go north or south? He didn't have to go home and wait like some idiot for his wife to waltz in, blithe and casino-blinded, so he turned the car south toward Eagle Run—Evil Ruin, where he would find his wife. He didn't mind being a caveman about it and dragging her out if he had to. He felt as stunned and inarticulate as one when it came to understanding what she was up to, and what had happened to his marriage, which was now all evasion and excuse.

But as he crossed the state line, and Mystic approached, his plan began to seem pointless. What was he hoping or not hoping to see or do? It might only make things worse, and Mira more determined. He turned back to Providence, defeated. After a while on the highway, the hospital rose in front of him like a feverish patient sitting up in bed. Steam belched from the industrial laundry. He took a detour past Brindle to assure himself that it was dark and safe. But the lights were on and blazing on the second floor. The front door was unlocked and his entry unnoticed.

He hadn't been in the building since late September, when he fixed a dripping faucet in the upstairs studio. Now he saw how the spine of bulbs that ran through the gallery, some burned out, threw a beaten shadow over old newspapers fanned on the floor. A few dispirited pastels gazed out from the walls. A couple of dented soda cans sat on the dusty platform. The room had the feel of a bus station minimally attended to, a place to pass through and leave from. It was shocking to see it neglected. Mira's attention to Brindle, to all the details of her life, had stumbled badly. A sour taste flooded his mouth. He left the gallery and found his wife in her office reading something on her laptop. Her head rested in one hand while the other tapped a pen against her cheek. The whorl of hair at the top of her skull had a kiss of pale scalp at its center. Her head shot up when he said her name.

"Owen. My god, you scared me," she said, and whipped off her glasses. She closed her eyes and took a calming breath. Her lips paled. "Wait. Aren't you supposed to be tutoring now?"

"I bagged it. The kid was too stoned to hold a pencil. He kept nodding off." The wicker chair screeched when he sat down. "Actually, I got canned by the boy's father. That was after I told him that his son was more interested in getting high than getting into college."

"And he fired you?"

"I got the 'I don't think this is working' line. Which is code for 'This is too fucking humiliating for me to deal with.'" He felt strangely moved now by the father's disappointment. "I didn't think you'd be here."

"Why not? I told you I'd be here tonight," she said. She put her glasses back on and gave him a determined look. "This morning, don't you remember? You were at the door, just about to leave for school, and you had some jelly on your chin. I wiped it off and told you I had a late class. Life drawing?" She opened her hands to show there was nothing to hide. "Remember? Bare boobs? Paying students?"

He remembered how she'd touched the spot of raspberry and sucked it off her finger, how he'd tried to read some kind of remorse in her gesture but felt nothing more than the November morning air biting his neck. "It doesn't matter."

"No, it does matter," she insisted. She tapped her mouth with two fingers. "It matters that I'm here when you assumed I was somewhere else—at the casino. I don't lie to you, O. I always tell you where I am and exactly what I'm doing and where I'm going."

"Yes, well, that's the problem, isn't it," he said. "What you're doing and where you're going."

"Get a grip, Owen. This is crazy." Her glasses slid down and she pushed them up again for the clearest view of him. "Maybe you don't want to listen, or hear me, but I do tell you everything."

He couldn't point to all the untruths or small distortions on her part, but he sensed they were everywhere, like the sanguineous vapor of rust in the air at that minute. Like the battered state of Brindle. He took in the room with the shelves listing under piles of old art magazines, paints, brushes, bottles of glue, stacks of faded construction paper, abandoned pieces of pottery, jars of markers, too many of them missing tops. Mira had once bought twenty boxes of German colored pencils from a guy selling art supplies off the back of a truck. There were only two left. The first time she'd brought him to Brindle, Owen had been hit by a potent mix of nostalgia for his elementary school art room and his attraction to her. He'd told her he wanted to make love to her on the table amid the pipe cleaners and Popsicle sticks and gummy erasers. She was passionate about every smudgy handprint, lop-sided pot, and still life. She believed in the power that came from creating something, and she had made him feel everything—the creation of a new life for him—was possible. And it had been. To fall back into his gloom was unthinkable. He wasn't going to allow it. He'd die first.

"You're not always where you say you'll be," he told her. "Sometimes I call in the middle of the day and I can't find you."

"But you know me, O. Half the time I don't answer the phone. Half the time I can't even find the damn thing. That's nothing new." She came around to him, straddled his knees and put her hands on his shoulders. Her face was at his neck. She was angry but trying to hide it. "What exactly are you so worried about? That I'm going to become some kind of addict?" Her laugh on his skin, in his ear, was almost mollifying.

"It's possible," he said. "It happens all the time."

She pulled back. "Right. Look at me. I'm a real degenerate." She shook her head and wagged her tongue. "Tell me honestly; do you really think that's going to happen?"

He didn't answer but instead put his hands under her shirt and ran them up her back.

"You know you're being more than a little crazy about this, right?" she said.

He felt the fight within her to appease him, to assure him, but to hold her own at the same time. He wanted her to feel the fight within him, too, and he gripped her tightly enough to make her gasp. Her breath battled him against her ribs. He knew he could hurt her—he was very close to it. His fingers pressed into her spine. She started to say his name; he wouldn't loosen his hold. Marriage was not always about being in agreement, but sometimes it was about only that. O, she breathed. Above them, a chorus of chairs scraped across the concrete floor and he let go. Her reprieve—she jumped off. She straightened her shirt.

"Wilton's up in the class," Mira said, and pointed to the ceiling. "You know how he's always looking for something to do? Why don't you go up and take a look and let me know how it's going."

Her tone was squeezed and false. He was ashamed for having tried to hurt her, and for how easy it would be. They both knew what had just happened, how close he'd been to violence. The proximity was sickening. He took the stairs that ended in a small landing where he could stand unnoticed and calm his breath. His control was a battered flag. When he looked in, the studio was bright and glaring. He recognized the model from before. It wasn't her expression of implacable boredom, but the rejection in her pose, half thrown, half discarded, that was unforgettable.

"I don't care what they say," Wilton announced, "but this is a hell of a lot harder than acting."

The words hung in the air. A stool scraped, then another. Owen could see only a slice of Wilton from where he stood, and the shoes and ankles below the easels of the others. Someone dropped a piece of charcoal that pinged on the floor. Paulette, a long-time instructor with a gray braid that reached down to the small of her back, soundlessly wove her way between the students.

"In acting, at least they give you the lines," Wilton added.

Paulette told the model to take a new pose. Pages of sketch-pads flipped over, a flock of birds taking off.

"Here I have to make those lines up myself. So much tougher," Wilton continued. "My question is, how do you ever know what exactly it is you want to say?"

"Would you be quiet? Please?" one woman said. "Do you hear anyone else talking?"

"Excuse me." Wilton teased out the words and waited for the appreciative murmur from the others. "I didn't know there was a ban on talking."

"What are you, a ten-year-old who has to keep talking even when no one responds?" she said.

"I wish I were ten years old," Wilton said. "I'd have longer to get this right."

The sanctimonious silence cracked. Paulette tugged uncer-tainly on her braid. The woman was disabled by shyness. The faucet still dripped.

"Is there a rule against talking, Paulette?" a woman asked.

The model scratched her forearm. She looked like she was thinking about dinner or what she had to do tomorrow. She flicked at something that had landed on her folded belly.

"How can there be a rule against talking?" Wilton said. "That's un-American."

"How totally, completely, fucking irritating," the scolder said, her feet balancing on the toes of her serious boots.

"Oh, well," Wilton sighed, the pleased, seductive pest. "I tried."

He tried and he succeeded; the others in the room were now enthralled.

Owen went downstairs and found Mira in the gallery, stuffing garbage into a bag in a hurry as though she'd just realized what the place looked like—to him. She yanked the ties of the bag shut, and went out to the Dumpster. He followed her into the cold as she heaved the thing up. The arc was short and the bag hit the side of the Dumpster. It split and papers escaped in the wind. She didn't try to catch them but looked at the river and the hill rising behind it. A single rat had found something to eat, its red eyes flashing. It started to snow and Owen opened his coat around his wife.

"Are you in love with him, Mira?" he asked.

"Shit," she said, exasperated. "How can you even ask me that? You're ridiculous."

"Really? Because I'm trying to understand what this is all about. It feels like love, Mira, something crazy enough to make you do this, to sneak around, to jeopardize what you have. To do this to me."

"Enough. I'm doing nothing, and I'm not sneaking anywhere, and I'm not doing anything to you. God, would you let me breathe?" She pushed him away.

By now the drawing students were clomping down the stairs, and Mira went back inside to say good-bye to them. She was professionally bright-eyed. Wilton was in the thick of the bunch, saying good night and holding the door open for them like the place was his. When he spotted Owen, he clapped his hands together.

"How wonderful. I didn't know you were going to be here," he said. "I thought you were out teaching."

"I was." Owen gave him a cool look.

"Listen," Wilton said, "what that class needs is more men. You have to come next time. There's a dangerous estrogen overload that can't be good for anyone's art."

"All the great male artists had too much estrogen, didn't you know that?" Mira told him. "Estrogen dominance, it's called. It's why they screwed everything and drank too much. It's why not one of them was bald or thin."

"That's some theory," Wilton said. "Maybe I don't have enough estrogen. Maybe that's my problem."

When Mira asked him to show what he'd drawn, he held his pad to his chest. "Not a chance."

The model, puffy in a red jacket, appeared in the foyer, gave Mira a quick wave, and left. Wilton trotted after her, and they talked out on the steps, the door open and letting in the cold. The woman had her car keys out already like a warning against Wilton's flirtation, and she shifted with disinterest. She tolerated him for as long as it took for the traffic signal at the end of the block to cycle through green to yellow to red.

Wilton came back in with doggish disappointment. "I struck out," he said.

"So are you going to show us your work now?" Mira asked. "You're embarrassed. That's kind of sweet, actually, kind of endearing."

"Oh, it's not modesty," Wilton said. "It's shame."

Mira slid the pad away from Wilton, who didn't protest. It was always a game with them. They bent over his drawings. In his rudimentary sketches, Wilton had managed to give movement to what was still, elasticity to what was brittle. He'd captured the deeply erotic appeal of the model, and her look of disdainful boredom, almost as if it had been aimed directly at him. He'd made her breasts rise off the page. Wilton wiped the charcoal dust off his hands and declared the work to be shit. Mira hadn't spoken.

Wilton's talent was enviable, obvious, immense, not at all raw. Who knew what the man could have done with his life?

"I saw your daughter the other night," Owen said, softening toward him at that moment.

Wilton's face was lit with expectation. His body tilted in Owen's direction. "Tell me everything," he said.

Owen huddled in his down jacket as he stood over the grill and used a long fork to poke the pulsing coals. Behind him, Mira and Wilton talked in the kitchen's lemony light and waited once more for Anya. Wilton's slicked-back hair made him look shiny and marsupial, and he wore a white apron from the steak company that said "I'm the Man with the Big Meat." Mira's face was flushed, and she'd pushed up the sleeves of her black sweater. A row of pearly buttons ran between her breasts. Despite the cold of early November, she had wanted to duplicate the summer dinner Anya hadn't shown up for in July, because this time the girl was absolutely coming. She'd called her father the day after Owen had told him about the visit. Earlier, Mira had retrieved from the basement a round paper lantern her parents had used at their parties and hung it from a branch. The silhouettes of dead moths were imprinted on the inside. When Wilton had delivered his nervousness and his white box of meat in the afternoon, Mira had assured him that each part of the meal had its own particular flavor of reunion: seriousness in grilled meat (forget the carcinogens), affection in the sweet beads of couscous, optimism in the beds of lettuce, blood in the tomatoes and the tangy drops of vinegar. And possibly bitterness in this smoke roused by a sudden, strong wind Owen turned away from. The paper lantern swayed like a full moon gone crazy.

A shadow shifted. Owen scanned the yard's impenetrable

corners. The pea gravel mumbled underfoot, the dried leaves eddied around his ankles. Mira and Wilton had moved away from the kitchen window, and the surrounding houses were turned inward. This disregarded outside, shelter to smash-and-grabbers, raccoons, and coyotes, was the wild territory of city life. Cold breath hesitated at Owen's mouth and tensed. A branch snapped, the leafless lilac bushes screeched against the carriage house, where something inside was swinging behind the glass. Owen's heart hammered. He held the tongs like a club. At the back of the carriage house, overgrown bushes and hissing thorns hooked his pants. One of the glass panes in the door was smashed, and the in-rushing air had set things swinging and shifting: there was no one inside doing it. Still, someone had tried to break into the carriage house. But who knew when? Yesterday? A month ago? At the same time the house had been broken into? He already knew he wasn't going to tell Mira.

When he heard footsteps on the gravel and came out from behind the bushes, he saw Anya stopped at the top of the driveway. She was wrapped in a long coat with a scarf over her head like some kind of doomed countess. Wilton rushed out the back door, throwing the apron behind him. His arms were a riot of motion. He slowed to smooth his wheezy breath, his shirt, touch his hair, lift his shoulders and let them drop again, shake his wrists out. The man was running through his entire repertoire of misgivings. A sob bubbled up out of him like the sound of a ball bouncing down an abandoned hallway. He could have been trudging through sand, begging for water, for how hungrily he moved, and his daughter just a mirage. Wilton put his hands on her shoulders, kissed one cheek and then the other, and pressed his face against hers. He bent at the knees, cried, and dropped even lower. Owen glimpsed Anya's heartbreak at this man falling at her feet while her arms were limp. She looked stunned.

Owen was sure he would never see another meeting like this, but it was too much, and he went inside where Mira was slicing cucumbers. She was pretending this was like any other night, when it must have taken everything for her not to watch the meeting of father and daughter. He didn't know what to say or what to explain—about the break-in and how besieged it made him feel or how the reunion in the driveway filled him with envy. To regain what you thought you'd lost. She would understand what that meant, but she didn't look up at him and he didn't speak. He watched her knife make careful cuts.

"May we come in?" Wilton asked, appearing in the doorway with Anya behind him.

Mira put the knife down and grinned. Her ability to be so instantly bright and enthusiastic was striking. Had she learned the poses from Wilton? "We've been looking forward to meeting you for a very long time," she said, and didn't so much shake Anya's hand as hold it. "And you've already met Owen."

"Nice to see you," he said. Anya looked as though she'd been blindsided.

Wilton's grin was stiff and he couldn't still his hands. "They've heard me tell a million stories about you."

"There can't be that many stories," Anya said.

"Okay, so I repeat myself sometimes." Wilton tapped his temple. "I'm almost an old man. You haven't seen me in a long time."

"And you haven't seen me in a long time either." She smiled coolly.

"That's very true. But here we are now."

When Wilton moved to lift her coat off her shoulders, she

stiffened. Wilton waited, poised with a pinch of wool in each hand. It was an instant of humiliation that Wilton, for all his great acting ability, could not pretend his way through. Anya finally let her coat slide off and then held it draped over one arm as if she wasn't planning on staying long. A thick black turtleneck sweater and black pants made an anonymous and mournful outfit. Her hair was pulled back severely with a silver clip. It was too much, too harsh. She tried to ignore her father's voracious gaze. For Wilton, the memory and the reality might take longer to merge, and in an awkward burst, he pointed out the apple pie on the counter that Owen had made that morning. His voice was clattery. It was like watching a blind animal bump around in a cage. When Owen picked up the platter of steaks to take outside, it tipped and spilled a long line of blood on the floor.

"I'll get that." Wilton grabbed a towel and kneeled.

"My family has a dog." Anya looked down at her father on all fours not far from her pointy-toed boots. "He's always around to lick up stuff like that, cereal, crumbs, blood."

"Arf, arf." Wilton wagged his ass as if he had a tail.

Owen had an urge to kick him.

"My four little brothers can make a pretty good mess. The dog comes in handy."

"Ah, brothers," Wilton said, as if this was something remarkable about her he'd just learned. He put one knee up and heaved his body on to it. He lacked his usual fluid grace, and it took him a moment to stand.

At dinner, Anya's cheeks quickly grew red from the wine, and she circled a finger around the neck of her sweater to loosen it. Wilton refilled her glass. Neither daughter nor father ate much, while Owen and Mira packed in their food as if they could devour all the awkwardness in the room. Mira tried to draw out Anya, and soon Anya was describing family vacations, brothers, dogs, noise, and a bounty of happy details.

"Where I grew up, the driveways are lined up like this," Anya said, and chopped the air into even plots of blacktop. She turned to Wilton. "My dad's a lawn freak, works on the grass every weekend."

Owen suspected that she knew exactly what she was doing by throwing her sunny history at her father, calling that other man "Dad." She was showing Wilton every way his absence hadn't mattered. He looked like he was biting into glass.

"I just hire people to do that for me," Wilton said. "Does that count?"

Anya looked at Owen, a private look, he thought, one that asked for ballast. Mira noticed and shifted in her chair.

"Four little brothers," Mira said. "They must adore you, the sophisticated big sister."

"Actually it's only three. One died two years ago. He had a brain tumor. Sometimes I still say four."

Wilton's mouth dropped open. "I didn't know. I'm sorry. How awful. And your poor mother." He shook his head. "My god, poor Linda."

The mention of Anya's mother, the woman who was their connection, and whom Wilton had known in a way that would always be a mystery to their child, was a reminder that there could be no benign conversation here, not really.

"She's okay," Anya said.

Mira got up to refill the pitcher at the sink and let the water overflow. "What I want to know," Owen said, forcing himself to look away from his frozen wife, "is what it was like watching your father on television."

Anya tore at a piece of bread and rolled the crumbs into tiny pellets. "I wasn't allowed to watch a whole lot of TV. My parents thought there was too much junk on."

"Definitely true." Wilton raised his glass. "Good for them."

"But I watched at friends' houses," Anya said. "Up until I was eight, I used to think Bruno—the character of Bruno—was my real father. It was confusing."

It was a sweet and painful confession. Wilton made a cap out of his cloth napkin and put it on. The red corners stuck up like ears. The silence screeched. Embarrassed, he pulled the napkin off and put it on his lap. "I'm the real one, by the way. The real father."

"The other day, I was remembering when you used to—"

Wilton leaned urgently toward his daughter. "When I used to what, sweetheart?"

"Swim in your pool. I'd jump off the edge."

"You'd do that over and over, for hours. I'd stand there and catch you."

"And you had some toys in the pool, beach balls, rings, things like that."

"Lots of them." Wilton smiled. "I tried to get something new every time you came over."

For the first time since she'd arrived, Anya looked directly at Wilton. "You used to take me to parties," she said. Her eyes narrowed. "Sometimes I had to go to the bathroom, but I didn't know where it was and I was too embarrassed to ask. I peed in my pants once."

Wilton lowered his head for the next blow. "Why didn't you come find me?"

"I was five years old." She moved her fork across her plate. "A baby."

"Yes, you were. You were a lovely child," he said dolefully. "I wanted to show you off."

"I had to hide my underwear under someone's cushions." Anya's resurrected shame flamed her face. "I thought they'd be hidden forever and no one would ever know."

Wilton's hair touched his plate. Tears slid onto the tomatoes. "I'm sorry for all I've done wrong, Anya. Sorry, sorry, sorry."

She was disarmed by his crying, and she looked again at Owen for help, but what could he do? Her confidence had unraveled, and her hair had come loose from its clip and hung around her face. Wilton made the only sound in the room.

"I should go," Anya said, up already, thanking them for dinner, and peering around for her coat.

"You don't have to leave so soon," Mira said, her head at a plaintive angle.

"So this is fine. Our getting to know each other again like this. Fine that we take it slowly." Wilton threw his daughter his last good try. She looked like she was considering a kiss or a hug for him but chose neither, putting on her coat instead when Owen gave it to her. She stuffed her hands in her pockets.

"I can't tell you what it's meant for me to see you tonight," Wilton added. "And whenever you're ready to do it again—if you are, that is, if you are—then please call me. I'm always available, anytime. I won't push you. We'll do this at your speed." He spoke to the back of her head as she left through the kitchen door and went down the driveway. "I won't push, Anya," he called. "Good-bye, good-bye. I love you."

In the morning, the forks Mira and Wilton had used to dismantle the pie after Anya left were laid down like weapons. Neat piles of crumbs were evidence of the talk that had gone on long after Owen had retreated to his study. He'd taken his work and his squid pen over to the couch with him, but had done nothing but listen to the unintelligible murmurings of their conversation, the tones of their consolation. When he opened his eyes, it was just before six o'clock, and he couldn't remember having fallen asleep on the too-short couch, his legs thrown over one arm and now cramped up. Mira must have come in and covered him with the blanket on this, the first night they hadn't slept in the same bed.

He made coffee and went outside. The morning was cold and brilliant with the last turning leaves. Everything was in the sharpest relief. The night's dampness had eaten through the paper of the lantern and left it lacy with holes, wire ribs holding fast. In the yard over the back fence, a stubby dog barked until a woman in a bathrobe appeared in a doorway to call him back. In five years, this was the only time Owen had ever seen her, though her raspy voice was familiar, some smoky sound he'd been hearing forever in the shallows of his sleep. Her bathrobe was open at the chest, and one breast revealed itself as she whistled for the dog. She saw him watching her, clutched her robe shut, and went back inside.

He went to the back of the carriage house, reached through the hole in the glass, and opened the door. Pieces of broken glass crushed underfoot. The air smelled of chilled wood. Stuffing exploded from old cushions, home to mice. There were dressers, tables, a couple of wicker chairs like the one Mira had in her office at Brindle, and everywhere, dust, dead leaves rolled like cigars, mouse droppings. More than anything or anywhere else— the house, its contents, Mira even—time had stopped in here

when her parents had died. Whoever had tried to break in had lost
the nerve, spooked by the nighttime theatrics of the chaise cushion thrown over the rafter like a carcass. Bicycle tires gone flat
drooped like slack intestines. He maneuvered through the junk
to feel under the dead weight of a rolled-up carpet for the gun
his father had given him. It was still there. His forefinger touched
the metal through terrycloth and he drew back his hand as if he'd
been stung. He didn't know why he'd kept it—an absurdity like
having a pet cobra. Mira assumed the thing was buried deep in a
hole in the Cape Cod woods.

He sat down on the rolled carpet and drank his coffee. The
dust swirled inside, the trees swirled outside, and wind breathed
in and out of the open door. He felt the same nervous thrill he'd
had as a boy when he took *The Noble Front,* a book of war photographs by his father's friend, into a hidden spot among the
locust trees. He knew that the tingling in his skull and stomach
and bowels was not about the gruesome pictures of the dying,
dead, and wounded, but about being alive. He didn't think he'd
ever felt it as much as he had then, shaded by the ropy trees
and their lozenge-shaped leaves. Eventually, he'd burst out from
between the trees, breathless, as if he'd just dodged death himself. It was inevitable now that he would picture Caroline in
her distressed posture on the restaurant floor, her gray skirt at
her waist, one shoe off. Were her toenails painted? And when
he saw himself kneeling next to her, he had that same gasping
sensation of being alive and of being very close to death. It could
still come. He waited for it. He tasted the sea. Brine bubbled
in his skull. Something crashed behind him. The coffee cup
fell and shattered. Something was breaking branches, whisking
against the clapboards, scattering the pea gravel. He knew the

gun was there. The sides of his vision narrowed to a point: a man in the open doorway, dark and featureless, but unmistakably Wilton.

"Are you okay?" Wilton took a step forward. "Are you sick? Say something. Is it your heart? Are you having a heart attack? Should I call 911?"

Owen struggled to find his breath as fear retreated and left sickening sweat in its place. Here was Wilton, the man who always appeared in doorways. "What the hell are you doing out here, creeping around like that?" he croaked.

"Was I creeping? I saw the open door, I was checking to see if everything was okay. I was being neighborly." He smoothed his hair into compliance and leaned against a table. Wilton wore a not too clean white robe over his clothes. A gold insignia of a hotel was stitched on the breast pocket, an emblem of more luxurious days.

"But you can't see the back door from your place. You were watching me," Owen said. He took a deep breath, and thought: that fucking gun. This was not his life. He wondered if he were going crazy.

"Well, yes. But not intentionally. I've been awake all night. I've been watching everything. I've been thinking." Wilton circled his toe in the dust. "What if Anya decides that last night was it, that she doesn't want anything more to do with me? Do you see why I couldn't sleep?" He took something from his robe pocket and displayed it on his palm. "I found this in the driveway."

Wilton could not have written this any better, Owen decided; here was the romantic, sentimental lore of Anya's silver hair clip. "You found it."

Wilton's eyebrows lifted. He knew what he was being suspected of. "Yes, I found it. Anya's magnificent, isn't she? A beautiful woman—when she was just a little girl I missed all those years with her, Owen. I can't get them back. Do you know what that's like, to lose an entire part of your life?"

"Actually, I do," Owen said.

But Wilton was single-mindedly about himself, winding up, his voice rising, his hands moving. The sun twitched in the yellow leaves. "What do I say to her?" he asked. "How do I talk to her? How do I get her to love me again? You have to help me figure this out. What do I do?"

"Tell her the truth," Owen said. "Tell her what happened. That's what she wants to know. Tell her what you did."

Wilton's slammed his hand on the table. "No. That will never happen. I already told you that. Do you understand? What would be the purpose? It would be the end. She would never see me again." Wilton's voice softened. "You and Anya seem to have some connection, all those looks you were giving each other."

"There were no looks."

"I think Anya trusts you," Wilton said. "Will you help me, please?"

"I don't want Mira to go the casino again. Don't ask her to go with you anymore."

"I thought we were talking about Anya."

"I need Mira to stop. Now."

Wilton stared at his feet. "What does she say about this?"

"It doesn't matter what she says. This is what I'm saying."

"I don't want to get in the middle of you two." He shook his head. "That's never a good idea."

"You're already in the middle." Anger ached in Owen's chest. He didn't speak easily. "I'm worried she has a problem."

"Like a gambling problem?" Wilton's laugh was round and

brutal. "My god, Owen, of course she doesn't. That's ludicrous. Besides, it doesn't happen just like that." He snapped his fingers. "I can see how worried you are, but you don't have to be. You've concocted this whole thing. Would I let something happen to her?"

"Mira's changed." He hated to reveal his fears about Mira to Wilton, but who else knew her so well?

"Actually, she's very consistent. She has her routine. She has a glass of bubbly water, a few pretzels, then maybe she plays the slots for all of ten minutes. Then she finds me and we leave. It's a distraction, that's all. Harmless."

"A distraction from what?" Owen asked.

"Come on. She's your wife. You know the pressure she's under."

"Do you give her money?"

"Do you mean to play with? Never. Do I pay for the drinks? And the gas? Yes—and why not? The casino and I have an arrangement these days, a small financial one—for my appearances. Nuts, I know, that they'd want an ancient face like mine. But it's all about demographics, and the place is filled with the right kind. These people know exactly what they're doing." He gazed at the rafters, a pose of infuriating evasion and calm. "You're upset about nothing."

"And you still give Brindle money."

"I give lots of money away, you know that. And yes, Brindle is one of those places. And why shouldn't I?"

"Do you understand how this backs Mira into a corner? How can she ever say no to you?"

"Easily. Mira doesn't let anyone tell her what to do. Look, I love both of you. You've made everything possible for me."

"This isn't an acceptance speech. I don't want Mira to go there again. Do you get it?" Owen said. "Do not ask her again. You want your daughter in your life? Then stay out of mine."

Wilton pulled his dingy bathrobe tight around himself and left. Owen taped cardboard over the shattered windowpane and, back in the house, got into bed next to Mira. She was asleep, unaware of how he was shaking.

7

The kids rumbled in from the cold. In these first moments of the morning, many were still hopeful that the day might deliver something extraordinary. They might do better, understand more, feel differently, or be freed from the classroom forever. Theirs was the last age of magical thinking, and this is what he loved about them. This is why he'd become a teacher, though he'd gradually understood it wasn't enough. Other kids knew from the minute they opened their eyes that the day was already lost. Owen noted, as he did every morning, who wasn't dressed warmly enough, who was wearing yesterday's clothes, last year's too-tight sneakers. Whose pants had the shine of brand-new, whose nails were dirty, who had the vacant, restless look of the hungry, whose neck was scrubbed, whose hair was filthy. Who hadn't gotten enough sleep, who was lost, who was adored.

In the paper that morning, a city official had called the city's public schools "a sorry state of affairs." Had the man actually seen the exploded urinal in the boys' bathroom, or the flaking ceiling paint in the cafeteria that sometimes fell onto the food, or the gym with half its lights blown out? Had he seen the bombed-out shells of some of the teachers? Had he felt the moral strain of meting out endless discipline and getting nothing done because of it? Every day there were substitute teachers in the building who Owen knew he would never see again and seasoned teachers who sat like driftwood washed up at the front of the room. By midmorning in his class, he could watch the optimism of one kid teeter, then another, and another.

Kevin, doubting eyebrows and skin the color of aged gold leaf, was the first to tip that day. The arms of his gray sweatshirt rode high to reveal wayward wrists as though he were trying to escape his own clothes. That the boy hated school was the least of it. When Owen had called his mother three weeks into the start of the year, he hadn't even finished his diligent sentence before she said, "I can't make him do anything either." The boy was distressed and distressing, full of rage if provoked. He was busy reforming a paper clip into its original set of U-turns, his head so low he didn't know Owen was looking at him.

"Mister," Danielle said. "What's the matter with you?"

He'd been staring at Kevin, his mood dreamish but not dreamy at all. Owen turned over the book he'd been holding and read to the class from the back of it. "'*Go Slow, Children Crossing*, by M. Andrew Peterson. A mall is planned for the lot across the street from Barlow Middle School where generations of students have hosted their annual winter festival. Will they stand in the way of growth and new jobs in order to preserve tradition? The students must confront what progress and change mean to them.'"

Boring, someone yelled. He agreed. He took his father's new book, *The Reflecting Pond*, from his bag. He yanked at his tie, felt his stomach rumble.

"'The particular turn off Route 6 was rarely used except by blueberry pickers,'" he read. "'In season, and at certain times of the late afternoon you could smell the berries from the highway. When my son was young, we picked buckets of the fruit, which we ate by the fistful.'"

The kids were silent, but their silence was not always easy to decipher. It was likely some had never seen a blueberry, didn't know they grew on bushes, so how was any of this meaningful to them? For a few moments, he was lost in a way he hadn't been since his very earliest days of teaching. Was this the end for him, then—had he come full circle to cluelessness? Teaching was an act of faith—had he lost that now, too?

Just then the fire alarm kicked on, like his personal warning to get it together, the clang so familiar to the kids that it lacked any urgency. One day it was going to be the real thing, and they'd all still trudge out of the building like zombies. They pushed back their chairs, obedient now that the alarm meant liberation, and he led them into the thick flow down the stairs and outside. Teachers and students and the people from the front office and cafeteria workers rubbing their hands in see-through plastic gloves gathered on the west side of the school next to the parking lot. Mrs. Tevas gave him a nod and whispered something to the principal.

Everyone turned to look at the stoic, unflappable building. No flames, no smoke. There never was anything. Across the street, a woman waited in her open front door and watched the shivering mass of her daytime neighbors. Mrs. Bogan, a math teacher, pawed through the crowd of kids demanding, "Where's your jacket? Where's your coat?" Owen went to the back of the pack where Kevin, always apart from the others, was gouging a hole in the hard-packed dirt with his sneaker.

"What are you digging for?" Owen asked.

"Huh?" The boy's lips were purple in the cold.

"What are you hoping to find down there?"

Kevin was wary of attention and too ready to be punished. He covered the hole with his foot. He would wait for Owen to move on before he resumed digging, and in the meantime, he'd move as close to disappearing as he could. The boy's teeth were chattering, but he wouldn't accept Owen's coat or connection; there was one student every year who made Owen feel deeply inept like this. The kids bounced around trying to keep warm. Girls pushed boys and they all pressed up against one another, laughing and moaning like nervous cattle. The fire trucks arrived and the men clanked into the building with their wide, slapping boots. No one was in a hurry. This was leisurely inferno theater. Owen watched as Spruance burned with imaginary fire and flames stuck their tongues out. It wouldn't be a terrible way for the school to go. On the faces of the teachers and students, he saw that this was the moment of real magical thinking—a dignified end to a troubled school.

It was when he'd gone upstairs to the bedroom the evening before that he'd stepped on the single earring, nestled under the rug, close to the bed, rounded under the red weave and a pile of Mira's discarded clothes. It was an inch of gold sunburst with a fine-size diamond in its center. Heavy, pretentious, matronly, nothing Mira would ever wear and nothing he'd ever seen before. He waited for the earring to tell him what was going on with Mira. But wasn't this how a wife was supposed to discover that her husband had a lover? The forgotten earring, the wrong-colored pubic hair on the sheets, the satin bow ripped off the bra. But for the husband who suspects his wife has a lover in the form of a casino? Where was evidence of that? He slipped the earring into his pocket.

So this is how you begin to know who your wife is. To start, you look for something particular of hers, a book that might have found its way into the drawer of her bedside table where her diaphragm hibernates in its bubblegum pink case. Between the pages of *The Portrait of a Lady*, which she's been reading forever, might be an ATM slip showing a withdrawal from their account or a note she'd written to herself, errands on the back on an envelope. A bank statement, a canceled check, a tally of what she'd won and lost. He was doing what too many of the sincerest websites instructed the suspicious and the worried to do. He'd gorged himself sick on their checklists at home and in the library at school, Mrs. Tevas sighing conspicuously as she shelved unread books. How do you know your mate has a problem? The addict won't tell you the truth, so you look for her lies to take shape, to have mass and color and sound. You try to figure out what was going on in her head when she left her mother's gold watch on your crowded bureau amid the wrinkled neckties, coins, notes, a scattering of pens and dusty antacids. It's not something she's done before, and what was she even doing there to begin with? What was she looking for? You extract a key from the pocket of her jeans left on the floor for days, but because you have no idea what it opens or closes, you reach again into her strangely warm pockets and pull out a balled-up silver wrapper that you open up, fold back to its rightful shape and sniff; a stick of peppermint gum.

You slip the key into your own pocket next to the earring that pokes into your thigh like a nettle. You hold your wife's clothes to your nose hoping to detect a combination of her almond soap and her own sweet smell, but the denim stinks of smoke at the knees. Why the knees? Has she been kneeling in an ashtray, scrounging for filthy quarters? You drop the pants back on the floor and stop talking to yourself; you don't want to wake up again in the middle of the night, a boulder on your chest trying to tamp down your panic. You look next door at the house that's predictably dark; her crime still has an accomplice in Wilton.

Owen burrowed through a bag of Mira's hanging on the closet door, and found a fireball candy, ticket stubs from a movie they'd seen months before, decomposing tissues, a scallop shell, a tampon, a lipstick. Mira was all around him in particles and breath and details, everywhere in this house but still elusive. He was a thief now, stealing trust. He went to the bedroom at the rear of the house that had been Mira's as a child. It looked out onto the backyard. At first, he couldn't figure out why she'd lived back there for so many years in one of the smallest, coldest rooms, with a pipe standing duncelike in the corner, when there were other rooms that were brighter and bigger. But he understood now that it was farthest from where her parents slept and argued and made each other unhappy. Being back here without the ubiquitous wallpaper must have felt like entering another country, one without an overblown, assaulting aesthetic. What if he told Mira he'd move back here himself unless she stopped going to the casino? What if he left their bed? Would it even make a difference?

The walls were scarred where tape had pulled off the paint. She'd hung up terrible posters as a kid, vivid photographs of nature with inspirational commands on them—*Soar high! Explore! Celebrate!*—simply because they drove her father crazy. He didn't understand her sense of humor. He offered to move real art into her room, give her something worthwhile to look at instead of that garbage. She was smarter than that, he'd said. Owen pictured Mira lying on the bed reading in the same way she did now, a book resting against her bent knees, her glasses slipping down her nose. At sixteen, she'd had sex here for the first time.

The bed sagged when he sat on it, but the springs met resistance from something underneath, and he pulled out a box the size of a phone book covered in cream-colored fake leather with a small bent gold clasp. The inside of the lid was furred in balding red velvet that surrounded a blemished square of mirror. There were chunky clay beads in the compartments, thick plastic bangles, smooth black stones, and notes on lined paper folded into tight quarters, which he unfolded: *I like you. She wasn't invited. I am so bored.* He'd stumbled upon—no, he hadn't stumbled anywhere, he'd gone looking—the few things in this house that were truly Mira's. Stuff that had no value to anyone but her. In this house, Mira had seen how swiftly life passed. She'd seen generations die under this roof and then lived among their immortal things, their coats still on hangers in the downstairs closet, their hand towels still waiting. He pictured her at the slots at that moment, time completely forgotten, stopped. "When I'm there," she'd told him last week, "everything is right then. There's no earlier or later." He imagined her mesmerized by stimulation, stuporous even in the rush of it. He'd read that some women had orgasms when they played the slots. He pictured Mira with the tip of her tongue on her upper lip, her feet balanced on her toes, her mind numb with rapture in front of a machine. It was like watching her kiss her lover, watching her lover put his hand up under her shirt, put his mouth on her breasts, spread her legs. It was a sickening, dead-end feeling.

When he put the box back he saw another one, similar in shape but covered in real brown leather. It had a heftier clasp that had also been pried open and bent. The key he'd found was not to this lock. No girlish, papery stuff here, but gold bracelets, pearls, platinum pins. Ridiculous pirate booty. He'd never seen anything like it. It was dazzling. The chilled pearls slithered across his palm. He touched his tongue to an emerald's facet, bounced the heft of a ring. It was all boastful stuff, a means to display your wealth, that Mira had pushed under the bed like old shoes along with the dust balls and the missing socks. It must have belonged to a line of Thrashers, and then, in an instant, it had belonged to Mira. He would have closed the box, slipped it back and left the room with only an unsettled sense of being a stranger in this house, if he hadn't spotted the sunburst earring's match. She'd been here recently, digging around in this treasure chest. She'd brought it into the bedroom. Was she seeing what she could pawn or sell to fund her time on the slots? How else was she doing it? Their joint account was intact. Wilton had said he didn't give her money, but he had also agreed that morning in the carriage house two weeks before that he wouldn't go with her to the casino anymore, and how had that worked out? Wilton needed his fix of recognition and fawning as much as Mira needed to play.

His squid pen was gone. He'd blamed his own chaos for it, but now he wondered if Mira had taken it when he didn't think she'd even known it existed. But of course she'd known; she knew every single thing in the house. He put the earring back in his pocket, leaving its forlorn twin alone in the box, which he slipped under the bed. Mira's car crunched down the driveway and he watched the headlights sweep over the backyard, then shut off. Her keys jangled hesitantly at the back door. She must have noticed the light on in this back room and sensed he was right above her. They waited for the other to move first. He held his breath, felt her heart beating in his, and detected her presence more powerfully than he had in months. It was all calculation between them. How to move, what to say, what not to say. Who would take the first step.

Her key slipped into the lock. He knew exactly what she was doing: dumping her bag on the floor, pulling her arms out of her coat, leaving the sleeves inside out, prying off one shoe at a time with her other foot, pretending this was their old routine. Dinner, an evening together alone. No Wilton. She called for him, but he didn't answer. She banged through a couple of cabinets. When she called again, he came down the back stairs and met her in the kitchen. They kissed breezily. She didn't ask him why he was using the back stairs, or why he'd been in the back room. She had the urge for a baked potato and chattered about her day at Brindle while he sat at the table, dumb and droopy. Did he want a potato, too? He shook his head; he'd lost his appetite. She fluttered around the room, clumsy with distraction.

Later that night, she made him a startling naked offer, stepping out from the shower and only half drying herself, her body beaded with water. She stood over him where he'd been watching her from a chair, unable to be anywhere but where she was but still unable to say anything. She dripped onto his knees, kissed his neck, let her wet breasts rub his chest. He thought of his tongue against the emerald and how cool the gem had been. Her skin would be too hot for him, too revealing. He was cold; he didn't want her. He didn't move as she snaked off his pants. She smelled like chamomile. He wanted to push her off, but his erection betrayed him, and she took his prick into her mouth. He was powerless with her, always had been, and came in a rush of sorrow.

He wanted to crouch down with the memory as the firemen clomped out of Spruance. Teachers corralled the students back inside. Owen touched the single earring in his pocket, frigid against his fingers. He considered putting it into Kevin's shallow hole, filling the hole with a clod of tired dirt and a few stubborn strands of grass, and tamping it down with his foot. But in the end, he couldn't.

On Friday night, Owen woke to find Mira standing at the foot of the bed, the bloom of moonlight behind her. He wasn't sure if she was in some kind of an insomniac daze at midnight, but when he inched up on the pillow, her eyes followed him. She took a blanket from the back of a chair and put it around her shoulders. Outside, it was only black and white.

"I can't sleep," she said. "I was just watching you. To see how it's done. Hoping to maybe get some pointers." She gave him a rueful smile.

"Come back to bed. You're shivering."

"Wilton told me what you said to him about not going to the casino with me anymore. I was so angry at first, O, and insulted, I didn't even want to see you. I'm not a child." She sat on the edge of the bed and swept his hair from his forehead. "I was thinking about how terrible it is—for both of us—that you don't trust me. I don't want to make you unhappy."

"Then stop. It's so simple."

"Take me."

"Take you?" He laughed at her dirty talk.

No, she said, smirking, she meant he should take her to the casino. "You're awake now. And I'm clearly and permanently awake. You've said no every time I've asked you to come, but you have no choice tonight. I'm going to show you everything so you'll stop worrying. Let's call it a date."

Strangely hopped up, she whipped the covers off him. He was reluctant to go for every reason, but he'd been resistant for too long. How could he explain why he hated the place when he'd never even been? They dressed and left the house, whispering in the driveway as if the hour were illicit. The heat was slow coming on in the balky car, and Mira covered up the bottom half of her face with her scarf. Her eyes had that flash of intensity and purpose, but it was her mouth Owen needed to read her by. He pulled down her scarf, and she pressed her fingers to her bottom lip. She would be someone else tonight. After an hour, Eagle Run rose up from nowhere—enormous, metallic, and startling in its ugliness. Mira directed him to drive to the top level of the parking garage where she and Wilton always parked. In the wind, two empty plastic bags chased each other across the frigid expanse of concrete. The glare from the buildings was a wall. Beyond it was a stand of rangy, compelling pine trees. In the other direction there was a faint, sulfuric illumination, like a landing strip.

In the elevator, a female voice asked them if they'd remembered to lock their car.

"It's the voice of God," Owen said. "This is a religious experience. People lock their cars, change their money, and pray for the best."

"Something like that," Mira mumbled.

When the elevator doors opened, Owen followed Mira down a hallway wide enough to decompress hundreds of bleary-eyed gamblers on their way out. At this hour, though, there were only a few dazed stragglers intent on avoiding eye contact. They watched their feet leading them home. Soon Owen got his first assaultive whiff of air freshener and money and heard the incessant chiming.

Mira led him past the crowded playing tables where people perched on their seats. There were cages where you could change your money, and behind the bars, women who looked like disheartened grandmothers. Everywhere, eagles were carved into fiberglass tree trunks, and bright yellow suns rose a hundred times. Owen found it difficult to put the spaces together; he couldn't draw a map of the place in his head. He didn't know where the center was, but he also knew that disorientation was exactly the point. They encountered pockets of noise—and always that rolling, burbling chiming—and greater noise, but never any silence, not even in the bathrooms, where music was piped in over the urinals. Slipping in and out of the shadows with angelic bearing were women in baby blue uniforms and sneakers pushing cleaning carts loaded with sprays and brushes. They were quick to mop up spilled drinks and ugliness.

It was hard to tell the seasoned casino-goer from the novice, or even the winner from the loser. Women stuck together, while the men were more often alone. A young couple dragged their three miserable children behind them. Misshapen bodies ruled— bellies straining against cowboy shirts and tees, flesh bulging at necks and wrists and under chins. Big, flat feet. Even thin people looked distended, and the pale looked paler. Mira said the light distorted on purpose so that nothing was entirely familiar; it was why people came back and back again. Her face looked boneless and flat, her hair spiraling crazily. Her red down jacket was garish. Above them, a giant eagle the size of a Corvette was ready to pluck its fatty snack from the crowds. To Owen, the place was immaculate and filthy at the same time, opulent and cheap, exclusive and indifferent. It was a lure and a lie, a waste where desolation was made shiny. Hope and desperation were the only real things about it. Who were these people who came here? His ability to imagine the lives of others shut down. How could Mira stand this? It made him feel already dead.

She showed him the line of restaurants, and the display tank of enormous lobsters in the window. The people eating, even at this hour, were single men mostly seated at tables meant for two. On the lower level, they looked into the day-care center that posted its rental rates for kiddie socks, its price list for diapers and juice. You paid by the hour, like a motel. The days of leaving the kids in the car, the window cracked just enough, were over, Owen said. The word "experience" was everywhere. *Enjoy the experience! Live the experience! Experience the experience! It's an experience!* It seemed like the right word to Owen, the experience, whatever it was, was something done and passed through. Unless you came back for more.

"I had a student whose mother worked here for a while," he

told Mira. "Housekeeping in the hotel. Twice she found someone dead in a room. Once an OD, the other time the man had hanged himself from the shower rod. She said it happened all the time."

"Sounds like an urban myth to me," she said.

"No. I saw the woman's eyes and she couldn't fake that." He recalled her deep black Haitian face locked in a permanent gloss of shock. The men had come to save themselves, she'd said, but it hadn't worked out. Or had it? She'd come in to talk about her daughter's grades and had spoken of this instead, because she couldn't get it out of her mind. "When you check in to the hotel, do you think you can ask for a nonsuicide room just like you can ask for a nonsmoking room? Which ones have the better views? Do you want a view of the woods when you're about to off yourself, or do you want to look over the parking lot and the service entrance and smell the exhaust from the kitchen fan?"

Mira looked at him. "I'm so glad you're keeping an open mind."

She led him to the waterfall that flowed over turd-colored rocks. Drinkers faced it at the bar as if it were one of the world's greatest wonders and not something much closer to a burst water pipe. It reeked of chlorine. This seemed the worst of all possible hours to show him the casino; what good could ever be happening? How much despair could he take in? But none of it seemed to faze Mira. It was as though she saw things entirely differently.

"This is where I sit with Wilton," she said, and touched two stools. The glass bar showed streaks from a dirty rag, and the bartender gave them a bored look. Mira said that sometimes she had water or a diet soda, and Wilton had a glass of wine. Sometimes there were peanuts, but other nights there were pretzels. You just never knew. She was making fun of him now with her details. Here people recognized and fawned over Wilton, she explained.

Some wanted to talk to him, tell him about their lives, and he listened as though it were all fascinating stuff. He made people feel important and heard; he made himself feel loved that way. Sometimes a woman grabbed his elbow and clucked at him while her husband stood off to the side like an embarrassed little boy. None of this meant that his fans had his name, or the name of the show, right. He posed for photos with them, his hands squeezing their thickened waists to make them blush and feel pretty. Sometimes Mira took the picture, waving the reluctant husbands in. Sometimes Wilton zeroed in on a single woman, his long figure bent over hers for hours, his face hopeful.

"And then? After your drink and pretzels and photo ops? Show me what *you* do," Owen said. "I want to watch."

"You sound like some kind of pervert," she teased. "*Show me what you do. I want to watch.*"

Mira took him onto the floor. Owen thought they looked like a couple of shoplifters, still in their coats and sloppy clothes. Brass and neon reflected in her glasses as she changed twenty dollars. The slot machines were shiny and buffed, grouped in clusters like grazing cattle. Players were randomly scattered, but he suspected there was nothing random at all about where they'd chosen to sit. Animals, humans, slot machines, Wilton at the bar—no one ever wanted to actually be alone, though what could be more lonely than this picture? Is this what his wife liked? Old women were as bright-eyed as raccoons. A few old men smacked buttons with the heels of their hands. They stared at the machines with bitter underbites. Mira ran her hand over the backs of the red plastic seats. Her mood was subdued, but he also thought she was playing too hard at being cool and untouched. She led him to another herd of machines. Here, each looked like a temple, wider at the bottom, built in piled units, peaked at the top. They were shrines of metal at whose feet you sat and whose illuminated belly displayed your fortune. She sat down in front of one.

"Do the machines understand you? Do they talk to you?" Owen asked. "Do you talk to them?" He'd read that the compulsive players believed in their own magic—where to sit, how to count, what to intone. If they won, it was because of something they'd done, and losing was only a distraction. It was not about money after a while; it was about the rush, the action. The brain chemistry changed and took over; they were helpless then. He'd read about it all, and he got none of it.

"I'm not delusional, O," she laughed, and made sure he noticed the ancient woman at one of the machines. Her spine was arched, her face practically in her lap as she fed a plastic card that was attached to the strap of her bag by a pink coiled leash into the machine.

"Oh, that's kind of sad," Mira said.

She took off her coat and hooked it over the seat next to her. She liked the slots with the reels, she said, and looked into the machine's bright face. Owen fed a coin in for her and watched her fingers curl around the ball at the arm's end. She pulled, and the reels spun and clunked into place.

"What are you feeling?" he asked.

"What am I feeling? Are you a shrink now?"

"Just tell me."

She tapped at her bottom lip. "I guess it's like when you're waiting for someone to come home and you finally hear a car door shut. There's that second before you know if it's the right door, the right person. It's all about that instant of expectation." She pulled the arm again and the reels spun unprofitably. "And then it's over." She shrugged. "And that's it. Harmless as hoping. See? There's nothing to it."

Owen had waited many times for her to come home from here and had listened for that flawless sound that was her determined footsteps on the gravel. It was a moment that could fall to disappointment or rise to enchantment. She was right: that instant of expectation was brilliant and always, necessarily, fleeting. It was what made you come back for more of everything. But hope wasn't harmless.

The man on Mira's left and the woman on her right were enthralled by their own motions of hand to coin to slot to arm or button. They watched the spinning wheels but seemed almost not to notice or care what was happening. Mostly, they looked bored. Their expressions reminded him of the dreams he'd had when he was sick as a kid, repetitive and indistinct, of trying to work something out but not getting there and not really caring. One man sucked at a drink through a straw and put in another coin.

Owen sat down at the end of the row to watch Mira from a distance. Her attention was poised on the action, and her hand reached to pull the machine's arm. When her winnings clanged into the tray, she snatched them back and played again. It was too easy to simply hate the place for all the obvious, elitist reasons, but he hadn't understood what his unease was made of until he saw Mira wrapped in pure solitude at that noisy, concentrated moment. She didn't notice anything around her, not even that he'd moved away. And this is what she wanted, what she liked. He had the chilling sense then, one that froze him to the seat, that he loved his wife more than she loved him, and if need had anything to do with it, he needed her more, too. He might collapse without her.

When he looked away, he spotted Walter, the chemistry professor he knew from the pool at the Y, wandering alone between the machines just like the way he swam—slow, heavy, an old, perseverating manatee. The man clearly wasn't happy to have been spotted, and he gave Owen a fully blank look that went beyond embarrassment or even acknowledgment, before he walked in the other direction. This place at two in the morning was a vector for bad news and sad stories, and everyone just wanted to be alone. Owen was aware of how unobserved and almost invisible he felt, though he also knew that he and everyone else were closely watched. You were never fully on your own here, though your ruin was entirely yours.

Finally, Mira looked up and waved Owen over to take her place at the machine. The seat was temperate from her body. He remembered how she'd told him one night that she liked the seat to be warm because it was like the whisper of someone else still with her. At the time, it had seemed like the loneliest idea; now he understood the need for another presence, even the fleeting suggestion of one. The most public act here was also the most private. The machine was a gleaming Buddha, clearing its throat. Hopeful fingerprints smeared the glass. If I touch it once or touch it twice, if I leave the whorls of who I am, will I win? Will I understand what drives my wife? Mira fed in a coin for him. With her hand over his, she pulled down. The resistance was just right, the resistance of pond water and of that first instant when they fucked. His prick twitched in confusion. The arm sprung back and the reels spun and dropped into place. It felt like promise, but he also knew that a computer had already decided the outcome by the time the reels were set spinning. Mira had to know that, too, but what was any knowledge worth here? It was only a liability to think too much. Mira dropped in another quarter. This time, she took his hand and placed it on the glass belly to feel the reels in motion—at the base of his skull and spine. Another quarter, then another, and with her hand still over his, she pulled until the money was gone. She was the one playing. He was just the body on the seat.

"You see, O?" Mira said, her eyes strangely unfocused. "It's nothing. Everything's fine. I'm fine. A few dollars and some luck—or not." She seemed to take his silence as collusion and shrugged. "Tell me that you've never felt you wanted to step out of your life for an instant. Life is too real for me sometimes. Everything I see, and such unbearably sad stories everywhere I look, the whole world suffering. If you take it in, you'll explode."

"But you have to take it in, Mira. That's what being alive is about. You can't act like it doesn't exist."

"But it's too much for me sometimes," she said. "I'm not tough like you. I can't live with it all the time. I can't carry it around." Her lower lip began to tremble, and he thought she was about to cry.

They left the slot machines and wandered past the coffee shop just opening. On their way to the elevator, they passed a man on a bench who sat like a refugee, with two sleeping children. They were a living cautionary tale, bad public relations. At the parking garage's first blast of cold air, Mira realized she'd left her coat behind. She said he should get the car and meet her at the front entrance. A few minutes later, he pulled into the circular drive at the main entrance. A man in an Eagle Run uniform knocked on his window and asked if he needed any help.

"I'm waiting for my wife." Owen said.

"Okay, but you're going to have to move your vehicle." He bent down to take advantage of the warmer air coming from the car.

Vehicle. The man was really a kid, probably fresh out of high school, acne running next to his sideburns, stuck with this shitty job and shittier shift. "When she comes, I'll move."

"I'm sorry, sir, but you're going to have to move now."

"Give me a fucking minute, okay? I'm not blocking anyone.

There's no one else here. Look around. I told you my wife would be right out—and she will."

The kid straightened and all Owen could see of him were his fingers flexing in his shiny black gloves before he bent into the warmth again. "It's just that a lot of people are waiting for their wife or husband or whatever. Do you see what I mean?" He glanced over his shoulder and then appeared to take stock of Owen's troubled face. "And they don't come out, not for hours sometimes. You look upset. A few minutes, then you're going to have to move."

Owen was struck by the patience a job like this must require to assuage many more losers and assholes than winners. The boy slapped his arms to keep warm. To his left was the too bright casino entrance with a few blinking people coming and going. To his right, just past the circle, was the dense and oddly comforting stand of tall pine trees dusted with the first falling of snow that he seen from the garage. Mira was taking too long. She couldn't be lost in a place she knew so well. The boy nodded and resolutely waved him on. To him, Owen had become another pathetic story, another hopeful spouse, but he was wrong, wasn't he? Wasn't Mira simply looking for her coat?

Owen drove around the complex that spread farther than he'd imagined, past the garage and the hotel's back entrance, the busy service end of the operation, the parking lots, and the lit-up shuttle bus making its rounds like a demented animal. He drove in circles. He took great gulps of air. Being inside had made him feel like dying—and sometimes dead already. Snow fell in his headlights. He drove up to the front entrance again, but still Mira didn't appear. The next loop around began to tangle him up in confusion. He didn't know if he should go in and look for her, and he couldn't call her because she didn't have her phone, as usual.

But more than that, it was clear she didn't want to be found. He sped through the turns and watched the snow fly off the hood of the car. What was she doing? His single, panicked gulp returned with a frustrated bark. It wasn't her notion of this trip, or the trip itself, or the time they'd spent at the machines, or what she'd shown him that meant something; it was these precise minutes when she was inside and he was not. These minutes when she was deciding not to come out just yet. Was she trying to decide if she'd tell him the truth? And what was the truth anyway? Was she in trouble? Was she a liar? He knew nothing, he understood less than that. Misery fogged the windshield and the inside of the car was humid with cold sweat. He banked too fast on the next loop, nicking the back tire on the curb and sending the car fishtailing in the snow. He felt himself veering toward danger too easily, and he slowed down. Almost thirty minutes later, Mira appeared at the front and got in the car, as if nothing had happened.

A mile away from the casino, Owen pulled to the side of the road and turned ferociously to his wife. "Where the hell were you?" he demanded.

"I'm sorry, O. I totally lost track of time. I was watching a blind man play 21. It was amazing the way he could read the cards—"

"Shut up, please. Just stop." It was almost a good story, but he didn't believe her. "What is wrong with what you have, Mira? What is wrong with our life that you do this? That you want to do this?"

She looked to her right at the snow. "It's coming down fast. The driving is going to be awful if it doesn't let up soon. If you don't get going."

"What is wrong with me?"

"This has nothing to do with you," she said, and placed a tentative hand on his leg.

"Of course it does. How can it not? I'm part of your life, aren't I?"

"Yes," she insisted.

"I'm just trying to understand this, because if I can, then maybe I can give you what you need. I can help." He put his head back and closed his eyes. The snow whispered around the car. "But you have to tell me the truth. No more lying. Are you in trouble?"

"No. No. No. You have to believe that." It was awhile before she spoke again. "Look. You've asked me not to go anymore, and I get now that's enough—because it's what you want. And that's what we're here for, isn't it? To make each other feel loved?" She sounded more resigned than convinced. "I'm done. I promise."

"We'll get you some help," he said. "You'll go see someone."

"Is 'someone' code for shrink? God, I don't need help because there is no problem. Isn't what I just said enough for you?" she snapped. "The only thing I need is some sleep. I'm so tired of this."

"So am I," he said.

Maybe Mira didn't know herself what she would or could do anymore. Owen's relief was cautious but open, and he appreciated the remarkable insistence of the season's first snow, and his wife already asleep before they'd even hit I-95. He drove carefully on the unplowed roads, white and smooth ahead, and on Whittier Street, where an inch of untouched snow lay on the sidewalks and roofs and balanced on the telephone wires and branches. No one else was out at this hour, and he and Mira would be the first to leave their footprints when they got out and went inside the house.

8

Wilton named their visit to Cape Cod a "historic excursion" and "a pilgrim's progress," four of them squeezed into Owen's Honda on Thanksgiving morning. Between father and daughter, like silent ambassadors, were three pies in pink boxes that Wilton had ordered from Vermont. Bottles of wine rattled around in the trunk. Wilton kept up a ramble of mind-numbing commentary on the view from the Braga Bridge in Fall River, the houses of New Bedford spread out like vinyl-sided Easter cakes, the long swoop of highway by the canal. He glanced at Anya, but she held on to her indecipherable smile. Wilton began to read the highway signs and billboards and describe the clouds; he couldn't stop making some noise to be heard. Owen was tempted to pull over and shake him, tell him not to try so hard, to shut the hell up for five minutes. Instead, he bore the pressure of Wilton's knees bumping up against the back of his seat and into his kidneys. Mira had offered Wilton the front, but he'd wanted to sit in back with his daughter. His hair rose in a static plea to be loved.

Since that first dinner together, and after standing Wilton up a few times, Anya had finally met her father at the Bright, a coffee shop across the street from her apartment. Wilton had re-enacted part of the meeting for Owen and Mira, playing both parts with painful perception, reciting their strained, banal dialogue. He burned his tongue on his tea, he whacked the table when he crossed his legs, Anya looked up like a rabbit each time the door opened as though there might be someone to rescue or shoot her. She didn't talk much, while he talked too much. Wilton was no star to her, no celebrity, no hilarious television doofus she might be loosened up by. She might require him to play the part he had no real talent for: the nothing, the no one to her. Still, it had been easier than Owen had expected to get Anya to come with them today; he'd made the case to her on behalf of Wilton's heart, as though it existed outside of the man, a free-roaming, orphaned thing. As they'd stood in front of her apartment where he'd gone to find her one evening, she'd twisted her scarf around one hand and agreed with Owen that they should let Wilton think he'd proffered the invitation first. They would keep this meeting between them. She looked past him to the water and the blinking gas tanks and said she was trying to be nicer to Wilton, but it was hard when there was so much she didn't understand about why he'd so completely disappeared from her life. She wasn't sure she even liked him. From the way she thanked him, Owen knew she probably believed he was looking out for his friend with this advance work, but his motives were not generous. The equation was clear to him now, no longer a hypothetical. If he brought Anya to Wilton, then Wilton might not lure Mira back to the casino with his need for sympathetic company. There it was. A trade.

Mira had been asleep since Swansea. Since their trip to Eagle Run two weeks before, she'd been saying she felt flu-ish, but her illness lurked below the surface and refused to reveal itself. She dragged through her days and came home from Brindle exhausted. Owen played her eager nurse. He babied her with movies and homemade soup. He read out loud to her from Edward's book and lit a fire in the bedroom fireplace that filled the house with smoke. He washed her faded nightgown by hand so it would be fresh for the night. She'd been determined to rally for this Thanksgiving trip to Brewster to meet Edward's girlfriend.

Wilton leaned into the front seat. "Is Mira all right?"

"Still asleep," Owen said.

Her neck was flushed and sweaty. In the middle of last night, Owen had heard her on the stair landing, where she must have stopped to watch the sharp rain falling between the houses. When she got back into bed, her feet were icy but her skin was overheated.

"Are you worried about her?" Wilton asked. "Do you think she should see a doctor?"

In fact, he'd felt some relief from the worry he'd carried around since the summer. He didn't mind that Mira was mysteriously unwell or that her insomnia was flaring. He suspected casino withdrawal, with its attendant side effects of shame and remorse. He wouldn't mind if the symptoms lasted for a long time. In the evenings, he canceled his tutoring sessions at the last minute to be with her, and at night he pressed himself against her hot back and closed his arms around her. He felt they'd passed through something very dangerous.

Wilton spoke to Anya carefully, like her translator. "Mira hasn't felt well for a few days. What do you think?"

"Me?" She laughed. "What do I think?"

"I thought maybe because of medical school," Wilton said, chided, as Owen received another sharp knee to the kidneys.

The sun was a pucker in a colorless sky. The overhang of trees on 6A, a cool green umbrella in the summer, was a web of black branches in November. Katherine's tentacled condo complex, Ocean View, was one of the many built in the last few decades that always triggered a round of contempt from Edward. The man didn't understand why this part of the Cape had become a vector for retirees. The winters were long, windy, and bleak. People drank too much and a few took to beating one another out of boredom. These bird-watching, water-coloring, concert-going, lecture-attending, adult-learning, book-clubbing white hairs didn't know what they were in for, he said. In the summer, they lined up with their visiting grandchildren at the ice-cream stands, Grandpa clutching his ass-worn wallet, squinting to read the flavors and the jacked-up prices on the board.

Owen was amused that his father, made fickle by love, hadn't mentioned that Katherine lived at Ocean View. He'd given Owen only the address, not the name. Blocks of identical units spread down a wide slope to the bay that lay like a blue sheet kicked to the end of the bed. Weathered gray buildings were set into the landscape with the regularity of dentures. Dead leaves played on the tennis courts and covered pools. The wind was clattery coming from the beach, but there was also deep silence here. Owen imagined Edward restless and itching to be let out. The pond was a riot of life by comparison. A few other cars circled the development, and couples with children in the back strained to read the street names tacked sideways on posts. It was as if they'd all been summoned to a secret meeting at an undisclosed location.

"I see the water," Anya said and laughed at her own enthusiasm.

Mira inched up and rubbed her eyes behind her glasses "We're here already?"

"Already?" Wilton said. "You missed the whole trip, you poor thing."

Edward appeared in the doorway of the unit in his usual dust-colored sweater and baggy chinos cinched with a belt. He looked like a castaway. It was so rare that Owen ever saw him anywhere but in his own house or in his own woods or pond, that at first he didn't see how comfortable his father was there, waving like a host, leaning against the doorway. A wobbly baby—Katherine's grandson, Owen assumed—appeared behind Edward, passed by his legs and waddled across the square of lawn that twinkled with frost. It took Edward a moment to realize what was happening, and then he bent with his arms out as though he were about to chase a chicken. The baby held his flapping hands up by his shoulders and shrieked as Edward roared behind him. The kid had speed and purpose and moved to the car. His thin hair and Edward's lifted identically in the wind.

Mira, who'd been leaning down to pull on her boots during the baby's escape, opened her car door at the instant the child came flush with it. The timing was exact, the sound of the baby hitting the frozen winter grass with the back of his head was stomach-turning. Owen saw just below the door, the bottoms of the baby's feet in yellow socks flecked with leaves. Owen rushed out of the car and around to where Edward had dropped to his knees.

"Okay?" Owen asked. "He's okay?"

The child's eyes were open and looking at the clouds zooming in off the water. He blinked, and then seeing Owen's alarmed face hanging over him, started to cry. The wail was furious, sore at being thwarted and full of indignity.

"Oh, shush, Petey, you're fine," Edward said and scooped the kid up in a single movement. "He's fine. You just went boom, right?" Edward turned the breathless baby to face the sea. "Look, the water." The baby's new howl was the sound of a passing airplane. "Should we look for boats? Do you see a boat? A bird?"

Mira got out of the car. A bloodless, white circle ringed her mouth and she looked a hundred years old. "He's all right? Is he, Edward?" she asked. "I didn't see him!"

"Babies are tough little buggers. It takes a lot to hurt them," Edward told her. "He's fine, it's not your fault. He's getting cold out here, though, so I'm going to bring him inside." Calmed, the baby put his head on Edward's shoulder and looked up shyly at Mira. "Listen, Mira, sweetheart, please don't worry. He's really okay. Remind me to tell you about some of Owen's falls. Take your time, take some deep breaths. I'll take care of your friends." He led the others inside.

"I could have killed him," Mira said to Owen as they walked to the water. "I could have. I'm out of it. A second earlier, a little faster and—"

"But you didn't. It didn't happen. Crisis averted. Tragedy dodged. Don't think about it."

"I just need a couple of minutes before we go inside. Get my head together." In the longest exhale of low tide, two figures walked on the sandbars. "I had the strangest feeling before, like I was looking down at the baby on his back and at myself, unable to move. It was if I were seconds ahead of the moment, as if I'd already lived it and saw myself useless. It's a scary feeling." Mira shivered the picture away.

"It's over."

"I want to tell you something, O."

Was there ever a more ominous beginning? Seagulls screeched.

"I lost some money. At the casino. I told you before that I didn't, but I did," she said. "I was too embarrassed. Not much at all, a few hundred dollars at most, but still. I want to be completely honest about it."

Lost: a blameless word. Lost like a winter glove fallen out of a pocket, lost like a thought or a passion. "The money doesn't matter. You're done now. You're not going back."

"I know you've been wondering," she said, "and looking in my things, poking around."

How had he imagined she wouldn't notice? Did he not know her at all? He fished in his pocket for the sunburst earring and held it out to her. He'd carried it with him every day.

"Oh! I thought I'd lost it." She said it had been her grandmother's. She reached for it but changed her mind and drew back.

"Take it," he said. "I found it under the bedroom rug."

"But I looked everywhere."

He pressed it into her reluctant hand. "It's yours, Mira. You do with your things what you want—sell them, pawn them, give them away, whatever you want. It's your stuff, your money. Just don't fucking lie to me about it. I can't stand any more of that." He sweat in the cold like a sick man.

"You think I'm selling the jewelry?"

"I don't care if you are, Mira. That's what I'm saying. But tell me the truth."

"The truth? I dropped the earring and then I couldn't find it anywhere. I thought maybe I'd somehow managed to get it hooked on something. I looked everywhere."

"Not everywhere. It wasn't so hard to find."

"It was for me." She pulled her coat hood up and turned to the water. Her face was entirely hidden from him in a puffy red frame. "You want to know what I was doing with it? I'd put on one of my mother's fancy old dresses, some jewelry, makeup, high heels. I was dressing up. I do that sometimes just to see what it feels like to look the way she'd want me to. I know it sounds pathetic, but it's a completely private thing, Owen, and I've been doing it my whole life. I don't have to explain it." White clouds blew out from inside her hood. "And now that you've made me tell you—all your interrogations, your suspicions, your hounding, your invasion. You've humiliated me, made me feel so ashamed." What had started out as her admission was now her furious defense. "I can't have anything that's just my own anymore?" She turned and started up the slight incline toward the condo.

Owen took a direct hit from the wind as he watched her. The image of Mira moving through the house in another woman's clothes—her mother's—playing at being someone else altogether, was strange and painful. Owen knew her less, not more, despite her revelation. Her private act was a form of captivity; she could not escape who she was. She waited for him at the condo door where a wreath of silk maple leaves and miniature ears of dried corn had been hung. She looked at him to say something, and when he didn't, she knocked disappointedly. A few kernels of the corn fell out like loose teeth.

Katherine appeared, flustered and amused, as if she'd just heard a dirty joke but didn't entirely get it. She grabbed their hands. Hers was rough. She was about Mira's height, solid, with short gray hair sculpted around a ruddy, earnest complexion. There was something sensible and direct about her—she made Owen think of a nun who, if she needed to, could chop wood in a blizzard or tend to bees. She was dressed like Edward, though her clothes were of a more recent vintage. She said their names, solemn as a vow, and kissed them both. "I've wanted to meet you since the first time Eddie talked about you. I knew I'd like you." She pulled them inside. "Isn't the water gorgeous? It's the best time of year. In the summer, this could be anywhere, but in the winter, every day is a little different and exciting. You never know what's going to wash up."

She introduced them to her son, Brady, who looked to be close to fifty, and his much younger wife, Lynn, who appeared closer to Anya's age. They both sat serious as cement on a brown couch that took up most of the boxy living room. Protected between them, the blond baby drank from a bottle and watched the football game on television. They didn't change their defensive pose; they knew what had happened outside, and they were going to hold it against Mira. Rey stretched out on the carpet as though he'd always lived there. There were framed photographs of nature's geometries—sea grass, a horseshoe crab, a shingle of sand—on the walls, but no fuzzy-bordered family portraits.

"I'm sorry about before," Mira started. "I didn't see your baby. He's okay?"

"Not really. He's got a bump on the back of his head," Lynn said.

"So what's Petey's favorite team?" Owen asked, cutting her off. Why should Mira let them punish her when she'd punish herself plenty?

"He's eighteen months old," Brady said. He cast an unfriendly eye at Mira, who took a seat next to his wife. Still wrapped in her puffy coat, her face wild and windblown, Mira couldn't take her eyes off the baby, as if at any minute his real injury was going to reveal itself—with her name written all over it.

"Oh, please, Brady." Katherine dismissed him, as she hooked her arm in Owen's. "Don't be such a tight-ass. Have a sense of humor for god's sake."

A counter separated the living room from the yolk-colored kitchen where Edward, wearing an apron, was talking and pouring drinks for Anya and Wilton. Anya gave Owen an intimate smile and held his unwitting gaze until he yanked himself out of it. For an instant, he'd felt an exotic, warm pull. It was clear that Wilton had seen it happen.

"Come with me, sweetie," Katherine said, and pulled Owen into the tiny dining room.

Owen recognized his father's quirky touch in how the table was set, silverware and glasses and napkins placed at odd angles, disequilibrium his own idea of balance. Owen liked that Katherine hadn't felt the need to fix it. Two small and dusty plastic figures of pilgrims, man and woman, stood in the middle, waiting for the company to sit down. Katherine's things—her furniture, her clothes, even herself—had the shine of well-used and frugal attention. Nothing extra, nothing wasted. A wide view looked onto the bay that had turned frothy under the clouds.

"They built this place with the view from here when it should have been there," she said and ticked her head at the living room where Mira was still frozen on the couch. "Who spends time in a dining room? It doesn't make any sense. They did get the bedroom right, though. I can see the water from my bed, last thing I see when I close my eyes."

"And a nice thing to wake up to."

She looked at him as if what he'd said was full of hidden meaning. "Yes, you know about that, don't you? The pond is lovely. I can see why Edward's so attached to it. Funny to be attached to a body of water, isn't it?"

"Yes—especially when it's so indifferent to us."

"When we met, Edward reminded me of some animal that lives in the trees and watches everything without ever moving his head. Just the eyes go from side to side. You're a little like that."

"A monkey, maybe?"

She squeezed his arm. "The eyes, dark like yours, the hair—" She reached up to brush his back. "How can I describe it? Primal? No, that's not the right word." She shrugged and gave up.

She was intent on taking him on the full tour—though you

could see the whole thing from one pivoting spot—and they went into the single bedroom. There were matching nightstands on either side of the tightly made bed, one with an electric clock, the plastic aged yellow like old teeth, the other with a radio that leaked a repetitive traipsing of classical music. Edward's wallet and keys were on the bureau. There was a portable crib set up in the corner. Katherine sat on the bed and motioned for Owen to sit next to her.

"Your father told me that you don't talk much," she said. "That's okay, by the way. I don't think we all need to be talkers. I want you to know that I'm the one who gave your father the gun."

"I'm not sure if I should thank you or not. We're not exactly gun people." His fingertips were itchy with the memory of the thing hidden in the rug. "Not at all, in fact."

"It's fine. I don't like violence either. Some people do, you know."

Edward called her into the kitchen to taste his sweet potatoes. Owen leaned back against the pillows and stretched out on the bed to give the view the same horizontal gaze Edward might give it. He wanted to see what his father saw. Edward had been without a woman's attention for a very long time, and now it appeared before him as effortlessly as this vista. It was beautiful and boundless, and something to envy. He could easily fall asleep.

"Ah, excuse me," Brady said. Owen shot up. "I was going to put the baby down for his nap." He pointed at the crib in the corner.

"Sorry. I was just—" Heat crept up his neck.

"I know. Checking out the view. My mother wants everyone to like it as much as she does."

"That's understandable. It is pretty spectacular."

Brady sat on the bed with all the careful effort of a middle-aged man. The baby was almost asleep on his shoulder, his mouth pulsing with dreams. Veins mapped the boy's fluttery eyelids. "So, our parents," Brady said. "Interesting."

"Right. Our parents." Owen hovered his hand over the baby's warm back. Brady gave him a nod of permission to touch. "We're practically stepbrothers."

"Not really."

"I was joking."

"They're moving fast," Brady said, undeterred and humorless. "Too fast, if you ask me."

Brady's disapproval made Owen think about the man's own story. Was this his first or maybe third time around in marriage? He was stocky like his mother, but had too much padding; his clothes were just a little too tight. There was no play in the guy—he was all swollen seriousness.

"I don't think so. They seem happy to me," Owen said.

"My mother was attacked years ago by one of her students in the school parking lot at night. No one knows what happened exactly because she wouldn't say and she wouldn't press charges. She spent over a week in the hospital. She could have died." He went to the crib to put the baby down. "I'm telling you this because my mother's a very tough woman. And she knows how to protect herself."

"Good to know."

Why was Brady telling him this? Was it some kind of warning, and a way to say his mother was not a woman to be screwed with? It was Brady, after all who'd given her the gun, Brady who also tenderly pulled a blanket over his baby.

Beyond the bedroom window, Owen saw Edward, Katherine, Wilton, and Anya standing at the head of the beach stairs. Brady began to sing a breathless tune to the baby as Owen left. Mira, still on the couch, eyes closed, had taken off her coat but clutched it to her chest. Lynn was locked onto the television and didn't look up. Owen went down the road to the stairs. Katherine had taken Wilton and Anya to the sandbars and Edward watched them through the binoculars.

"You've been talking to Brady," his father said, and gave him the glasses. "He's a gloomy little shit, isn't he?"

Owen laughed. "Pretty gloomy. I don't think he approves of you two kids. Says you're moving too fast."

"So I've heard."

"He also says his mother's not to be messed with."

"I've heard that, too."

Through the binoculars, Owen followed the progress of the others in the thickening mist. "Can I ask you something? Did you have girlfriends all along? When I was kid, when I lived with you, and I just never knew?"

"Oh, sure," Edward said. "You never met any of them because there was never anyone I was serious about. Kids get all sorts of funny ideas, and I didn't want you think this one or that one was going to be your mother or move in with us. I think we did pretty good, just you and me. I didn't see the need for anyone else, long-term, that is. Short-term's another matter."

"Amazing. I had absolutely no idea." All those treks his father had taken in the late afternoons—was he really getting laid then?

"That was the point," Edward said, pleased with himself.

The others came back from the beach, breathless with the cold. Inside, Wilton looked startled, his expression blown open by the bay. Sand clung to his eyebrows and cheeks. He watched Anya too closely—how she loosened and then pulled her hair back with the silver clip, how she adjusted her black sweater, how she turned away to check her phone, how she went into the kitchen to help Edward. Katherine orchestrated the seating, assigning water views to Wilton and Anya. Lynn had a glassy look of displeasure, while Mira blinked herself alert. Brady went at the turkey with a stern knife.

"I'd like to say something," Wilton announced, rising theatrically from his chair and holding his glass. "We're very grateful to be here in this beautiful place, not far from the first Thanksgiving, in fact, and at this table, and with all of you, our new friends. But especially, I want to thank you for including *my* family—me and my daughter." He turned to Anya, and the sand on his face sparkled. She glanced at Owen and raised a reluctant glass. Wilton waited for her to look at him, but she wouldn't.

"Yes, to you two," Mira said, exploding into the silence. Her voice was too avid and sharp. "And to Edward and Katherine."

Wilton didn't sit, still waiting for Anya to look at him, and his face changed from expectation to disappointment. When he took a sip of his wine, his hand shook.

"Watch out, you're spilling," Anya said to him. Her tone was more sympathetic than scolding.

Two islands of red stain spread on his pale blue shirt. Wilton sat. His daughter had made him look old and useless, his touch for charm gone. Edward, who'd once called white bread the devil, stuffed a soft cottony roll smeared with margarine into his mouth. He was going to try and swallow all the tension in the room. Katherine took his face in her hands and kissed him gratefully, the crumbs on his front transferring to hers.

"Christ. Teenagers," Mira said, laughing—with relief, Owen thought. "Get a room."

"Eddie's moving in," Katherine announced.

"Are you serious?" Brady put down his fork and looked at his mother. "You haven't known each other very long. Don't you think this is a little fast?"

"Not too fast at all. When you're my age, just because a year goes by quickly doesn't mean it isn't still three hundred and sixty-five days. Long enough," Edward told him. "You have to be willing to make a change at our age, because if you're not willing, then you've written off the future and you might as well be dead already."

"But what's the hurry?" Brady asked.

Edward ignored him and spoke to Owen as though it were just the two of them at the table. "I'm all alone on the pond these days."

"I know you are."

"Even Porter's gone now. Sometimes I think about that guy who died in his house in the woods, and his dogs got so hungry locked in there that they finally ate him."

"Is that for real?" Lynn asked, finally animated by something. "That's foul."

"Can't be true," Brady told her.

"But it's absolutely true," Edward said.

"Rey prefers dry food," Owen told his father, "so you don't have to worry about that happening." At the mention of his name, the dog got up and stuck his wet nose in Owen's hand. "Anyway, I think this is great news."

"I think it's great, too," Anya said, and looked again at Owen. "Very romantic."

"Yes," Mira said, her eyes moving between the two of them. "Very romantic."

The baby began to cry, and Brady retrieved him from the bedroom. When he brought him back to the table, Edward held his arms out for the kid and buried his face in the baby's belly. Owen saw how easy and contented his father was with the child. He had a flash of memory—his father holding him at the pond's edge, his father inching into the water, the feel of it reaching his own chest, the beginning of life in the water, the introduction of named pleasure.

After they'd cleaned up and sat through their post-meal stupor, they took a walk to the golf course. Katherine and Edward linked arms and Anya walked next to them. Owen and Wilton followed—the others were back at the condo—but Wilton was slow and dour and they fell further behind. By midafternoon, dark waited to rush in and sea mist coated Owen's face with a briny wax.

"The ants have been let out of the ant farm," he said, noting the other families walking, stuporous and cold.

Wilton stopped to catch his breath. His face folded into a grimace as he put his hands on his knees and sucked in the air. His ears were bright red; he was too vain to wear the orange wool cap Edward had offered him. His bare ankles looked like pure white bone.

"You all right, old man?" Owen asked.

"Old man?" Wilton bristled uncharacteristically. "Don't call me that." He watched the others cross the road to the golf green and its undulating paths. Anya was describing something with her hands and dancing backward so she could face Edward and Katherine. "Look at my sunny daughter talking up a storm. A real chatterbox," he said, bitterly. "She's said more to those two on this walk than she's ever said to me in all this time. And she doesn't even know them. When she was a little girl, she used to tell me every thought in her head."

"That was a long time ago. She doesn't know you now."

"She knows me," he snapped. "I'm her father, aren't I? What's to know? I'm the same person I always was."

"Be patient. You're asking a lot."

"You seem to be some kind of authority on my daughter. You

two obviously have some private understanding. You look at each other all the time, in the car, at the table, even on this walk she keeps turning around to look at you. All those meaningful glances." He grabbed Owen's arm. "What do you know?" he demanded. "What has she told you? What have you told her about me?"

"Jesus, what's the matter with you?" Owen shook him off.

Wilton's eyes narrowed in the wind. "I thought you could help me, you could help me get her back—but you've turned out to be no fucking help at all. In fact, just the opposite. You've made it worse."

"No fucking help? I was the one who got her to come today. I told her it would make you happy. I did it for you."

He walked away from Wilton. The man was desperate to be forgiven by his daughter for something he wasn't ever going to confess to her. Maybe it was never going to work. At the complex's clubhouse, Owen cupped his hand against the glass to see the residents' many grandchildren cannonballing off the sides and into the pool. He heard their shrieks, saw their tucked bodies. In the window's reflection, he watched Wilton bend again to find his breath, then turn to go back to the condo and the soothing comfort of Mira. Owen watched the man take a right on the road instead of staying straight until the next turn, and he didn't run to correct his friend's mistake.

9

Downtown was emptying out at 5:30 on a Tuesday. Owen watched the Department of Corrections van back out of the courthouse lot and slide into traffic. He couldn't see through the dark windows, but he knew those inside could see him. At Kennedy Plaza, people waited for their buses, some forced to stand beyond the reach of the skimpy, overcrowded shelter. They perched on the curb with the tilt of impatience. In the soft rain, nylon parkas gleamed like rock and shopping bags slumped on the pavement. Christmas decorations, left hanging into January, still festooned the decidedly unfestive plaza, a criss-cross of slushy walks bordered by winter trees and ringed by the city's few tall buildings. At one end, the glass elevator of the Biltmore rose over the park and a cluster of wet men hanging out by the waterless fountain. This center of the city—scene of frequent high school fights and, recently, the death of a drug addict who was run over by a bus that refused to let him board—was gazed upon indulgently by City Hall. The building's ornate façade presented a perverse kind of civic pride. We might be provincial and historied with corruption, but this is who we are, the city proclaimed. Providence—the entire state, in fact—was without pretension but full of self-importance.

Owen passed the skating rink on his way to the Donnell

Building, which he'd been summoned to by Mike Levi. He assumed Mike was going to fire him for not showing up to one too many tutoring appointments. He deserved it, after all. Squealing skaters were undeterred by the rain. Overbundled, they moved across the ice like Frankensteins. He'd watched Wilton move the same way down his slick, ice-coated driveway a few days earlier. He'd had a lean, distracted look and shivered in a sweater that hung open at the neck. The man wasn't made for winter. Mira said Wilton kept the thermostat in his house turned up high to blast hot air into rooms he never even entered. It was a profligate and lonely luxury.

Mike's company, Educational Excellence Consultants (EEC—sounds like *eek!* Mira had pointed out once), newly occupied the far corner of the third floor. The elevator still smelled of someone's lunch and old coffee. He felt the stuffy, adenoidal silence of office buildings. The view at the end of the hallway was of the low backsides of other buildings, the tops of revolving doors and heads emerging one by one, without umbrellas. On the walls of the reception area, where Owen waited for Mike to get off the phone, were framed letters from grateful parents, thanking EEC for helping their daughter realize her potential, brightening their son's future, building their child's confidence. The testimonials were breathless, written as though Mike and his corps of tutors, coaches, and advisors had heroically pulled these already too advantaged children from the academic trash heap. For some of the parents of his Spruance students, struggle might have already gripped and staggered their lives, but more than anything, they wanted to spare their kids the same disenchantment they'd faced. In that, they were no different than these letter-writing, gushing parents, but the other disparities were astounding. Last month they'd sat opposite him on parent-teacher night, waiting for assurances that everything was going to be good in their child's future. "Your son, your daughter, can do anything," he said, both always true and untrue.

"So you like those letters or what?" Mike asked. He spoke with a sharp Rhode Island accent.

"Spectacular stuff. Clearly, you're a genius."

"Twenty-seven years in the public school system and not one parent ever wrote me a thank-you note. Well, maybe one. I got plenty of no-thank-you notes, a few fuck-you notes."

He hiked up his pants with mocking self-importance. He was like the city—proud but a little disheveled, and mostly likable. Mike had been a devoted and inventive teacher, but he'd also gotten rough with a couple of kids at Spruance in his last years there and had been forced to take a leave for a week or two. He said what he thought even when he knew it would get him in trouble. His marriage to Faye had taken a pounding because of it. He'd put on a lot of weight, and for a time he drank too much. He'd finally left when the classroom window he'd been trying to open shattered and ripped a long, deep valley down his arm. He'd been hurried away in an ambulance, smiling as if he knew this was the only way he was ever going to get out of the place.

Mike led him back to his office and took a seat behind his desk. A motivational poster of enthusiastic clouds hung on the wall. *Fly High: Soaring Is Just Another Word for Success.* The same kind of poster that had been in Mira's childhood bedroom.

Mike saw what he was looking at. "I know, it's awful. A present from Faye. Have to put it up. But I don't have to look at it. You do." He laughed and then leaned forward, pressing his hands together. It was a gesture of seriousness Owen imagined the man probably used with his clients, and it made Owen smirk.

"So, Owen."

"So, Mike. You don't have to say it. I know. I've missed a couple of appointments."

"More than a couple." Mike looked down at the paper in front of him. "Eight, in fact. And those are just the ones I know about. Your counting sucks, by the way. Good thing you don't teach math."

"I feel bad about it."

"No, you don't. Don't bullshit me."

Owen shifted in his chair. "Fire me, and we can move on. We can go get a beer, talk about something else."

Mike put up a hand to stop him. "What makes you think I'm going to fire you?"

"Because I screwed things up for you. I deserve to be fired. I'm asking to be fired."

"Such a martyr. Look, I just explain that you are a rogue employee. I say the good ones usually are, that you just have to be broken in." He mimed snapping a whip. "That goes over well. Makes us look human but effective." He took a sip of his coffee and frowned. "What do you think about working here, with me? You and me. Full-time. The business is growing like you wouldn't believe, and I need some help, expanding services, running seminars, setting up satellite offices, marketing. The economy is in the toilet, but this is recession-proof. You have no idea how popular this idea of success is. Lots of very ambitious parents out there."

"Anxious parents," Owen said. "Rich parents."

"Does it matter? You're too good to be stuck at a shit-hole like Spruance. It's a waste. The whole system's broken, it's chaos, it's unfixable. All those things you have to do, and none of what you should really be doing. It's like patching a hole in something that's just going to tear again. No teaching gets done, am I right? I'm offering you something real here, better, a good way to get out."

"Teaching gets done," Owen said. "Maybe not in the usual ways, and maybe not everything that's supposed to be taught gets taught, but it's not pointless."

Mike's shelves held SAT prep books and study guides, expensive promises between soft covers. Owen knew teachers who threw whole years and classrooms full of kids away, others who stood as vacant as burned-out houses. But there were good ones, too.

"I'm there in that room every day, and I care about what goes on."

"You care. That's nice." Mike smiled and put his arms behind his head. "Very sweet."

"Maybe I don't want to get out," Owen said. "Ever thought of that?"

"Okay, you can bullshit yourself all you want, but tell me this— what are you actually teaching those kids?" Mike asked.

Owen hesitated. "Hope." He wasn't sure he'd ever said it out loud before. It was what Mira believed it was all about. Since she'd stopped going to the casino, her zeal for Brindle had reignited. At dinner now, on the nights she didn't stay late, they swapped stories about their students. They were careful with each other, and it had some of the feel of early, swirling romance. He was hopeful about his marriage, too. "It's about teaching the kids to have expectations for themselves. Because no one else has expectations for them."

"Come on. You sound like my fucking poster. You sound like a campaign slogan. When did you get so sentimental? Be serious."

Owen laughed. He liked Mike's challenges. "I am serious. I'm getting them to tell the stories of their lives and of their parents' lives. It's just too bad that any conviction sounds false these days. Earnestness is just a ruse now, right? Or is it just you who's gotten so cynical?"

Mike leaned forward. "End of the year, they're going to close Spruance."

"That's an old story. I'm not sure I believe it anymore."

"Believe it," Mike said. "It's going to happen, and you'll be farmed out to who knows where. Seniority could kill you. You'll become one of those permanent roaming subs, five different schools a week and no one even says hello to you. You'll be a zombie—waiting for his pension."

Because Mike had lived in Rhode Island forever, he had access to information others didn't. Like Mira, he picked up news just by tasting the particulates in the city's air. Owen pictured the school building sitting empty on its barren rise, like a junked car on cinderblocks.

"I've called you a hundred times and I never get you—or Mira either. I leave messages and you don't call back," Mike said. "What's going on with you?"

To his left, Owen saw the twinkling end of a construction crane. The skating rink was opalescent and emptying out in the heavier rain, but two skaters persisted. "I've been busy. It's letting up now. No more missed sessions, I promise."

"All these years and that's what I'm going to get from you? That you've been busy? Look, I've been married forever. I know the deal. You have that look—scared and pissed off. Go ahead—tell me I'm wrong." Mike put his hands flat on the crowded desk among the papers and the granola bar wrappers. "Tell me."

"We had a bump. But we're okay."

"A bump. How benign. But if you say so. I give up." Mike shook his head. The front door of the suite opened and set off a chime in the outer office. "Listen, I have to see this person—interviewing for an assistant—and I haven't even read her résumé yet. Where the hell is it?" Mike pushed through some papers and then walked Owen to the door. "Think about the offer. It's a good one. Call me."

"I will."

"No, you won't. And I'll have to hunt you down, but that's okay. I'm used to it. You're a piece of work. I shouldn't put up with you, but I do." He gave Owen a sloppy handshake.

In the reception area, a woman read the letters on the wall. Her long wool coat, the color of mice, had jagged wet patches at the shoulders and water wicking up at the hem. Her damp hair fell in a familiar, golden swoop on her shoulder. "Joy?"

"Oh." A blaze rose in her face. "Owen."

"You know each other?" Mike asked.

"Of course. Joy works for Mira," Owen said, but confusion had begun to bloom in his chest. Joy wouldn't look at him. "At Brindle."

Mike looked from one to the other and claimed he needed a few minutes to do something in his office. He left them alone but didn't shut his door.

"Joy, what's going on? Are you looking for a job?" Owen asked. "Does Mira know?"

"What?" Water collected on the rug under the tip of her umbrella. "Mira laid me off. Three weeks ago." Her lower lip trembled. "Didn't she tell you?"

Mira hadn't told him. His head buzzed, and he was having a hard time understanding what Joy was saying to him now—that it was about money, that Brindle was broke, that Mira couldn't pay her or the teachers anymore. How was that possible?

Joy gave him a cold look. Sometimes Mira would be gone in the middle of the day and couldn't be reached, she explained. The kids showed up from Noah House and Mira wasn't there to work with them. There was nothing to feed them or their disappointment, and they ran around the place, hungry for everything.

"I'm sure she just got caught up in something," he said. His impulse to cover for Mira made him reel.

"She takes Brindle's money, and she knows I know," Joy said. "I know where she goes, too. She plays the slot machines."

"That's not true," he insisted.

"Yes, it is. With that friend of hers. The famous actor."

"He's not famous."

Joy's mouth tightened in a way that brought back the moment at the fundraiser when he'd embarrassed her about Wilton. If he'd expected she was going to cry for herself here, the humiliation was all his. She was steely, while a man lied to by his wife is the expendable, foolish one, the one to feel the most sorry for. Joy looked at her wet boots, the leather stained with tide lines of salt, and then she went into Mike's office.

Owen left downtown and drove to India Point Park. The wind rocked his car. It was too cold to get out, and he couldn't see much of the bay except for a frill of fluorescence and an occasional whitecap. Other cars were parked like his at contemplative angles to the surf, and he suspected that many chapters of the human heart were being written in that squally hour. It was no easier to admit the truth about yourself than it was to admit the truth about the one you loved. But he was a coward and Mira was a liar. She'd stolen from Brindle; she was reckless and out of control. He'd convinced himself of the return of their happier life, and maybe Mira had convinced herself of it, too, but none of it was real. She'd lied so often that the lies had become the truth for her. What had looked like caution between them now appeared as evasion.

If tonight was the life-drawing class, as Mira had reminded him that morning, and Wilton was a member of it, what was his pad doing in the backseat of Owen's car like some kind of

stowaway? Was there even a class anymore? Was there even a
Brindle? He reached back for the pad and threw it out, propelled
by his long, furious roar. The wind lifted the pages over the water, and then they disappeared into the dark. His throat was raw.
When he got home hours later, after stopping to drink and watch
a basketball game in a bar on Wickenden Street, Mira was in bed
with her head turned away from the door, one arm hanging to the
floor, the fingers curled into a soft fist. He wasn't sure she was still
asleep, but it didn't matter. He kneeled on the floor by her head.
The alcohol tingled his sinuses and made his eyes tear. He could
stay like this forever and he'd still never know his wife.

He lifted his face to see the moon slip in at the top right corner of the window. The light revealed generations of Thrasher
fingerprints on the panes. Everything else was indistinct but this
instant, and those fingerprints, and his wife's steady breathing.
This was not his house. Maybe this was not his wife. He pressed
his cheek to the floor that was composed of a million ancient
splinters pressed together. He felt the permanence of the house
below him. He smelled the stink of smoke and grease on Mira's
skin and knew that this scent would have the power to knock him
over years later.

Another night, and Mira was gone. Owen had come outside to
witness the eerie late January phenomenon he loved—a smudgy,
reluctant moon behind purpling clouds. It made him think the
earth was in freefall—and saved at the last moment. The marvel
would only last a few nights, and then it would be gone until
next year.

"Hey, Owen. Are you always lurking back here in the dark?"

He turned to see Anya on her father's porch. "Look up," he
said. "Look at the moon."

She did and was unmoved by it. "I wanted to surprise Wilton."

"Not home," Owen said.

"Besides, I needed a break from studying before my head explodes."

Piles of student work on Owen's desk had not been touched for weeks. "I was thinking about making something to eat. You hungry?"

"I'm always hungry."

She came off the porch and pushed through the heavy snow. Random divots glowed. Inside, she took off her coat. Like her father, her long body in a chair gave the impression of lassitude. In truth, they were both alert to everything. She was wearing a yellow-and-black-striped wool cap that was tight on her skull. Wilton had bitterly mentioned the hat because he was sure it belonged to Anya's boyfriend. Not that he even knew if she had one or not. Owen complimented her on her pink sweater. Color on her was surprising and made her look even younger.

"A present from Wilton," she said and plucked the material at the neck. "Every single year, a cashmere sweater for my birthday. I thought it would be a nice gesture to wear it—this is the first time—but it's so itchy. I think I'm allergic to cashmere. Is that even possible? And this color. It's girlie-girl, so not me."

"Girlie-girl," Owen repeated. The moon had made him reckless. "Like bubblegum."

"More like undercooked pork." Anya looked around. "Is Mira here?"

He bent into the refrigerator and spoke to its empty shelves. "Actually, Mira and your father went to a casino."

"A casino? Why?"

"I don't know—why does anyone go to a casino?" He shut the refrigerator. "Mira plays the slots and your father has a drink and talks to his fans, and then they come home at a nice, reasonable hour. They go all the time."

Her head angled to the left. "You're joking, right?"

"Not joking at all. You can ask them about it yourself, but they may not tell you the truth. At least Mira won't." He laughed queasily.

Anya scratched under the bumblebee hat. "Is this funny? It doesn't sound funny to me."

"It's not," he said. "It's just the opposite. I don't know why I laughed."

Anya looked baffled, her mouth drawing in as if to contain her doubt. It would be easy enough for her to assume Wilton and Mira were sleeping together and the casino was just a moronic alibi they gave. If only that was all this was, a series of dumb, unoriginal fucks they'd get bored with eventually. They were in love with each other, in a way, after all. Owen thought maybe he had been a little in love with Wilton, too, for a time. How could you not love the one you confessed to and who confessed to you? The one who seemed to belong only to you when you were with him?

"Mira plays the slot machines?" Anya asked.

"Devotedly."

"She doesn't seem like the type, you know—confident, beautiful, totally together. The kind of woman who makes other women feel like a useless mess. I'd think she'd just find the whole thing way too tacky and ugly. I mean, look at all this, the house, you."

"Right, look at me."

Anya fiddled with his keys on the table; the conversation suddenly felt very intimate to him. She plucked at her sweater again. The skin at the cashmere neck had blossomed into red blotches. He sat down and pulled her striped hat off, surprising her. Static snapped around her head. She'd cut her hair short, revealing the graceful, emphatic line of her jaw. She looked at the hat in his hand. Owen brought it to his nose and inhaled. Sweet, sweaty, dampish wool.

"What are we eating?" she asked, and grabbed her hat back.

"Nothing. Turns out there's not much here."

"We'll go to Wilton's then," Anya said, bright with her idea. "There's always food there, and he said I should go in any time I want. To make myself at home, he said."

They put on their coats and at Wilton's door, Anya lifted up the front mat for the key. Owen remembered the first night he'd told Wilton, who still had his California vigor back then, that this was a bad idea. One of Alice Jessup's nurses stood across the street having a cigarette, one foot up on a snow bank in the bitter cold, watching them. Otherwise, the street was empty, moonscaped by ice. The smudged moon had disappeared. There was an almost clinical smell inside the house, and the chill had nothing to do with the heat that blasted through the grates, but with the aura of impermanence. No meals had been cooked here, no wine spilled, no cushions puckered from body weight. No art, no sex, no tears, no parties, no books, no life. Just waiting.

Owen hadn't been inside for a couple of months, and now in the front room, an uninviting, boxy couch faced a very large television. A masterful remote was the only object on a glass table. In the kitchen, a single mug was in the sink. There was a lime-colored blender with packing material still around it, a toaster without any fingerprints or crumbs loitering at the base, no tea-kettle, no can opener, no pictures, no junk, no shoes at the back door, no tossed rag, no bottle of aspirin or vitamin C. Only boxes and boxes from UPS and FedEx, some opened, others not.

"It's hard to tell if he's coming or going," Owen said. "What is all this stuff?"

Anya's eye was caught on a box of giant oranges, each piece in a tissue paper nest. "He tells me that he doesn't need anything, that his life has always had too much crap in it. But then he orders all this shit he doesn't even bother to open. Or eat. Makes you wonder why he bought such a big house." She picked up an orange. "What's he thinking?"

"He's thinking, it's all for you, the house and everything in it. He thinks you might live here with him," he said. "That's always been his plan. He has no work, no purpose except for you. What did you think this was all about?"

"I don't know. But I'm not going to live with him. That will never happen. He's delusional. What's he going to do, buy a new house every time I move?"

"Maybe. He's an optimist. You're the only thing he wants."

"Am I a thing? Like the blender? Well, he wants too much." Anya began to poke around angrily in the cabinets. "I didn't see him for all these years, and now he thinks this is going to happen? We'll be a happy little family?" Her sweater lifted to expose a sliver of skin above the waistband of her jeans.

"Yes, a happy little family."

She shook her head. "You know, my brothers would love a house like this. They could turn it into a gym or a skate park. This house needs lots of kids, not just one person. It's such a waste." She opened the refrigerator and pulled out pickles, cheese, and vacuum-sealed envelopes of meats. "Wilton's hopeless as a father. I hope you know that."

"I think I do."

"Everything there is to do wrong parentwise, I'd say he did. And still does. Did you see him on Thanksgiving? I could barely breathe." She slapped down the last package on the counter, took a knife out of a well-stocked block, and sliced into a salami. She examined the first claret piece flecked with white fat and green peppercorns. "You know he abandoned me basically, just dropped out of the picture one day. I was young, and I don't remember it, really—I was just aware that all of a sudden he was gone."

"Your mother took you to another state."

"God, don't defend him! Is that what he said? That it's because we moved? He wasn't interested in being my father and that's the truth. And now, when he doesn't have a career, he's a has-been's has-been, he decides that it's time? It's like he's got some terminal disease and we're in a bad movie and have to reunite so he can die in peace." She paused and thrust her jaw out. "He never asked if I wanted him here."

"You wrote him a postcard."

"One postcard. That's it. I wrote that I needed some money for school. I never hid that." She sliced more rounds of salami until she'd sliced the entire sausage. "My mother thought it was better that he was out of the picture anyway. She thought it would be too confusing for me, but I could have handled it. People handle much more than that every day. My story is not the worst. I don't feel sorry for myself."

It was distressing to know the truth about what had happened in her life when she didn't know the truth herself. The real story was wounding, but any more so than what she already believed?

"Then why did you come tonight?" he asked.

"I don't know," she said. "I really don't. I don't know what I'm supposed to do."

She pierced the plastic pouches of cheese and smoked salmon and then examined the messy bounty on the counter. They fished around in jars of pickles and slippery marinated mushrooms, cut into a loaf of bread shipped from Virginia, and made enormous, dripping sandwiches. It occurred to Owen that Wilton must have been throwing out uneaten food for months, waiting for the guest who never showed up. They took a bottle of wine and their plates to the couch in the living room. When Anya turned the television on, Owen was grateful that it still had the power to suck up his attention. Men in skimpy bathing suits jumped from one inflatable lily pad to the next, each falling with an ignominious splat. Anya's laugh was low and throaty. She lowered a marinated red pepper onto her tongue and swiped the oil from her lips. She halfheartedly blotted where she'd dripped onto the pale wool of the couch.

"Can I ask you about something?" she said. "Is Mira an addict? Is that what you were saying before?"

He nodded, he shrugged, he held up his open palms, he was full of mixed signals. When he touched Anya's cheek, she froze. He wanted to put a hand on the back of her long neck and on her allergic clavicle, on her long thigh until he felt the inner seam of her pants. The peril was dizzying.

Anya stood and went into the kitchen. He was left with two men trying to ride a giant tree trunk down a muddy hillside, his own hand in midair. He thought it was time for him to leave.

"Take your glass," Anya said, reappearing to turn off the television. She gestured with a new bottle of wine. "I want to show you something."

"I should go. You're a little drunk."

"So are you. Come on."

Maybe that's all this is, Owen told himself, too much expensive wine, too much salami. He followed her upstairs. Her pants creased beckoningly as she climbed, the air stirring around her. They might be caught by a returning Wilton, but what were they doing but making themselves at home? And wasn't that what he'd always wanted, Anya here? They stood in the doorway of an empty room with a fireplace at one end. There was a single

log in the grate, an old newspaper thrown on top. He told Anya
that this room was where the previous owner had slept and died.
She located the spots where the legs of the bed had stamped the
wood over the years. She lay on the floor in the imagined bed, her
hands by her side. She wanted to see what the woman had looked
at all those years—two cracks merging into an X on the ceiling.
In the next room there was a glass-and-chrome desk, a simple
wooden chair, a laptop, a mug of pens, neatly stacked blank paper,
an address book, and in the corner, a towering stack of the white
Styrofoam boxes Wilton's steaks came in.

"I have no idea why he keeps these," Anya said, pinging one
with a finger. "But I have no idea why he does most things. He's a
very strange guy."

They went into Wilton's bedroom, which Owen hadn't seen
before. Had he pictured such a vast bed with a troubled tangle of
sheets? There was no telephone by the bed, no clock or dirty socks
in the corner. No bathrobe, pills, or spare change. Nothing on the
walls. There was only a television, bigger than the one downstairs,
and beside it, a pair of scuffed slippers on the bare floor.

"I think he spends hours and hours watching television," Anya
said. "Watching himself, mostly."

She sat on the edge of the bed and pulled herself up to the
wall that served as the headboard. There was something monastic about the room and the entire empty, echoing house. Anya
looked small on the bed, a lone passenger on an ocean liner.
Her feet wiggled in striped socks. She touched her earrings. "See
these? Wilton gave them to me last week. Waited outside my
apartment to ambush me with them." Gold teardrops. "They belonged to his mother, or so he says. I never met the woman."
She stared at the blank screen and sipped her wine. "My own
grandmother. She's not alive anymore, apparently. I've never met

anyone in his family. I don't even know if he has one. Isn't that weird? My mother doesn't know either. Maybe he exists, but was never actually born."

"Sprung from the ether," Owen said.

Anya wavered between anger, curiosity, and sadness when she talked about her father. Owen imagined it had always been a tough balance for her to maintain, and that it had made her unpredictable. Her friends would say they didn't really understand her. She scratched her irritated neck. Owen went to the other side of the bed and sat down so his back was to her. He faced his own bedroom across the way. He'd left a lamp on and saw the books on the shelves, the restless blankets, clothes everywhere. He couldn't remember when he and Mira had last spoken there, or what they had said to each other.

Anya turned on the television. A movie—two men in the cockpit of an ascending airplane—was huge and bright. It was like being in the front row at the drive-in. He drank from the bottle of wine as the plane dipped and turned. His bones softened pleasantly. He moved next to Anya and stretched out his legs.

"You should take your sneakers off," she said. "So you don't get the sheets dirty."

But the sheets already gave off a sour odor and were tinged gray, signs of an unwashed and transitory life. Wilton could leave all of it in a moment, attached to nothing, attached to Anya by a filament. Owen didn't take off his sneakers. Anya sloshed wine into her glass. Splashes spread into stains on the sheets.

"This is what I wanted to show you," she said and worked the remote. Beeps and twitters emanated from the set, until a roster of all the episodes of *Ancient Times* appeared.

"The sacred archives," Owen said.

"He watches them over and over. Look, you can see which one he watched last."

The show's theme music came on with its circus-freak melody, and he hummed along. Bruno Macon, young and tight-skinned in a dandyish seersucker suit and polka-dot bow tie held a wriggling mouse by the tail. Owen vaguely recalled the episode, though he couldn't say what came next. Did he remember this from his childhood or from a night Mira had turned it on? It was like being able to see only an inch in front of your face. Bruno gazed into the mouse's eyes and chattered away. Anya held the remote in the air as if she might suddenly decide to obliterate her father. Wilton turned away from the mouse and looked out at them from the screen. He saw Owen with his daughter, saw how Owen was sensing the heat of Anya's leg against his. His eyes widened. He screamed and dropped the mouse.

Owen touched a scar under Anya's chin. "How did you get this?"

"Every kid in America has a bathroom scar. Smack against the sink."

He wanted to lick the drop of wine at the corner of her mouth. There were a million reasons not to kiss her, but he kissed the wine in the crease of her lips. He kissed the other side of her mouth. He touched her neck where it was irritated. She held her breath, then rolled away from him. She stood with her hands on top of her head as though she was trying to keep her ideas from flying away.

"We have to clean up before Wilton comes home." She gestured impatiently for him to get up. "Now." She blotted the wine stains with a napkin. "What are you doing? Get up, get up!"

The feeling of the kiss trickled away like the end of a flash flood. He wanted to call Anya back to the bed. What if Wilton did discover them? Let him find the two of them on his bed. But Anya was turbulent and insistent—he'd done this to her, riled her up—and he followed her downstairs. They screwed the lids on the jars, swept the crumbs into the sink and washed them down the drain. But they'd opened the packages and sliced into the bread and spilled red wine. Anya could clean up, but she couldn't erase the evidence that she had been there. She might mean for her father to know he'd missed another opportunity, while the real opportunity still terrified her too much.

"I'm sorry about before," he said. "I shouldn't have done that. Kissed you. I wanted to, though. I wanted to very much."

She gave him a measured look and put the key back under the outside mat. "Maybe, but you were thinking about someone else."

He never thought he'd be the kind of man who waited in the dark for his wife. Tonight, a week after he'd kissed Anya, he wasn't sure if he was going to appear in the hallway when Mira thought she wasn't being watched, when she assumed he was reading, or working on his students' papers, or even sleeping if it was late enough, giving off his bready scent under the blankets, or if he was going to rush her and slam her against the wall. Press his hands against her shoulders, maybe her throat. Hurt her, make her wince and cry, drop her keys, drop to her knees. The house would shudder with his violence.

But a thunderous bursting out of the dark was not his style, not something he would do, yet the option still waited for him like a fine suit in the upstairs closet. He was just looking for the right occasion to wear it. He saw violence's upper hand everywhere. It was at school—Kevin had pierced the upper arm of classmate with a pen and been expelled—and on the news, in the world, and he noted its sheer chaotic precision. Violence wasted no time on interpretation or discussion. It just did its fearsome thing. But he'd seen too much of it already—he wouldn't take it for himself.

On this Tuesday, three weeks after he'd seen Joy at Mike's office, he'd been sitting in the dark for hours. He'd turned off all the lights. His eyes had adjusted to the darkness, but Mira would be blind when she came in. He would be able to see what her expression really was, not the one she tried to appease him with when she lied about where she'd been, when she lied about Brindle and everything else. She'd be tired, too—she was always tired these days, too tired to fight, to talk, to face him. It was the February cold, the ice, the wind that did it, she'd say, a long day. Wouldn't he just leave her alone for a minute? It was her period, it was Brindle, it was her students, her insomnia. Even in the dark, he would be able to detect the glitter of excitement on her skin, even as she tried to wipe it away with the hem of her shirt. In the mornings now, he'd watch her pick up the clothes she'd taken off the night before and inhale their odor the way you might when you hoped to detect the scent of a lover. Hers was an innocuous sniff though: she had no real lover, but he was as jealous as one.

The room's silence buoyed him. It was like a childhood night on the pond, when his solitude felt almost like confidence. None of those dead Thrashers, their cells and touch all around him, approved of what their daughter was up to either. They were on his side. The lights of a passing car swept over the drawing of Mira as a girl, and then she was gone. He would have liked to know what she saw when she looked at herself these days and if she noticed the new tiny grains of deception that were popping up on her forehead like pimples. Anguish had thinned the skin under his own eyes, revealing his muscles at feverish work, as if he spent all day watching ants crisscross the room. His students looked at him like he was a corpse and he was about as animated as one. He knew someone should fire him, but no one was paying any attention. He had just turned forty, and he was less defined in all ways. If he were to turn on the lamp, he would catch himself in the act of aging, the skin loosening when he flexed his fingers, bagging where his joints recessed. Decay was speeding up now. It was only when he made a fist that youth came back.

An animal—an opossum, a dog, a coyote—rummaged in the blue recycling bin at the side of the house. Its paws tapped the ice in a rapacious code. Mira might run over the scavenger when she pulled into the driveway. She might feel the explosion under her front wheel and detect the life of something extinguished rising in the night air, but she wouldn't know anything until the morning when she saw the pulpy evidence on the snow. And then she might pause to think about how it was that she hadn't noticed. He moved into the other front room to sit in a deeper armchair. He was a man somewhere out of television's panorama of domestic life, part of a cast of characters, grinning politicians, tight-assed teachers, sexpot secretaries, class clowns, office dumbbells, greedy landlords, demented grannies. He was the sitcom, a sweatered Pops waiting for his child to come in, post-curfew—the son with beer on his breath, the daughter with her shirt buttoned up wrong. The light would go on with an unmistakable tsk, and his line, delivered with all the serenity of a saint would be, "Do you know what time it is?" By which he would really mean, "Do you have any fucking idea what it's like to sit here while you're out there? How could you have left me to get old and worried like this?" All those concerned, fuming fathers in their upholstered perches—wasn't the true story that they were just angry about their own captivity, their life slipping away?

He touched the brocade of the armchair, raised like burns,

and extracted a long hair from between the cushions. A few days earlier, a hair had floated down from nowhere when he'd been in the kitchen, and yesterday when he'd been looking in a back linen closet for—well, he couldn't recall now what he'd been looking for, except some part of Mira that led him to places he'd never explored before—a hair had fallen across his forearm. It had spooked him. He'd been slipping his hands between the piles of expertly folded, chilled sheets that hadn't been used in decades. He'd touched the ancient crumbling bars of Cashmere Bouquet soap someone had hoarded. There were pillowcases stitched with initials in such baroque script that he couldn't make out the letters. He'd found himself standing there when the copper filament of hair appeared. He'd gripped a pillowcase and pressed it to his mouth with the kind of whimper that belonged only to the cheated on, the abandoned, the betrayed, the lovelorn. All of which he was.

He heard Mira's car turn down the driveway and the engine roar before it went quiet. Owen pictured Mira and Wilton sitting in that stunned silence that always met you at the end of a long drive. What appeared in a flash before the headlights went off was the burgled carriage house with its dipping double doors, its clapboards picking up a more innocent white from the snow. What Owen wanted to hear was two car doors opening and closing. That brilliant moment of return. There was only one, though, and then the melancholy shuffle of Wilton making his way home on the ice. Soon, Wilton would catch his own reruns. Every night was a reunion for him.

From the window Owen watched Mira in the car staring ahead. He followed her as she got out and walked to the back door, then turned around and walked to the front. Owen froze in the hall by the stairs, his hand on the sculpted post. He backed up. Should he ambush her now like a thug or move back to his chair like the father? He was neither of those things. His heart flip-flopped. Her key slipped into the lock and she stepped into the darkness. He sat on the stairs.

Mira turned on the Merchanti lamp. No *tsk* but some fumbling and *shit*. She'd dropped her keys. He was feet from her and said her name.

Alarmed, she turned to see him. "O! What are you doing?"

His eyes stung. "Turn it off."

"But then I can't see anything."

"Turn off the light, Mira." His words were low and deliberate.

She did, and when she came to the stairs and raised her face to him, it appeared to be swimming out of the black, a body rising to the surface. She would go on acting as if she didn't feel his anger, and went into the front room, forcing him to follow. She plopped down in the armchair, which hissed under her.

"You were sitting here, weren't you," she said, patting the seat beneath her. "It's still warm. I can feel you. Nice."

"I've been waiting for you."

"I'm not late," she said, as if tardiness were the sole crime of the night. She evaded him expertly. "In fact, I'm earlier than I said I'd be. I was cleaning up the studio. It was a mess, but I'd had enough. I'm exhausted. And hungry. Is there any dinner?"

"No Joy to help you?"

"This is too weird, talking in the dark like this. I can't see you."

He didn't want her to see him. He wanted to press himself into her body but stayed away. "I know Joy doesn't work for you anymore," he said.

A car sighed in passing. "Right, because I told you."

"You don't tell me anything."

"I did tell you. She was stagnating at Brindle. I've been saying it for years, haven't I? I love her, but it was time for her to leave

and do something different. She should have *some* ambition. She
would have stayed forever if I hadn't made her go."

"She told me you laid her off because you couldn't pay her anymore."

"That's just not true. Can I go now?" she asked, but didn't move.

"She said you take Brindle's money to play the slot machines.
That you've taken it all, in fact. There's nothing left."

She let out a long, exasperated groan. "Please tell me she didn't
say that. What a totally shitty thing for her to do. She must be
incredibly angry at me." When she stood, he told her to sit.

"Is it true?" he asked.

"Jesus. Of course not."

"How can you do it?"

"Do what?"

"How can you look at me and lie like that?" He stood behind her
now, his hands tight on her shoulders. "Why is it so easy for you?"

"Look at you, O? I can't even see you."

"How do you do it?" He paced the room. His eyes throbbed,
his face was hot, his hands were cold. He picked up a round pa-
perweight from a table behind the couch. In the dark, it looked
black with a thousand air bubbles like stars glowing inside. It
had the satisfying heft of a strongman's baseball and he threw
it against the fireplace. A chip sparked off, but the thing didn't
break. It rolled, imperfect now, onto the rug. Mira didn't react, so
he picked up a bowl with a glaze like blue ice, another vain and
pointless object, and it exploded against the wall. He felt the deep
pleasure of destruction. When he pulled his arm back to throw a
vase, Mira was up and caught him by wrist.

"Don't," she hissed. "Don't you dare. That's enough. I get it."

Her small hand was nothing on him, and he broke her grasp.
"Why shouldn't I?" He threw the vase and it burst in a thousand

musical pieces. "I mean, what's the worst that can happen? I'll get in trouble? You'll become a fucking liar? An addict?"

"I don't know what you're doing, but please, O, just stop."

"I don't know what you're doing either. But I'm not nearly done. There's so much more, and this is so gratifying. A whole house to destroy." He stood over her and used his size against her. "What I'd like to do, Mira, is throw *you* against the wall."

"You're scaring me." Her shoulders drew in protectively.

"Too bad." He punted a porcelain dog he'd always hated. The house had never heard so much noise, including Mira's indignant and helpless cry for him to stop. "Go ahead, throw something, break something yourself," he screamed. "See how good it feels. Let's break everything so we can get out of this terrible house."

Mira huddled on the couch, her knees to her chin, her hands covering her face. For a while, Owen didn't move, and then he straddled her. His knees sunk into the soft cushions around her.

"Make love to me," she said, her face still hidden.

He didn't answer, or move, and felt her humiliation sinking under him. He wanted to shame and break her. Her smell was heartbreakingly familiar.

"Then get off me," she said, but he wouldn't. She struggled uselessly for only a second. He felt how weak she was against him.

"I've asked myself what's going on in your head when you look at me and lie to me. But that's the wrong question, because you don't see me at all. Is that how it feels to you? That I'm not even real? I don't want to do this anymore. You're killing me."

He could recount to her every untruth, every evasion, every assurance and mollifying gesture of goodwill, everything she'd kept from him, but what did it all come to?

"If you ever go again," he said, "I'll leave you. I swear I will."

He hadn't known he was going to say it. He hadn't even known it was a fully formed idea until it came out of his mouth. The most violent threat of all. He watched his words float like a bright spot after a flash, and he knew Mira, still trying to hide herself under him, was trying to follow his threat, see where it landed and what it was made of.

10

He passed the front desk of Extended Stay with his head down. He'd had enough of the staff welcoming their dogged guests with chocolate chip cookies in greasy brown paper sleeves, molten from hours under a 60-watt bulb. Since moving out of the house three days before, he'd eaten too many, and they'd begun to collect in his gut. There was a dispiriting burned-sugar smell in the lobby, partially masked by the disinfectant an employee applied to the furniture and door handles as if dejection were contagious. Owen couldn't tell the men on business from the men in marital limbo because they all had that same disoriented look. He had it, too, like someone who's discovered he's gotten off at the wrong exit and can only wait it out so he can turn around again. He was one of many who'd driven by Extended Stay a hundred times on benign domestic errands without ever imagining he'd be living here, slipping a plastic key into a lock that opened the door to his new home. Owen had seen only one woman in the place, a flash of heel and tapered ankle.

At night, he heard the highway running east and west behind the building. On one side of Extended Stay was Ocean Wave Dental Associates, and on the other was the mysterious American Arbitration Association. People entering either place looked scared. Over dinner at Tokyo Joe's, he told Mike Levi, his only friend it seemed, that Extended Stay was somewhere between root canal and a forced compromise. Both places left you feeling totally fucked with.

Mike took a sip of beer and again offered the converted bedroom in his basement that over the years had served as refuge from the marital frontlines for a number of people, including himself once or twice. Owen thanked him, but said the prospect of sleeping in someone's basement hideout was too depressing.

"Like that place isn't?" Mike said, pointing to Extended Stay. His fingers were greasy from dumplings. He'd thrown his brown tie over his shoulder like a leash.

"It's supposed to be depressing," Owen said. "But the worst thing would be to die there. The endless extended stay."

"Who's talking about dying? Lighten up, for Christ's sake. This is all going to blow over. Come on, eat something. You look terrible, by the way."

Owen's room on the first-floor rear had a midget kitchen with plates and silverware for three, a television parked in front of a stain-proof couch with cushions that were sewn to the frame. The arrangement suggested the smallest number of variations in human behavior. Eat, watch, sleep, shit, shower, shave, repeat. Maybe turn off the TV once in a while. He had to get out of there. Udon arrived like a wormy haystack stuck with pink shrimp and florid strips of imitation crab. Their waitress was a middle-aged black woman in a droopy kimono that revealed her white bra strap. A sound track played pinging, metallic music—aluminum pie plates left out in the rain.

He had left the house when Mira wasn't there—he didn't know where she was that Wednesday afternoon. It occurred to him as he sat in his car, his bag next to him like a sulking passenger, that you could measure your place in the world, you could see who you were by where you could go when trouble made you leave. Who would make the pullout couch for you, who would blow up the air mattress, who would say, "Stay as long as you need to" and "Help yourself to whatever is here"? A little while ago it would have been Wilton, but not now. He wanted to kill the man. Refuge wasn't possible with any of his colleagues at school, or the men he swam with, or even his father, now ensconced in bayside heaven. And it wasn't really possible with Mike either, despite his offer of the basement. The fact that, at forty, he had nowhere to go was sobering news of his own making. He regretted it. Mira had called and asked him to come home. He waited for her confession about Brindle, but none had come.

Mike looked up from his plate. "You having an affair? Who are you fucking?"

Owen laughed. "No one. No affair, no fucking. Sorry to disappoint."

"Then Mira—who's she fucking?" Mike clicked his chopsticks together. "No one? So, what then? What's the problem that's so big that you move out?"

Owen's intention from the beginning of the evening was to tell Mike about Mira. But disgrace was the smell of tempura in old oil, of cigarette smoke lingering just outside the entrance. It made him queasy. His wife was in deep shit and he had failed to save her. How was that for a confession? He sat back against the booth.

"Mira's a compulsive gambler," he said. "An addict."

"Come on. You sure?" Mike dabbed his mouth, an uncharacteristically delicate gesture that spoke of his alarm. "No shit?"

"No shit. I swear."

"Okay, okay. So what does a person do about that?" He was ready to fix this. Everything could be solved. "You get her into some program, some rehab thing, right?"

"What does a person do? First a person begs and pleads and offers help and then a person moves out, because what else can he do? He loves her, but a person's wife, it turns out, is someone he doesn't know very well."

"Well, Christ, whose wife is?" Mike clicked his chopsticks again and looked across the highway at the Extended Stay, lit up in the cold dark.

There was chair tilting, snoozing, and pencil chewing during last period. Owen read to his class long after he should have put the book down and had them working on their vocabulary lists. He took stock of their faces, but he couldn't always tell who was listening and who wasn't. His work in this room had contracted into a nut he could roll around in his mouth but not bite into. He looked at the ones who squinted, who needed glasses but couldn't afford them. The radiators hissed. He put down the book and tried to lift a window. This and his groaning was a ritual by now that made the kids laugh.

"One day I'm going to get this thing open," he told them. "You'll see." When they tear the place down in the spring, he thought, and I can walk over the remains and smash them with my feet. When I'm either back with Mira—or not. He gave up and opened the classroom door. The air in the hall was cooler and silver gum wrappers eddied in a breeze near the stairwell.

"Hey, mister." Jacqui's voice bounced down the hall. The tongues of her white high-tops flapped as she carried a baby, a flurry of pink in a car seat. "You want to see my baby, Crystal?"

He stuck his head in his classroom and told the kids to read to themselves. He shut the door behind him. "Of course I do. Very much."

"You don't want nobody to see me?" she challenged. Her clothes were too small, the blue denim pulled a taut white across her thighs. He wasn't sure how she could breathe with her waistband cutting into her like that. She could be twelve or twenty with the lip gloss and the snap in her voice.

"They're reading," he said. "But how are you, Jacqui?"

She looked at the classroom door. "So what's the book about?"

He told her it was about a single mother sent to bed with cancer while her son learned to fend for himself and his younger sister. What was it with these idiotic books and their endless pairing of tragedy and optimism? Were they somehow supposed to be inspiring? He crouched by the baby and its glorious, squished face. Her lips mouthed the words of sleep. He touched the indent of her knuckles, and the smooth plain of her forehead, the sea-washed black hair in a flat whorl.

He thought about how little he knew about Jacqui, who'd done this astonishing thing, having a baby, or any other of his students who opened for him only the narrowest view onto themselves. He wanted to know how they saw themselves in the world. Jacqui had been looking in the classroom and turned to Owen, who was still crouching. A comb had been plowed through her glossy hair and left perfect furrows. Having a baby hadn't changed the skeptical, feisty line of her mouth, and some acknowledgment passed between them that for all the difference in their ages and stations, she had something he didn't have, she'd experienced something he hadn't.

"She's beautiful," he said, and stood.

"I know. They won't let me bring her here, though. So that's why I got to go to a different school. But I wanted you to see her, so I came." She picked something off her sleeve, a woman's weary gesture, a dismissal of men. "I was a good student, right? I was good in your class?"

"I liked having you in my class. You always had something in-teresting to say. You're a smart girl." A smart woman? A stupid girl? What the hell have you done?

She clamped her hands on her hips. "Then why didn't you get me a card or a present or something?"

Should he have delivered pink carnations and Mylar balloons? Mira would have said yes, that's exactly what he should have done; this is Jacqui's life, not yours, and it has nothing to do with how you feel and nothing to do with the scenario you've imagined for her.

"I should have. I'm sorry. I have to get back in," he said, his hand already on the door.

"Yeah, you should have." Hurt became accusation. Her head jutted at him in pursuit. "You don't have nothing more to say?"

"I'm glad you came by." He gave her a chilled smile.

"Right."

Jacqui picked up the car seat and it banged against her leg as she made her way down the hall. Back in the classroom, he looked out onto the street and saw a dusty gold minivan idling in front of the school. Jacqui's mother was at the wheel and she flicked her cigarette onto the ice. The kids, unusually quiet for the mo-ment, watched him. He told them to take out pens and paper and shut their books. Those who hadn't already done so slapped them closed for maximum bang. There was rustling and griping, things dropping on the floor, pens that suddenly didn't work. If you were in a classroom long enough, you'd begin to see how entire chunks of time were thrown away.

"I want you to describe yourselves twenty years from now," he said. "What you'll be like and where you'll be and what you'll be doing." He sat on the edge of his desk. He wanted to know that they'd be okay in the future. He knew not all of them would be.

"How are we supposed to know?" Lily asked.

"You don't know," he said. "You have to imagine, look ahead."

"So it's not true?"

He smiled. "I don't know. It might be true. It might not. You'll have to wait and see."

Hadn't he, at their age, always tried to imagine his future?

A few puzzled faces looked at the ceiling, while others had already started writing. The more they cared about what they were doing, the tighter they drew in an arm to protect their work. What he had in mind was for them to envision something beyond this afternoon. He would read their sentences later in his room at Extended Stay, and he'd try to get some measure of the distance between what they said they'd have—because it was always, in part, about *having*—who they said they'd be, and who they were now. In the past what his students wrote was sometimes confessional, sometimes fantastical, and there were times when he hadn't been able to tell the difference. Many of their stories had shocked him with their lists of tragedies, but the sunny stories had shocked him equally with their optimism. Marcel looked up and gave him a charming smile. He was a smart and resolute kid, perplexed by his rowdier classmates. Next to him, Oscar, back from a day of suspension for fighting, hung over his paper with his head on a fist. Owen bent down next to him. His paper was blank except for the words "I want."

"You want what?" Owen asked.

Oscar's shoulders lifted. "I don't know."

If you lacked everything, what did you want most? The boy didn't pick up his pencil again. *I want.* Did that say everything? In ten minutes, the bell would ring and the kids would explode out of the building. It was a long time for the kid to stare at *I want* and not be able to go any further.

Owen returned to his desk. It was ancient, heavy wood, scarred and stained and burned in spots from the days of classroom smoking. Teachers who'd once sat at this desk had left their marks in the drawers, talismans, souvenirs, things taken from kids and never returned: a butter knife, pepper spray, a flip book of a woman undressing. Owen didn't know what he would leave at the end of the year. When he looked at the kids, he felt like he was by the pond on a breezeless day, trying to detect the unseen forces that touched the surface and made the water ripple and tap the shore.

He sat in the Bright opposite Anya's apartment. It was just after five o'clock, and he hoped to catch her coming back from class. He wanted to say something about the kiss, but he wasn't sure exactly what. Across the street, a man sold fish from the back of his pickup. This was the same guy he'd bought fish from years before when he'd lived in Fox Point. Glistening, black-eyed fish, on the cheap side, smelts lined up like slices of greased metal on beds of ice. Owen had scribbled down a recipe the man had recited for him. It was the first dinner he'd made for Mira in her kitchen. She'd been fascinated by the way the bones pulverized between her teeth.

At the front counter of the Bright, a woman whose dark bangs shaded her forehead stumbled on a corner of the threadbare rug and tipped her mug of coffee. She yelped and spun her hand around like she was trying to unscrew it from her wrist. Owen jumped up with some napkins. She thanked him, and then sat at the table farthest from him where she took a textbook from her bag and began marking it with a highlighter. The place was scattered with people like her, students of something, hybrids, transplants, gentrifiers who might live in the neighborhood but clearly weren't from it. No native would enter the place, with its bad neon art for sale, its gluten-free brownies. Even the name wasn't right. He knew what it was like to be in Fox Point, but not of it. When he'd lived there, the neighborhood had been comfortingly cool to him, as though it already knew he wouldn't be staying long. It had been indifferent to his despair, its pride and dark dealings undeterred. It was still that way.

He took his father's book from his bag. On the cover was a photograph of the ocean during a snow squall, and he recognized the tiny speck to the left as the shingled, porched house that was on the highest bluff above the sea in Truro. One winter, the ocean had surged over the dunes during a storm and wiped out the road leading to the house. It had also buried the parking lot that teemed with cars jockeying for spaces in the summer. The next day, his father had taken him out—to see the earth changing, he'd said. They'd hiked up through the cold sand to the porch so they could look back and measure just how far the storm had pushed the land. The dunes slid into the marsh. Owen was more interested in peering through the seams left between the glass and the plywood of the boarded-up windows. Inside, there was a single chrome chair in the middle of a room. Owen knew he'd seen something he wasn't going to forget. "Look," his father had urged him, pointing to the road, "it's going to be a major job to clear all this." A new landscape would emerge. But inside was the story of a life—whose chair, whose marooned house? Every inch and detail had been someone's intention. Now Owen realized that this was what the empty rooms in Wilton's house had first reminded him of, the inability to ever know all the facts that make up a person's history. Mira's rooms were crowded, and still she was unknown to him.

Outside, a few shivering teenagers loitered in the well-lit playground. A skittish man, fists jammed in the pockets of an army jacket, came inside. This was the man from Brindle's party, the same man who'd stolen the clay dog. Persecution thickened his gaze, and Owen could see that he carried an ancient, wordless grudge. The woman who'd spilled her coffee glanced at him. It must have been the flash of her purple scarf or her cherry-red glasses that made the guy veer toward her.

"Do you mind?" she said. "Moving back a bit, giving me a little space?"

"I'm not doing anything." The man sounded like a pissed-off kid and took a step closer.

"Just move back. A few feet. That's all I'm asking." She returned to her book, but her knees bounced under the table.

People glanced up and then down again, ever curious, but never really moved these days. The man flexed his hands in his pockets. Owen pushed back his chair. He felt none of his old reluctance. He liked the fact of his height.

"Maybe you should just leave," he said.

The man was instantly acquiescent, no fight to him at all, which made Owen an instant bully. He put his hands up and backed up. "I'm going," he said. "Calm down, big guy." He gave Owen the finger. "Cocksucker."

The bells on the door barely spoke when he closed it behind him. A couple of people shook their heads and went back to what they'd been doing. Out on the sidewalk, the man drifted across the street where the teenagers cut him a bored glance. Owen turned back to the room, but no one would look at him. The girl behind the counter scowled.

"You didn't have to do that," the woman with the purple scarf said. "He's a pain, but he's harmless. He would have moved in a minute. I think you kind of have a problem."

"What's that?"

"Forget it."

"No, I'd like to hear it." Was he going to bully everyone now?

She took off her glasses. Lines appeared at the corners of her eyes. She was older than he'd imagined. "You're one of those self-appointed defender types. Look, someone would have bought him a cup of coffee eventually, and he would have left. That's how it works here. He's a regular, and who are you? I mean, have you ever even been in here before you lay down the law and act like an asshole?"

"You looked like you needed help."

"But I didn't."

Owen had confirmed for her and for everyone else in the place what they'd suspected about him from the minute he walked in: that all big men are aggressive dogs straining at the leash. When he looked outside again, the man in the army jacket was on the corner talking to someone in a buttery suede coat, long hair whipped up by the wind. It was Wilton who fished some bills out of his pocket and handed them over. Wilton's approach to the door was as theatrical as the other guy's departure, and the bells played a cascade of sound. He surveyed the place long enough for a few people to acknowledge him. Wilton was a regular, it appeared.

"This is a surprise." He gave Owen's shoulder a squeeze. "May I sit with you? I'll be right back."

On his way to the counter, Wilton said something to the woman with the purple scarf and she glanced at Owen. Wilton nodded. At the counter, he leaned on the glass display case and rested his chin boyishly in the web of his fingers as he flirted. He came back with a cup of coffee and pulled out a chair, angling himself in order to get a view of the street—and Anya's apartment. "Now, tell me why you're here."

"Why are you here?"

"Ah." Wilton sipped his coffee. "Sometimes I wait for Anya at this hour. If she wants to see me, she comes in. If not, she pretends she hasn't seen me. No more dates, no excuses or standing me up. None of her waffling. I'm done with that. Even a masochist has his limits. That's one of Anya's classmates over there, by the way." He motioned at the woman with the scarf. "She thinks you're a menace. I told her you were a pussycat." He laid both hands flat on the table, and his expression turned to concern. "How have you been? We haven't talked in a while."

As a kid, Owen had been tossed around by the strongest ocean waves, and for those moments underwater he couldn't tell which way was up. That was the sensation he had now, caught in some dangerous tumble with this man.

"How the hell do you think I've been?" he said.

Wilton sat back. "Well, yes, Mira told me that you'd left. I'm very sorry to hear that. You love each other very much, that's clear. I know you'll work out whatever it is."

"Whatever it is? You know exactly what it is."

Wilton pressed his hand to his mouth, one of Mira's gestures, and shook his head, but his attention was drawn to a car that pulled up across the street under an oily column of light. A young guy got out and stood on the sidewalk while his passenger hauled something from the backseat. There was Anya's bumblebee hat bobbing above the roof of the car. Her friend was talking, clearly urging her in some way, and she kissed him on the mouth to quiet him.

"That's the son of a bitch who's sleeping with my daughter," Wilton said. He wasn't thinking about Mira at all, and maybe never had been. She'd been a diversion—they both had been—while Anya was the real thing.

Anya ran across the street and into the Bright, spotted her

friend and waved, and then turned as if someone had whispered behind her to pay attention. Distress crossed her face. She pulled at her earlobe. Her eyes met neither man's, but lingered instead on the space between them before she turned and left. Wilton gave Owen a cool, competitive look.

"Now we'll never know which one of us my daughter doesn't want to see anymore," he said and got up to leave.

Owen shuffled. He was late to his first class, having once again mistimed his waking, his showering, his Monday morning commute from Extended Stay, but in no real hurry either. What kind of trouble could he get in anyway? At the far end of the lockers, Mrs. Tevas was taping up a poster that said: *Reading Is Traveling Without Ever Having to Leave.* The words floated above something that looked like Emerald City.

"But don't you think leaving is a good thing sometimes?" he asked, holding up a corner for her.

She glanced at him, patient but not particularly playful. She took in his wrinkled shirt, the crumbs from the donut he'd gobbled in the car. "I hear you need a place to stay for a while."

If he passed her desk in the library at certain times, her eyes looked gold. Now they were dark and exacting, and she was the holder of information about him that she showed no discomfort in having. Information, gossip—an entitled and potent Rhode Island mix that flowed from certain taps. Mike obviously had told his friend, the principal, who'd told her friend Rosalie Tevas.

"That's true—for a while, nothing permanent."

"You hope," she said.

"Yes. I hope."

She finished taping up the poster and swung the roll of tape around her finger. She knew of a furnished apartment, top floor of a house in Fox Point he might be interested in. "Nothing permanent," she stressed again.

After school, Owen went to the Ives Street address. Mrs. Tevas answered the door. She hadn't told him this was her house. She'd changed out of her work clothes into a purple warm-up suit. He felt as if he were seeing something he wasn't supposed to see. Without her heels, she was even shorter, which only made her more commanding. He remembered how he'd seen her fiercely confront a student who'd threatened her. She'd pushed the kid up against the wall, grabbed the neck of his shirt, stuck her face in his. Her husband, George, passed behind her and gave Owen a cursory look. As she opened the door to the apartment upstairs, the late winter gray fell into the concern on her face. The furniture belonged to her son, she explained, as did everything else in the three rooms. The poster of the World Series–winning Red Sox. The URI beer mugs on the bookshelf, the cacti in tiny pots. This was his place, spotless, with the caustic odor of Ajax in the air. Even the old chenille bedspread with little white balls was perfectly even.

"He's a Marine, in Iraq," Rosalie said, hesitant to step into the room. "He could come back any time, and then you'd have to—"

"Decamp. I understand," Owen said. George paced around the floor below. "It's temporary." The word was hopeful for everyone. Everyone would go home. He was six houses down from the Bright and could see a corner of Anya's apartment.

"I used to live in this neighborhood, around the block actually, when I first came to Providence." He wanted to tell her more, but she was snapping her nails. His story wouldn't mean anything, and now she knew enough.

"Everything you need is here," she explained. "No smoking. No dog."

"Nope, no dog."

"Or cat. George and I are right below, so no—" She paused and absently touched the door lock. "No loud noise."

They nodded at each other, an exchange between people who didn't know each other at all but were now going to be living very closely. She would take only very little money from him. After all, she said, she knew what he made.

"I'm very grateful for this," he said. "My wife and I—"

"Fine." She put up her hands; she didn't want to know his problems. Her clock and calendar were set to her son. "If you could keep it neat. George comes up and cleans, vacuums, dusts. Waters those things. He might still want to do that."

"He doesn't have to. I'll keep it clean."

"He might do it anyway." There was no doubt that this was exactly what George was going to do. Owen suspected that the man did not want him in the apartment at all.

Later that night, after he'd brought his things over from Extended Stay, he watched the cars slide by on Route 195, and beyond, the gas tanks banked on the edge of the bay with their crowns of red stars. He wanted to remember what he'd felt years before looking at practically the same view. It was possible he'd felt nothing then—or so much the same thing as he did now that it was undetectable. In bed, he sensed the imprint of Rosalie's son on the mattress. Owen was a body double, a place-holder. His beating heart was someone's good luck, and he was glad for that. The street sounds were familiar still—wisps of Portuguese, little kids up too late—life unlike the aristocratic, chilly hush of Whittier Street. He'd stopped thinking of Mira for a few minutes. And then there she wasn't, not in the bed with him, not standing at the foot of it in one of her engaging insomniac wanders. Not telling him on the phone she wanted him to come back. It was, for a second, as though he'd never met her, he was back here starting all over again, and only dreamed that he might someday be with her.

Weeks before he'd left, he'd told Mira that he'd go to Ellie Cotton's memorial service with her, and last night she'd called to ask if he would still come. She was hoarse and she didn't want to talk. Ten days had passed since he'd moved out, and the house was alien territory already. He paused at the front door. The UPS truck pulled up in front of Wilton's and cut the engine. The usual driver emerged with a stack of boxes, which he placed on the porch, but this time he dropped them and rushed away as if he didn't want to have to talk to Wilton. The thuds of Saturday's delivered booty drew Wilton out. At one in the afternoon, he was in his dingy white bathrobe, his face in its private sag.

Owen didn't want to be spotted by him. And not in a jacket and tie like he was some sort of suitor. He let himself in. The house was stuffy. There were two plates on the table painted with dinner's red and green remains, two wineglasses. Mira's napkin, always in a tight ball, was under a plate rim. Morning hadn't happened in the house yet—no coffee cup, no newspaper, no keys tossed on the counter to show that Mira had been in and out. A vague sense of dread followed him upstairs. Already the smell of heating dust rising from the carpets was part of a memory. He was revisiting, not visiting. There was a time I lived in this house, he said to himself. Mira was still asleep. She'd thrown off her nightgown and the blankets, and her body was huddled in a punishing chill, her hands stuck between her thighs. Blue veins ventured across her skin.

He sat on the edge of the bed. His fingers hovered above her shoulder. He traced the spiral of her ear. When he said her name,

Mira didn't wake up so much as emerge from something dense and sticky. Was she hungover? She rolled onto her back and pulled the blanket up. Its tattered satin edge rested on her upper lip. He wasn't prepared for how he felt seeing her for the first time—breathless, light-headed, willing to give up everything to come back.

"Hey," she said.

He couldn't bear to look at her any longer—or have her look at him. "We don't have to go to this thing. The woman's been dead for months, so it's not like she's going to notice. You never even liked her."

"I have to go." Mira sat up. The skin on her arms looked too white. "I want to see her house without her in it. See what that's like. You don't have to come."

"I told you I would."

"But that was before." She put on her robe.

"I'm here now. And I have a nice tie on. That doesn't happen very often."

"I hate this, you know," she said, as she went into the bathroom and turned on the shower.

Owen waited downstairs in his study. Forgotten student papers were still on the desk. He'd give them all 100s at this point. He searched again for his squid pen, wriggling his fingers around the shallow back of the drawer, but didn't find it. Mira came downstairs wearing a shapeless black dress and black boots. Her face was splotchy, as though she'd scrubbed it. She hoped she looked appropriately funereal even if she wasn't at all mournful for Ellie Cotton, her father's lover. She swiped on some deep red lipstick, and they walked silently to Power Street.

The dead woman's living room was packed with people who'd taken on the hush of a memorial service. The correct stance was a gaze averted from everything, a two-handed hold on the caterer's gold-rimmed coffee cup, a shaking of the head when there was nothing left to say, the pinch of a triangle of sandwich. Mira, a pro at these things, had gone to funerals and wakes with her parents when she was a kid, while life on the pond with his father didn't include traveling anywhere for any death. If you lived far enough away from everyone, then you never had to attend a funeral, his father said, as a selling point for solitude. Or stand mute at a sick bed, or smile at a wedding, or clap at a retirement party.

Last year, Owen had gone with Mira to a service for a friend of her mother's, at the Slavin Memorial Chapel, which sat on the corner across from the Y. They'd lingered on the walk bordered with leggy impatiens that, like the line of aging patriarchs in their fine clothes still smelling of mothballs, held on even in November when their stalks were thin and translucent. Owen had been immensely moved by the gathering and the solemnity of the morning. His father had been wrong to cut himself off from this part of life.

For some in the room now, conjuring up the appropriate mood wasn't so easy though; there was plenty of other people's current grief and troubles to go on about, and plenty of happiness, too. Pictures of grandchildren were slipped into hands like drugs. Good news was whispered—a condo in Florida, a show at the Art Club—while the bad news was said out loud. Cancer. A daughter's divorce. Mira joined a circle of women. Jim Peabody, a stiff who had been a close friend of Mira's father, approached Owen. He leaned in when he said that Ellie and Thrasher had particularly liked the lunch hour—"if you know what I mean." He winked at Owen.

"No, what do you mean?" Owen asked, though he knew exactly what the man was saying.

"Screwing," he whispered, and made a poking motion with his finger.

Owen was struck by how Peabody, who was now examining the tip of his striped tie, assumed Owen knew about the affair. It was likely everyone in the room did. It gave Owen some sense of what Mira's father must have been like: suspiciously well-shaven like all the men here, a bastard, a boaster, careless with people, entitled. Owen watched a woman stroke Mira's cheek. It was the gesture everyone always made at the motherless child, for luck maybe, or for their own consolation. Another woman touched Mira's hair. It had never occurred to Owen that she needed and liked this attention, and that their past was hers, too. That her mother might be part of them still if she were alive. If the women thought she looked particularly sad as she leaned into their comfort, they couldn't imagine the nature of her own private distress.

When the circle dispersed, Mira came over to the bench where he was perched on the silk cushion. "You saw the coven?" she asked. She took a sip of his coffee. "I spent a lot of time in this house when I was a kid because Ellie and my mother were best friends. I used to play with the twins. That's what everyone called Mack and Conrad—the twins." She nodded toward Ellie's two grown sons in dark suits who stood just inside the front door, ready to greet people but more eager to get them out. They were clearly impatient with a woman who kept thinking of one more thing to say to them about their mother.

"They're putting the house on the market next week," Mira said. "If you grow up in Rhode Island, you either can't wait to get out or you can't imagine living anywhere else. There's no in-between. Too bad they couldn't have combined events today: memorial and open house. Saved on the refreshments."

"They could call it 'You say good-bye, and I say, how much?'"

"Maybe I should have left, too, O, gone somewhere else. I skipped that step. I was always here. I still am here. Do you realize that I haven't seen anything in my life?"

"We could go somewhere else," he said. "Anywhere. We don't have to stay."

His words floated right by her. "Did I ever tell you that after my parents died, Ellie asked me to come live here with her? Can you believe it? That's guilt for you. People think they can just erase it, but it sticks around forever." She paused. "You wanted to leave the pond, didn't you? You didn't want to stay there forever."

"I remember being seven or eight—very young—and out on the water on my raft," he said, "and thinking I would leave someday. But kids—they're supposed to think they're going to live with their parents forever. They don't see the end of anything, not even the day at bedtime. It's too terrifying. Did you hear what I said before, Mira? We could go anywhere. We could live on the pond." The idea gripped him. He saw her standing at the head of the arbor, the water behind her. It thrilled him.

All the reasons he'd wanted to leave the pond—its pewter winter broken only by cawing; its flash of summer, which brought more enviable lives—had become all the reasons he'd take Mira back there with him now. He didn't know how it would work, but he could keep her safe there.

Mira's tear fell onto her boots. "It's crazy," she whispered. "People think I'm crying for Ellie, but I'm not. She was such a bitch."

"Then why are you crying?"

"For us. But more for you now, such a lonely, motherless kid. I want to take care of that boy. I wish I could take care of that little boy. I'm crying for him. That I didn't know him. That I can't know him now."

The air had disappeared around her. Owen turned her away from the curious crowd. He got their coats and pulled Mira through the kitchen, where platters of food rested on cheery red counters, and out into the backyard to avoid the lugubrious twins at the front door. Mira, still crying, stopped to look at the birdbath erupting with winter's detritus. On Power Street, at the high point of the hill, they looked over the city and at the new construction that spread across the horizon. Mira, red-eyed, pointed out what had changed in the last decade. He knew he could live here for the rest of his life and still never feel this was his, not in the way she did. They started down the hill to Brindle; she wanted to show him something. On the slick cobblestones just before Benefit Street, she slipped and took his arm. The aristocratic John Brown house looked down at them.

"Ellie's heart killed her," Mira said, as though they'd been talking about the woman the entire time. "Fitting for her because she had a ticker like a cunt—wrinkled and greedy."

Owen laughed. "I'm sure the twins would have appreciated hearing that about their mother."

"They should put it on her headstone. 'Here lies a greedy cunt.' Do you think they know I saw their mother with her legs spread and my father between them?" She stopped. "Do you know how my mother finally found out about Ellie? We had a fight and I told her. It was the meanest thing I could think to do, so I did it. I wanted to hurt her so she'd fight back. But she wouldn't. Ever. I hated that about her. I had no respect for it. She could be so passive." They crossed South Main Street and made their way down to the river.

"She claimed she already knew," Mira went on. "Maybe she knew about other women my father had fucked over the years, but not Ellie, who was her friend. She was trying so hard not to

be humiliated. And I was trying so hard to shame her. I even in-
cluded the lovely detail of oral sex. It was my father I should have
been angry at, but I was angriest at her. She was living with a liar
and a cheater and she didn't do anything about it. I could see how
my father hated her for it."

Squares of ice floated by, like discarded pizza boxes. Owen
imagined Mira's parents slinking in and out of overstuffed rooms,
dragging their resentment with them. It seemed to him that he
and Mira had been colonized by their ghosts, and now they were
also playing out the single story the house allowed.

"You know what my mother and I had been fighting about? I
wanted to live in a dorm my senior year. I wanted to get out so
badly, and my mother didn't want me to go. I think she didn't
want to be left alone with my father. So I tried to make her hate
me. I told my mother about Ellie two days before she died." She
ran her gloved hands along the railing. "You're going to think I'm
melodramatic, O, but I know that's why they had the accident. My
mother had been walking around the house like a zombie, leaving
a trail of used Kleenex everywhere. She'd go into the bathroom
and run the water so no one could hear her wail. She'd go up to
the third floor into the closet. But of course we could hear her.
You know how the sound runs up and down the pipes—you can
hear everything. My father pretended that nothing was wrong. He
swiveled in his desk chair. He talked on the phone. There was a
party they'd been invited to. My mother didn't want to go because
she was too upset and her face was wrecked, but my father said
that people would talk if she didn't show up.

"He blamed me for having said something to her in the first
place. I'd made all this mess. He'd confessed nothing to her and
then played on the fact that she cared way too much about what
other people thought of her. So she went to the party. She had

me clasp her necklace for her, which I think was something of a truce. This was the first time we'd touched or said anything to each other in days. And then there was the accident that night on their way home." She put her fingers together as though she were still struggling with the clasp of the necklace, trying to make the last connection.

"Anything could have happened. Who knows? Maybe a deer on the road or your father had too much to drink." He wanted to envelop her, protect her from pain. "You didn't make it happen, Mira."

"I'm not going to change my mind, O. This is something I just know. I could have kept Ellie a secret, but I didn't. It could have gone differently, but I wouldn't let it. I can't change that."

"Why didn't you ever tell me this before?"

"Would you have loved me if you'd known?"

She charged ahead to the pigeoned underpass at the bottom of Wickenden Street. She didn't stop on the bridge, but hurried to Brindle. It was only at the door that she hesitated. From the way she looked left and right, it was possible that she might change her mind and not go in at all. She picked up some trash and scraped a cigarette butt into the gutter with her foot. Owen sat on the granite steps out of the wind. Cold rose up his spine.

She unlocked Brindle's door—if she didn't do it now, she said, she might never do it at all. Owen felt like he was being taken to identify a body. He was afraid of what he might see. There was grit under his shoes, and no echoes of activity. The air was chilled and pulseless. He followed Mira to her office. Out in the icy back parking lot, the Dumpster overflowed. Other people were dumping their garbage there now, she told him. She hadn't paid the hauling bill—because she couldn't.

"I want to tell you something," she said. "Brindle has no more money. None at all. It's done."

The wind inflated a trio of plastic bags caught on the fencing as he waited for her to say more. Traffic moved by the river at Sunday's desultory pace, and she was silent, staring at the garbage. He went up to the studio where stools were pushed in a corner, easels tipped. On the shelves, corpses of clay lay under white sheets. The faucet he'd fixed once dripped and dripped. He took the last stairs to the roof and sat on the bench with his back against the bulkhead. In a few minutes, Mira appeared. She didn't go to the edge to look down or out but instead sat next to him.

"I lost all the money," she said, finally. She could have been speaking to the clouds tumbling in or the finch tiptoeing on the ledge, for how airy her voice was. "Everything Wilton gave Brindle—almost seventy thousand dollars—and then what was left in the account." She paused, and forced her eyes to widen. "But I can get it back. I know I can."

"Do you hear yourself? 'If I can win this one, everything will be okay. I'm close, I know it's going to happen. Just one more chance.' It's not going to happen, Mira. It's done. It's over. You lost."

"I'm going to lose Brindle."

"So you lose it."

"Look what I've done, O. Look what I've ruined." Her voice rose. He could hear how tight her throat was. She leaned back against the bulkhead and closed her eyes. She was breaking down. "Oh, my kids! Those poor, poor kids. What have I done?"

"Not you," he insisted. He saw it clearly now. "It's what Wilton's done."

She shook her head and then covered her face with her hands. "No, he didn't do anything. I did it. All me."

"But he holds out more and more money to you, and he knows you won't refuse it because you can't."

"That's crazy."

"Brindle is your baby, and you've lost it, Mira. And when Wilton couldn't get Anya, he took you instead. He bought you. Do you see that? Everything was fine before Wilton."

"Everything wasn't fine."

"It was. This is his fault."

"No, I couldn't breathe, O. I was suffocating."

She stood and went to the edge, taking in everything in front of her. Her history was laid over the grid of these streets and the seven hills of Providence. Maybe she couldn't see farther than that, or take a deep enough breath. Maybe he'd held on to her too tightly, but what else could he have done? She didn't turn or call after him as he left the roof. He made sure that the front door locked behind him so that if he changed his mind about what he was about to do, he wouldn't be able to get back in. He didn't know how long she would stay up there, but he didn't have to worry. He knew she wasn't interested anymore in how far she could lean over without falling. She'd done that already—and she'd fallen as far as she could go.

The air inside the carriage house was brittle from the long, absolute winter, and the cold smothered the sounds of a diminishing Sunday afternoon. Between the rug's heavy folds clotted with dead leaves and insects was the gun in its swaddling. The metal was warm, all hard lines and black shine, but still strangely feminine. Owen knew its odor, a whiff of a different life. The idea that he would point a gun at Wilton was absurd, but he saw that violence was what he'd been inching toward. The possibility had been growing in him for a while. But to even pick the thing up would be to play a part in a bad movie, to be the man who shot the thief in his house, to be not himself, to give up everything of himself. Violence was something alien and not his, but here he was, his fingers on the metal, electrified and sick to his stomach.

Mira said things hadn't been fine before, and that she couldn't breathe. To hear this was a cold shock, and Owen pulled his hand back from the rug and sat on the cold floor. Thoughts smashed around in his head as he wondered if Mira was still on Brindle's roof looking down and thinking what to do next, and maybe how to save herself. He recalled how Caroline's mother, in the city to clean out her dead daughter's things, had asked Owen if there hadn't been something he could have done to save her child. The question had stunned him, but he knew what she was asking: Wasn't there some way he could have spared Caroline and gotten himself killed instead? He didn't answer her, though the answer was yes, there was always something different you could have done from the moment you woke up that morning. She'd come to do the sad job on a thinly lit May day, and he was woozy with the idea that the people he saw out on the street in the pale sun would trade his life for the life of the one they loved, that if someone had to die, they would choose him. Caroline's parents wouldn't hesitate to chose him over their daughter. It was nothing personal. Save the one you love.

He stayed in the carriage house until he was shivering and his mind had settled, and then he let himself into Wilton's house with the key under the mat. He yelled for Wilton, instantly hoarse, as if he'd been calling for hours. After a few minutes, Wilton, in his sorry-looking bathrobe, took aged, limping steps down the stairs, his hand clutching the banister. His drawn face was puffy and his cheeks were tracked with creases.

"Oh, Owen." He pushed his hair back. Clearly, he'd been asleep. "Was my door open?"

Owen held up the key. "I told you it was a bad idea to leave this under the mat. Someone could walk right in."

"I know, you're right. I never learn. I'm impossible that way." In his chatter, Wilton struggled to be alert and gauge the mood of the visit. "I was just napping. But I see I've missed most of the day. Was it a nice one?"

"Not particularly," Owen said. Wilton's belt was loosely tied, the robe open above a V of pale bony chest. Below, his prick parted the material like an actor peering out from between the stage curtains. "Tie yourself up. No one wants to see that."

Wilton looked down at himself. "Sad, but true. Maybe I'll just get dressed, but it's so late now, maybe I won't even bother. Is it coffee time or drink time?"

"Drink."

Wilton went to the kitchen and spoke with his back turned. "I've been so tired lately. Hence the napping. My body's natural rhythms are off."

"That's called being unemployed," Owen said. "Hence the napping."

"I'll admit it. I have become something of a bum."

Wilton had grown old since he'd moved to Providence almost a year earlier. Owen pictured the way Wilton had popped up off the couch, agelessly wrinkle-free and on the ball, after that long, boozy first night they'd met. Disappointment was eroding him. He left the lights off, as though to hide the damage.

"You look a little tense," he told Owen. "Everything okay?"

"I'll take a drink."

"Right. Coming up." Wilton sifted through the bottles of wine, looking for the right one.

Owen wasn't sure what he was waiting for. He had not intended to play Wilton, but he found that some of his resolve had retreated and that already he was mourning the loss of his friend. But Wilton had always been more the idea of a friend than the actual thing itself. The kitchen was crowded with more new appliances still in their packaging. There were unopened boxes, a woman's wool winter coat with the tags still on, shrouded in plastic. The bounty was like wedding gifts for a couple who'd already split up. Two carafes of olive oil, wrapped to their waists in bubble paper like topless contestants, sat on the counter. Wilton noticed what Owen was looking at and quickly held a carafe out to him.

"This is for you," he said. "Actually, they both are. Made by monks in Italy, so virginal in every way. What do I need olive oil for? You're the cooks. I can't even boil water, as you know."

Wilton's ability to detect the undertones in a situation was still not at full force, and he was flailing some, evading Owen's eye. He always tested the atmosphere before he said too much, and in that way he pulled secrets out of you, let you speak first, let you tell all. But there was no solid self there in the shadowy kitchen, only one that responded. Wilton's bones and blood were made of other people's stories, and the weak spots in them were his incitements. His ability to change and shift had nothing to do with the fact that he'd been an actor; he was a man without a self. It was hard for Owen to say he knew him at all, but easy to say he'd been duped.

He smacked the bottle out of Wilton's hand, and it rolled under the table, intact. The gesture had been effortless, and already made him feel not less than himself but more of someone else. His body thrummed, his fingers tingled. It was too easy. Wilton looked down at his empty hand.

"Okay, I guess that means you don't want it then." He wasn't going to react or give himself away before Owen did. "Did I tell you how I fell the other day?" He touched his hip. "I'd show you, but I'm not sure you'd want to see. I've got the color of every race. I should be a poster boy for the UN." He mimed how he'd slipped on the carpet in the Bright and fallen against the corner of a table. "They wanted to call 911 but I wouldn't let them. It seemed too undignified. My friends helped me up."

My friends. Who were these people? Wilton turned from the wine and took vodka from the freezer and poured it into two glasses. It was metal going down Owen's throat.

"Why don't you take your coat off," Wilton said, "and we'll sit in the other room. I'd light a fire if I knew how to get the fireplace to work." He held up the bottle of vodka. "And we'll take this bad boy with us. Just in case."

Wilton opened a closet in the front hall and brought out a suede coat the gold color of pond sand. "I know you've admired mine for a while, so I got one for you just like it." He held it out to Owen, a second chance for him to accept a gift. When Owen didn't move, he draped it over the back of a chair, an expensive, coercive pelt he gave a consoling pat to. "There. It's yours if you want." He pulled his robe to cover his knees when he sat. "You're dressed up. A party?"

The vodka cauterized Owen's sinuses. "Memorial service." Wilton said he was sorry to hear it. "Don't be. Mira hated the woman. She used to fuck Mira's father."

"And he used to fuck her, I imagine. Those things sometimes go both ways." He gave Owen a patient smile. "You're not much of a conversationalist today."

The room was hot and arid. "Did you know that Anya and I ate dinner here not so long ago?"

"Is that so?" Wilton sipped prissily at his drink.

"She came to see you one night, but you weren't here. You were out with Mira, of course. At the casino. We had a bottle of your wine."

"I hope you enjoyed it." Wilton slapped the back of his neck as though he'd just been bitten by something. He looked at his fingers to see the bug's remains.

"We watched some *Ancient Times*. In your bedroom. On your bed."

"Good thing you had the wine, then. Television is always much better when you're a little altered." Wilton raised his glass to the blank screen of the living room set.

"We spilled on your sheets."

"Did you? I didn't notice." He was trying to play it unflappable, but his face was beginning to show apprehension. He shifted on the couch and grimaced. "Very painful. I'm taking some pills for my hip. I probably shouldn't have had that vodka—I feel a little woozy. I might just lie down for a bit. You don't mind." He stretched out on the couch.

"Anya told me all about her family, her brothers, her dad. Sounds like she's had a very nice life. She's done perfectly fine— better than fine—without you. You were never missed, she said. Not for a second."

Wilton opened one determined eye. "Get me a glass of water, will you? And find some crackers. I think I should put something in my stomach."

In the kitchen, Owen looked over at his house and saw that Mira wasn't back. He pushed away the notion that she might still be on the roof, now fully frozen with self-recrimination and cold. The picture made him ache for her. He found a box of crackers and filled a glass with water. He watched Wilton sip and nibble and throw one arm over his eyes.

The furnace kicked on and off with a shudder. "Don't you want to know if Anya and I fucked?" Owen asked.

Anger was the essence of all men. Not the eruption of it—any goon could flail his arms and fists around, any goon could point a gun—but the holding in of it. It was the cultivation and harvesting that mattered, and the taste of that perfect, intense fruit. Wilton sat up and placed his empty glass on the table, and the tiny ping it made was the only sound of his rage. Owen would match his control.

"This isn't you talking. I'm surprised at you, Owen. You're a much better person than this," Wilton scolded. "Too smart for this kind of nonsense." He hoisted himself off the couch, went to the front door, and opened it. "Go home. Go make up with Mira and stop all this moving out craziness. Go home. I have to lie down now. I'm not feeling well."

When he saw that Owen wasn't going to leave, he closed the door and limped upstairs, as if it didn't matter to him one way or the other if Owen stayed. Soon Owen heard the shower running, and when it stopped, he went up to Wilton's bedroom, where the man stood naked in front of his closet. It was sad to see the gray-ish droop of the man's ass, the vulnerable dip of the small of his pale back. The bruise on his hip was a florid Cape Cod sunset. Wilton tried to step into a pair of pants he slid from a hanger, but he was in pain, awkward with modesty, and damp from the shower. He hobbled around on one foot until he landed on the bed, his pants stuck at his knees. Covering his lap with a pillow, he sighed.

"You give so little away. I still never know what you're thinking after all this time," he said. "With Mira, on the other hand, it's easy to know what's on her mind, easy to know when she's hid-ing something. Look." He fluttered his fingers on his bottom lip. It was a perfect imitation of Mira. "It's her *tell*. But you—you're hidden, even to yourself. You don't know what you think." Wilton stood and pulled up his pants. "You don't know what you want. That's a problem.

"Hand me that shirt, won't you? The fact is," he went on, "and I say this with the greatest affection and respect, you have no balls. You're passive. Even Mira thinks so, not that she loves you any less for it. When I told her your story about the shooting, and how you'd acted like a coward, she asked me if I thought you'd have done things differently if she'd been the woman in the restaurant with you that night instead of Caroline. She wanted to know if I thought you would have saved her instead of yourself. I think she's jealous of Caroline, actually, how the woman still has such a hold on your psyche." He spoke to his reflection and ran a hand through his wet hair.

"And what did you say?" Owen asked.

"I said I wasn't so sure."

I would have saved Mira, Owen told himself. I would have done anything for her. I still would. That's what I'm doing now. "My wife—" he started. He felt control shifting to Wilton, and he tried to pull it back. In his second of hesitation, Wilton cut in.

"Yes, I know. You think Mira's in trouble. I don't know, maybe she is, maybe you're right about that. But if it's money, I'll give her what she needs. That's the simplest part. That can be fixed tomorrow. If Mira needs help, we'll get her help. Everything can be fixed."

It was tempting to think everything could be solved with a large enough check, apologies and compassion dealt all around, trips to a therapist, weekly confessions in a fusty church basement, just a big fuck-up by all of them. They'd look back and smirk at the mess they'd made; they'd been too incautiously excited. But Mira would never be the same, and his marriage was broken. If he stayed, he'd always live with a liar, and how would he get past that? Her betrayal ached like the flu in his bones, in his jaw, his eyes. Wilton went into the room where his desk and laptop were. His imbalance from the bum hip had mysteriously disappeared. Owen seized the idea that he'd been fooled again.

"Some things can't be fixed," Owen said from the doorway. "You can't fix things with Anya." He saw Wilton's shoulders lift slightly, then fall again.

"You don't know that." Wilton stared at his computer screen.

"Yes, I do. It's what Anya said." The gun was a useless menace, after all, when words could better rip Wilton apart. "So what's left for you now? The older you get, the fewer people are going to know who you are, and soon no one will remember, and you'll be just some batty old fuck who claims he was on television once. You'll have done nothing with your life, left nothing, not even a daughter who thinks of you as her father, a daughter who wants nothing to do with you."

The computer threw light onto Wilton's thin fingers trembling on the keyboard, as though they were about to type his way out of this.

"I've seen how it works," Owen went on. "People look twice at you not because they admire you, but because they can't believe a man would spend his life being an idiot and a clown—and who now just hopes someone will recognize him. It's pathetic, actually. They wonder where your self-respect is."

"Self-respect?" Wilton laughed and wheeled his chair away from the desk. "It's a slippery beast. Do you really think most people wouldn't trade places with me in a second? That they wouldn't act the fool just to be on television? It's a national pastime, making an asshole of yourself. Just like you're doing now." He paused. "I think you're making the old 'we're laughing at you, not with you' observation, which makes you sound like the batty old fuck."

When he tried to stand, Owen pushed him down. With his hand on Wilton's shoulder, he felt how much stronger he was and how he could crush him.

"You seem to have forgotten one thing," Wilton said, as though the idea to sit again had been his. "That I'm your friend. We've depended on each other, helped each other, confided in each other."

"I told Anya what happened," Owen said, and watched as

Wilton, for the first time, looked resigned, not to his helplessness, or to Owen's twitching muscles, but to the inevitability of this hour when everything would collapse. It was as if he'd been waiting for it all along, from the moment he'd arrived in Providence.

"I don't believe you."

"Well, you should." The floor beneath Owen's feet became a cloud. Anger was transporting him, lifting him. What he wanted Wilton to see was that death was less terrifying than the moment when it was still being decided. When the gun was in your face, and it might go off.

"No, I know you," Wilton said, trying a last appeal. His expression said that he knew Owen would always be a coward. With the chair in the center of the room, Wilton had found his stage. "And I know you wouldn't do that."

Maybe Owen wasn't capable of much in the end; he couldn't threaten the man with death. Death was easy by comparison to living with the threat of being killed. Death was gone; pain was being alive. He took a swing at Wilton's face. The contact of skin against skin and bone against bone was dense and satisfying. He itched to do it again, to pummel the man. But Wilton had fallen off his chair, head bent, legs twisted under him, one wrist cocked against the floor, his robe open. This was the final, humiliated slump as Owen stood over him.

"Get up," Owen said.

"I can't."

"Get up," Owen commanded.

Wilton ignored his angry bark, rolled onto all fours and crawled into the bathroom, hoisting himself up first on the toilet, then the sink. He examined his purpling cheek and nose in the mirror. He spoke to Owen's reflection.

"I could use some ice." Wilton ran water in the sink and watched it circle down the drain. "Do you know that's the first time I've ever been punched? Lots have wanted to before, but you're the only one who's actually done it. I didn't know you had it in you."

"I told Anya about the accident."

"So you said." Wilton touched the twisted skin under his eye. "Maybe I'll even have a shiner. That's dramatic."

"Do you know what she said? She said, 'Of course. He always chooses himself first, and always will.' And after that? She could barely talk, she was sick with the truth. Remember the day we were in the Bright and she saw us and fled across the street? It was *you* she didn't want to see. You saw her expression. How else does a child look at a parent who's tried to kill her? She doesn't want anything to do with you. She wishes you'd never moved here, she wishes she'd never written you that goddam postcard."

With Wilton still hanging over the sink, Owen went downstairs. He took off his own coat and put the suede one on. It was luxurious and heavy.

Wilton stood at the top of the stairs looking down at him. "Tell me you didn't," he pleaded. "Tell me she didn't say that. Tell me."

Wilton had been that first shadow in the lungs on the X-ray, the first sound of dripping water behind the wall, the first sniff of mold coming from the basement. Wilton had appeared the first time Mira turned on the television, and he was that electric sizzle haunting the air after the set had been turned off. He was Owen's first prescience of ruin by the lilacs a year ago.

"She said all of it. Every word." He hesitated. "Anya wishes you weren't alive."

Wilton spoke, but it didn't seem to be at Owen anymore. "Then maybe I should just go. I should disappear and pretend I was never even here."

"Yes, why not?" Owen said. "Go all the way. Kill yourself and don't fuck it up this time."

Wilton stared at him open-mouthed. He didn't have anything to say now. Owen felt disturbingly calm as he left the house, as though the riot had passed through his neighborhood, leaving the damage behind. He let himself into his own house through the back door and waited for Mira in the kitchen. The air was stale, and the tangerines in a bowl on the table wore sweaters of mold. Soon he heard Mira's footsteps crunching on the snow, and her hesitation as she discovered the door was unlocked. She would have seen the light on but wasn't sure who was inside. In his rush to the door, he scared her and she ran.

"It's me," he called. "It's just me."

"God, you terrified me. Don't do that." She stood at the far end of the yard and looked up at the starless night.

"Come inside."

Her hand was at her chest. She was tight with the slow ebbing of fear, and then her face softened into something that looked like relief. "You're back?" she asked. "Are you here to stay?"

"I just wanted to see that you made it home."

"Did you think I wouldn't? Don't go, please, Owen. I've told you everything. It's over now. Stay."

But he wanted to be in his apartment in Fox Point on Mrs. Tevas's third floor. He wanted to go back to where he'd begun when he came to Providence, so that maybe he could see what it would be like to start over again.

12

O n the Friday of vacation week, the elementary school across the street from the Bright was childless and closed up tight, a bank of snow blocking the door. The front mural was scabbed over with ice. Owen could have made coffee in Mrs. Tevas's son's Mr. Coffee and cooked himself something in one of the boy's pans that George Tevas had arranged by size in the cabinet with all handles pointing in the same direction. But the smells of cooking in the apartment made his landlords antsy, and each time they turned up CNN as though to block the odor and the reminder that it was still not their son upstairs. Owen understood that he was not meant to actually live too much up there. When he'd been at work, George had come upstairs to clean. It unnerved Owen, but how could he stop the man?

He had become a temporary regular in the Bright in the two weeks since he'd left Mira, but it was no friendlier a place to him than it had been. He picked at his muffin, a dry mulchy thing left over from the morning that the woman at the counter had chosen for him. She'd witnessed his bullying of the man in the army jacket weeks before and she wasn't going to forget it. *Enjoy,* she'd said, serving him the rock tipped on a plate. Anya's classmate, who was often in there, was studiously icy. There were other spots he could have gone to sit in his self-exiled state, but being here was some kind of way to stop time while he waited for Anya. Fox Point had welcomed him back in its perfectly indifferent way. He hated and loved the neighborhood for its reminders of his darkest times when he'd found himself shivering in the heat, hungry but unable to eat. The coin-op laundry had puffed endless sweet steam, and the houses were covered with the octopus suckers of satellite dishes. Not much had changed.

On the corner where he and Mira had first met, a dog without a collar sniffed a snow bank. It was a summer night back then, Mira on her gearless bicycle trying to track down the kid with the sticky fingers. I was ridiculous, she'd later said, and admitted that she'd been showing off for Owen, trying to look tough and determined. Last night, she'd called at 2:00 a.m., the time completely lost to her until he'd pointed it out. In the apartment below him, the television had still been on, keeping its twenty-four-hour vigil of the wars. From the way Mira's voice echoed, he imagined she was up on the third floor, but he didn't ask; he didn't want to know. She said she hadn't seen anyone in days, not even Wilton, who hadn't come by and whose house was often dark; she hadn't been to Brindle or anywhere. She didn't ask Owen to come back; he sensed that she was waiting him out in her penitence. He hadn't been able to get back to sleep after the call, suffering his own form of withdrawal from her. He'd been sitting in the Bright for hours, and the day had slowly drained away down the slushy gutters.

Anya appeared in the noisy doorway and made her way over to her friend. Owen had been waiting every afternoon to see her, and to see how far the lies he'd told Wilton had spread. Had Wilton talked to Anya and begged her forgiveness for a crime she didn't even know he'd committed? But she looked untouched and beautiful, laughing at something as she unwound the thick wool

scarf from around her head. Ruin had fallen all around her, but
she didn't know it. Her father was not on her mind. When she
and her friend looked over at Owen, blood rushed to his face. He
could only blink dumbly at Anya for how he'd used her once again
to get what he wanted. His nerve grew weak at the knees—he
didn't know what he would say to her. She came over and rested
her hands on the back of the vacant chair where he'd put his
suede jacket.

"What's going on?" she asked. "Please tell me that Wilton didn't
send you to spy on me."

"He didn't send me." Owen's mouth was dry.

"But isn't this his coat?" She gave the thing a quick tap.

"No. He gave this one to me."

"But it's just like his, right?" She looked out to the street. "The
other day, when I saw both of you in here, I couldn't come in. It
was too much. I can't have him following me or waiting for me,
just lurking around for a glimpse. It's too creepy. It's like my own
father's a stalker."

"Have you talked to him recently?"

"Not in a while, a week and a half, two maybe? He calls, but
I've had exams. I ignore him." She looked out at the street. Owen
couldn't tell if she felt guilty about dodging her father. "You think
I'm being ridiculous about all this, about him, don't you. You think
I should just be nicer, more forgiving."

Owen imagined Wilton convalescing in his bed at that moment, considering what to do next, where to go. "Will you sit for a
minute? I need to talk to you."

"Now?" She glanced back at her friend. "We were just about to
study." She lowered her voice. "She thinks you're hitting on her, by
the way. Supposedly you're always here looking at her, and once
you even threatened to beat up some guy for her?"

"No on both counts."

"That's what I told her. You're married, for one thing. And Wilton calls you the Peaceful Diplomat. He told me about some fight you broke up at school, how you made the kids shake hands afterward, and now the boys are friends." She might be leery of her father, but she'd begun to quote him, a thread of attachment growing tauter.

"It wasn't exactly brokering peace in the Middle East," he said. "I didn't do anything except tell them to cut it out."

Anya smiled, ran her fingers over the jacket, then pulled out the chair and sat. "Okay. I'm sitting. What's up?"

"I left Mira." Anya's face drew back in surprise. "I'm living here now. In an apartment at the end of the block." He decided not to add that he could see her apartment from his own.

Anya picked at his forlorn muffin. "Your leaving doesn't have anything to do with what we did, does it?"

"We didn't do anything."

"We kissed."

"We were drunk. It was nothing."

"Don't be an asshole. If you're married, then a kiss *is* something. Even if you're not married, it's something. It was something to me." Her mouth pinched tight and she started to get up.

"Look, you're right. I'm sorry, I am an asshole," he said, and touched her hand. "Sit, please? I left because of Mira's gambling. I left because she wouldn't stop going to the casino and playing the slots, and she's in trouble. I left because she's been lying to me." Why did he want her to know all this?

"And you're telling me this because?"

"Because I don't have anyone else to talk to." He hadn't known it was true until he said it; he was without friends. He stood and reached for his coat. His movements were jerky and abrupt; he was fighting with himself. "I don't know why I'm doing this. Just forget it. I have to get out of this place. I'm sorry."

"God, relax. Take a deep breath. Just hang on for a minute."

Anya went to speak to her friend, who threw another convicting glare at Owen. When she and Owen left the Bright, Anya took his sleeve and pulled him across the street to her apartment on the second floor. The dark stairwell stank of cat piss. In the living room, sprawled on the careless furniture, her two roommates watched television. One of them was Peter, the man he'd seen Anya with that day outside the Bright. He was wearing the bumblebee hat and a suspicious look. The guy was in love with Anya, and she was offhanded with him. The other roommate, Diana, exuded shatterproof tension. They were all med school classmates. Anya led Owen up another set of stairs that ran behind the dirty kitchen; it was clogged with empty plastic shopping bags and old newspapers. Her room was a small square, deeply angled under the eaves. But it was a girl's fantasy in many ways—he knew this from reading student stories entitled "Where I'll Live"—with satiny pillows, fluffy comforters, framed pictures, scarves, beads, candles half burned, and a hairy white rug. The air smelled of cheap vanilla. Had Wilton seen the room with its listing walls, he would have insisted that she get a different place—preferably one she could stand up in, and one that wasn't a firetrap. In his house, she could have her own floor of rooms.

"This is the only spot where I can actually stand up straight," she said, posing in the center of the room as her head touched a tasseled pyramid of pink and green silk hanging from the ceiling. Her single bed was against one wall, under an eave and pushed into the corner. When Owen sat at her desk, the back of his head hit the eave's sloping wall with a solid thud. Anya, who lay on her side on the bed because the angle of the ceiling made anything else impossible, laughed as his sinuses bubbled and his eyes shivered. The pain made him strangely more attuned. He noted the dip between her shoulder and hip, a deep, powdery swoop that made him feel the exhilaration of sledding down a steep hill. He thwacked his head again to make her laugh more, and to see and feel more. He felt the weight of his body in the chair, the long length of his legs pointed at her. He smelled her—bookish, salty, and faintly like pine.

"Is Peter your boyfriend?" Owen asked.

Anya smirked. "I wouldn't call it that exactly."

"What would you call it then—besides none of my business?"

"Unclear. Sometimes we sleep together, but I don't want a boyfriend. They take up too much time."

"He seems to think otherwise."

The way she wrinkled her nose made him remember how young she was. The conversation stalled in the bedroom's intimate air. They barely knew each other. Owen forced himself to look away from her laundry slinking over the sides of a basket. He picked up a silver-framed photo by her bed—a man, a woman, four boys, Anya. They appeared enviably ordinary in front of a white garage with a basketball hoop. Anya's mother, the woman who'd had a child with Wilton—that alone was extraordinary enough to consider—was a middle-aged athletic-looking blonde in a polo shirt tucked into baby-yellow bermuda shorts. One arm was around her beefy husband's middle. The sun gave his bald head a paternal glow. Anya's brothers were all bones and huge knees, grinning in braces, long shorts, and chunky sneakers. She stood behind them, her height—Wilton's long body—the one thing that set her apart from the others. If this family had come to the pond when Owen was a kid, he would have made them take him home with them at the end of the summer. They were perfect, lots of white teeth and tanned forearms.

"That's my family," Anya said, reaching to take the photo back from him. She named her brothers and angled the picture away. Owen knew she was protecting herself in some way from him. "I miss them."

"I'm sure you do." In a second, I'll say what I need to say and then I'll leave, he told himself. He wasn't sure where to rest his eyes—they kept moving back to Anya.

"Can I ask you something? Something Wilton told me about you?" she asked. A square of red silk hung over a lamp, and the glow that hit the highs of her face made her look fervent. "He said you were in a restaurant once and the woman you were in love with was shot in a robbery. He said you charged the guy with the gun, but it went off and hit your friend. He said you were holding the woman when she died. Is that all true?"

The only truth was that he'd put his hands under Caroline's head so her hair wouldn't get dirty on the sticky tiles.

"What did you say to—?" Anya asked.

"Caroline. "

"What did you say to Caroline?"

Her name in Anya's mouth made Caroline seem alive, if not right in that room, then in some other city: all had turned out well. Owen felt a flutter of panic that he couldn't remember what he'd said to Caroline. Her eyes had stayed open as her body grew heavy.

"I said, 'I love you.' I said, 'You're going to be okay.'" He didn't say either of those things, and anyway Caroline would have known they weren't true; it was there in the way she hadn't looked away from him. Maybe he'd said nothing.

Anya blinked determinedly. "I'm sorry. That's just an awful story. I don't know how you ever get past something like that."

"Maybe that's not the goal at all." Owen said.

When someone downstairs left, the house shook. Owen watched a plane thread through the evening sky. Anya's cell phone rang, and while she didn't answer it, she kept an eye on the thing. When it rang again a few minutes later, she showed him it was Wilton and turned her phone off.

She gave Owen a sheepish look. "I don't always pick up."

Wilton's presence, caught there in the phone on the bed, prodded Owen with urgency. "I want to tell you the truth," he said.

"About?"

"Look, I didn't love Caroline," he told her, "and she didn't love me. I don't know why I told you otherwise. I didn't do anything to protect her, and I didn't say any meaningful last words. I didn't tell her she'd be okay. I pissed myself and cowered. That's the real story and the real me, not your father's account."

"Why would he make it up then?" she asked, angry.

"Because he wants you to believe people are more admirable than they really are. That he is more admirable, that I am, too. That people won't ever let you down or do wrong by you or have bad motives. That even tragedy makes a good story. He knows it's not true, but he wants you to believe people don't do terrible things to each other all the time, that we're not all cowards when it comes to saving others."

"Who doesn't want to believe that?"

"I'm not sure I believe it anymore."

"I think you've just forgotten."

Anya inched closer to the wall to make room for him on the bed. She asked him to lie down with her. The soft mattress closed in around them like a hand. He wasn't aware he was crying until the freckles on her neck blurred and drifted. He needed to shut his eyes and pretend he was floating on his back on the pond. His hair fanned out on the surface. Anya, like water, swayed against the nerve endings on his scalp. The bed dipped and turned. He told her he was imagining swimming at the pond and described the place to her. She said she'd like to see the real thing some day, maybe take a swim there, too. He moved his face to her ribs, and through the cotton of her top, her breast fell against his cheek. The sensation was of a passing sunfish, a change in temperature, a shifting current. He stirred his hand in the water and took a sip of it. Anya touched his forehead, the bridge of his nose, his chin, and he was diving, invited in by a pond dweller. He was under, with the pressure against his eyes and ears, and he heard his heart walloping away. For an instant, he was perfect.

But he couldn't breathe. He was not on the pond; he knew where he was and exactly what he was doing. His craving for Anya twitched in the tips of his fingers, the tip of his penis, his legs and feet. He moved her into the angle where the slope of the ceiling met the bed and pressed against her. He sensed peril waiting at the base of her throat, incaution thrumming like a guide wire on a bridge. He moved his head to find the moon in the window and fell off the bed.

It was a long way down in free fall—minutes seemed to pass—until he heard the crack of bones and wood and then felt the back of his head smack the hairy white carpet. It was like taking a nap amid sheep. When he tried to sit up, his left hipbone jolted, and there was a sickening click of the rearrangement of joints. He lay down again. Anya leaned over the edge of the bed, and the way her hair curtained her face, she seemed far away. What had just happened was either funny or pitiable, and they waited to see which one. When Anya said his name, her mouth still had the

gloss of prekiss. He decided that now he might as well believe
in the better stories, because where had his gloom ever gotten
him? It had suffocated Mira. Maybe everything could be fixed, as
Wilton had said. He laughed up at the tasseled silk that hung over
him like an exotic sun shade.

"Holy shit," Anya said, laughing with him. "Are you okay?"

"A single bed. I'd forgotten what those are like."

"Monastic," she said. "Meant for one. Just tell me something.
Was that an accident or your way out?"

Owen rolled onto his knees. When he finally stood, he put on
his coat and kissed Anya's forehead. "I shouldn't be here," he said.
"I know that much." He would get to Wilton and apologize, and
would make sure Anya never knew what had happened. And he
would leave her alone.

"I know. It's been a weird day for me, too." She rolled onto her
back and threw an arm across her eyes, the gesture just like her
father's. "But I know I don't want to do this again. You need to
figure things out."

She didn't look at Owen as he left her room and then her apartment. He walked through the neighborhood with his hip sending
sparks down his leg, and then down to India Point Park by the water. He warmed himself by picturing the tall urban grass that grew
between the rocks in the summer and the occasional tall ship that
passed by on its way to Newport or Boston, its sails flashing impul-
sively in the sun. The shoreline rumbled south past the hospital and
the gas tanks and the Big Blue Bug. Atomically bright spotlights
hovered over repair crews working on the highway. Yards away, two
men seemed to be making some kind of deal.

In the apartment, he found that George had visited again while
he'd been out. The man had the timing of a jewel thief. The bathroom gleamed antiseptically. The pot Owen had left in the sink

had been washed and put away. Even the student papers on the table had been straightened, and the pencils and pens lined up like soldiers, the radio pushed back in the corner, its aerial de-telescoped, the handle wiped. In the bedroom, his clothes had been pushed into a corner and the bed had been made with the chenille spread. One part of the edging was torn, his fault, and a chenille ball whisked the floor. It must have irritated George every time he saw it. Owen felt invisible in the apartment, any trace of him wiped away, disinfected, and vacuumed up, which was all okay and how it should be. It was how he felt about himself. He took some aspirin and a sleeping pill well past its discard-after date, and lay down on the bed but did not get in it. He might not get in it ever again. He didn't exist here—he was just an idea of himself. He would sleep, he would dream that everything was going to be just fine. He would wake up and do what he had to do to fix things.

He blinked at the dark ceiling and didn't know where he was or how long he'd been asleep. A chenille ball rested in the corner of his mouth. Where was his glowing bureau, the battling roses on the wallpaper and the searing point of the streetlight outside his bedroom window? Where was his wife with her hand curled on his chest? Where were the locust trees, the bayberries, the catcalls of frogs? His phone was ringing and he leaned over to the floor and dug around in the pockets of his pants.

"O." Then nothing but the sound of the sea. "O? Are you there?" It was Mira with that breathless expiration of his name. "O, the car, the goddamn car. It's dead and I'm stuck here."

He didn't understand. Where was the clock? Where was she and why wasn't he with her? He reached behind for her and felt the cold touch of wall. This was not his bed, not his wall, but this was his wife. He pounded his skull with the heel of his hand to dislodge the murk.

"O. Say something."

Her voice cracked. She was on I-95, on her way home from the casino, though she wasn't sure exactly what part of the highway she was on, not even if she was in Rhode Island or Connecticut because she hadn't been paying attention. Owen sat up, light-headed. He went into the kitchen. The clocks on the microwave and the stove, though resynchronized by George, still ran minutes apart by the end of every day and now read 1:14 and 1:19. Mira was by the side of the road and she couldn't see anything on the other side of the guardrail. The fog was too heavy. She was terrified—of the road, the dark embankment, of being stuck there in a blizzard. She begged him to say something. Downstairs, the TV murmured. He heard a truck passing Mira and pictured the stretch of highway going both directions and cut down the middle by a velvet belt of exiled trees and desperate bramble.

"I'm alone," she said shakily.

"Where's Wilton?"

"He's not with me." He heard the useless click of the ignition, and then what sounded like her batting her keys. "He was before, we came together, but he isn't now. Will you come get me?"

"Do you know what time it is? Where the hell is he?"

"I don't know where he is," she said, revving up in frustration. "But I'm scared. Could you please come?" He asked again where Wilton was. "I left him at the casino and I drove for about twenty-five minutes, and then I thought I should go back and get him, but I couldn't find him anywhere, so I turned around again. Please, O. I'll tell you later. Just come get me. Please!"

When he went downstairs, George opened his door a few inches. Owen gave him a silent nod and went around back where his car was parked and two cats huddled in conference by the garbage cans. The temperature had risen eerily and the streets were hidden in fog. His wipers smeared the glass, and light burst into spikes on the highway. He could guess the number of times Mira had made this same trip, and yet she still didn't know where she was? There was nothing to notice, she'd once said about the drive to the casino: no wild building, no cross with plastic flowers on the side of the road to mark a death, no rest stops with two cars pulled up next to each other. She only knew where she was going and where she was coming from and who was in the seat next to her. She used to observe everything, he thought, and everything was once interesting to her. The heaviest disappointment began to sink him, and his hands strangled the wheel for rescue. The fog was terrible. He could see only a few yards ahead. No other cars cleared the way for him.

Half an hour later, he saw her car, just a shadow through the fog, on the other side of the highway. He took the next exit, circled back, and pulled up behind her in the breakdown lane. On the other side of the guardrail was a steep embankment ending in a tureen of swirling fog. Mira watched him in her rearview mirror, and he watched her until she got out and climbed into his car. When he leaned over to buckle her seat belt because she was too dazed or too cold to do it herself, she thought he was leaning over to kiss her and offered her mouth. He pulled back and shook his head.

"Wilton disappeared," she said. She was shivering in the blasting heat. "I couldn't find him anywhere. I looked and looked." Her eyes were gargoyled and her tongue tripped on her teeth. "I don't know where he went."

"He took a room. Maybe he met someone. He's okay."

"No, I don't think so." Mira insisted that something was wrong.

How easily she and Wilton had gone to the casino again tonight, as though nothing Owen had said or done mattered. As though he hadn't moved out, as though his marriage—and Brindle—weren't devastated. In the dip ahead, red and blue throbs swept through the white haze in a volley of patriotic colors. He knew that whatever was going on was assuming in Mira's mind the shape of Wilton. Her hand pressed to her mouth as a policeman with a flashlight waved them past. Two cars in strobed brightness and shadow were in the right lane, one station wagon overturned, one bent at midsection and facing the wrong way. It was impossible to tell smoke from fog. Owen thought he heard the very distant whine of sirens, but it was only Mira sucking air in through her teeth. He must have passed the accident going south and not even known it. The drivers might already have been dead.

"We have to go back and look for him," Mira said. "He was acting strange and unhinged and a little crazy. I've never seen him like that. Will you turn around?"

"Not a chance. I think you're—"

"What, overreacting? You didn't see his face, O. He fell the other day and bruised his cheek badly. His eye was almost swollen shut. He was limping. There's something wrong with him. He's sick." She hesitated. "He was talking about the end of things."

"Wilton will find his way home. He can take care of himself."

"He wasn't acting. You weren't there, O," she insisted. "He was talking about how he'd failed at everything, how he'd made a mistake moving to Providence and thinking Anya would take him back. He wasn't making any sense."

"He was drunk."

"He doesn't get drunk. How can you not know that by now? He was furious at me—about Brindle and what I'd done, furious at you that you'd moved out, furious at himself for being involved.

Furious at Anya. He wouldn't let me stay with him." She began to cry. "He said, 'Leave me fucking alone.' It was horrible."

Owen didn't speak.

"He was the one who asked me to go with him tonight. He begged me. I didn't want to, I told him I couldn't ever go again, that I'd promised you, but he insisted. Just one last time, he said. I've made a mess of everything." She clapped her hand over her mouth. "It's all my fault. And now I've lost Wilton."

"He'll come back," he said, uncertainly. Mira couldn't be consoled.

In all his rambling fury, Wilton had not told Mira about Owen's visit. Why had the man kept quiet? The city came into view with the rise of the hospital and the stacks of the power station near Brindle. Owen got off at Eddy Street near the hospital. If they parked across from the emergency room, the hopeless cases from the car accident would soon be wheeled in. He felt the emptiness of having witnessed a tragedy and being unable to do anything about it, give comfort or even stand witness to the final conveyance. So he didn't stop, but drove back to Whittier Street, which was luminous in fog tinted green from Alice Jessup's nightlights.

13

Mira asked him to stay with her, and they were still awake, waiting for Wilton to come home or call. Mira held a cup of tea gone cold and kept an eye on his place.

"I shouldn't have left him." It was her incantation; she'd said it a hundred times already. "He tried to call Anya a couple of times tonight, but she wouldn't answer. I think he finally gave up any hope that she might move in with him."

"She was never going to move in with him," Owen said. "That was pure fantasy, wishful thinking."

"Maybe, maybe not." She pulled at the neck of her threadbare Brindle sweatshirt. Her arms looked thin and vulnerable. "We don't know."

I know, Owen thought. He listened for birdsong, a car, a bang through water pipes, something real instead of the morning's boundless worry. Finally Mira went upstairs to lie down. As he wandered to stay awake, he saw that Mira had been on a cleaning jag since he'd last been there. Every object had been lifted, cleaned under, and put back, but not in precisely the same place as before. It was as though his acuity were painfully sharp for the first time in the house, and he saw that his tenure there had been only a blip in its long history. The dust ring that had gathered around him for almost six years of marriage had been whisked away. If he turned fast enough, he could catch his own afterimage as a wisp. *So this is what it looks like without me, this is life without me, and how it goes on,* he told himself. What Mira had been doing was returning the house to the way it had been before him, when she was its sole caretaker and before she believed, if only for a while, she could actually have a life here with someone else, with him. In his study, he stretched out on the short couch with his legs draped over one end. His fatigue was dizzying. When he tucked a blanket into the seam where the cushions met, his fingers touched something cool and he extracted the squid pen from the leathery depths. He couldn't imagine how it had gotten there.

The way Mira said his name when she woke him was part dove, part moan, an insistent force of O, O, O. She hadn't changed her clothes, but she'd washed sleep from her face, and the way her hair was pulled back made her alertness appear forced. "What if he doesn't come back?" she said.

"But he will." Here they were, back in this same discussion, as if they'd never taken a break from it.

"You can't say that. You don't know how he was acting."

"But we know he's done this before, gone away sometimes without our knowing. He's not required to tell us or check in with us. I can't talk about this anymore, Mira. You have to stop."

She looked stunned. He could reassure her that Wilton was okay, and he could come up with a million plausible reasons for why he hadn't come home last night, but he wouldn't believe any of it himself. The dread he'd been fending off all night now charged him. He hobbled off the couch, pushed past Mira, and went into the bathroom where he vomited—sleeping pill, Anya, a million bad decisions, Mira. He hid the noise with running water.

"You all right?" Mira asked when he returned.

He wouldn't look at her. "Just tired."

She sat in the desk chair and leaned back. "Do you know why Wilton doesn't leave any lights on when he goes out?" she asked, looking over at his house. "So when he comes home, he doesn't have to face that second of disappointment when he realizes there's no one waiting for him."

Mira swiveled to face Owen. "Did I ever tell you how I wasn't allowed in this study without my father's permission, and if I did come in, he couldn't wait to get me out? He'd clear his throat and fiddle until I left. It was so wrong. Sometimes when he wasn't home, I'd sit in this chair and touch all his things, his papers. I opened his drawers and felt all the way in the back, looking for something. It was thrilling. I'd never keep a child out of my room, never. I'd invite them in and show them everything." She let the chair tilt forward—enough of the past. "I have to go back and look for Wilton," she said. "Will you come with me?"

He agreed, and by the time they left the house, the first sunlight insulated the telephone wires that ran along the highway. After a silent hour, the casino rose like a steel-hued fortress not meant to be approached in the morning. It was all angles and glass and unkind seams. The engineering and mechanics were hidden on purpose; the whole place was trickery.

"This is exactly where I left him," she said, stopping under a fake cedar when they were inside. She ran her finger down the fiberglass trunk. The recorded sounds of skittering breezes and birds hung in the branches. The abandoned plastic cups, the flecks of wrappers and napkins, the disillusioned wanderers, and the piped-in smell of bacon and coffee gave away the early hour that was otherwise hidden. A woman in a tight blue uniform ran a rag back and forth over a chrome railing. He couldn't believe he was back in this place. In her open jacket and untied red sneakers,

Mira looked almost destitute, and so did he. He followed her as she went in one direction and then turned as she went the opposite way. He scanned every face; they looked eerily alike. Mira crossed the bridge over the waterfall's river and gestured to the bartender. She used her hands, one high above her head to describe Wilton, the other to pat the stool next to her. The bartender gave her the kind of smile that meant he was going to be professionally polite and tight-lipped. He shook his head and turned back to filling bowls with pretzels.

"He's not allowed to discuss other guests," Mira told Owen. "He used the word 'discretion' with me. Prick. People don't quite get the idea that someone is missing. If you choose to disappear, are you still technically missing?"

"He's not missing," Owen said. "We just haven't found him."

Owen checked at the hotel reception desk, though Mira had already called them several times. A woman also used the word "discretion," then relented after he pleaded with her. She looked furtively on her computer for Wilton, though he could have checked in under any name and paid with cash or gotten the room comped. Mira suggested that they patrol the halls of the hotel, floor by floor, and press their ear to every door. What sound did she imagine they'd be listening for? They walked the casino again, past the gaming tables and a busload of women who fanned out in some kind of military maneuver, charging their posts, purses pressed under their arms. Mira was purposeful in her avoidance of the slot machines, while he watched for any sign from her—a twitch, a hand over her mouth, her hand looking for a coin in her pocket, tracing the seats. Nothing. She might as well have been passing cinderblocks for how the machines—and the people who played them at this hour—moved her now.

"Wilton could be anywhere, but I think he's nowhere," Mira

said after a couple of hours. "His space just feels empty, O. I can't explain it. He's not here, he's not in the world. I know it's crazy, but I feel it."

Owen sensed Wilton's profound absence, too. It was nothing he could explain either or confess to her, but it was like a sound or smell that you don't notice until it's gone. And then you realize the sound wasn't ever the wind, or the smell of the ocean, but all along it was someone breathing close to you.

Mira had been desperate to come, and now she was desperate to leave, pulling him away by his hand. Her breath fluttered; she lost her way and had to turn them around. She stopped to look at a child sleeping on a bench, an adult's coat thrown over him for a blanket. Back in the car, Owen slowed to look at the stand of pine trees across from the main entrance. The temperature had risen into the sixties. The woods were an untouched boundary, striking, fully green in the winter, an instant of antidote, dripping. In this moment of unexpected beauty, Owen saw that Mira's fear was fully his now—Wilton was nowhere.

When they turned onto Whittier, the street was jammed to the end with a line of idling cars. Another pulled up behind them, boxing them in. Owen's hands levitated from the wheel. Mira inched up in her seat. She'd called Wilton's cell and house phone over and over, knowing that if he were home, he'd answer. He never liked to let a call go, because who knew what it might offer or ask? And it could always be Anya. The notion that Wilton might not pick up because he couldn't, and that this traffic had somehow to do with him, hit both of them. But they didn't hear what they expected to hear outside: radio squawks, the orchestration of rescue or resuscitation. They heard kids laughing instead.

In the bulbous back of a minivan in front of them, two heads and four hands appeared, two little girls waving wildly, sticking their fingers in their ears. Mira waved back, her thumbs in her ears, her fingers fluttering. She wagged her tongue. Owen loved her for this. She made a quacking duck out of her thumb and forefinger. Three balloons lifted into the blue. There was nothing tragic going on here—unless pink balloons were a distress flare— nothing at all to do with Wilton. The world went on no matter where he was.

Mira got out to see what was happening and came back ten minutes later. "It's a birthday party. Alice Jessup's great-grandaughter," she said deliberately, determined to get the tumble of generations right. "Kids everywhere. The truck that was delivering one of those inflatable bouncy things got stuck in the middle of the street, wedged right between the cars on either side. Snapped off the side mirrors and then couldn't move. It's really something, one of the best driving fuck-ups I've seen." His wife, the archivist of abysmal Rhode Island driving stories. "Wilton's not home."

"You looked inside?"

"No. The key wasn't there, but I rang. Anyway, you know he'd be outside watching the action if he were home. These little kids would thrill him. You're going to have to back up if you ever want to get out of this. It could be forever before they get that truck out. They might have to airlift it—or cut it apart with the Jaws of Life."

She instructed the cars behind him to back up. She stood at the intersection directing traffic, this resolute woman in red running shoes, this mayor of the street. No one knew this neighborhood better, no one felt they belonged here more than she did. She waved him back like he was any other car, and he drove around the block to park closest to the other end.

When he walked back up the hill, children and their parents milled around the street examining the wedged truck in front of the house. Many were shedding sweaters and jackets and looking for somewhere to dump them. A small pile grew on the steps up to Alice Jessup's. The season was prone to freakish spells of warmth and people drank it up. Tinny music played in Alice's backyard. The truck driver was a stooped kid, miserable and disbelieving, his lower lip hanging slack. His partner sat in the passenger seat of the truck smoking, as if to say none of this was his fault, he was just waiting for quitting time. The driver kept touching the seams where his truck met the parked cars. The side of the truck announced Partee Tyme!

"Tough squeeze," Owen said.

"Yeah. Seems like it." The boy took off his Friars cap in the universal sign for bafflement and whacked his knee with it. "I hate this fucking neighborhood. These streets, they're ridiculous, too narrow."

"Definitely not designed with trucks in mind." The kid looked too young to drive anything. Owen took a closer look at him.

The kid glanced at Owen and then quickly away. But Owen had seen enough of his face to know that he knew him. Not his name at that moment, but some vague sense of where he'd sat in Owen's first classroom years earlier. And what did the kid remember of him? That he was a mess that year and sometimes stared at nothing for long stretches, that he lost his way when he was talking, that his pain was catching and the kids couldn't wait to escape from the room. Owen wanted to tell the boy now that there wasn't much a person couldn't get past if he wanted to, that this day would pretty soon be shrunk to almost nothing, a speck to keep in a drawer or a pocket. But the kid was speaking into a cell phone now, and he'd turned his back to Owen.

The inflatable castle had been unloaded and put up in Jessup's backyard and an occasional child careened against its walls. A blindfolded girl swung a plastic bat at a piñata with murderous intent. The yard was dotted with mounds of melting snow. He couldn't know if Alice upstairs was aware of what was going on below her, if she heard or sensed anything, or if the kids had been dragged into the medicinal stink of the sickroom to pay homage to the world's oldest human who probably didn't even look so human anymore. Maybe ancient Alice was the best entertainment of all, the real magic of a very long life.

Mira appeared next to him. "Look," she said, excitedly. "Look at Wilton's. The packages that were there before are gone. He's back."

They rushed across the street and knocked on his door. The grinding and shrieking of the truck being extracted from the parked cars was deafening. Amused police and a crowd of gawkers and kids watched the tow truck try to drag the Partee Tyme! truck backward. Owen expected to see Wilton's expression—part seduction, part calculation. Maybe he'd already be back in his filthy bathrobe, his face smooth from a shower and a shave and smelling like the expensive oriental grapefruit soap he'd once given to Owen. "Everyone wants to smell like a fruit salad," he'd said. Owen's heart beat apprehensively. He would take the man aside and apologize, he'd say he'd lied about it all. When the door opened, the sound was of mutual surprise—and disappointment.

"Oh," Mira exhaled.

"Oh," Anya said, looking first at Owen, then at Mira. "I thought you were my father."

"And we thought you were him." Mira peered around Anya into the house. The packages were pushed against the wall. "Why would he be knocking on his own door?"

"Because I have the key."

"So he's not here." Mira drew out the words, and Anya took full note of Mira's inspection of the room as they stepped inside. "I've been calling. Why didn't you answer?"

"It's not my house, so why would I? Anyway, I just got here." Anya turned to Owen. "What's going on? Where's Wilton anyway?"

"We're looking for him," Mira answered. She wasn't going to be shouldered out. "He didn't come home last night."

"Come home from where?" Anya asked Owen, pointedly ignoring Mira.

Mira looked puzzled by Anya's obvious iciness, but she persisted with her. "He'll be really happy you came by to see him. He's been hoping for this for a long time."

"Come home from where?" she asked again.

"Your father and I went to the casino last night," Mira said. "He wanted to stay, so he did."

"And you left him there?" Anya asked her.

"Yes, I did, but that's what he wanted. I shouldn't have, but I did."

"Look, the guy's not a child, not some invalid," Owen insisted, stepping between the women. "He can find his way home. Hire a cab or go anywhere else he wants. He doesn't have to tell any of us where he is or what he's doing."

"I can't believe you still go to that place," Anya said, speaking around Owen to Mira. "After everything that's happened, everything you've ruined. That's really fucked-up. You should get some help."

Mira looked from Owen to Anya to Owen, and her mouth disappeared into a bloodless seam. Owen moved his wife to the door, then down the steps, and told her to go home.

"You told her about me?" she asked. She squinted in the sun. The street was festively busy with people coming to see the wedged-in truck. "Why would you do that, O? You don't think I'm ashamed enough?" She hesitated. "And when? When did you see her? When did you talk to her?"

"You've been gone a lot," he said. "And I don't live here—"

She started to say something but held back. Her eyes pulled down at the corners as though she were figuring something out and it was becoming more and more clear to her. She turned away from him, but instead of going home, she crossed the street and stood in Alice Jessup's driveway, watching the party and the careening kids. Owen turned back to Wilton's where Anya was waiting at the door. He moved her back inside.

"Don't do that," he warned. "She's my wife."

"You don't act like she is," she said, but she wouldn't look at him. Her confidence was a fake, and her attack on Mira had left her shaky.

"I know," he said.

"Look, I just want to talk to my father," she said. "I want to tell him I'm sorry for how I've been acting. I know he's been trying with me. I've been mad at him for so long, I don't know how else to be. Some of the things you said last night made me feel I could try a little harder, cut him a little slack."

Owen looked at the places in the room where he'd done all the damage to the man—and to his daughter. In the dark, his crimes would always glow fluorescent.

"I don't know where he is," he said.

Anya looked at him blankly, hiding herself from him, and then turned on the television. She lifted an indifferent hand when he said he was going. She was going to wait there for her father.

He needed some sleep and drove to Fox Point. Taking the stairs to his apartment above Rosalie's, he stalled at the niche that held a vase of silk roses and waited for the heaviness to drain from

his legs. Someone was moving around upstairs. There was a faint
scraping across the floor and a rhythmic squeak of something sliding back and forth. Were people screwing so tentatively in the
bed under the white chenille? The door was open a few inches
to reveal George on his hands and knees, scrubbing behind the
toilet. The tub was filling with a cloudy soup of Ajax and water.

"George, you don't have to do this. I'll clean the bathroom. I'll
clean everything," Owen said. "Please. It's so early."

"I didn't hear you come back last night." The back of George's
bristly neck was red. He adjusted his rubber gloves over the
sleeves of his Patriots sweatshirt. "I don't mind." He dunked his
sponge in a bucket and resumed scrubbing the spotless tiles. "It
gives me something to do."

Owen sat on the edge of the tub. Caustic steam stung his eyes
and ate away at the back of his throat.

"You going to sit there and watch?" George asked.

"I might." Owen's sneakers had left gray slashes on the wet
floor and he leaned over to wipe away the dirt with the heel of
his hand.

"I never saw anybody who liked to watch me clean." George
scratched his chin with a rubber finger. "Excuse me." He motioned for Owen to get off the tub and put the lid of the toilet
down, like an usher showing him to his seat. "Here. So you don't
get in my way."

"Breathing this stuff will kill you," Owen said.

"Something's got to kill me eventually." George plunged his
hands into the water and took a breath of the bleachy bouquet. He
opened the drain and coaxed the blue silt down. "Let me ask you
something. It's none of my business, but I figured if you're sitting
there on the can, I can ask. You going to work this thing out with
your wife? I ask because my boy's going to need his place soon and

I wouldn't want to push you into the street. Rosie wouldn't either. But we might have to." He collected his sponges and bucket. "I'm not trying to rush you."

"I understand. And that's great news—he's coming home."

"No date yet, but soon, I think. I just have a feeling about it. Look, you're not going to get any marriage advice from me. I got nothing for you in that department."

Owen smiled. "That's too bad."

"Right. I don't do that kind of cleaning," George said.

He disappeared at the stair's turn. The man's touch was everywhere. It was impossible now to ruin this order by sleeping on the bed with the bedspread he'd already torn, so Owen lay on the floor on a pile of clothes. If a normal day had twenty-four hours, this one had a hundred times that many. Later, when it was just turning dark, he opened his eyes to see a bat circling in front of the sparkling night window.

14

On Thursday afternoon, Owen tried to swim at the Y. He waited for the moment when he would give in to the water and the water would give in to him, and he'd be weightless and, with any luck, empty-headed, too, for a bit. He locked his focus on the screen of bubbles the swimmer ahead of him kicked up. He'd often imagined that if you could take some measure of the vapor above the pool, you'd discover what was in the minds of all the silent swimmers.

What wafted from him now was an unsteady, combustible mix. Wilton had been gone since Friday, almost a week. Mira had filed a missing-persons report on Monday morning—last to see him and best to know him—but was that too late? Or too soon? Wilton was an adult, the police had reminded her, and if he wanted not to be found, he was allowed. Owen's conversations on the phone with Mira—nothing in person since that moment on Wilton's steps—had all the qualities of a fragile alliance: necessary information, suspicion, self-preservation, a wish for another way.

Earlier, when Owen had called her during his lunch period, Mira had recounted for him again the questions she'd been asked about Wilton when she'd filed the report: Was Wilton mentally or physically impaired? In need of medical attention? Emotionally unstable? Suspect of foul play or victim of a crime?

"All of the above? None of the above? I mean, if I knew the answers . . . ," she said, trailing off.

They asked each other if they even knew Wilton well enough to say if disappearing was something he'd do. If they'd known him for only a year, could they actually say what was in or out of character or history? Certainly Anya, who now came and went from her father's house several times a day, didn't know him any better than they did. As Owen had stood outside the teachers' lounge and heard the low riot of children surging up from the basement cafeteria, he'd told Mira he didn't understand why more people simply didn't walk away from their lives for a time—or for good.

Fifteen minutes in the pool, and the sound of his breathing and the slavish industry of his limbs had failed to settle him. Everything was a struggle. Wilton was riding on his back and pushing him under, squeezing his lungs with his narrow fingers, grabbing his ankles, filling his goggles. Owen's arm smacked down hard on the plastic lane divider, sending a current of pain down his spine. He swallowed a mouthful and came up gasping. He was afraid of the water all of a sudden and knew that if he stayed in the pool, it might kill him. He scrambled out. In the shower room, three boys from the swim team threw purloined shampoo bottles and flip-flops at one another. Owen had watched them for years here at this hour, seen them grow from scrawny to less scrawny, and the understanding had always been that Owen would pretend they weren't there snapping towels, throwing wads of paper on the ceiling, spilling soap on the floor, taking anything left unattended, and in exchange they would pretend he wasn't there. He closed his eyes under the hot water. His body was taking a daily beating from fumbles and falls; remorse tattooed him.

Something slammed into his balls and he folded over with

white, explosive pain. The tile floor swam in front of him. He was
going to puke. His chest and stomach were being pulled inside
out. He crouched. The shampoo bottle spun at his feet. Across
from him, the boys were frozen with their backs against the wall.
As if on cue, they dashed for the pool door, but Owen snatched
one kid back by his bathing suit. The boy struggled on the slick
floor as the waistband of his suit cut into him. His friends, fascinated and glad it wasn't them who'd been captured, watched from
the doorway.

"You little shit," Owen hissed. He held the boy by the twisted
arm. The kid was made up of twigs and string, easy to toss.

"It wasn't me." The boy looked at Owen's size inflating above
him.

"You little bastard."

Owen wanted to punish the boy for all the times a wad of wet
paper had landed on him, for all the boys' boasting about pissing
in the pool, for how they turned grown men silent and complicit.
Some men had been just like these boys once—and if they hadn't
been, they'd secretly wanted to be. Past and present could not
share a locker room peacefully, and Owen tightened his grip on
the kid, hard enough to feel bone, and it felt absurdly satisfying.
His balls throbbed. He lifted a hand to slap the boy. But the life-
guard, a skinny teenager, appeared then in the doorway with a
band of kids pressing up behind him. He had hoped never to be
called into service for more than the occasional whistle-blowing
for running or roughhousing, and his look was so beseeching that
Owen let go of the culprit who sniffled and pulled up his suit.
Owen got dressed quickly and jammed his things into his bag. He
wanted nothing more than to get out of there. Mrs. Paul at the
front desk yanked her door-knocker-size earrings in disapproval.

Outside in the March wind, water from his wet hair dripped down his neck and under the collar of his suede coat. All these years working with kids and he'd never lost it with one before now. But once that happened, he knew, you were done. From then on it was all about temptation and holding back—when the swiftest solution to every problem was right there in your hands. Use it once and you'd use it again and again.

"Mr. Brewer? Wait." The Y's director rushed after him.

For years, she and Owen had only ever smiled at each other in passing, maybe talked briefly a few times, and now she was saying that she'd just been told what had happened, that he'd put his hands on a boy who'd been terrified and bawling when he came to her office to call his mother to pick him up. His arm still showed the evidence of Owen's grip. She knew the kid was a pain in the ass, but still. Owen was a teacher, she said, he had to understand how these things worked. He felt sorry for her out there in her wrong-season suit in the cold, and her attempts to be fair.

"So you're not disputing this?" she asked.

"No, you have it right. That's exactly what happened."

Her face was kind and uncomfortable. Cars maneuvered in and out of the tight lot, and kids peered at them from behind the building's smeary glass front door. "I have to ask you not to come back. I'm sorry. I know you've been coming here forever, but do you understand?"

He said he did, and that he wouldn't be back, she didn't have to worry. That was it then—gone. No more swimming, no underwater friendships, no watery daydreams. Soon there'd be no place left in the city he was welcome—not his house, not Rosalie's son's apartment. Soon, Spruance wouldn't even exist. Across the street, at the Slavin Memorial Chapel, new graffiti arched above the discreet sign on the side wall that read "Back Entrance for Deliveries." A man in a white shirt and black pants scrubbed at the kindergarten-colored spray paint with a soapy brush.

Disgrace rose up in Owen like a fever. He was mauling kids now, and shaking and sorry—for what he'd done to the boy, for how he'd let everything lead to that one moment poised on the edge of violence. He walked to Whittier Street and his wife.

The yard service was just finishing up at Wilton's and load-ing the last equipment and men into the back of the truck. For a minute, things appeared normal and ordinary. There was the expensive activity, the whisking away of noise and mess, Wilton's porch was clear of delivered boxes as if he had brought the loot inside. But he knew Wilton wasn't there, wasn't back.

He let himself in through Mira's back door and took off his shoes. The kitchen was evidence of her worry—newspapers slid-ing off the chair onto the floor, used tea bags like animal drop-pings left on envelopes, in the sink, on a stained napkin. Upstairs, he saw the same disturbance in the wrestled bedsheets and blan-kets, books kicked to the end of the bed, one pillow still holding the indent of Mira's head, like a fossil. Her car was in the drive-way, but she might have gone for a walk, though by now it was nearly dark out, night closing in too early still. The house blazed with a hundred lights left on, and he turned them off as he went from room to room. He was looking for Mira but also playing the part of the intruder. The air shifted, disgruntled when he opened and closed doors on the privacy of objects.

The third floor was dark, but stray light ran in pale yellow lines down the hall. In one of the rooms, he sat on the bed and looked into Alice Jessup's room across the street. The curtains were open, and the old lady was in a chair watching television. In all the years he'd lived here, he had never seen her. A nurse placed a tray on the table in front of her and tied a bib around her neck. At a distance, her features seemed collapsed into skin. The nurse held a spoon in front of her mouth. Once, a young Alice must have looked back at this house and waved to Mira's grandmother. Did she know now what had changed over here or anywhere in the world? She might still believe her girlhood friend was at this window, sneaking in the maid's room, and waiting for her to wave back.

Owen leaned against the wall and heard noises behind the plaster—mice, wind or a branch tickling the slates, or something more methodical. He went down the hall, past open doors and the back staircase with its abysslike drop, to the backless closet. He turned the glass knob and faced the thickest, warmest black. His hands and feet went cold. He couldn't see what was in front of him, so he got down and crawled into the closet. He said Mira's name. A splinter slid into his hand, another into his knee. She didn't answer, and he called her again.

"O?" She couldn't catch her breath. "O?"

He couldn't judge the distance, and when he reached out for her, his hand met only air. "Move toward my voice, Mira."

"I can't."

He crawled further in, and when he reached her, felt how her knees were pulled up and her back was bent into the steep angle where the roof met the corner walls. She had found the smallest, sharpest point in the house and folded herself into it.

"What are you doing here?" Owen laughed.

"It's not funny," she said, though he could tell she was relaxing, smiling. "I thought someone was breaking in."

"It's just me."

"No, earlier. This afternoon. I was—"

"You've been in here since this afternoon?"

"Yes, and I actually wished I had the gun your father gave us. I would have used it. I would have killed someone, I swear. I'm losing it."

He tried to sit, but he was too big for the angle. He stayed at her feet, his hands at her ankles. She was not always strong, and not always the one to pull another from anguish. He rested his forehead against her knees and she touched his head.

"It's pretty awful in here," he said, still against her, and not wanting to move. He felt calmer than he had in a long time.

"I warned you. It's the place of last resort."

"For me, it's the carriage house." He told her about what had happened at the Y, how he'd hurt the kid and been exiled.

"How are we going to live through this waiting for Wilton?" she asked.

He said he didn't know and, taking her by the wrist, crawled out with her.

"God, I hate this closet," she said, before kicking the door shut. Her curls were covered with cobwebs and Owen told her to stand still so he could lift them off.

Later, when they were sitting with the remains of dinner and the bones of conversation, Owen was sure he'd imagined the knock on the door until he saw Mira freeze. They were jumpy, fiddling too much, strangely shy with each other since they'd left the closet and stood in the light. Could their collective hope make Wilton appear now just as he had the first time at their back door? They stared at each other until Owen got up.

"Can I talk to you for a minute?" Anya said, the cold yard behind her. She seemed about to step inside but saw Mira and drew back. "Out here? Alone?"

"No, come inside. Talk in here. With both of us."

"It's okay, O," Mira told him. "Whatever she wants."

Owen followed Anya onto the bricks. They stood with their backs against the clapboards for warmth. "Have you heard anything?" he asked.

"No. I saw you through the window," she said. "I thought you didn't live here anymore."

"You're freezing. Come in or at least let me get you a coat."

She shook her head. "I just wanted to tell you that I called some people in Wilton's address book, but no one's heard from him. No one's spoken to him in years. What's he been doing all this time? Who has he been with? Do you think anyone has ever loved him?" she asked, her voice pinched and rising.

"You're shivering. Come inside, please."

Anya refused. On the other side of the back fence, the woman with the yappy dog passed by, talking on the phone. It was so perfectly ordinary that Owen longed to hop the barrier and be taken in. He knew that Wilton could see the things other people had— wives, husbands, lovers, children, dinners, a sense of what a day was worth and where you were needed, and who was waiting for you, a glow over a front door—but he couldn't have that for himself. Wilton had been most real to his daughter as an idea, as the notion of abandonment. She'd been so loyal to an absent father that she hadn't known what to do with the present one.

"Mira left him at that fucking casino," Anya said. "I just don't understand that."

"He wanted her to leave him. He told her to."

"It doesn't matter. You don't leave someone if you think they're not safe alone or in trouble, even if they want you to. How can you forgive her for that? How can you forgive her for anything she's done?"

"Because I love her."

In the glow pouring over them from the kitchen window, he

saw how young she was and, now, how determined. "I just wanted to let you know I'll be sleeping over there, in case he comes back. In case you see lights and think he's home."

Anya returned to her father's house, and Owen watched as light after light went on. Inside, Mira stood at the sink. It was clear she'd heard their conversation.

Owen put his coat on. "I should go."

"It's a good question, you know," she said. "How can you forgive me? For anything, for everything?" She turned to look at him. "Why did you come by earlier?"

Owen sat at the table; he didn't have the will to leave, but maybe the will to confess what he'd done, what he'd told Wilton. Mira might never forgive him if he told her, but she might not ever forgive herself if he didn't.

"I wanted to see you," he said.

She gave him a gentle smile. "You can stay if you want."

He knew she didn't want to be alone in the house, so he slept that night in her old bedroom in the back. The bed sagged against the booty under the springs. He woke later to Wilton's voice, deeply relieved to know the man was finally back. He had taken a vacation from his life, and who could blame him? Tomorrow Owen would apologize. But too soon he realized he was hearing Bruno Macon, not Wilton at all, and his lungs deflated, his throat closed. Down the hall, Mira was watching reruns of *Ancient Times,* her useless remedy. Next door, Anya was doing the same thing, and the gray and blue shadows of Wilton on the screen lived it up in the space between the two houses,

Three days later, there was still no word from Wilton or the police. Owen had left Spruance after lunch, claiming a stomach bug, and now he drove down Route 6 to his father's house. The bare trees revealed what summer foliage always obscured—raw new construction and old houses faded into gray, streets that curved against the bay on his left and the ocean on his right, everything dusted with winter sand. The waterfall at the miniature golf course was off, its cataract blocked by a patch of black plastic. The drive-in screen loomed over the deserted parking lot.

How was it possible for a man to just vanish? Could Wilton slide off a bar stool at the casino, leave a fifty as tip, check into a hotel and check out the next morning, and there be no record of any of it? Could he push through a set of glass doors at the casino entrance without anyone ever seeing him leave? Could he take a cab to a motel, have a shower, get some ice from the machine, watch some free cable, and not only kill himself but also hide his own body? A detective had told Mira that bodies weren't so easy to get rid of, they held on stubbornly to their place in the world. They—or some small part of themselves—almost always showed up eventually in one form or another. Wilton was officially a missing person now. To Owen, though, Wilton was hovering somewhere between lost and found, still undecided about which way to go.

Owen had allowed the car to wander over the center line and now he yanked the wheel back. The tires squealed. Another car honked. Owen tasted the salt of fear. This was the season of fatal head-ons, the end of winter losing against the insistence of spring and drivers made inattentive by their own impatience. Everyone out here knew at least one person killed this way. The brother of a friend, the husband of the third-grade math teacher. As a kid, this was the season Owen sat in the classroom and willed the trees to burst into blossom, while through the open windows, he could hear the cars on Route 6. On this Wednesday afternoon, the roads had only a dribble of traffic and "See You in June" banners swooped across restaurant doors.

His ringing cell phone made him cringe. He wasn't ready for any kind of news; he wanted to float in that time when nothing was known and everything was still possible. Mike Levi was calling again—Owen had been dodging him for weeks. He'd too easily canceled his tutoring sessions at the last minute, amazed at how bountifully he lied to his students: a family emergency, a minor surgery, a school meeting. They never suspected him of dishonesty. He didn't have the face for it, apparently. At Spruance, he was not quite so prolific with his fictions, but he didn't need to be. His body was present at the head of the room, which was some kind of sad but useful standard by which job performance was measured in these last months of the place. He spent his class time reading *The Call of the Wild* out loud and letting the sleepy ones sleep, the dreamy ones doodle. He brought them food. He told them stories. He had some vague sense that someone in charge would eventually come into his classroom and catch him and throw him out on his ass. That it hadn't happened yet was almost a disappointment, and certainly an indictment.

In the warm weather, the strip of land that ran down the middle of the dirt road to his father's house was tall with grass and wildflowers that musically played on the underbelly of the car. But the grass was still dormant, and the road unattended. Large ruts hadn't been filled in, and some of the stones he and Edward laid every few years to hold the silt in place had been washed away by winter. He parked between the twisted locust trees. The eucalyptus smell in the air was heady, and soon, the sound of mewing reached him like a hundred violins playing on the other side of the pond. The bushes shivered with kittens. They appeared from around the house and from under it, circling his ankles and hooking their skinny tails over his shoes. They were fanged and starving. In the past, Edward would not have let the cats grow feral, fuck with abandon, and give endless, slippery birth. The kittens were evidence of how quickly a man's place gets taken over when he leaves it. His father had moved in with Katherine, and the cozy habitat of a woman was his natural world now. There would be softness and mystery to explore, and he might ask himself why he'd waited so long for it.

Owen looked for some cat food inside, but everything edible had been cleared out. He drove to Dutra's, where he bought bags of cat food, bread, peanut butter, a six-pack of Rolling Rock, some licorice, a can of baked beans. He joked to the man behind the counter that his selection looked like what you'd buy if you were planning on running away with a lion. It was the same man who'd always worked there and who never showed any signs that he recognized Owen.

"You'd need a can opener if that's what you were going to do," he said, humorlessly tapping the tin of beans.

At the house, Owen used a collection of clamshells for bowls and filled them with the greasy pellets of food. The kittens swarmed, and the sound of their crunching rose in the trees like some horrible banquet. When they were done, they wobbled off to the last patches of sun. In the room where his father wrote, the desk was clear and the single bed, which had always served as a landing pad for junk, was bare. An Indian print bedspread was faded in a line where the sun hit it. Three of Rey's tennis balls waited in the corner. The stillness of the place was an enticement for Owen to see his life a little more clearly. He'd come here for that.

The pond was pewter. As he stood on the beach, the reflection of the trees on its surface grew narrower, and very soon what was mirror would be all shadow. He walked the perimeter and wasn't surprised to see that since Porter's death the path had become overgrown. Edward had no reason to walk it anymore. Everything had changed and neighbors accused one another of trespassing and small crimes these days. According to Edward, they could pull out the maps they'd gotten from the county office showing exactly where their indisputable property lines were, where their floating docks were allowed. Some of the houses had been fussed up with skylights and decks. Still, winter debris collected at the base of their doors. Halfway around was Porter's old place, cleaned of furniture and the man's collection of nautical charts and bird photos. A few feet of old orange carpeting in the bedroom had been peeled back to reveal water-stained plywood. The house steeled itself for demolition.

Past Porter's was the house that had been going up the summer before. It was enormous, glass and cedar with a strange buffed metal girth that rose over several neatly planted topographies. The place sat directly on the path. Owen saw no way around it. A woman appeared in the kitchen window. He wasn't close enough to know if she was the naked companion of the barking, naked man on the dock, but she had the same brilliant orange hair. She put on a white apron and began to work at the counter. A loose ponytail ran down her back. He heard faint strains of Latin drumming. With his father at Katherine's, this woman might be the only person on the pond now, except for him. When she looked up, as if she'd heard his thoughts, he darted back.

The only thing to do then was turn around and go back through the arbor that was dotted with silver winterberries. But he didn't want to—and he was angry now because his plan had been to walk the entire circumference. He'd had it in mind for a while. He didn't understand how the house could claim its place so thoroughly and indifferently. He hadn't considered swimming, but now he was compelled to. His jacket was the hardest to take off; it introduced that first blast of cold. His fingers were stiff at the buttons of his shirt, his belt, his boxers. He was naked when he took the gun from his pants pocket. He filled his lungs and talked himself in. His body clenched, his skin drew next to his bones, and his balls retreated up as he forced himself under where it was warmer than the air. He couldn't take a full breath, and the cold made him laugh in short barks. He swam to the center of the pond, his stroke off-balance because of his grip on the gun. His breathing slowed and his organs huddled for warmth; soon his stroke relaxed and the iciness was glorious. Everything in his head was easing out, floating away on the surface, and when he dove, the bottom of the pond rose up to him. He'd never seen it before because he'd never dared to go that deep. He touched the ancient fronds and the nodules on sunken branches. When he looked up, the sun sat on the water. The bottom was under his feet, and he was all right. He let go of the gun, watched it sink until it was gone, and then rose to the top.

The woman from the house stood on the beach, a bright red coat over her apron. She held a blanket and yelled at him. "Get out. It's too cold. Are you crazy?"

"Yes." It took most of his energy to answer.

"You okay?"

"Yes."

His joints began to creak, half frozen. The cold was seeping in through some crack in his body. He didn't know what he'd intended, taking this crazy swim—instead of just chucking the gun into the water as he'd planned—but he saw just how stupid it was. Stupid and perfect. He was exultant, alive, thrilled. But the water was lethal and fear was all over the woman's face.

"I don't like this. You're making me nervous," she yelled and gestured him in. "I'll call the police if you don't come out." She crossed her arms and waited. Her feet were bare in the sand. "I mean it. Get the hell out of the water."

He swam toward her and when he rose from the water, his arms and legs were rocks. The woman took steps back from him. She was the same woman from the dock. She took in his nakedness, his shrunken penis, his face and his size, and tossed him the blanket.

He'd begun to shiver uncontrollably. "Thanks. For coming down. For seeing me."

"You're not going to do it again, are you?" she asked. "Because it's nuts. You know that, right? Dangerous. It's not what people who are okay do. Are you okay?"

"Yes."

"Are you trying to kill yourself?"

"No." His teeth clicked against each other as he picked up his clothes.

"You need some help anyway."

"Probably." But maybe, he thought, all I needed was the weight of the water.

He would have told her the whole story just to tell someone, but he could barely talk. She looked beyond him, and he turned to see his father on his small half moon of beach. Edward's stance was crooked and confused.

Owen thanked her again and waded in the shallows and reeds around the pond to his father. He felt as though he was burning up and freezing at the same time. As he sensed a shift in the weather, Edward would have sensed that his son was in trouble and come to the pond. He looked at Owen as if, above every other question, he was trying to understand how his boy had turned into this naked man with a blanket around his shoulders. How his son had just emerged from the water.

"It doesn't take long to die in this temperature," Edward said furiously. His hand was a claw digging into Owen's arm. "What the hell were you thinking? What's wrong with you?"

Owen's teeth banged. His father, who didn't know that a gun lay under the precious surface, who would have retrieved it himself if he had, pulled Owen through the arbor. Up at the house, he turned on the outdoor shower and held his hand under the water waiting for it to warm. Steam frothed over the enclosure. Owen saw kittens eyeing them from the bushes. He stepped into the searing spray.

Edward watched him, too angry to speak at first. "What's this all about, Owen? You better tell me. You better talk."

"I can't stop shaking." Owen was getting colder instead of warmer. His knees knocked together. He stumbled. His body might break into a thousand slivers of ice. "I can't stop." He heard his voice slurring. He wanted to sleep.

"Okay, relax." Edward stepped into the shower and rubbed Owen's back. He put his arms around him. "Just relax. It's okay. Whatever it is, it's okay. You'll be okay."

The water ran over Edward's head and soaked his clothes as he kept up a steady tone of soothing. Owen wanted to sleep; he felt halfway there already. He leaned against his father. When his shivering finally loosened its grip, so did Edward, who went inside, the door slapping after him. As though he'd just woken up, Owen noticed the bottle of lavender shampoo on the bench, the rose body wash, and a pink razor—Katherine's presence—and he felt brought back to something hopeful. He dried himself and went inside. Edward was at the stove, heating the can of baked beans. He chewed on the licorice. He pointed to Owen's clothes on the couch. He'd folded them, while his own wet things huddled on the bedroom floor and he'd put on a pair of shorts that were too small and a sweatshirt. Owen dressed and leaned over to scratch the dog.

"He's gotten fat," Owen said. He didn't know what to say to his father.

"He's a lazy condo dog now," Edward said. "I see you fed the cats."

"It's like some experiment gone terribly wrong out there. Your cats are fucking like crazy and ready to eat each other."

"I didn't forget," Edward said. "That's why I came here in the first place—to feed them. I didn't expect to see you, much less in the water." He spooned the beans into two bowls, brought them to the table, and banged them down. "Damn crazy idea."

"You don't have to feed me," Owen said.

"I like to feed you, you idiot." Edward poured them each a glass of scotch. "I don't get to do it very often anymore, so just let me. Even if it's just a can of beans." He tested them with the tip of his tongue. "When you're ready, you'll tell me what's going on."

"Talk to me first," Owen said.

Edward told him about life at Katherine's and the robust social scene, which he didn't participate in as much as she would like him to. He was proud of his own stubbornness and of how ordinary their disagreement was. A man in the complex, a former publishing bigwig, had asked him to write a book about how the elderly can find meaning in nature.

"He's a moron," Edward said. He nodded at Owen's untouched food and told him to eat. "There's no more meaning in nature than there is in anything else; it's just another way for old people to keep their minds off dying. Look at potholes or lampposts if you want, or landfills, or nuclear power plants, or the war, or a city bus. And the natural world? It's all about dying when you've outlived your usefulness. Make your eggs, your seeds, your off-spring, your flowers, and that's it. You're finished, plowed under, dried up, eaten, and shit out. There's nothing romantic about it." Edward was unmoved by his own description. "Besides, I don't have a lot to say on the subject."

"Right. I can tell." Owen laughed. "No opinions."

"I have precisely two words: pay attention. That's what it's all about. Pay attention. It doesn't matter if it's the ocean or the mail-box." He blotted his mouth with his sleeve. "Now your turn. Talk to me. Tell me."

Owen started his story with the present—Wilton's disappear-ance more than ten days ago—and worked his way back to the beginning. *And before that,* he heard himself saying, *and before that, and before that.* He'd arrived at the beginning, just he and Mira one night about to have dinner in the kitchen, when Wilton appeared at the back door. He'd also arrived at the end, where the tragedy was his fault.

"I lied to Wilton about his daughter. I told him we'd all be better off if he wasn't around anymore." Owen said, and then hesitated. "I told him to kill himself." The words backed up in his throat and he looked wildly at his father.

Edward put his hand on Owen's cheek. "No, you don't have that power," he said. "Do you remember that little red double-decker bus someone sent you from London? I can't even remem-ber who it was now. Anyway, you were crazy about it. You took it everywhere, to school, on walks, to the store. You slept with it. You must have been about six. Then one day we went out in the boat and you dropped it over the edge. On purpose."

"It wasn't on purpose." Owen could still picture the red rect-angle sinking out of sight, the regret burning in his chest.

"It was entirely on purpose. You hung it right over the edge and

opened your hand and let go. I watched you do it. I was amazed."
He opened and shut his hand. "I thought you did it because you
wanted to see what would happen—not to the bus, because that
was obvious—it was long gone to the bottom; you knew how that
worked—but to you. You wanted to see what would happen to
you if you lost something you loved that much. To see what you
could bear."

"And what happened?"

"You whimpered for a bit and then I think you were relieved.
You knew you loved it too much, that it was only setting you up for
disappointment—if and when you lost it—which you inevitably
would. Something that perfect couldn't last. You were a magical
boy, but too old when you were so young. No kid should have to
understand that. You don't have the power to make a man kill
himself. What Wilton did—if he did anything—he did because
he wanted to."

"What was your marriage to my mother like?" *My mother*—he
hadn't said those words in years and they felt false in his mouth.
My mother, never Helen, a name he'd always found at odds with
his image of her as breezy, long-haired, bare-footed.

"I adored her," Edward said. "But she bounced around a lot in
her life. I knew that she would eventually leave me and take you
with her. I'd expected that from the beginning. I didn't expect her
to die."

"Why did you wait this long to find someone else?"

"Oh, Christ, Owen. You were that someone else. You were so
much more than I ever expected to have. You were enough. What
did I need anyone else for?"

Owen went to the couch, put his head back, and shut his eyes.
He was shivering again and his head ached. He said he had to get

going, he had to teach in the morning, and Edward should not let
him fall asleep.

"You're not going anywhere. Listen to me," his father said. "You
have to stop thinking you can control what happens, that you can
keep everyone safe, Mira included."

Edward told him to get up and led him to the bedroom. He
pulled back the sheets so Owen could get into bed. He piled another blanket on top of him. Later, Owen found himself in dizzying disorientation—was this his house, his apartment, his childhood, his old age, his wife, his mother, his father, no one next to
him? He forced himself to get his bearings. In the other room, his
father was asleep in the chair, Owen's suede coat thrown over his
lap. It was just after 5:00 a.m. and he had to be in the classroom
in a little more than two hours. There was the pond, the birds
just rousing, the inch of light over the tree line, the kittens faintly
insistent at the door, and his father like a sickbed visitor whose
chin has fallen onto his chest.

Trouble hung over the school, and it was clear that morning that
the news was out. Spruance was officially over, finished at the
end of the year. The few teachers in the building early exchanged
doleful greetings and nods, as if they'd met one another on the
sidewalk going in to Slavin's for a funeral. With death coming,
there would soon be nothing left but last gestures. Owen's stomach gripped as he moved between the kids in his classroom.
What remained of the school year was damned and ruined, and
it seemed to him that what a teacher really had was expectation. Not necessarily talent or that vague concept of vision, but
some measure of faith. But that was done for now, because you
couldn't tell kids that school had nothing to do with the building

they came to every day, the banged-up stairwells, the dripping bathrooms, the stink of the boiler, the smudgy trophy case with the oldest wins just outside the front office. It had to do with all that, and everything that was theirs. He loved the students who tried and those who didn't. The kids couldn't imagine themselves anywhere but Spruance—even those who couldn't wait to leave as soon as they arrived every morning—because how could you imagine your own exile? If every day they said they were bored, what they really meant was, *I can't do this. There's too much else in my head and body.* If students and teachers could be scattered and sent to the four corners of the city, then what did any of this matter? As he took attendance, he had a hard time meeting the eyes of those who would still bother to look at him. They asked him if he knew what was going to happen to them, and he told them he knew nothing. They knew he was lying.

At the end of the day, he found a good-size group of kids still on the front steps. He wanted to think they were appreciating the beautiful afternoon, stretching out on the granite, or that they were commiserating. He tried to think of something consoling he might say to them, like "You're all going to be just fine." But the crowd was not interested in him, or in the bulldozer of school reform rumbling toward them, or the dogs humping across the street, but in the standoff that was taking place between two girls. They swiped at earrings, necklaces, the necks of low-cut shirts. They kicked and pawed and the crowd egged them on. And when they saw Owen, they stopped and walked away. They might have wondered, what was the point now of beating each other up? It was their giving up like this that most upset him.

Anya was watching from across the street. If his first impulse was to believe she had some news about her father, he saw from her strangely distant and gauzy expression that she didn't. He looked away from her. The buses pulled out, and on the front patch of meager grass a teacher bent to pick up garbage. Her slip showed at the back of her thick thighs as she reached down.

"I figured something out and I wanted to tell you," Anya said, when he crossed the street.

He suggested they walk. He wanted to get away from the school. In the five days since he'd taken his crazy swim in the pond, the trees had begun to swell. The sun twitched behind the branches as they walked, and Owen felt that nothing jarred quite so much as pain on a glorious day. The sky held the kind of light that made you think Providence was the right place to be and you might know everyone you passed. A steady thwack of tennis balls came from deep in the neighborhood. Blocks from Spruance, a group of his students had gathered on and around a bench in front of the too precious Child's Hour Preschool. The kids had chosen a beautiful spot—who could blame them?—touched by vague hints of green, faced by expensive, shining houses. He asked the kids what they were up to; the consensus was nothing, and in any case, they were much more interested in Anya.

"So if you're up to nothing, you should probably go home," he said, and gestured with a shake of his wrist to get them off the bench.

They balked and moaned and made a big show of it. Behind the doors of the preschool, a woman nodded at him as if she understood how they were both burdened by children. Her small charge was rolling around on the floor in a tantrum. The kids started up the hill, a group too wide for the sidewalk, so they spilled onto the street. One boy slid his foot along the impeccable edge of the granite curb.

"Why can't they sit there?" Anya asked. "That's not allowed? Why, because they're black?"

"It's much more complicated than that," he said, but in many ways it wasn't. He believed he was protecting them from contempt and suspicion, but maybe he wasn't. Providence could also be the very wrong place to be, backward and distrusting.

"They should have told you to go fuck yourself."

Owen lacked the will to fight with her, and they were silent until they'd arrived at Wilton's house. "What did you want to tell me?" he asked.

"I've decided something," Anya said, looking down at her twisting hands. "I decided that when Mira deserted Wilton at the casino—"

"She didn't desert him."

"Okay, when she ditched him. Is that better? Okay, when she abandoned him, when she ditched him, he met a woman, and he's been caught up with her this whole time. He's fallen in love and he flew to Prague or Costa Rica and they're in some state of romantic amnesia. He's lost track of the time; he's not used to people caring about where he is. It hasn't occurred to him yet to check in, but it will. And then he'll call. And he'll be fine."

Her scenario stopped Owen cold. It was a fantasy that she was going to sell to herself and to him, but it was ridiculous, made up out of nothing but regret and a wish.

"It happens all the time," she insisted. "People disappear for only a few reasons. They get lost, they get killed, or they fall in love. And he hasn't been in love in a long, long, time. This is what he wants, someone to love and to love him back. Stop shaking your head, Owen. Just stop. And don't dare tell me I'm wrong." She eyed him angrily.

"I just don't think—"

"You don't know him any better than I do. You don't know anything about him."

"Anya," he said. "This is not your fault."

"Did I say it was? This isn't about me," she said. "My father's fine. He's in love. What's the matter, don't you believe it's possible?"

She extracted the key on a string from under her shirt where it lived against her skin now. She opened the door and slipped behind it.

15

In the thirteen days her father had been missing, Anya had slept in Wilton's house every night; Owen had slept in his Fox Point apartment. Back at the house to meet Mira, he watched Anya from the kitchen window. A kitten on the end of a red leash prowled on its belly in the wet grass of Wilton's yard.

"This is what she does all day. Paces and obsesses over that cat," Mira said, coming to stand next to him. "It's hard to see, her keeping vigil."

"That's what we're all doing, isn't it?" he said. "Just waiting?"

He knew Mira was keeping her own kind of watch, one that involved distraction and neglect. Her hair was flattened on one side of her head and she looked tired. The house had a stuffy, anxious smell. It needed airing out, the junk mail and newspapers tossed, the coats and shoes picked up from the hall floor, half-full crusty jars chucked in the garbage. He felt the house picking at him with its needs, an insistent old lady.

"Anya doesn't sleep," Mira said. "I see the lights go on in the middle of the night when I'm awake. It feels like we're the only two people in the world and we're both watching *Ancient Times*. It's sad."

Mira was trying to conjure Wilton again, to draw his essence from the television, as she believed she'd done in the beginning. She told him how Anya wouldn't talk to her or even look at her, despite her attempts over the fence. Did she want dinner, company, a walk? Did she have something she wanted to say? Needed something at the store? The only thing Anya wanted, apparently, was for Mira to leave her alone.

"It's a terrible feeling to be hated like this," Mira said. "Despised. I don't blame her for blaming me. I was the last person to see Wilton. I left him. But still, does she think this is what I wanted?" She gulped down her distress.

She was wearing a very bright white shirt over blue leggings and green sneakers. It was an attempt to be bright, but it tried too hard. The shirt was huge on her, the hem whisking the backs of her thighs. Owen touched the stiff collar and felt her freeze up as his finger brushed her neck. On this Saturday morning, she had asked him to go to Brindle with her to pick through the ruins—a salvaging expedition, he imagined.

"The shirt was my father's. I found an entire drawer full of them still in their packaging. I think he had a shopping disorder. I mean, look at this house. He was a shopaholic."

"So everything is an addiction these days," he said coolly, still reeling from how she'd responded to his touch. "Maybe it's not disease, though, maybe it's just pleasure, just single-minded desire. Maybe there's nothing to cure but selfishness."

"Maybe." She looked quickly at him and then down at her feet. "I lied to you, and you should always detest a liar, O," she said. "A liar is not someone you want to be with, believe me."

"But the lying is over," he said.

"Is it? You're still not living here and Wilton's still missing. I don't know the truth about anything."

He followed her into the hall where she began jamming things into her bag. She couldn't find her glasses or her keys and searched under the newspapers, under the table.

"I don't know why you don't hate me and blame me for everything, too," she said. "I hate me and blame me."

She was on her knees, her face hidden. She'd been hiding from him since he'd come in. That she would stay on the floor like this, trying to bend herself into something inconsequential and unseen, was too much for him. "Blame me, Mira," he said. He forced himself to say it again—so she would at least get up. "Blame me. Hate me."

Slowly, she stood. She found her glasses in her pocket and cleaned them for too long with the front of her shirt. She held them at a distance, looked at him through the lenses. Nothing was clear; she wiped again and fixed on him.

On that night they'd first met on Ives Street years before, when the boy who'd stolen money from Brindle had finally showed up, Mira got in the kid's face and asked, "Why do you think what you did is wrong?" The question was imperturbable and patient, and it didn't take long for the kid to break and fess up. As she examined Owen, he had the sudden, chilling sense that she knew exactly what he'd done and said to Wilton all along. That she'd always known, had learned everything the night Wilton disappeared and was waiting to hear him say it. She was waiting for him to confess and release her. And if he didn't, well, this is how she would punish herself, this was what she deserved.

In the benign Saturday morning sun that made the oak look newly oiled, maybe what he'd done wouldn't appear so terrible. Maybe Mira would see it for just what it was—his way of pulling her back from the edge. A house alarm began to wail across the street. It happened often enough now that there was nothing urgent about it anymore, but the noise was a rope winding through the air, choking them quiet. Owen went out to the driveway. Anya was on her father's porch steps. The cat's leash tightened as it snooped around in the bushes. The alarm went silent, but the sound still throbbed in Owen's ears.

Mira appeared and waved to Anya, though she knew she'd get nothing back. In the car, Mira asked, "Did you sleep with her? Is that what I should blame you for?" She was practicing casualness, settling her bag onto her lap, and snapping in her seat belt. He could feel a furious heat coming off her.

"No." He sped out of the driveway and onto the street. He loved the moment just before the car crested the hill and the city came into sight, but now it came too quickly. He'd missed the instant of expectation.

"Wilton thought you did," Mira said. "He talked about it that last night. He said it was his fault because he'd pushed you two together—he'd wanted you to help him with her. And then I saw it too the other day, the way she spoke to you, the way she looked at you and you looked at her."

"I said no, Mira. Jesus. Did you hear me?"

She stared straight ahead, and when they'd reached the bottom of the hill, she spoke. "Do you remember how, when we first met Wilton, we used to talk about him all the time together? And then suddenly we didn't anymore because it was all secrets?"

"We each had our own private life with him."

"It doesn't really work, though, does it." Mira pushed her hair onto the top of her head and let it fall. "He gave us what we wanted—some excitement, some nice wine, a new friend for each of us. A lot of flattery—too much of it, too easy."

Because we always want more, Owen knew, we bank on it to head off the sadness coming at us, that first glimpse we have of the end. On North Main Street, a banner strung between the trees announced that it was Roger Williams's four-hundredth birthday, and the long scarf of park dedicated to him was busy with celebrants bouncing in the chill. The twang of live music scratched through the air. A cluster of balloons straining on a string dipped low in a sudden gust and hit the side of the car with rubbery thuds. Traffic was stopped by a cop who let a long train of shiny-suited cyclists cross. Some of the riders wore pictures of children on their backs, or names and dates of dead ones. Across the river, the tail end of the cyclists appeared around the base of a building.

When the last cyclist finally passed, they headed over the Point Street Bridge, where the hurricane barrier looked like a bird paralyzed in midflap. Owen pulled into the lot behind Brindle. Four parking spaces belonged to Brindle, and all but one were taken. Anything left fallow for too long in the city was grabbed up, and this was free space. And the Dumpster was for free dumping, but he could see that it was empty. He'd expected to see a massive mound of it spilling onto the ground and recalled the feasting rat sheltered from the snow and the legions of black plastic bags lined up against the outside wall.

"Where'd all the garbage go?" he asked.

"I paid the bill I owed and they came and hauled it away."

"How? You don't have any money." He turned to her. "What did you do? Did you play again?"

"Play? No, Owen, I did not *play*. I don't *play* anymore." His anger had surprised her, but she was ready to fight back. "And screw you for asking me."

"It's a fair question," he said.

"No, it isn't," she snapped. "Not now it isn't. The day Wilton disappeared was the day I stopped forever. My god! What do you think I am?"

She got out of the car and slammed the door. Owen didn't know what she was or what compelled her. He didn't know who she was any more than she knew who he was. You imagined your spouse's virtues when really you should imagine their transgressions. Whether or not she ever played the slots again, she was changed for it—they both were. Just how, he wasn't yet sure. The shift might take years to reveal itself. But maybe the same wasn't what I should be after, he told himself. Inside Brindle, he watched Mira stomp through the gallery

"Where did you get the money?" he asked.

She stopped to look at how leaks under the front windows had feathered the wall below the sill. "You look away for one second and this is what happens," she said, tracing the damage with a finger. "Time moves very fast when it's going downhill. I've spent so many years here and put so much into this place, put everything into it, in fact. Probably more than I should have." She was talking to herself. "I don't want to lose it. I'm going to have to start all over, from the beginning, but that's okay, I think."

"Tell me where you got the money."

She considered Owen, her expression revealing nothing. "I sold something that belonged to my mother. A bracelet. She never liked it anyway."

That she'd done what she'd said she never would was a sad relief to Owen. He opened the front door to let some warmer air in and listened to the oceanic roar of the traffic on I-95. To his left, two women approached from Point Street, walking briskly with their arms hooked in this unfamiliar neighborhood. They yelled for him to wait and picked up their pace. He put them in their late fifties, expensively dressed in sharply pleated pants and bright jackets that pinched their waists. Silk scarves were knotted at their necks. They exuded fitness and some giddy quality of liberation from men and children.

"Thank you," the silvery blond woman said, breathlessly. "We've been calling and calling and no one answers."

Her friend gave Owen a generous smile. "We're thinking of taking a class. Can we look around?"

"Brindle's closed now," he said. "I'm sorry." Their perfume was a strong, confusing bouquet. "You'll have to come back."

"No, come in," Mira said, moving up from behind him. She ushered the women past Owen. "We're just doing some renovations," she explained, instantly bright and chatty. He was struck by how effortlessly she switched her mood. "That's why it's such a mess. And you know how these things go. It's taking much longer than we expected."

"I know how *that* goes," one of the women assured her. "But you'll be open soon? We wanted to take a drawing class. You know," she glanced at her friend, "with a model. Life drawing."

Mira explained that the class would start in the late spring. She pulled a notebook from her bag to take down their information. The women said they'd heard good things about Brindle. Mira's pen was poised, but Owen knew she sensed their sudden reluctance. The disheartening air of the place had begun to leach into their lungs.

"The place is going to be beautiful," he said. "You'll see. And the light in the building is amazing."

"This will change your life," Mira said, placing a hand on one woman's aqua forearm. A different picture, and this woman could be her mother. "I swear it will. There's nothing like drawing,

painting. You'll start seeing everything in a different way once you
learn how to really pay attention."

The woman was startled by Mira's intimacy and her intent,
colorless gaze. You could feel Mira was looking inside your head
at a time like this, and that her hand was on your heart and not
just your sleeve.

"How?" the woman asked. "How will it change my life?"

"You'll have to find that out for yourself," Mira tossed off, click-
ing her pen for emphasis and laughing. "That's the mystery. Then
later, you'll have to tell *me*."

Her answer was no answer, really, but it satisfied the women.
Mira had planted the suggestion that seeing differently could
transform you. The notion was simple and anyone could swallow
it. You didn't have to know anything, have anything, come from
anywhere. It was the same idea he offered his students every year
and every day. Maybe he'd try it himself, a different way of paying
attention, a different view of life. The women talked for a while,
blinking in the sun, before they wandered back to where they'd
come from, no longer hooking arms. Owen locked the front door
and followed Mira upstairs to the studio.

"I know you think I'm full of shit, O, but I meant what I said
out there about getting Brindle back. I'll sell what I have to sell
to do it."

He pictured their house empty of all its valuables, the wind
whipping through cleaned rooms. "And how about the part about
changing the women's lives?"

She turned around to smile at him. "Well, *that*—who knows?
It's always possible, isn't it? I can't offer a guarantee. People want
the change to be like an earthquake, but more often it's a tremor
they don't even register until much later."

There was nothing false in how her mood had shifted. She still came to life in this place. He sat on a stool facing the model's deserted and scuffed platform. There was a half-eaten muffin on the shelf, reminding him of how hungry he was. His appetites were either huge or nonexistent. He needed a shower and some food.

"That muffin over there," he said, pointing to it. "You're going to get roaches next."

Mira handed it to Owen. She tapped it with her ring: clay, glazed white and cakey, complete with blue dots for blueberries. "One of the kids made it," she said. "Pretty convincing, apparently."

She sat on the model's platform and leaned back on her elbows. The sun hit her face and she closed her eyes. "Sometimes I think Wilton's turned into vapor," she said. "I see drops of him collecting on leaves and beading up in the mirror. He's the water on the outside of the bottle. He's the fog on the inside of the windshield. He's on my glasses. I can wipe him away and he comes back."

She was talking about death. Owen had begun to see Wilton's scattering everywhere, too—on the aging faces of the women earlier; in the sight of George's dutiful hand dusting the shelves in the apartment, always losing his battle with the dirt and war; in the way some of his students looked hopeful in the morning, their eyelids flecked with optimism. Mira spread a blanket over the platform. She lay down on her side, facing away, and asked him to lie down with her. But he was stuck where he was and wasn't sure he wanted to lie next to her, because how could he ever get up again if he did? He traced her figure in the air. He didn't know how to draw or paint or do anything else she taught others to do. He didn't know how to make much at all. He felt like a man of very small abilities. His finger followed the upsweep of her legs to the sharp fall of her hip, the rise again of her ribs to her head as she supported it with a hand. She looked over her shoulder at him.

"Anya thinks Wilton's in love," Owen said. "That he met a woman that night and the two of them have gone off somewhere. That he's so in love he's forgotten about everything and everyone."

"That's what she should believe," Mira said, after a minute. "That's her idea of how it works—that love makes you forget everything, that love can save your life."

"What do you think happened to him?" he asked. "Where is he?"

Mira turned to face him, and her pose reminded him of women on the pond's crescent beach in the summer, languid and half-dazed by the heat. He etched the line of her chin and neck, the mouth, the swoop of her breasts, the flat of her stomach, the gullies of her hip bones that disappeared under the waist of her pants. He drew in the air and felt the contact of his finger against the line run hot up his spine. She took her glasses off. Her head was down, and her shoulders rounded forward. Her bare toes curled and uncurled. He lay down on the platform and fit his body against hers.

"I don't know what's happened to him," she said.

Owen's mouth was just above her ear; he didn't have anything more to say.

"Where is he?" She tried to roll against him, but he didn't want her to see his suffering. "I don't blame you for anything, O. Come home to me, please, O."

He said he would—he was ready.

16

Chocolate and sugar mixed with the sweet honeysuckle and damp earth as Owen turned the car off Route 6 and onto his father's road. The air smelled like birthday cake, he said. He tried to catch Anya's eye in the rearview mirror, but she stared resolutely into the trees, one arm resting on the cat carrier she'd brought to carry home one of Edward's wild kittens in. A week earlier, she'd watched as her own cat was snatched up by a coyote in Wilton's backyard. In the morning, she'd shown Owen the red collar that lay coiled like a vein in the grass.

"Maybe we're on Cake Cod, not Cape Cod," Mira said. Her terrible stab at humor—and her failed attempts to reach Anya—made her shift uneasily in her seat. "Edward always makes his own birthday cakes. They're kind of magnificent. Wait till you see."

The silence was enormous. Owen parked between the locust trees and scrambled out of the car; he couldn't get away from the tension between the two women fast enough. He closed his eyes against the fluttering shadows, inhaled the scent of new leaves, silt, wet bark, tadpole ooze, the ammoniac sting of fish. Then his car alarm went off—the opposite of the painful silence but just as loud. Was it habit that made him automatically set the alarm, even when the women were still in it. Or did he really want to lock the women away? He laughed at his mistake and their surprised cartoon faces behind glass and turned the alarm off. Mira smirked at him; she found the unintentional the most amusing, too. But Anya was stony and stood against the car as if she were ready to leave in the next second, no need to take another step forward into the day. Edward and Katherine rushed out of the house and formed a shield around her as if they'd agreed on this unified compassionate front beforehand. Katherine stroked Anya's hair. Rey stuck his head in her crotch. Edward scolded Owen about the noise.

The pond was as high as Owen had ever seen it. Sun spiked up from its floor, the moon sleeping in the woody depths. He couldn't say exactly what had changed inside the house. There were still the bleached, almost indecipherable photographs thumbtacked to the wall, the faded couch with its ripped cushions decorated with animal hair, and his father's reading chair frayed from decades of ideas and cats scratching. There was his father's listing birthday cake on the table, rose-colored, dotted with gumdrops, unrestrained and beautifully hopeful.

"Do you see? We got rid of so much stuff," Katherine said, opening her arms to the room. "All those shells, rocks, those animal skeletons and feathers. It was your father's idea."

Here was the end of the Museum of Natural History. Katherine squeezed his arm; the day would be made up of these small touches of commiseration.

Outside, Owen and Mira watched Edward take Anya to the arbor to find a kitten. He peered into the bushes and parted the tall grass, Anya leaning over with him. Two cats leaped away. Edward tried another bush, then another. He whistled and clicked. With his longer absences from the house, the animals were no longer desperate for his food or his company. Owen was struck by the realization that his father was most likely never going to live here

again, and this marked the end of a part of his own life, too. He
didn't know what would become of the place. He spotted a stack
of plastic boxes partially hidden by the propane tank and the dormant trumpet vine. He showed Mira. Edward's collections from
the house, not thrown out but not quite kept either, and probably
hidden from Katherine.

"My father's way of leaving without fully going," he said.

Mira sighed. "I love this place. Who could ever really leave? I
could see us living here."

Owen wondered if she meant it. After lunch, they squeezed
into Katherine's ancient Camry with its pine-stinking tree hanging from the mirror and went to look at the ocean waves at Head
of the Meadow Beach. Edward twisted to talk to the backseat and
detail for Anya what she was seeing along the way: the variety of
trees, a new house that had violated building codes and he hoped
would be torn down, a summer resident's large garden he disdain-
fully said was cared for by paid hands. A faded cross on Route 6
where a high school kid had died last year in an accident.

"One of the most dangerous roads in the country," he told her.

Katherine drove fast and loose with one hand hooked on the
bottom of the steering wheel. She took turns wildly, forcing Owen
against Anya, then Mira. He was stuck between them with his
knees almost at his chest. Large sections of asphalt at the beach
parking lot had collapsed and sand flurried around in their de-
pressions. The place was deserted—it always was, except in the
teeming summer. The cinderblock bathrooms were stoic at the far
end. Edward delivered his somber update: more erosion.

"A few decades from now with the way things are going, who
knows what the place will look like. Fortunately, I won't be around
to see it. Everybody zipped up?" he asked. "Hats? Gloves? The
wind's fierce. Mira, you zipped?"

"Zipped," she said.

She got out first and pretended to be blown away by the wind, her feet running backward faster than she could keep up. Her arms windmilled and she grew smaller and smaller in the haze of sand and afternoon. When she came back to the car, her nose was red and she was out of breath.

"It's a bitch out here," she yelled through the wind. "Be careful!"

This false clumsiness and the acting were unlike her—and much more like Wilton. It was disconcerting to watch. Was she hoping for the same easy affection and laugh he always got from his acrobatics? Was she still just trying to thaw Anya out? Her playfulness only seemed to sting Anya more. They crested the pale sliding dunes to see the water, a stormy blue expanse with enormous rolls. Owen inhaled greedily. It was impossible to tell what was the sound of the water and what was the wind. Even Edward realized it was useless to talk and gave up his attempts to educate them anymore. Katherine took pictures, waving people into better views. She forced Anya and Mira to stand together for one, Anya's head tilted away from Mira. Edward shivered, his face frozen into a grimace of pleasure. Tears from the cold spilled down his cheeks. He mimed to Owen that he'd forgotten his hat in the car, and Owen mimed back that he'd go get it. Anya had pulled her striped bumblebee hat down almost past her eyes. Only Mira ignored the cold as she bent to examine something on the damp, sloping sand. For a moment, they were each alone.

The wind in the parking lot was gentle in contrast to the gale on the beach, but the sand still pinged as it covered the car in a fine dust. Owen imagined that if they left the car there long enough, it would eventually disappear. Inside, he reached under the front seat for Edward's hat, which had been kicked there by his enthusiasm. Owen's cell phone rang, and he fumbled for it with his cold hands, dropping it into the seam of the seat. All rings were urgent when you weren't expecting them. He shouted into the phone as if he were screaming down a hole.

The voice on the other end was making sure it had the right Owen Brewer. A cloud dipped behind the dune and the grass stood still. And what a brilliant, exhilarating toothpaste blue and white the air was at that moment. Owen had never seen anything like it. The man explained that he was a homicide detective in Manhattan, but why, Owen wondered, was he calling from New York? He squeezed himself behind the front seat, contorted on the car floor. He focused on the scattering of sand on the mat, the single grains.

"We have some news," the man said.

"Hold on."

Owen reached to lock the doors. If the man on the phone used the word "found," what would that mean? Found like a hat kicked under the seat, found like the earring under the rug, found like something you'd buried in the schoolyard? *Found* was something that couldn't reveal itself. Found was a body. "Okay. I'm here."

But he was suddenly dense and couldn't understand what the man was saying. The noise in his ear was too loud. "I don't know what you're talking about," Owen shouted. "What about Wilton?"

"Wilton? What's Wilton? I'm talking about Rumford. He's the one."

Owen pictured the detective leaning into the phone, speaking more deliberately now, as though Owen was addled. A confession, the man said. Rumford was a boaster, an idiot, a blabbermouth, and what did he have to lose talking about how he'd shot a woman years ago in a restaurant, when he was going to spend the rest of his life in prison anyway for killing someone else?

"Rumford?" Owen asked. Having a name for the shooter was a terrible intimacy. He wished he'd never heard it. He watched the wind blow the grass horizontal. "Rumford?" he asked. "Not Wilton?"

"Christ, yes. Rumford. Correct."

Owen had believed Caroline's killer would never be caught, that there were lots of people in the world who simply got away with the very worst things. The man's free-roaming presence had always been a part of his weather, he understood, but now that he had a name and was caged, Owen didn't feel relief. He felt oddly vacant.

"Did you have to call me?" he asked.

"Have to? Look, I thought you'd want to know. Most people do." The detective was tired of Owen and closing up the conversation by speaking to someone he was with, and then he was gone.

So the ending was as mundane as could be. The lucky break was always tepid—and nothing more than luck. What did he care if the guy was in prison? Better for Owen to imagine the story and its players and die with his version of things tucked under his tongue, so that he might tell it differently in another life. He folded up the news, put it away, and went out to the dunes again. He wondered if the others would be able to read his face and see something different, but they had gone down the beach and close to the water's edge. Edward was wearing Anya's hat, while her hair lifted into the air.

Later, when they got back to the house, Mira fell into a weighty sleep on the couch with her legs pulled under her, and Katherine and Edward went into the bedroom. The cold had worn them out, but Owen was antsy. While Anya pretended to be engrossed in one of Edward's ancient *Audubon* magazines, Owen walked to the shoulder of Route 6, where he stood for a while, watching the sporadic late Saturday afternoon traffic pass. A car came out of the pond road, a monstrous white SUV driven by the woman with the red hair. She turned right in the direction of Provincetown without noticing him. He tried to imagine what they would have said to each other if she'd stopped. The news of his phone call was shapeless still, nothing he could pull out and show. He wanted to toss it out on the highway and watch it get run over.

Mira and Anya were setting the table for dinner when he came in from his walk.

If one woman put down a fork, the other moved it; one refused to yield to the other. Mira orbited Anya, mumbling, pulling her bulky sweater tighter round her. Anya said something back.

"Well, I'm sorry you feel that way," Mira said, suddenly fierce. Edward and Katherine had emerged from the bedroom and were looking on drowsily. "But you're probably right: you shouldn't have come."

The silence was punctuated by the dog's wheezy fart. "Well put, Rey," Edward said.

"Let them talk, Eddie," Katherine scolded. "For god's sake, stay out of it."

Anya backed up to a wall. "You should have stayed with him. What kind of a friend leaves another when he's in trouble?"

"You don't think I know that?" Mira folded a paper napkin, her fury contained in that controlled motion. "I won't ever forgive myself for that. I think about it every single minute."

Anya watched Mira's careful movements, and seemed, for an instant, to soften. She looked down at her feet in the gray socks Edward had given her for warmth. She also wore a sweater of his—stretched-out, the wrists and neck moth-eaten. The wind hissed as it slipped into the house around the windows. "Did he ever talk to you about me?"

Mira stopped and looked at Anya. "Are you kidding? All the time. You have no idea how much he loves you." Owen could tell that Mira was considering some hard piece of truth—and whether she should give the softer lie to Anya instead. "He thought things were going really well between you two. He knew your getting back together, your moving in, wasn't going to happen immediately, but he was always hopeful. He wanted to let you do it the way you wanted, even if it took a long time. So yes, he talked about you. Everything else was just a diversion. He thought you were much nicer to him than he deserved." Mira's look said she thought otherwise.

"I wasn't nice to him," Anya said and ran into the bathroom. Minutes passed as they listened to the water running in the sink.

"Do you think she's crying?" Edward whispered.

"I imagine she is," Mira said.

"It seems to me that's exactly what she should be doing under the circumstances—having lost her father," Katherine said.

"Not lost," Owen insisted. "Just missing."

Edward shook his head. "You don't really believe that anymore, do you?"

Mira's gaze was intent on Owen, asking, *Yes, what do you believe?*

Tell her, Owen urged himself, tell everyone what you've done, what you said, how you betrayed the man, how you told him to kill himself, and he'd likely done just that. He imagined that if he applied all the pressure in his head and chest to his words, he could turn them into diamonds he might hand out instead as recompense. Edward gave him a sideways glance. Water splashed in the bathroom. Release them, he told himself. Release Mira and Anya.

Anya came out of the bathroom and dabbed at the water on the front of the sweater. She gave the room a forced smile and sat at the table. "Just so you know, I heard everything you said," she told them. "But my father's in love and he'll be back."

Her resolve—her sunny, romantic scenario—muted them, and at times the silence in the room took flight and squawked in relief across the pond. But soon, loosened by the wine Edward kept pouring into her glass, Anya began to describe what it was like sleeping in her father's almost empty house, how she saw shadows and heard noises all the time, and how she didn't understand how Wilton could have lived there by himself. Her cheeks were red. She swiped her hair behind her ears. Mira didn't look up.

"Most people aren't meant to be alone," Katherine told her. "If they were, they wouldn't fall in love. It does have a purpose." She smoothed Edward's hand. Her presence beside him at the table made its point; she would protect Edward from everything.

When Katherine brought over the listing cake, they sang a rousing rendition of "Happy Birthday." They made the noise of a hundred people. Edward blew out the single, yellowed hurricane candle and cut huge, sloppy slices. They picked gumdrops out of their teeth. Mira went out to the car and returned with something in bright wrapping paper. When she put it in front of Edward, he drew back.

"It's a present. It's not going to bite you," Mira said. "Open it."

"I don't need a present."

"No one *needs* a present," Mira said. "That's the point."

Edward pushed the package at Anya. "Then you open it."

She pushed it back. "But it's not my birthday."

Edward unwrapped the gift with excruciating care, lifting each piece of tape off the paper. Mira had given him a Chinese bronze crane, about seven inches tall, with swooping tail feathers. It was one of those entirely familiar objects that had been on the mantelpiece in the bedroom forever, but one that Owen had never stopped to really look at. He knew it—but he didn't know it. What did it mean that Mira was giving her things away?

"It's very beautiful," Edward said and put the bird in the center of the table. "Thank you."

"It's not useful, you know," Mira told him. "It doesn't do anything. It's just to look at, a thing."

"I'll have to get used to that," Edward said.

Owen stood. "I need to tell you something." He waited for their gaze. "When we were at the beach before, I got a call from a detective in New York." Mira's hand flew to her mouth, as if she didn't want the words about Wilton said by anyone. Anya's head was down, but her eyes were lifted. "They found the gunman. The man who killed Caroline."

Mira's hand was still over her mouth; Owen hadn't said the words she'd wanted to hear.

Edward leaned back in his chair and a smile lifted his face. "Now this is a damn good birthday present." He waved his fork in the air. "So he'll go to prison."

"He's already there," Owen said.

"And with any luck, someone will kill the prick in his sleep. No, actually, when he's awake so he can see it coming, so the last thing he knows before he dies is fear. Maybe it will happen when he's in the shower, or on the toilet. A knife into the neck. Great, goddamn great news."

"Eddie. Where do you get these ideas?" Katherine said.

Mira looked at Owen. "This is amazing, O. After all this time, they found him. You must be relieved."

Her tone was as intimate and naked as though they were the only two people in the room. Owen also heard her distance. He remembered Wilton's counterpunch story, true or not, about Mira, and how she'd asked him if Owen would have saved her if she'd been in Caroline's place. He wondered if it was this question that had driven her to risk everything, to see if he'd pull her back. Wilton had called Mira jealous, but Owen knew it wasn't that; she was afraid she'd slip away, like Caroline had, while he watched.

He returned her look. "I haven't thought about it in years," he said.

Edward let his chair fall forward and he slapped the table. "That's bullshit, Owen," he roared. "Of course you have. You were always thinking about it, every minute of your life since it happened. It *made* your life. It *was* your life." He was oiled with wine and sentiment. "You're going to live forever now. Nothing's going to happen to you. Isn't that right?"

"Edward, honey," Katherine soothed.

"Isn't that right?" he asked again. "Tell me."

Owen nodded. His father was right; Owen had always been thinking of the shooting, and of what he did and didn't do, every minute since. He'd always been waiting to do things differently and better the next time, but he'd stalled. He'd seen how close the end of life was, and how the edge was always in sight, and he'd been stuck because of it; he hadn't moved. When he sat, Mira put her warm palm on the back of his neck.

"A child can think about a parent's death, but never the other way around," Edward said, ignoring the tears collecting on his chin. "My son has known four missing people now. His mother, the man with the gun, Caroline, and now Wilton."

"My mother wasn't missing," Owen said. "She was dead. Big difference."

"The dead are always missing," Edward said. "We don't really know where they've gone."

"But the missing aren't always dead," Anya announced. "My father is not dead."

It was as though they'd forgotten about her, and it was her voice that made them notice her again and how she looked, wild with grief.

Mira got up and stood behind Anya. "Oh, sweetheart," she said. She hesitated and then bent to kiss her on the head. Confusion framed Anya's face. She was not impervious to kindness. She looked pleadingly at Owen, but he could say nothing. Mira stayed with her hands on the girl's shoulders. "We have to start thinking that he might be."

Edward took a big bite of cake and spoke with his mouth full, spewing crumbs in his strange excitement. "What you girls need is a ride in the boat tomorrow morning before you go home," Edward said, his mood so high it might finally burst through the roof. "This time of year, for only a few days, you can see straight down to the bottom of the pond. It's remarkable, like the whole thing's lit from the bottom. It will help us all."

Down at the water in the early morning, Edward, who was still elated from the night before, took off his flannel shirt and dried the rain from the seats of the rowboat. It was a funny, gallant move, stripping half-naked. His stomach was distended in the way of old men, his chest fuzzed with white hair. He directed Mira, who'd taken the oars, to row to the far left side of the pond where the reeds grew thickest. Anya held hard to the sides; she didn't know how to row and she was shivering in the cold. Owen told them to wait. He ran back up to the shed and came back with two ancient orange life jackets, stained with mildew and the silhouettes of insects.

"Come on, O. That's no fun," Mira said. "I hate those things. And they smell."

"But you have to," he said. "You can't swim."

"Who said anything about swimming? We're boating. Stop being such an old lady and give us a push."

Owen dropped the life jackets and he and Edward pushed the boat out. For a minute, Owen imagined that Mira and Anya were feeling that first thrill of the solid flow of water coursing under them.

"Come on, old lady. Let's leave them alone." Edward put his hand on Owen's shoulder as they made their way through the arbor back up to the house. At the top, where the fragrant overhang of spring branches blocked the sky, Edward stopped to catch his breath. He'd buttoned his shirt up wrong and one side of the collar whisked his ear.

Edward went off to look again for a kitten for Anya, and his voice calling for one faded down the road as flashes of the yellow plastic cat carrier snapped through the trees. Owen stood at the window and watched Mira and Anya lean over opposite sides of the boat and look down. He wondered if Mira was telling her about the pond dwellers now, if all this time, she really had seen something, maybe not what he'd hoped she'd see, but something of her own. Mira straightened up, and then Anya did. Mira was clearly trying to explain something while Anya shook her head. The water rippled as Mira stirred an oar. There were a million conversations that could be going on out there. They might even eventually forgive each other.

Mira moved the boat around the pond and stopped in front of the new house. They watched it for so long, that Owen knew something must be going on there. Maybe the woman with the red hair had come down her path to talk to them—about crazy naked men who swam in the cold. When Mira had the boat in the center of the pond again, she turned to watch a bird swoop in to pluck something from the water. Anya grabbed one of the oars. Mira snapped back. Her own single oar still rested on the water. The trees around them bent in to get a better look. Mira offered the other oar to Anya, but she shook her head. Mira seemed to be explaining that they weren't getting anywhere this way as the boat began to twist and drift. After a few minutes, Mira inched farther and put her hand on Anya's oar. But Anya was stronger, bigger, and she jerked back. Mira refused to let go even as she was being pulled off her seat. Owen's eyes blurred. The women were fighting and tugging. Their palms would be full of splinters. And then Anya let go, raising both hands in sudden surrender or victory, and Mira fell back off the seat. The oar handles pointed at the sky like the green soles of her sneakers. She had hit her head and wasn't getting up. The stink of blood streamed through Owen's sinuses as he left the house and ran toward the pond.

But then he saw Mira pull herself back onto the seat. She was bent over and couldn't or wouldn't lift her head. Finally, in a slow recovery, she stood and saw Owen at the head of the arbored stairs, and when Anya dug the oars in hard, Mira fell into the water.

Her entry was soundless. The surface barely noticed her. She was that light, that distressed. Owen froze with the realization that he wasn't moving. Anya yelled and he tripped down the stairs and onto the sand, and then the water was at his ankles, his knees, a stab in his balls, his chest, as he swam to Mira who was about sixty yards away, a head rising and then disappearing, mouth open, mouth shut. Her sweater floated around her like a cape of deadly leaves.

His own clothes weighed a thousand pounds. His limbs ached. When he reached Mira, he grabbed for her. Her lips were purple and her scalp was a transparent white. She fought and cursed at him to stop, to let her go, but he had a handful of sweater and an arm across her shoulders to pull her in.

"Get away from me!" she screamed. "You're drowning me."

Her hand raked his face, and her nails tore the skin under his eye. The pain wasn't his then, or when she kicked him in the gut a minute later. His head went under and he swallowed a lungful of pond water. He believed he still held her still, feral in her fear, but what he held was cold, clear water. Her own panic was going to sink her, but she was out of his reach, thrashing her way to the beach, all dog paddle and determination. She stumbled out, gasping, and kneeled on the sand. Rivers ran off her.

"You were pulling me down," she wailed at him. "You were going to drown me."

"I was trying to save you." Owen was vaguely aware of Anya still out on the boat, oarless and twisting. He didn't care.

Mira stumbled up to the house. Her waterlogged sweater dragged over the ground. Katherine and Edward stood confused at the top of the path as she brushed by them and he followed. Mira turned on the outdoor shower and struggled to undress, but her clothes sucked at her skin. She waved Owen away. She ripped and tugged at her pants, her socks, her underwear. She screamed in frustration, then whimpered and sat down. Finally, she let him lift the shirt over her head and she leaned over his bent back as he pulled off her pants. She stepped under the water and he closed the wooden door and stood just outside it. Cold had moved into his bones; there was ice behind his eyes, and a headache stomping in.

"I can hear you freezing out there," Mira said. "Come in with me."

"I can't," he said. She'd thought he was trying to drown her.

"Yes, you can." She opened the door, pulled him in, and undressed him as he'd undressed her. The water seared the scratches on his face. A bruise bloomed on Mira's shoulder, and when she lifted up her hair, he saw a raw red scrape on the back of her head. She tensed when the water hit it. They heard Edward down at the water shouting instructions to Anya to free the boat that was now caught in the reeds on the far side of the pond.

"She tried to kill you," he said.

"No, she didn't. She didn't mean to do it. I was angry at something she'd said. It was an accident." Mira's words were final and forgiving. She would blame no one but herself. "I know better than to stand in a boat."

Owen spoke to her back. "That day I left you on the roof at Brindle, I went to Wilton's house. We had a fight. I hit him. I told him that he'd ruined our lives." The hot water was beginning to run out, and Mira shivered against him. "I said that I'd told Anya the one thing he didn't ever want her to know—a story about what had happened years ago. The story you don't know. I wanted to kill him with it. I wanted him to kill himself over it."

"I know."

He tuned her around to face him. "What do you know?"

"I know what happened when he had Anya in the car, when he'd tried to kill himself and her. He told me that last night I was with him. But Wilton didn't believe you'd told her. He said you were too good a person, that you wouldn't do that to her. That last night I saw him? He was moved by everything you did for me. He knew you were trying to save me. He said he'd never been loved the way you love me. What devastated him was the fact that he'd never had love like this and never would. That it was too late for him. That's all he was looking for. Anya seems to get that."

"Why didn't you tell me you knew?"

"I was waiting, O. I thought that if you finally told me, it also meant you'd forgiven me for what I've done. And if you didn't ever tell me, then I'd have to live with that."

Wilton had protected him. Owen crouched down. He saw the backs of Mira's legs, her ankles with their sculpted tendons, the lip of water around her heels.

"Why did you leave him there, Mira?"

"Because he wanted me to. It's the only real thing he's ever asked of me, O. It was what he wanted—to send me back home to you. He begged me to go."

Owen pressed his face to the back of Mira's legs, and they stayed like that, the water growing quickly colder.

Soon, they heard Katherine yelling for Owen, and he ran from the shower to meet her at the top of the stairs. Edward had gone into the water, she told Owen anxiously, to pull Anya back in the boat. Anya couldn't figure out how to work the oars and was going in circles. It was too far, too cold, he was too old, Katherine insisted, her worried words tagging Owen down to the beach. Edward's stroke was strong and competent, and he'd been doing this forever, but nothing was going to assure Katherine that he was okay. Owen dropped the towel from around his waist and went into the pond. Edward had stopped a few yards from the boat, and Owen caught up to where his father was treading water.

"Did she send you out to check on me?" Edward nodded at the beach where Katherine stood, squinting to see them.

"She did."

His father's broad, shut-eyed smile was something beyond delight, a simple pleasure in knowing that someone was watching. Edward waved at Katherine and then looked at Anya, who was waiting in the boat with the oars inert in the water, her hands in her lap.

"Christ. Who doesn't know how to row a boat?"

"I'll get her," Owen said. "You go back in."

"There hasn't been this much action on the pond in years," Edward said. Life was more vivid all of a sudden. "Porter would have loved it. These new people could care less." He flipped over and started a splashy backstroke to the shore and Katherine.

Owen swam up to Anya. He had her take up the oars and toss the rope into the water. He pulled the boat, a smooth, familiar weight, up to the shore and hid his nakedness behind it when she got out. She didn't say anything to him but hurried up to the house. When Owen got back, his father and Katherine were in the shower together, complaining about the lack of hot water. Inside, Owen wrapped himself in a blanket from the couch. He heard Anya talking to Mira in the bedroom. Anya was breathy with apology, but there was also some element of excitement at what had just happened and what she'd done. The strain was over now. They were all very much awake. Her father was still missing, and everyone in that house knew he wasn't going to reappear, but she'd let some weight tip off the boat and sink to the bottom. She would have to write her own story about her father.

17

Anya had offered them anything they wanted from Wilton's house but urged them to take the television from his bedroom—which they did. Owen imagined all the nights Wilton must have unfolded himself on his big messy bed and clicked the thing on. At his feet was a version of himself in a linen suit and silk tie, feckless and permanently youthful. He was at his best there on the screen, maybe a genius. But in his head, when he turned himself off, the night would descend indifferent to celebrity and talent and invite all kinds of regret. His loneliness could make fire all by itself in the dark.

For now, the television sat in the hall outside their own bedroom, while Owen took down the wallpaper. He'd thought that they would have been done with television after everything that had happened, but Mira wanted it—a useful reminder of the lovely confusion about what was real and what wasn't. Liberated after a century behind rosy paper, chunks of plaster fell in puffs of toxic dust. The walls would have to come down to the studs, a job for the summer, Owen knew. A hole opened up to where the air was warm and fusty with the breath of another century. He'd heard of people finding love letters and confessions, stashes of money, bottles that were empty except for the gold stain of dried booze, behind old walls. He pressed his eye to the hole; maybe he'd discover in there some understanding of how it was that life could pick you up and toss you around and still return you to the place you'd started. Because here he was, just where he'd been a year earlier, as if he'd done nothing more than leave his chair to get a glass of water.

When he drew back from the hole and the rush of yeasty air, he saw Anya next door. If you knew the father, did you know the child? There were the same oceanic, pale bare feet propped up on the porch railing, the graceful body balancing on the back legs of the chair, the unfocused attempts at reading. Always thinking, never really at rest. Anya pushed the hair off her forehead. If you'd known the father well—or maybe not at all—could you ever know this child? Did he want to know her? His grief for Wilton was borderless, his grief for her confined. She would be okay.

Six days earlier, Wilton's body had been laid out in a morgue in Hartford. According to the police, the car he'd been in, driven by a woman they assumed he'd met at the casino, forty-two, recently divorced, and with two teenage children, had left the dark Connecticut country road and slipped soundlessly into a deep, muddy marsh. Sunken, hidden by fog and cattails and the indemnity of private property and abandoned appliances, their tracks covered by new snow, the car had remained undiscovered until someone had come one early morning to dump a van full of old computers. Wilton must have thought, as the car slid off the road, what a fucking lousy way to go, what terrible luck when everything might just begin again, when they'd all survived what they'd done to themselves and to one another. He would have kept his eyes open as the dark water rose up the windshield and the mud locked them in.

Owen imagined that if you'd been on the tenth floor of the hotel above Eagle Run, unable to sleep that night after Mira had left Wilton, you might have seen this lanky, coatless man walk out with the beautiful woman, and you might have thought they looked ready for anything, arm in arm. You might have seen them laughing it up into the heavy fog as they waited for her car to be brought around by the pimply valet. You might have watched them get in, and seen the car take the long route past the parking lots until it disappeared from view. Maybe, if you'd seen them earlier, you might have thought it looked like love between them. But who would ever know what it was, or where they were going, or what route they were taking? Or why Wilton was in the car at all? You wouldn't have known they were entirely underwater and drowned when you finally managed to sleep.

It was three days ago that Owen and Mira had driven Anya to Maine, forty minutes outside of Portland, where Wilton's sister lived. On the highway headed north, empty on a weekday morning, Owen felt like they were chasing Wilton's body and that this was some sort of gruesome race, but for what prize? But the body had been delivered that morning and was waiting at Pineview Cemetery—how many Pineviews were there, Mira wanted to know, indignant with heartache at the dumb name—as were Wilton's sister, Susan, and her husband. The five of them, plus the casket, made an awkward group at the graveside, and later in Susan's sunporch with the green indoor-outdoor carpet, where the louvered windows were open and the noise of the street repaving ground on. There was a kind of stunned feeling in the room as they ate sandwiches to the sounds of a jackhammer. It was the same house, Susan told them, that Wilton had grown up in.

Owen searched Susan's face for any resemblance to her brother. There wasn't much she could tell them about Wilton, who'd been out of the house when she was still a baby. But the dead had the power to superimpose themselves, and here, after the morning spent standing by a deep hole and not knowing what to say to one another as the piney winds blew around them, Owen saw Wilton everywhere and in everyone. Susan looked like him around the eyes.

Wilton might have claimed to like how direct Susan was, how her bright, pedestrian geraniums reached for the sun, how there was a lack of pretension in any of this. Hers was the kind of life Wilton said he envied, but who knew if he meant it. Soon, Owen and Mira and Anya would get back in the car and drive the hours back to Providence, and they might all feel that this day had stumbled along and their stupor and sorrow had prevented them from asking the right questions. And that this was their only chance.

Owen had asked to use the bathroom, and Susan's husband was sent to show him where it was. Owen tried to picture Wilton in this low-ceilinged, compact house, sitting at the round table in the kitchen with the sunflower salt and pepper shakers and plastic tablecloth, his feet on the worn linoleum, his body relaxed in the tight living room. The view from the bathroom upstairs was of woods without end. It was an invitation of deep green amnesty. Owen would never know what Wilton saw in these trees growing up, or what he saw in the trees the woman's car crashed through, or where it was he wanted to go.

Owen left the half-stripped bedroom and the house and crossed the driveway to stand at the fence. Anya glanced up from her book.

"You look like a coke fiend," she said. "Or a vision of your future. Your hair is completely white. I can see every wrinkle in your face, even from here. You should see yourself."

"No, thanks. I don't want to witness old age just yet," he said, dusting himself off and explaining what he'd been doing.

"I think it would be interesting to see ahead like that. Get a preview of the next fifty years."

"That because you'll always be beautiful." He hadn't meant to embarrass her, but he had. Her strain of modesty was not Wilton's. "I know I'll look like my father. I'll have hair sprouting from the tops of my ears and out of my nose."

Anya gave him a soft smile. He sensed that they had only a certain number of words left to say to each other. Packages still being delivered to Wilton were piled up on the porch, and he offered to carry them inside for her.

"I was hoping someone might steal them. They just keep coming." Anya eyed the boxes warily. "Even the guys who cut the grass still show up, and I can't bear to tell them to stop. It's like they've come to the party, but no one's told them the host is dead."

Owen pushed through the gate. He made two trips inside with the boxes. The place had a picked-over feel to it—how much more had Anya given away, and why so urgently? What remained were the indents of chair legs in the rug, small squares of evidence that someone had once lived there. He thought of the outline of the former owner's bed upstairs. Anya was undoing piece by piece what Wilton had put together for himself and for her. His comforter was on the floor in front of the couch. Anya had been sleeping downstairs. She brought Owen a knife to open the boxes.

"No, you do it," he said. "Or you could just leave them unopened."

"I don't want any of it. I didn't ask for it, but everything's mine, anyway."

She kneeled to open the first box. She hesitated; her father's aspirations were packed inside. Here was a bread maker, boxes of chocolates, drinking glasses, three different kinds of vinegar, and another cashmere sweater for her birthday in two weeks. She sat surrounded by it.

"Maybe I'll miss it when the packages stop showing up," she said. "That day in Maine, I didn't understand what was going on, not really. Everything meant something else. Even the house didn't feel real to me. Who were those people I'm related to?" Her eyelids were violet and faintly quivering. "I feel like my father came from nowhere and disappeared into nowhere."

After Owen helped pack up Anya's car with stuff to drop off at Goodwill, he walked to Spruance. He stood across the street from the school with his back against chain link. In the weekend afternoon sun, the building was the color of yellowed paper smudged with erased words. There were still weeks left of the school year, but already the place looked shut down, unplugged and locked up. In every window, the faintest shadow of chicken wire embedded in the glass fell on the parchment shades. Weeds peeked out along the foundation and at the base of the wide, chipped steps. At the end of June, when the building would finally be closed for good, what was forgotten in lockers and desks and children's heads would stay there. Like the captive air behind his bedroom walls, the school's breath would have been witness to all sorts of history, but the kids wouldn't discover it; maybe no one would.

He hadn't known until then that he would stop teaching—maybe for a while, maybe forever. He'd lost faith in what he could do. If he watched closely now, would Spruance lean toward him even the smallest bit and ask him to change his mind? The clouds behind it held it steady. He had always been too interested in the lives of his students anyway, and how their families were arranged—one parent, two parents, grandparents, people called aunts and uncles coming in and out, neat, chaotic, full of the smell and sound of babies and spices, or softer with other syllables, Russian, Portuguese, Spanish, Thai, the foreign taste of something bready, peppery, sweet. He had heard terrible stories. He'd heard great stories, too, but he didn't always remember those as easily.

Earlier, he'd wanted to say something to Anya about her father, but she must have sensed something troubling and she'd dodged him. She'd had enough of him, of all of it. She wouldn't face him or give him the chance to speak. The wind had flattened her hair against her cheek. He reached out to brush it away, but she pulled back.

He hadn't intended to go to Brindle, but he walked in that direction. Mira had been going to work every day since Wilton had been found, determined to resurrect the place. He didn't always ask what she'd done there but waited until she told him; she was cleaning, she was starting off slowly, she was planning. Would he help? He didn't ask her about money, though now what was missing from the house was clearer to him. He remembered the etched-glass vase that was gone as though it had always been the first thing he looked at in the morning and the last thing at night. The house felt lighter for it, as though it might rise with him in it, instead of sink.

He walked with the peculiar feeling that he wasn't being seen. In Fox Point, the air gave over to the bay. The window in Rosalie and George's son's apartment was spotless and closed. The Bright was crowded with heads bent over to ignore the passing day. Wickenden Street was still sleepy in the afternoon; night would wake it up. The underpass was a drumroll of pigeons' beating wings. A truck rattled over the Point Street Bridge, the bridge rattled under the weight, and the handrail shivered beneath Owen's touch. Brindle's front door was unlocked, and he called for his wife. She wasn't in her office, or the white gallery that smelled of new paint, or the studio. Her car was not in the back lot. The blue Dumpster had been replaced by two modest army-green barrels. Maybe you made only as much garbage as you had room for.

He sat at Mira's desk, and though he wanted to, he wouldn't read what was on top, not the letters or the notes she'd written to herself. He didn't pick up the phone to find out where she was. He had to believe she was coming back soon, that everything was fine. Her black jacket with the red zipper, the one she said that morning she wasn't sure she was going to need, was balled on the seat of the wicker chair. The desk was too small for him and his knees banged the underside. If the rest of Brindle was clean and cleared to start over, the office was still crowded with piles, old pottery, dried hydrangeas gone violet with dust. The skull of a rabbit Edward had given her. In this, Mira hadn't changed. Owen didn't think he'd ever spent time in the building alone. The sounds of the city settling were what Mira had heard for years. He was intrigued that in this room she'd turned her back on the river and looked into the core of the building instead. She'd always waited to see who was coming in.

He was enormously tired. The storm that had been inside his chest was leaving. In this unresolved hour, he went up to the roof and leaned against the still-warm brick of the bulkhead wall. In a few hours, people would crowd the bars that lined the other side of the river. Bubbles of music and heat would rise from cars. He moved to the edge and gazed down at the sidewalk in front of Brindle. At the other end of the roof, he looked down to the empty lot, and behind it, the few square yards of undeveloped land—weedy, sparkling with empties, hemmed on four sides by chain-link fencing. He could plant city tomatoes there and give them away. He'd seen pictures of buildings in other downtowns that had hung on against development, buttressed by skyscrapers, office buildings, warehouses, stores. Clapboard houses that were blown on by the exhaust fans of twenty-four-hour diners or sandwiched between a fish market and a dry cleaner. In bed at night, would the inhabitants feel they lived in the very middle of progress? Brindle wasn't surrounded yet, but the city was already encroaching on it, widening and rising a little more every year. You could hear the city's growing pains at night, a splitting of the seams, the lengthening of bones under the grandest houses. In decades, Mira would stand on this roof and not have a wide open view of the river anymore. She might be looking into condos and offices, onto highway improvements. She'd have to look straight up to catch any piece of emptiness.

He was still peering over the edge when she drove into the spill of light in front of the building. He called for her, but she couldn't hear him. He groped on the roof's surface for a small pebble that might have been dropped by a bird. What he felt was a thin trail of pea gravel from the driveway at home. The tiny stones ended up in every room of the house, occasionally in the bed or the shower. It was up here, too, evidence of Mira's presence. He picked up a few pieces and let them rain down on the car roof. Mira looked up. She shielded her eyes from an imaginary sun, not yet the moon.

"What are you doing up there?" she yelled.

He liked the way her voice rose to him. "Waiting for you. Come up."

In a few minutes, she was on the roof. Illuminated in the stairwell, she looked small, and like the woman she was going to be for the rest of her life: open to what might awe her, humbled, no longer young. Her sculpted clavicle was both pedestal and art.

"It's a beautiful night," he said. "I'm watching the action."

She ran her thumb across his cheek. "You have something here. Dust. And in your hair. Everywhere in fact."

They sat with their backs against the ledge. He told her about the bedroom walls, about how he'd seen Anya. Mira took off her glasses and folded them in her lap. Maybe the view was better to her blurred. He asked where she'd been.

"Just driving around for a bit. Looking at the city. Not where you think. Not where you're afraid I've been."

"I'll always wonder." He wanted to believe she was telling the truth; what more could he do? "You know that."

"Maybe not always. But it's okay for now. You can ask, O."

"I don't want to."

He watched lights wash the brick building across the street and soak into the mortar. He put his nose to her neck and imagined he smelled the high, metallic stink of the slot machines. He knew he might always detect it, even when it was long washed away, even when it wasn't there. He stood and looked down again at the street. The height still scared him but there was something exhilarating about the wind blowing up in his face. He was ready to live with the uncertainty. His feet were steady. Mira was a good mystery. He wanted to feel the risk of love every day. It got the heart pumping. He might do something big. The wall pressed just below his knees. He teetered at the sight of the river running thick with diamonds. Mira said he shouldn't stand so close to the edge—he was making her nervous. His wife had saved him once before. Now she cupped her hands around his ankle to hold him down and bring him to her again.

Acknowledgments

I am enormously grateful to two women: Emily Cunningham, my exceptional and dedicated editor, and Jennifer Carlson, my remarkable agent, who always leads me in the right direction. Thanks also to friends and colleagues who read versions of this book and offered advice, endless support, and lots to make me laugh. To Michael, Tobias, Alexander—thank you, forever. You are my life.

About the author

About the book

Read on

Insights,
Interviews
& More . . .

Meet Hester Kaplan

Sometimes people ask me what it was like to grow up with parents who are writers. My father is a Pulitzer Prize–winning biographer; my mother is a novelist. Their friends were writers, too, and publishers, editors, critics, people whose lives revolved around books and writing and the business. Their talk was about who had written what, whose new book was magical or disappointing, whose publisher was rolling out the red carpet, whose publisher was quickly rolling it back up, who was still waiting to hear back from his agent and counting the minutes the phone didn't ring. They talked about novels as though the books were real life, about which character might be based on someone they knew, about scenes and image, about the power of poetry, the art of narrative, about language, tin ears, and talent.

I knew this because I listened carefully, but I also snooped. As a child, I hid under the table during dinner parties while the book and writing talk went on above me, and I watched as an esteemed novelist slipped off his shoe and caressed the ankle of the poet sitting next to him. I saw the jiggling leg of the man who admitted that sometimes, before he went to sleep, he reread terrible reviews of his new book. I saw what happened to the plumbing in the house after a tipsy poet reciting Elizabeth Bishop accidently dropped his pipe down the toilet. I heard the story of the furious writer who took an ax to the beautiful leather-bound copy of his own book his editor had sent as a present, stuffed the pieces in a mailer, and sent it back. Any one of these writer friends could show up buoyant one night and despairing the next. If I asked why someone seemed unhappy or restless or angry, my parents might say, "His writing isn't going well."

I understood what that meant because I saw my parents enter into something unknown and unpredictable with their own work every day. On good days, I heard the typewriter keys going at top speed for hours, but on others, I heard each letter put on the page with weary uncertainty. I heard the frustrated squeak of my mother's desk chair, and my father talking to Olive and then Buddy, the dogs who slept in his office, when ideas and words weren't flowing, I knew what it was like when my parents' new books arrived in the mail; there was great optimism and the smell of new ink in that box. But I also understood that that the writing itself, the sitting in an isolated room, the putting down of words every day was not the way I wanted to live. I announced that I would have nothing to do with writing. Or books. Ever.

Which didn't mean that I didn't find these writers and their stories fascinating and amusing, or that I didn't love going to New York with my parents when they went to see their editors. This meant lunch in a restaurant, and later, at the editor's office, an invitation to go into a large closet full of new books and pick what I wanted. I touched the shiny jackets, tested the unbroken bindings, ▶

66 I announced that I would have nothing to do with writing. Or books. Ever. **99**

inhaled the scent of a new book like an addict. I appreciated the heft of big books and the delicacy of small ones. I still do. My declaration against the writing life didn't mean that I wasn't secretly moved when my shy father let poetry and prose speak for him, coming into the kitchen during dinner to read a stanza of Whitman or a paragraph from Henry Roth's *Call It Sleep*. Or that when my mother asked me, at age twelve, to read a short story in *The New Yorker*, I wasn't left awed by its description of an empty, sparkling asphalt parking lot, and how that image had the power to make me feel deeply and curiously alone.

In my college freshman writing class, I turned in sloppy and poorly written papers. I was making the point to myself that I didn't care about writing— and that, in any case, I was no good at it. I would not be another English major who gushed about Molly Bloom, Lily Bart, sestinas, point of view. Anthropology was going to be my thing. But in my senior year, I found myself in a writing class describing an old woman living alone in a version of the apartment I lived in then. Nothing happened in the story, but I wrote that she lined up her pots and pans with the handles facing in the same direction. That single detail is what has stuck with me, my first attempt to create mood and meaning beyond and beneath what we see. That challenge—those words just out my reach—was the work I decided

❝ My declaration against the writing life didn't mean that I wasn't secretly moved when my shy father let poetry and prose speak for him. **❞**

I wanted to do. I had not found myself in the class as if by accident—I had taken myself there.

Still, I stayed away from writing for another decade.

I worked in publishing, in production and promotion because there were no aspiring authors in those departments, just people who liked books. But I was always aware that on the other side of decisions about book design or ad copy was a hopeful writer. And I knew this writer—I'd seen her wrestle, conquer, succeed, fail, and then do it all over again. I'd grown up with him. I began coming in early and staying late to write. It was a long time before I told anyone what I was doing, and I married that person, also a writer. Years later, I still feel that swaddling of privacy when I sit down to write, and I still hear the echoes of my parents at work, like faint, changing drumbeats. ◠

Inside *The Tell*

OVER THE PAST DECADE, I managed to find myself (as though *by accident*) in a few casinos, both the enormous, glitzy ones and the sad, down-on-their-luck ones. It's not because I enjoy gambling. In fact, I dislike it for the same reason some people love it: the excitement of risk. But there I was, wandering the floor, watching people at the tables, listening to the chiming of the machines and the sound of metallic rain as someone won at slots. I was especially drawn to those people playing the slots hour after hour, and wondered what enticed them and kept them there through their wins and despite their losses. I'll admit that playing the slot machines can be thrilling for a moment, but for me, it's not a good kind of thrill. It's like standing at the edge of a chasm, looking down and realizing that it wouldn't be so hard to fall.

I studied anthropology in college. I was in awe of Claude Lévi-Strauss. I heatedly discussed structuralism and *Tristes Tropiques*. I devoured *Yanomamo: The Fierce People*, a case study in cultural anthropology, as though it were a novel, and gobbled up other ethnographies. But I knew I was never going to *be* an anthropologist because my interests weren't scholarly. What interested me was more social, more personal, maybe more intimate: how people interacted; what happened when they strayed outside the norm and broke their contracts; how they understood, misunderstood, and formed their relationships with others. How a particular arrangement, formal and informal, small and large, functioned, and how it was different from any other. I also realized that my study didn't have to be of the Yanomano or the Dinka of Sudan; it could be of the people around me—family, friends, strangers on the subway, a boyfriend's parents, teachers, the women on my basketball team. Married couples. And, later, casino goers.

Casinos have their own particular culture. And for the women who play the slot machines—the majority of women who go to casinos choose the slots as their primary game—there is an inviting dynamic at work. Many women prefer the slots to table games because it allows them to be alone, to think or meditate, to go at their own speed without criticism or hassle. In *The Tell*, I wrote about Mira, a woman I thought I might know and admire in real life, and then I put her in front of a slot machine. I wanted to find out what would keep her going back to the slots, how she might get into money trouble, how she might hide the truth from her husband, Owen. Many of the women I talked to in researching the novel began playing the slots because it was fun, a way to release stress, an easy night out. For others, playing the slots blanketed their grief or offered addiction's instant gratification. Like so many of these women, Mira never imagined she was going to become a compulsive gambler or lose control of her life. She could ▶

> **❝ I also realized that my study didn't have to be of the Yanomamo or the Dinka of Sudan; it could be of the people around me. ❞**

About the book

not imagine how it could happen *to a woman like her.* Compulsive gambling can be devastating in any number of ways, and in *The Tell*, I wanted to know how it might test a marriage.

Every marriage is different, and *The Tell* looks at a single one. Mira's addiction, with its lies, betrayals, and secrets, threatens to destroy her marriage, which is built on the opposite notions of trust and honesty. Marriage is sometimes the context in which life happens; sometimes, as in this novel, it is the story itself. Marriage takes place within a room—and in *The Tell*, a large house of many rooms—a reminder of constancy, even as the marriage changes. As Owen deals with the damage Mira has done, their house, filled with a conflation of memories and responsibilities, holds and confuses him. Wilton, the seductive and ruthless new neighbor, wants what he thinks exists between Owen and Mira, but he can't ever really know what this marriage, or any other, is truly like as long as he's on the outside of it. Writing, like marriage and gambling, can also be a thrilling risk. Are you willing to see how far you can lean over that chasm? ❧

Further Reading

HOWARDS END, by E. M. Forster, begins with a letter describing the house at center of the novel: "It isn't going to be what we expected. It is old and little, and altogether delightful—red brick. . . . From hall you go right or left into dining-room or drawing-room. Hall itself is practically a room. You open another door in it, and there are the stairs going up in a sort of tunnel to the first floor. Three bed-rooms in a row there, and three attics in a row above."

The descriptions have a clipped cadence like excited footsteps that take me into this "altogether delightful" house, rushing me from room to room to get the layout. Now I stand outside for a full view as the letter continues: "Then there's a very big wych-elm—to the left as you look up—leaning a little over the house, and standing on the boundary between the garden and the meadow. I quite love that tree already." With this, a picture of the setting, inside and out, begins to build in my mind, and becomes the vivid physical world in which the characters—and readers— live.

When I am writing, my senses are on alert. A certain light falling over my desk becomes the light coming in through a character's bedroom window, and the smell of cooking from my kitchen uncovers a memory for another. Because much of *The Tell* occurs within Mira and Owen's spectacular and problematic Victorian, I found myself, in writing ▶

the book, returning to novels in which houses have the power to assure, unsettle, and reveal character. In Kazuo Ishiguro's *The Remains of the Day*, Stevens, the austere and scrupulous butler of Darlington Hall, recalls "distinctly climbing to the second landing and seeing before me a series of orange shafts from the sunset breaking the gloom of the corridor where each bedroom door stood ajar." In this moody and unusual light, he accepts the fact of his father's decline.

In Richard Ford's *Independence Day*, Frank, a realtor, visits his on-and-off-again girlfriend. When he arrives at her house, he finds that "Sally's is a place of peculiar unease on account of its capacity to create a damned unrealistic, even scary, illusion of the future . . ." He sees in the details of "bulky oak paneling, pocket doors and thick chair rails" a "false promise." He understands the ability of houses to fulfill or deny our expectations—when his continue to waver.

The structures in which we live—and have lived—reflect us. Their walls are what we wake and fall asleep within. Their closets hide us; their windows give us a view to the outside world, and let the world view us in return. Their history exists before we move in and continues after we move out. The paint spill, like something from a crime scene, on the back stairs of the house I grew up in is still an enticing mystery to me. The way the wind slams my office door in

66 Because much of *The Tell* occurs within Mira and Owen's spectacular and problematic Victorian, I found myself, in writing the book, returning to novels in which houses have the power to assure, unsettle, and reveal character. 99

summer thrills me. I trip over the hall rug but never move it. I imagine who sat where I am sitting now, who looked out this same dusty window onto the yard.

On first seeing Tom's house in *The Great Gatsby*, Nick says, "A breeze blew through the room, blew curtains in at one end and out the other like pale flags, twisting them up toward the frosted wedding-cake of the ceiling, and then rippled over the wine-colored rug, making a shadow on it as wind does on the sea." Illumination and levitation reflect Nick's exhilaration. Houses are indifferent to the lives within them, but in how we love, hate, care for or ignore them, they are reflections of ourselves—and our characters. They hold and recall lost time; they are for all of us estates of memory and intention. ∾